John H. Worcester

Memorial of Rev. J. H. Worcester, Jr., D.D.

containing a brief biography and selected sermons

John H. Worcester

Memorial of Rev. J. H. Worcester, Jr., D.D.
containing a brief biography and selected sermons

ISBN/EAN: 9783337264543

Printed in Europe, USA, Canada, Australia, Japan

Cover: Foto ©Raphael Reischuk / pixelio.de

More available books at **www.hansebooks.com**

MEMORIAL

—OF—

Rev. J. H. Worcester, Jr., D. D.

CONTAINING

A BRIEF BIOGRAPHY

AND

SELECTED SERMONS.

———

PUBLISHED BY
THE SIXTH PRESBYTERIAN CHURCH,
OF CHICAGO, ILL.
1893

EDITOR'S NOTE.

This volume has been prepared by order of the Sixth Presbyterian Church of Chicago, as a memorial of its love for the memory and grateful thanks for the services of its former pastor, Rev. J. H. Worcester, Jr., D. D. and is respectfully dedicated to all those, everywhere, who were instructed by his preaching, inspired by his example, and comforted by his counsel. The committee acknowledges, with gratitude, the kindness of Rev. Albert Warren Clark, D. D., Rev. P. F. Leavens, D. D., and Mr. B. C. Ward for their contributions to the biographical part of the volume. The permission of Pres. M. H. Buckham of the University of Vermont, and Rev. S. J. McPherson, D. D. of Chicago, to use their addresses, will be appreciated by all readers.

The sermons herewith presented are in no sense selected as superior to his ordinary efforts, but as representative of all in style, and as exemplifying the consistent unity of purpose in all his preaching.

Chicago, Sept. 11, 1893.

Alexander Forbes.

BIOGRAPHY.

JOHN HOPKINS WORCESTER, JR., was born April 2, 1845, at St. Johnsbury, Vt. He was of the Vermont branch of the eminent family whose name he bore. His grandfather was the Rev. Leonard Worcester, who was for nearly half a century pastor of the Congregational Church at Peacham, Vt. His grand uncle was Dr. Samuel Worcester, first secretary of the American Board. His father, Rev. J. H. Worcester, D. D., eldest son of Rev. Leonard Worcester, was pastor of the church at St. Johnsbury when John Hopkins Worcester, Jr., was born. His mother was Martha P. Clark, daughter of Deacon Luther Clark of St. Johnsbury. She was a remarkably lovely woman, of fine intellect, of a sweet spirit, and of devoted piety. She was the youngest of three sisters; the other two are still living (1893).

When but little more than a year and a half old his father was called to the pastorate of the First Church in Burlington, Vt., and thither he removed with his parents in the month of December, 1846. On the 23d of August, 1848, his mother died, and his boy heart had its first sad, deep sorrow. Although so young when thus bereaved, he never forgot his mother. Her bidding him goodbye and telling him to "love the dear Saviour," left an impression which he never lost nor ever disregarded.

On the Hopkins side he was descended from John Hopkins, who came to this country from England in 1634, first living in Cambridge, Mass. In 1636 he removed to Hartford, Conn., "being one of that company which made the notable journey from Cambridge, with Mr. Hooker at the head." In the fourth generation, Samuel Hopkins, D. D., married Esther, sister of the eminent Jonathan Edwards. His son, also Samuel Hopkins, D. D., was the great grandfather of the subject of this sketch. With such an ancestry we are prepared to understand the life of Mr. Worcester. He inherited intellectual gifts which, used as he used them, made him conspicuous for his mental grasp and "grip." But not less did he inherit moral and religious tendencies making attainment of a high order possible. Education and training can do much, but they can create nothing. The most they can do is to develope the native powers— to aid in realizing the potentiality which has its limit set before education and training begin.

Mr. Worcester's father being obliged, on account of his health, to spend the winter of 1850–51 at the South, the boy was left in charge of Rev. and Mrs. Rufus Case ; Mr. Case supplying his father's pulpit in his absence. Before his father's return he went with Mr. Case to West Lebanon, N. H., and remained there until his father's marriage, Oct. 1851, to Miss Catherine Fleming, a woman of fine intellectual attainments, and beautiful Christian character, then principal of a select school for young ladies. To her watchful and loving care and judicious training, the boy was greatly indebted, and the fond affection with which he repaid her care, was very remarkable. Being a frail child, it was not thought expedient to send him to the public schools, and so in his mother's school, of which, later, his father became associate principal, the boy was fitted for college.

He had learned the alphabet from picture blocks by the time he was two years old, and by the time he was three years old he had learned to read. A friend carrying him home on his shoulder one evening, when very little over two years old, was pleased to see him look up at the stars and repeat :

> " Twinkle, twinkle, little 'tar,
> How I wonder what you are,
> Up above the world so high,
> Like a dimont in the 'ky."

At his mother's funeral he was taken to the grave, and as he saw the body laid away, he burst into tears, saying, " Now I shan't have a mamma any more."

When he was about five years old, a minister's association was held at his father's house. As they were at dinner, and he was in the kitchen with the housekeeper, he opened the door and looked in. On the housekeeper's remonstrating, he replied: "It's customary, in Burlington, for little boys to peek just a little."

It seems that very early in life he had his mind set on preaching, for as a little boy it was a great delight to him to stand on the stairs and " preach."

The atmosphere with which he was surrounded in early life conspired to early maturity of his intellectual powers. Being an only child, educated in a young ladies' school, there was little to call forth or to give room for the development of those traits which usually characterize the boy. But he grew rapidly and solidly in mental strength. The spring before he entered college, as the snow was thawing, his father found him

playing in the water as it rushed down the street, and
laughingly said, "Oh, John, aren't you ashamed to be
dabbling in the water, and you almost ready to enter
college?" "Oh, no," was his reply, "I'm illustrating
the principles of Hydrodynamics." The few anecdotes
here given of his childhood and boyhood show the
maturity of his mind as well as the fine sense of humor
even then which charaterized his mature years.

He entered the University of Vermont at the age
of 16, and graduated in 1865 at the age of 20. During
his college course, Jan. 4, 1863, he united with the
First Church in Burlington. He never knew when he
became a Christian, but his Christian life in boyhood
was marked, positive, aggressive. He was one of the
founders of the Y. M. C. A. in Burlington. Of his
college life the following is from his classmate and
warm personal friend, Rev. Albert Warren Clark, D. D.

THE COLLEGE LIFE OF PROF. J. H. WORCESTER, JR., D. D., AT THE UNIVERSITY OF VERMONT, 1861–1865.

The invitation to write a sketch of Prof. Worcester's college days has brought up many delightful
memories. While deeply regretting that great pressure
of missionary work forces me to write in marked haste,
I cannot put aside the privilege and honor of writing
a brief account of Professor Worcester's life at the
University of Vermont. He was my most intimate
friend at college. Our friendship from the beginning
of our "Freshman" life, down to his last days in a
professor's chair was pure, intimate, golden, and un-
clouded by any misunderstanding.

An eminent Frenchman has said : "I always like
to know the domestic character and circumstances of

those with whom I have to do in the world : it is a part of themselves—an additional external physiognomy which gives us a clue to their character and destiny." This thought prompts me to say a word about the early home, the college home as well, of my dear friend John. An eminent divine in Connecticut once remarked at one of the annual Conferences of the Congregational Churches : "The first right of every child is to be well-born." The friend of whom I write was in every sense "well-born." Character is no accident. Blessed is he whose education began a hundred years before his birth.

A well known professor, now occupying a chair similar to the one vacated by Professor Worcester, re-marked playfully one day, as he looked at his first little boy : "It takes six generations to develop full and noble manhood." Behold the sixth generation of Worcesters in America : Dr. Samuel Worcester, first corresponding Secretary of the American Board, and Rev. Leonard Worcester, the grandfather of our friend, an editor, and for nearly fifty years the beloved and successful pastor of the church in Peacham, Vermont.

The seventh generation is still represented in the person of the noble and venerable Dr. Worcester of Burlington, Vt. Gifted, cultivated, conservative and yet progressive—just the man for father, guide and companion of our Professor Worcester. In his delightful home in picturesque Burlington, John Hopkins Worcester Jr., found invaluable help and inspiration in the presence and companionship of that modest yet highly cultivated lady who was to him from his seventh year a genuine mother.

In such a home, and in a town whose natural scenery is almost unrivalled, and at a university, small but grandly strong, I became intimately acquainted with the eighth generation of American Worcesters.

Professor Worcester was indeed "well-born", and well prepared for the college he entered in 1861. How well I remember the first recitation of the class of '65! The now eminent president of the University of Vermont met us—eighteen in number—for the first time on Thursday, Sept. 5th, 1861. He was at that time professor of Greek. At the head of our class, alphabetically, sat Atwater, now professor at Wesleyan University, Middletown, Conn., at the foot sat Worcester, younger in years than some of us, but even then wearing a calm, collected air, as of one who had a purpose before him, one who would reach it undisturbed by other aims. It was soon evident that one of these two men would be our class leader. From the first the boyish, yet manly, cultured face of Worcester attracted me. As a young man from the country, I was too shy to make any advances to the city youth, who, from the cradle, had lived in classic atmosphere. When on Sunday morning, the 8th, our class held its first prayer-meeting, I was glad to see among our number the fellow student, who was, so unconsciously to himself, attracting me. His exact scholarship in every department increased my admiration, and made me realize how imperfect was my preparation for college life. Although at graduation I had the honor to rank next to my friend, there was little in my first recitation to awaken in his bosom more than pity.

He seemed first drawn to me by the successful issue of a game of foot-ball.

When the Sophomores gave us the usual challenge for such a contest, no one was more enthusiastic in the line of acceptance and victory than he. In the severe and final struggle that followed, my well trained country muscle served me so well that John Worcester declared that the victory was largely due to me. From that hour our friendship was mutual. He was no athelete and yet no one enjoyed more than he our atheletic sports. He was equally enthusiastic in the class room and on the campus.

I recall with interest a vigorous game of base-ball. With more than usual eagerness he had "acted well his part." At the close I said to him "John where is your Society pin"? A look of pain shot over his face as he exclaimed: "Oh, it is lost somewhere on the campus". But, weary as he was, he exclaimed with his usual perseverance: "That pin *must* be found if we search for it a week." And found it was, to his intense joy; he was a great admirer of our college society.

Entering college, as he did, without a full experience of Vermont *academy* life, and as some thought, with a few airs from the girls' seminary, there was, at the start, a certain lack which was noticed not only by his classmates, but by the Sophomores. In those days many upper-class men believed in hydropathic treatment, and so, among the Freshmen, Worcester was one, who, according to the diagnosis of Sophomores, needed "water-cure." Entering the mathematical room one morning we were surprised and in-

dignant at the question in large chalk-letters: "Who
ducked John Worcester?" The next day he called at
my room looking very thoughtful: "Clark", said he,
"tell me honestly why you think the Sophs. selected
me for hydrophatic treatment." Some months later,
referring to the same subject he remarked: "That
pail of cold water was a blessing in disguise, it has led
me to ask myself some serious questions, and as a result my little wisdom has been the gainer." In the
summer of 1862 a large number of Vermont students
responded to the call of President Lincoln for volunteers to serve nine months. Patriotism sadly depleted
the attendance at the University at Burlington. Had
my friend's patriotic heart rested in a more vigorous
frame he would gladly have been with his classmates
"at the front."

When I returned from the war and found him on
his back with a broken leg, he greeted me with a
smile, remarking as he seized my hand: "Well, Sergeant, you see that Burlington is more dangerous than
a Gettysburg campaign; you come home without a
scratch, while I am on the list of the wounded."

The students from the University of Vermont who
had served nine months in the army expected, of
course, to join the class below them; but the faculty
graciously responded to the petition of the students, who
had remained in the college, and allowed us to rejoin
our old classes, with the condition, that we pass an
examination, in due time, in the studies pursued by
the class in our absence. His great kindness in helping me to keep step with the "Junior" class, while I
was at the same time making up "Sophomore" stud-

ies, I shall never forget. He was now the recognized leader of our class, not only in one department, but in all departments. This position he kept with great ease, and whoever was second to him, was so, "*longo intervallo.*"

Secretary Clark of the American Board, who taught us Latin, would commend the graceful translations of our "dux"; professor, now President Buckham, says among those, in the last thirty years who have had a most promising and brilliant college career, John Worcester stands easily among the first ten. Professor Marsh regarded him as one of the best scientific scholars. President Torrey listened with delight to his answers in philosophy. Professor Petty, if living, could tell you how the minutiæ of differential calculus attracted him, could tell you how, when volunteers were called for to compute the time of the next local solar eclipse, Worcester, with one other student, persevered to the end, while others, discouraged, stopped at the "Half-Way House."

In college he was one of the most effective writers and speakers, and yet at that time he needed the unrelenting pruning knife of President Buckham. Ah! but he was thorough with us. Did he not refuse to accept my first oration, quieting my wounded pride with the remark: "A fine essay, Mr. Clark, but I expect something more from you when we ask for an oration." Did he not say to Worcester: "You do not lose sight of your mark, but in your march to the goal you stretch out both hands and sweep in many things not needed." Our friend was man enough to feel the justice of the criticism, and from that time on his fellow students noticed marked progress ; he became in style more like Tacitus and less like Livy.

In our weekly debates in society-rooms he was gladly heard. The discipline of those days was one of the foundation stones for his historic speech at Detroit.

Professor Worcester's intense loyalty to his college, to the society of which he was a member, and to his special friends must not be overlooked.

As a student he was most loyal to the University and to its faculty. I do not recall one act that could be classed with the littleness and meanness that sometimes show themselves in college days. He was too noble to be small but he could be indignant, and he joined heartily in rebuking the class of '67 for an insult to our class.

In the various societies, religious, social, and literary to which he belonged, no one was more loyal and faithful than John Worcester. His love and loyalty to *special* friends should be mentioned even though it seem too personal for the writer of this article. It illustrates one phase of our friend's character. During the Spring term of Senior year the principal of the Vermont Episcopal Institute, at Burlington, was obliged to dismiss his first assistant. He applied to the President of the University for permission to engage one of the seniors to help him. The salary he offered for assistance in the forenoon was a temptation to a poor student. It was accepted very reluctantly by the writer, because of the necessity of living at the Institute. This did not sever connection with the college, but with the class-room and the daily life at the University. Worcester came to my room when I was

packing my trunk, threw his arms around my neck
and wept like a child: "Clark, this cannot be, you
must give it up, the war has bereft us of some of our
best men, and now you are going, this *must not be;*
what is college with you away from it?"

Similar devotion was manifested at the time of
our graduation. An effort was made by some to
secure, at my cost, a place in the honorary society,
"Phi Betta Kappa." College marks gave the place
to me, but on the ground that I had not been all the
time in college, another tried to displace me. Worcester was indignant, and exclaimed: "I utterly refuse to accept the election to the 'Phi Betta Kappa
unless justice is done to Clark."

I beg pardon for introducing such personal matters, but the sketch of Prof. Worcester's college life
demands their mention.

Nor can I forget that his *first public lecture* was
delivered in a school-house in Franklin, Vt., where
the writer was teaching in the winter of 1864.

This very imperfect sketch of Professor Worcester's college days must not be closed without additional
reference to his religious life at the University at Burlington. An eminent Scotchman has well said: "In
some, religion is like a gradual, general growth—the
growth of something that was always within them, for
they cannot go back with distinct consciousness, to
any time when they they had it not." This remark is
eminently true in the case of Professor Worcester. He
could not name the year, much less the day, when
he became a Christian. To myself more than to any
other fellow-student was given the privilege of know-

ing and watching the inner-life of our friend. From
the first he was chivalrously honorable in his dealings,
intolerant of everything in the shape of falsehood, and
ready, in the spirit of love and kindness, to act as servant of all.

It was a pleasure to see, all through his college
days, a steady and helpful growth in all that pertains
to spiritual life. In freshman year the sense of
"ought" was very marked. His religious life at that
period was, in a word, a conscientious reverance for
the "ought."

Joy in Christian life and duty was much more to
be seen in our last college year. At the Sunday morning class prayer-meeting, Worcester was never absent
without a good excuse. There is a room in South College that was witness to many of his earnest prayers
for unconverted classmates. That room could tell of
many a "still-hour" which helped to mould and guide
our lives. God be praised for such blessed memories.

The student's Bible-class taught with such ability
by Professor Worcester's father, was our first theological Seminary. Instruction adapted to our spiritual
needs and wisely calculated to promote symmetrical
growth was welcomed by none more heartily than by
the admiring son. When, towards the close of our
college life, the Y. M. C. A. was organized in Burlington, John Hopkins Worcester, Jr. was, of course, one
of its active members.

Does it seem strange that such a man at the time
of graduation was not yet clear that God was calling
him to preach his gospel ? He had a consecrated ambition and at the same time felt sure that law would

afford him a life of usefulness and success. His oration at the Junior Exhibition on "The future of eloquence in America," and his "Valedictory" on "Political Consecration," justly praised at the time by the New York Times, were in harmony with a struggle that for a time promised to America an able judge and statesman. He was a born leader, and could have won success in any professon.

Professor Buckham's baccalaureate sermon to our class on the text : "Behold I send you forth as sheep in the midst of wolves ; be ye therefore wise as serpents and harmless as doves," made a deep impression on Worcester's mind. With some of its stirring words, still ringing in my ears, I will close this hasty sketch. "The work of a Christian apostle is no pastime ; it is a life-long struggle with a foe, whose energy it will be hard to match, and whose cunning no wise man may dare to despise. We send you forth—Christ sends you forth—not to enjoy the luxuries of lettered ease, but to enter upon the severe campaign which truth is waging against error ; to receive hard blows and deliver harder ones. Meet the perversions of unsanctified intellect by superior intellect, sanctified. Go forth then, in Christ's name into the fields where truth is maintaining stern conflict.

Above all things, first, last, midst, and without end, aspire to that knowledge which will give both impulse and direction to all other knowledge—the true knowledge of God, by faith in His Son Jesus Christ."

ALBERT WARREN CLARK,

Missionary of the American Board, and Senior Pastor of the Free
Reformed Church. Prague, Bohemia, Austria.

Professor W. O. Atwater, of Middletown, Conn.,
mentioned by Dr. Clark, writes as follows:

My first recollection of John Worcester dates to
the time we were boys of 14 or thereabouts, in Burlington. I did not know him very well, as he lived at
one end of the village and I at the other, but I remember
him as a rather sedate and earnest, but kind and,
withal, genial boy. Our family left Burlington shortly
after and when I returned to enter college he was one
of the very few in our class whom I had seen before. As
the recollections of our college days come back to me
I think of him in the Latin recitation room with Professor Clark taking notes of lectures ; in the Greek examination in Herodotus with Professor Buckham, the
first examination which we passed and with regard to
the result of which we were all pretty anxious ; and in
the mathematical room with Professor Pettee where
John's ability and industry were especially prominent.

I remember very well how a fire broke out one
evening in the machine shop by the lake shore, not far
from where Worcester lived. The boys hurried down
there, of course, I with the rest, and as we were rushing
through Pearl street and had got nearly to the fire, we
heard that a boy had just broken his leg, and a moment
after we learned that it was Worcester, who in the
scramble had been tumbled over the steep sandbank
just above where the building was burned. He was
brought home and of course was kept in the house for
a number of weeks. It was shortly before the summer
examinations. I saw him a few days afterwards and
remember very vividly how he lay holding his analytical geometry, of which we had finished the larger part

in class, and said with a sort of grim determination in his voice : ' I am going to learn all there is between the covers of that book before I get out of this bed', and I have no doubt he did it. I shall never forget a composition which he read one day, in class, on the character of Paul. I thought then that he would become a minister and was sure he would be a good one.

Some years after graduation we were in Europe at the same time and met in Leipsic and later in Switzerland. His purpose in life had ripened with his character and I saw then that there was in him that which makes a noble, strong, and influential man. His later career verified the enthusiastic hopes of his friends, and in the unhappy struggle which has been going on for some time past in one of our great religious organizations, a struggle which, I fear, is not soon to cease and one in which Christian wisdom and Christian tolerance are so sorely needed, his influence on what, seems to me the right side, was already great and growing greater.

It is hard for us short-sighted mortals to understand why such men should be cut off in the midst of their very best activity in life, but it is not for us to question the rulings of that Providence in whom Worcester so firmly believed. We should rather be inspired by his example, as I certainly am, to labor with increasing diligence and increasing faith.

I hope some folks in the world may be helped to be worthier, more useful and happier, for this life and for the next, by what comes from the lives of some of the little company of good friends who were together in the class of 1865 at the University of Vermont. Of

that little company the name of one will certainly be
beloved and honored.   That one is John Worcester."

Rev. P. F. Leavens, D. D., of Passaic, N. J.,
says :

"I perceive on reflection that I shall best comply
with your request concerning the boyhood of our departed friend, if I simply summon my best recollection and write—*currente calamo*—what comes.   For
it breaks upon me with force that I was not a man
when he was a boy, but only another boy. To be sure
I was a few years older, as the calendar runs, but he
had advantages which set him up even with me, if not
ahead, in knowledge—at least in spiritual knowledge.

I am impressed with what our mutual friend, Rev.
Albert W. Clark, now missionary in Austria, writes as
to himself :   'What a host of recollections rise up in
memory as I think of our dear John.   In a thousand
ways our lives have touched and always in the line of
blessing to myself.' Yes, that tells the story. He had
a favored youth and he made it—probably unconsciously to himself—a blessing to the rest of us.

I must have come to know him when he was fourteen. I think it began in Sunday School. I sat in the
class of the elder Dr. Worcester and listened to remarkably instructive exposition of St. Paul's epistles.
In course of time I was drawn out to act as a teacher
and the boy was one of the number to whom I was
presented.   He certainly knew more than I of the
sacred Word, and we were fellow-students.

At length I knew him in his home, and there it is
I try in memory to reproduce my friend.   There was
everything finely intellectual in that atmosphere. Mrs.

Worcester's school for Young Ladies was justly famous. Both teachers and pupils there were the brightest of minds. This lone boy among them,—sometimes pitied, sometimes envied, I suppose—took a clear course and derived the utmost intellectual advantage from the situation. The father seemed to me in those days both a sage and a saint. As I see it from this distance he must have been in the prime of his years. He had been pastor but was not now : he had passed through much affliction, but now was in cheerful surroundings : he was grave in manner and measured in speech, yet keenly witty betimes, and so, taken all in all, he seemed a great father for the one child.

And every loop that opened to let a guest into wider knowledge of the family relations brought to sight learning, character, and aggressive religion. To me it meant glorious things that the father's father had been one of the pioneer ministers of Vermont. To this day I bare my head and do obeisance before the name of any among the first settlers of my native state. And the learned man who should have gone into the woods and shared the lot of the clearers of the forest, and had been their minister, and built their House of God, would seem to me worthy of triple honor, and sure to bequeath choice benedictions to son and son's son. My friend had a heritage above most of the children of the Green Hills, a heritage far beyond price.

On every hand in the family were preachers, evangelists, and missionaries. If it stirred my blood to read, how must it have stirred the blood of all that Worcester family to realize that one of them, the uncle of our dear friend, gave his life to the Cherokee Indians, and, in defense of their outraged rights, suffered imprisonment until he could maintain and secure his due privileges in the highest courts of the nation ! These things were the heir-looms of the family and the stories must have been the wonder-land of the glowing soul in the radiant boy. Have not the tales told at the fireside left lasting marks on all of us ? On no American boy could finer, nobler family traditions center than on the golden head of this fair child.

When the long summer vacations came and the girls were out of the way, he drew his friends to the house. That was grand for us. The spacious, rambling buildings ; the luxuriant gardens ; the absolute freedom ; the leisurely and uplifting talk—no wonder it rises in memory and starts a thrill of gratitude even at this late day. Here and there a distinct recollection stands out, like a glimmering light on a far-off, receding shore. Once the conversation ran about Chaucer and the father was telling us how to drink from that fountain head of English literature : again the drift was metaphysical, and he suggested that we would do well to read a certain new book which he pointed out, remarking that it was by an author over the sea named McCosh. It was the first mention I ever heard of that name which was to become so familiar. And here is a line from a letter in which the boy at another date is saying : 'My study is confined to French mainly, which I am seeking to familiarize myself with, in the thought that I may go to Europe sometime, in which case I shall need it.'

Can I not recall anything religious ? Nay, but I

cannot recall one single thing that was inconsistent
with religion. It was taken for granted, and I do not
remember that we urged him to give his heart to God.
I cannot make it seem to me that I ever thought of
him otherwise than as a child of God. And I am sure
now, as with all the might of memory I bring back
those days, that I was brought into contact with him,
not for anything I had to give him but that, in his
felicitous youth, he might be, as Clark says a 'blessing to myself.'"

Mr. B. C. Ward, an attorney at Newton, Ia.,
says of Mr. Worcester as a collegian :

"As to my impressions of the man, Dr. Worcester, while associated with him during Freshman year,
I can say this : He was the most brainy man in the
Class of 1865 and stood at the head in all scholarly attainments. There was good reason for this, because
he came from good stock. His father and mother
were cultured and intellectually strong, and they
spared no pains to give him the very best advantages.
Being brought up from boyhood under the very shadow
of the Vermont University ; accustomed to mingle only
in cultured society ; coming into contact daily with literary people, it was no wonder that he became manly
while yet a boy, and was inspired in his early years
with noble impulses and lofty aspirations.

With all his literary attainments, he was also
spiritual, having consecrated himself to the service of
the Master in early life. He was thoroughly conscientious, and nothing could swerve him from the path of
duty a hair's breadth. He abhorred meanness and

duplicity, and had no patience with one who was dis-
honest or insincere.

His serious mien and very dignified manner, which
was natural to him, caused some of his classmates to
think that he regarded himself as their superior, and
that they were not worth his notice.   Such, however,
was not the case.   The most humble member of the
class, coming to the College from his country home,
with but little culture, poor in purse, and so poorly
equipped in literary attainments that he felt discouraged when he measured himself with such a brilliant student as Worcester, even this humble student.
the writer of these words, found in Worcester, a warm-
hearted, genial friend, and a friend who was ever
ready to help, to encourage, to sympathize with those
who were placed in less fortunate circumstances,
Every student who proved himself worthy could have
Worcester's friendship.

Every member of the Class, now living, will acknowledge that by coming in touch with this noble
young man during those college days, his own ideals
of life's duties were raised, and his own life exalted.''

Through these words from men who knew him
well in his boyhood, we are enabled to account for the
man which Dr. Worcester became.   It needs but little
study to be well convinced that he inherited gifts of
mind from a gifted ancestry ; that his home surroundings were well adapted to bring forward to symmetrical maturity his inherited endowments, and that his
personal purpose was early formed to make the most
out of his native ability.

Noticeable among the traits which characterized him as a boy we find those sterling virtues, fidelity to duty, unflinching honesty, a readiness to help others, a prompt condemnation of every form of injustice, and of everything false, a courage and perseverance which rested only with duty done,—with victory won.

After graduating from the University he was for two years a teacher in the Seminary of which his parents were the principals. At this time he was much exercised about his future. He had marked out for himself the law as a profession. He certainly had unusual qualifications for success in that calling. His was preeminently a legal, a judicial mind. He also felt urged on by a demand from within him to take up the work of the Gospel Ministry. A genuine conflict raged in his mind. He did not wish to be a minister. Indeed, he very much wished not to be, but he was loyal to duty as it was made plain to him, and when duty became plain, personal preferences and regrets were at an end. To let himself speak of this struggle, at this time, the following from the pen of Dr. Leavens says :

Before my eyes now lies a letter written under date, Dec. 27, 1865. He had taken his college degree at the previous commencement, and had just recovered from a "long and severe illness." His observations about his illness have a tender interest, now that he has experienced the last trial on earth.

"Though very sick," says he, "I was never so low as to appear to myself, or, I think, to the doctor, as likely to die. Still I was brought more nearly face to face with death than at any time before within my recollection. Of course I was led to think much of religious things, and, as it seemed to me, I gained some ground in religious experience which I hope I may never lose.''

My young friend was now twenty years old. I was in my last year at Union Seminary, in its old location on University Place. I was feeling the stimulus of the course, under Dr. Henry B. Smith, as the most powerful uplift in my intellectual experience. I know not what I may have written to Worcester, but he replied very freely about his thoughts and plans. I quote his words literally as then written :

'' As for my future prospects . . . . . they are still uncertain. I suppose, however, that I have pretty much given up the idea of law, and with it, most of my ambitious dreams. The question now is mainly between teaching and preaching. My conscience, I confess, sometimes suggests the query, whether it is any the less a contest between selfishness and devotion than before, the selfishness having taken the form of a desire of ease, instead of a desire of distinction. I do not say that this is so, for I am not certain that it is ; I say that it is a query merely which sometimes suggests itself and one which I shall not seek to evade. I shall hardly attempt to settle the question, however, probably, until some experience in teaching and a year or two in a Theological Seminary have enabled me to judge better than I can at present of my qualifications for either profession. But I do feel, I will not seek to disguise it, an extreme reluctance to enter the ministry such that nothing but a sense of duty would lead me to think of it, and that I should be very glad to find that duty pointed in some other direction. It is not (mainly at least), that I recoil from the probable obscurity of the work, nor altogether that I dread its pressure. It results from an utter incapacity to realize, to feel, that any souls can be won to God, by anything that I can do or say, that have not been influenced already by other motives.

It is of no use to reason against such a feeling as this ; of course, I know the unreasonableness of it, and that the Spirit of God can impart efficiency to the weakest, as it must to the most powerful human agency ; but the feeling is one over which reason has no control, and which can only be removed by praying : 'Lord, help mine unbelief,' and struggling earnestly for a higher standard of piety and a deeper faith. It is in this way substantially that I am struggling to overcome it, and hope that when the time comes that demands a decision, I may not only be enabled to see my way clearly, but also, if it should be toward the ministry, to enter upon it joyfully and cordially. But however this may be, I feel satisfied that whether eagerly like Paul or reluctantly like Moses, I shall do whatsoever my Master shall show me that he would have me do.''

This was from the young man at twenty, written to be read in one of the rooms of that seminary, where afterwards he was a brilliant student and an honored professor, and from whose chapel his body was removed to the very house from which he had penned these forecasts of his lifework.

It is well that they spoke praises of his twenty years of noble service in the office of pastor ; well also to honor both his work and the promise of his career in the professor's chair. May his thorough and honest dealing with himself in choosing the ministry help other young men now in the throes of that strenuous debate to find the sure and joyous way!''

Although not consciously to himself, his future career was settled for the ministry when, in 1867, he entered Union Theological Seminary. In 1869 he went to Germany, where his time was spent chiefly in the study of the German language, and in attendance on theological and other lectures, first at Berlin, where he attended theological lectures of Professor Dorner, and afterwards at Leipsic.

In 1870, after the close of the University Semster, he visited Vienna, and then went from Germany through Switzerland to Milan, returning through Switzerland and Holland, (Paris being at that time besieged by the Germans,) to England, and after short tours in England and in Scotland, to his home in America.

In the autumn of 1870 he re-entered Union Seminary, from which he graduated in 1871. In the fall of this year he was employed as an instructor in the University of Vermont, and ''after proving his ability to succeed as a teacher he was called to a permanent place in the Faculty'' of that institution. But this invitation he felt compelled to decline. He still felt that he was called to the Ministry. Before graduating from the Seminary he had preached at South Orange, New Jersey, and in January 1872 he was settled as pastor of the Presbyterian Church there, having some time before accepted the call given him by that church. In this, his first pastorate, he remained until he was called to become the pastor of The Sixth Presbyterian Church of Chicago.

He was married on October 29, 1874, to Miss Harriet W. Strong, a daughter of Edward Strong, M. D. of Auburndale, Massachusetts. The union was a most happy one. Mrs. Worcester was eminently worthy of Mr. Worcester. In mental and moral traits, in earnestness of life and intensity of purpose they were much alike. It is no discredit to his memory to say that to her sweet spirit and womanly character he owed not a little of what distinguished him for strong, virile manhood.

During their stay in South Orange there were born to them four children, Edward Strong, Martha Clark, Leonard, and Katherine Fleming. Here, too, they were called to mourn the first break in the family circle, in the death of little Martha Clark, when a babe of only seven weeks and two days old. She died April 30, 1878. At this time and in this bereavement we get a glimpse of his home and his own heart. Writing to his friend Dr. Leavens, under date of May 11, 1878, he says :

"Yes, our home was very happy, wondrously complete it seemed, for a few weeks. And it is very happy still ; but a part of its sweetness has exhaled, to gladden us no more here . . . . . I have always counted children one of the greatest blessings of our earthly life. . . . . . Mrs. Worcester, I am happy to say, has borne this sorrow well, both physically and spiritually, and though she gains strength slowly still continues to gain steadily.

We both found our God unexpectedly near, and

gained some precious experiences of his love and power to comfort, which in a measure even now enable us to discern the light behind the cloud."

When shortly after this, Dr. Leavens was called on to mourn the loss of one of his children, Mr. Worcester wrote to him under date of June 15, 1879:

"I saw with great pain in the *Tribune* that you too have been called to pass through the same sorrow which came to us a year ago, and my first thought on seeing the notice was of your very kind letter written then, and of the comfort it brought us. I wish that I could say that now which would be as welcome and helpful to you as your words then were to me.

Your loss is even greater than ours ; for you had your treasure longer, and every day these little ones stay with us twists a new strand into the cord that binds us to them. Still there is no time when our children are not unspeakably dear ; and so far, we can say that we know what you are feeling now.

I rejoice to think that we also know what comfort you will find and what precious lessons you will learn in the valley of weeping. Some things I know you will find that will be very precious. You will find yourself bound by a new tie to your people,—to those with whom you have prayed by the side of their little ones fallen asleep, and to those whose sympathy has been your earthly help and comfort in this trial.

You will find a new and precious power given you to minister in such scenes in time to come.

You will find Christ dearer and his grace more real and more sure, and all the promises concerning them that sleep in Jesus more full of blessed meaning than ever before.

Such at least were our gains ; and I know that yours cannot be less. And though I often wish that my little girl were here, and as I see other children of about the same age that she would be, cannot help but think what a joy we have been missing all these months in not having the unfolding of that baby life to watch, yet those were experiences that I should be loth to give up, experiences that make those days now as I look back to them, seem days of holy joy rather than of pain."

As showing the fidelity with which he discharged all the duties of a Minister of Christ while with this church, the following touching tribute to his tender helpfulness to those who were not of his own church seems most appropriate. It was written by one whose heart he had touched and comforted, many years ago. His position in the General Assembly at Detroit in 1891, had brought him more prominently before the public than he had ever been brought before. Here is what is said of his quiet work while in charge of his first church :

"While Dr. J. H. Worcester's name is so prominently before our churches, will you permit me to add a word of praise, not of his scholarly attainments but of his character as a fearless, noble Christian.

About twelve years ago that dreaded scourge, scarlet fever, entered our home and claimed two of our little ones as its victims. After the death of the second one, our pastor, an elderly, delicate man, naturally feared to enter the house, so our physician, (a member of Mr. Worcester's church,) kindly suggested our sending for his pastor, saying he knew he would willingly come to us in our trouble.

Although an entire stranger to us, with a large
parish of his own, Mr. Worcester drove nearly three
miles to our home, and not only tenderly officiated at
the funeral, but aftewards called several times with
messages of sympathy and consolation from the only
true source of comfort in sorrow.

To us, in our deep grief and isolation, he seemed
as 'one sent from God,' 'an angel of light.' We rejoice in the honor that has been conferred upon him."

S. D. B. M. in *N. Y. Evangelist*, summer of 1891.

In all of his pastoral work here as elsewhere he
never hesitated to go with his message of consolation
and hope wherever it was deemed safe for a physician
to go.

He was pastor of this, his first charge, for eleven
years. Under his faithful ministry the church was
greatly prospered ; its membership was increased ; its
members were lifted up in their Christian life. Before leaving it for his second and last charge, a fine
new house of worship was completed and dedicated.

When he entered on his duties as pastor of the
South Orange Church he was not fully convinced that
he had wisely chosen the right calling. Even as late as
May, 1879, he does not seem to have been altogether
clear. In writing to Dr. Leavens at this time about
his disappointment over the failure of the efforts of the
preceding winter "for a higher standard of church
life," he adds : "You have greatly the advantage of
me, though, in one respect. You feel sure that you
are in the right track ; that you are doing the work
God wants you to do. I *don't*. I never have got rid
yet of the uncertainty which attended my entrance on
the ministry,—whether that is my work.

However, it appears to be my work just now.
. . . . . So there is nothing to do but to work
on day by day, and hope that sometime I may find
that the work has not been quite so barren of results
as it now seems to be.''

At what time in his ministry all doubt was cleared
away concerning its being the work God had chosen
him to do we cannot say. No declaration by himself,
no word from his pen has come to us on this subject.
That doubt had ceased before he became the pastor of
the Sixth Church in Chicago there is every reason to
believe.

The South Orange Church greatly regretted his
decision to leave, and only reluctantly consented to
unite with him in a request to Presbytery for a termina-
tion of the pastoral relationship to permit him to
accept the call of the Sixth Presbyterian Church of
Chicago.

The pulpit of the Sixth Presbyterian Church had
become vacant. Rev. Henry T. Miller had, on July
16, 1882, tendered his resignation to take effect
October 15th following, and Presbytery had taken action to dissolve the relation of pastor and people. A
committee to secure a new pastor had been appointed
and for some time had been at work to find a successor
to Mr. Miller when the name of Mr. Worcester was
brought to their attention. A member of the church
being in New York, on business, was asked by the
committee to go to South Orange and hear Mr.
Worcester preach and make report.

This report was so favorable and so well agreed
with what had come to the committee from other

sources that a meeting of the Church and Society was called and the whole matter laid before it. Power was given to the committee to call Mr. Worcester if deemed best, and, clothed with this authority, two members of the committee—Mr. J. W. Helmer and Mr. George H. Wells, visited South Orange and called on Mr. Worcester. From all that could be learned from those whom the visiting committee consulted, as well as from the judgment formed by hearing him preach, it was deemed important to have him preach to the Sixth Church.   As he was to be in Chicago to preach the sermon at the installation of the Rev. S. J. McPherson as pastor of the Second Presbyterian Church, on Sunday evening, Nov. 19, the committee tried to get from Mr. Worcester a promise to occupy the pulpit of the Sixth Church on the morning of the same day. To this he would not listen at all as the pulpit was vacant and his occupying it under such circumstances would, or could be interpreted as "*candidating.*"

He was informed that the church had clothed its committee with full power to call him to the vacant pastorate, and that call the committee then offered him.   This opened the way for less reserve in the discussion of the question, on his part, than he had, up to this time, exercised. Mr. J. W. Helmer, a member of that visiting committee, says: "When the committee called on him to invite him to come to Chicago, he seemed much surprised and not at all favorably inclined to consider the call.   The committee presented to him the field to which they invited him and urged such reasons as they could to induce him to come and see it for himself. In a very frank manner he replied:

'I have thought the time might come when it would seem desirable for me to make a change. This is my first pastorate and I have been here eleven years. It is generally thought better for a minister to change once at least, in his life, but I have no wish to go to a large city. I think I am better adapted to work in a village, or a small city. It is difficult for me to make new acquaintances, and the demands of a large city upon a pastor are such that I do not think it would be best for you nor for me to undertake them.' This was said with such transparent sincerity and earnestness, that the committee were still more strongly impressed in his favor. He frankly stated that he did not believe he possessed the gifts which would win people to the church. Whatever strength he had lay in the direction of training, educating, and building up those who had already been brought into it. So little did he seem to desire to undertake the work to which he was invited that, had it not been for the fact that he was to be in the city at the installation of his personal friend, Rev. S. J. McPherson, it was the opinion of the committee, he could not have been induced to visit Chicago for the purpose of looking over the field."

He finally consented to occupy the pulpit of the Sixth Church at the morning service on Sunday, Nov. 19, 1882, and did so, preaching the least acceptable sermon he ever preached from it. He spent a few days in Chicago, and led the church prayer-meeting on the following Wednesday evening, a practically unanimous call having been reaffirmed in a vote by ballot on the evening before. He would make no promises, and gave no indication of what his decision would be until he should have returned home and considered the whole matter with the deliberation which the gravity of the question demanded. In all of his conferences with the committee, with the Session, or with individual members, the question of salary was never mentioned by him, nor was any word spoken indicating what amount he would accept. He did make careful and critical inquiry about the work of the church as indicated by its contributions to the various Boards of the church and to benevolent objects.

In due time he communicated his acceptance of the call that had been made, and entered upon his work as pastor of his second and last charge, preaching his inaugural sermon on the second Sunday of February, his installation taking place February 13, 1883. He continued to be pastor of the church until Sunday, September 6, 1891, when the pulpit was, by order of Presbytery, declared vacant. He had resigned in order to accept the chair of Systematic Theology in Union Seminary, New York City, to which he had been elected. During the eight and a half years of his pastorate and work in Chicago, it may safely be said that the best work of his life was done. He had reached the years of mature life when he commenced it. The experience of his first charge was the substantial foundation on which he began building in his second. He was in the best of health during the whole time ; the demands of a large church in a great city called for the best which his matured power could give ; his personal sense of obligation in view of greatly enlarged opportunity, all united to secure from him the best and the largest work of his life.

What he was, and what he did, therefore, in Chicago will be the best exponent of the man. But the man is more than what he does,—greater than any phase of his work. It will therefore be in order first to note what manner of man he was.

Much has already been said of his inherited intellectual power, of his moral and religious bias, derived from a gifted and pious ancestry. It is a great thing to be the heir to such a patrimony. It is greater still to live so as to prove one's self worthy of it, and to improve it by greatly increasing it through well directed use.

In many respects Dr. Worcester was a remarkable man. His personal presence was striking. His face told the story of great thoughtfulness, intense earnestness, and frank, downright honesty. His reserve of manner probably led to greater misunderstanding of the man than anything else about him. He was judged by many as without warmth of sympathy, by some as haughty. He was neither. By a few he was judged as caring little for the company and the confidences of ordinary people, less gifted than himself. The exact opposite of this was the simple truth.

He was exceptionally *modest* in the best sense of the term. His modesty often amounted to embarrassing timidity; and in miscellaneous society his diffidence was extreme to the last degree. He shrank from every avoidable publicity at all times. This diffidence was unquestionably a great hindrance to him in many departments of his work. Young people, and people timid and diffident like himself, unavoidably misunderstood him and reached conclusions regarding him which prevented his acquiring the influence over them he otherwise would have gained. Thus judging there were those who delighted to hear him preach who yet shrank from meeting him face to face. When the University of Vermont, in 1885, conferred on him the degree of Doctor of Divinity, he shrank from accepting it, and urged his own people to continue to call him *Mr.* Worcester. From his friends he never wished to hear the title applied to him, and called the writer of this to task for having had D. D. printed on a pamphlet of his sermons. He had very little use for titles or for the personal pronoun of the first person.

He was an *intensely earnest* man. Life, with him, was a mission at all times. Opportunity amounted to obligation. Time was not money as so often falsely put,—it was life, it was opportunity, it was high responsibility. This intense earnestness,—this habitual looking on the side of responsibility left little time for the trivial things which fill up so large a space in the life of many. It is possible that it sometimes led him to judge small things as trivial which were really important, thereby preventing his wielding the influence over some whom, had he judged otherwise, he might have reached.

With all right thinking people time is precious. With him it was sacred. To use it, and use it all to the best advantage was his high duty. Every day had its duties,—every hour its share. Fully alive to the importance of every moment, he was always prompt in meeting his engagements. He would allow no one to waste time waiting for him to meet an appointment. Failure on the part of others to be equally prompt tried his patience and vexed him as scarcely anything else could do.

He was eminently an *honest* man. His abhorrence of all pretense and sham led him at all times to guard his words as well as his actions. This accounted for much of his reserve in speech. He would not over-state his feelings, nor pretend to what he did not feel. He had no supply of ready-made compliments ; no set form of greeting ; no meaningless terms of endearment. He was too honest for anything of the kind. This often prevented his saying much. He could not "gush." But he was not cold, he was not indifferent to the interests, or even to the judgments of others. Beneath a calm, but not a cold exterior he had a warm, a tender, a sympathetic heart. His known moderation of speech as well as his acknowledged honesty and sincerity gave added force to his expressed sympathy in time of trouble. His words spoken in the sick room or in the house of mourning are yet cher-ished as precious memories. If his words of praise were few, words of dispraise from him were still more rare. Charity was a foundation element of his hon-esty. If his sincerity led him to speak guardedly, his honest purpose forbade his judging hastily or unjustly. He was more severe with himself than with any one else, and much more severe than any others ever thought of being toward him. Frank commendation, when stated in terms of moderation, he appreciated and accepted. Adulation, or fulsome praise he could not endure. Criticism he always accepted with the best grace if honestly made. That it rarely led him to change was not because he did not consider it, but because he had so thoroughly considered what was criticized before it was done and had followed what to him was the only right course that, honestly, he could not change. There was no disrespect intended nor was there any want of appreciation of the value of the criticism from the position of the one who offered it, but simply an inability to accept it as his position had been clearly taken on the best judgment he could command. When he became satisfied that he had not chosen wisely, none could be more frank in promptly admitting it, nor could any one have been more grateful to those who led him to see it. His iron will made him exacting of himself, sustaining him in the performance of all that he conceived to be duty. He was naturally of an exceedingly nervous temperament although presenting an unusually calm exterior. It was sheer strength of will-power which preserved his outward calmness and which impelled him and sustained him in all that he did, and which ever made him complete master of himself. He was no petty tyrant as many men of strong will are apt to be. Indeed he was unusually considerate of others and readily found excuses for their failures which he would in no way have countenanced in himself. In the home circle he was tender, loving, confiding. He took peculiar delight in his children and entered into their amusements and diversions with great delight and enthusiasm. He took the greatest interest in their school work and always took delight in helping them. His clear explanations, with his ready power of illustration, lifted them over their difficulties. But he was equally considerate of their wishes where only gratification of harmless desire was involved. It was no small trouble to take their pet cat all the way from Chicago to New York, but he could not consent to leave it behind when his children wished to take it along.

He was naturally a *student*. His classmates in college bear testimony to his thoroughness in every department of college work. Others have made equally good records in college work, stimulated by a desire to excel their classmates, who, when the stimulus was withdrawn, ceased their effort and failed to distinguish themselves in after life. Dr. Worcester's ambition was to excel himself,—to bring his actual self up to his ideal self. This is only another phase of his honesty of character Nothing short of complete mastery of his subject,—the fullest obtainable information on all its details would satisfy him. One whose constant purpose is to excel himself can never cease to be a student and consequently never ceases to grow in mental strength and mental furnishing. With those whose ambition is only to excel others, study usually ceases when opportunity for comparison is at an end. With Dr. Worcester study was a constant delight. Knowledge concerning a new subject, increased knowledge of an old one were always eagerly sought. So it came that when he spoke on any subject he spoke clearly, forcibly, orderly, logically, exhaustively, for he had compassed the subject in his own mind ; he *under*stood it, and spoke from the fullness of one who was able to hold the subject up for view, for discussion, usually for settlement.

His wonderful power of analysis, his mastery of

clear statement were too much regarded as native endowments of mind.   No doubt his mind had an original
analytical and logical bias, much beyond that of most
men, but it was also well furnished for its task by careful study and patient research.   It may be assumed
that he believed the maxim of Seneca "All are sufficiently eloquent in that which they understand."
That he might understand he read widely, but he also
thought patiently and critically.   Through this thorough study and complete mastery of the subjects to
which he gave his thought, he was usually ready to
call up at once all he knew and had thought on a
subject, and to state all so clearly, so forcibly, so com-
prehensively that he rarely failed to carry his hearers
with him. In a degree not at all common, even among
trained scholars, his mind seemed intuitively to brush
aside all irrelevant questions, to eliminate all non-es-
sentials, and to state the simple problem thus freed
from its cumbrous surroundings, so clearly that his
statement of the problem was very generally its
solution.

He was a true *friend*.   He gave his heart in full
measure when a worthy heart was given in return.
None prized ingenuous friendship more highly than he.
His whole being spoke when he unbosomed himself to
one who could understand him and who thoroughly
sympathized with him.   In the intimacy of friendship
his natural restraint was forgotten, and he was
sprightly, full of keen but always kindly humor.   Few
men had greater capacity for genuine friendship.

As a *preacher* Dr. Worcester was peculiarly gifted.
His oratory was of a high order.   His thought was

always clear and strong, his choice of language through
which his thought was expressed was of the finest.
His treatment of his theme was comprehensive, logical, exhaustive. His appeal was very largely to the
intellect and the conscience. He made comparatively
rare appeal to the emotions. His wide reading and
careful study enabled him to flash light on the discussion of his theme by illustrations from nature, science,
art, and literature, as well as from the daily duties and
ordinary every-day experiences of the people whom he
addressed. His rhetoric was elegant,—always pure,
always strong. With great gift for rhetorical embel-
lishment he never indulged it except for the most
direct and pertinent purpose. His figures were drawn
from a very wide range and were always strikingly appropriate. Figures and illustrations were used by him
for their legitimate purpose only, and he never pursued either a single step beyond the point where it had
served its purpose. He was not and could not have
been what is regarded as a "popular preacher." He
had few of the gifts which attract large audiences, none
of those which attract the purely curious. He was too
close a student, too severely logical a thinker with too
much of a metaphysical bias in his habit of thought
and form of statement to entertain or to please. But
he was an unusually clear and forcible speaker. In his
masterful ability to analyze a complex and difficult
question, strip away all irrelevancies, place the several
parts in their proper order, and hold up and enforce
that which is essential, he had few equals and no superior in the Chicago pulpit. In handling a text or
a theme he wasted no time on the surface questions

and obvious truths. His penetrating mind dug deep and brought to view the richer jewels of thought which, but for his penetration, would have been overlooked.

More than most ministers he confined himself within what many would call a comparatively narrow range in his preaching. His inaugural sermon in the Sixth Church had for its text "I seek not yours, but you"; and his farewell sermon, from the text "For I determined not to know anything among you save Jesus Christ and him, crucified." All of his preaching during the years between these two sermons was true to the spirit and declaration of each. He not only felt, but he publicly said: "Christian preaching is concerned with but one thing, to make Jesus Christ known to men and bring them into touch with his living personality." If it is claimed that this view is a narrow one, here are his own words on the subject: "A narrow theme? Very well. But narrowness means concentration, and concentration means power. There are many things, in themselves worthy objects of study—history, science, statesmanship, literature—with which the preacher as a *preacher* has nothing to do. As a man they may interest him. And the more he knows of them, in other words the broader his culture, the better preacher, other things being equal, he will make. But these things are no part of his message. There are many public affairs in which as a citizen it is the preacher's business to be interested. But as a *preacher* they constitute no part of his mission. Just in proportion as he forgets the limitations of that mission and seeks to turn his pulpit into a lyceum platform for the

discussion of the sundry 'topics of the day,' just in
that proportion will he rob his ministry of all its distinctive power. The secret of that power lies in
keeping before the minds of men immersed in worldliness, distracted with doubt, beset with temptation,
burdened with care, in all its sweet attractiveness, its
manifold sympathy, and its divine majesty, the person
of Jesus Christ.

And the more intensely he feels the power of that
personality, and believes in its divinity, the less inclination will he have to do anything else. The ages of
gospel conquest, the ages of faith, have always been
marked by this sort of narrowness. It is when preachers begin to lose faith in a divine Christ and in an atoning cross, that they are impelled to resort to Shakesper-
ian readings and lectures on art and courses in history
and science for the improvement of their hearers. So
when a jet of steam issues from the safety valve of an
engine, so long as the expansive power which drives it
forth continues, it is narrow, almost cylindrical. Only
as that impulse is exhausted does it spread itself out
in all directions, a cold damp cloud, without form and
without force."

But the narrowness is apparent rather than real.
Closer study will easily reveal its breadth. It is wide
enough to embrace all of man's relations to God ; all
of God's love for man. But on this it will be best to
have his own words also. They are as follows :

"But if, at first view, we are struck with the nar_
rowness of the preacher's work, we are even more impressed on a second view with its breadth. 'Nothing
save Jesus Christ'! But the infinities and the eterni-

ties are in that theme.   God and man are there.

In Jesus Christ we have the ideal manhood ; and all that concerns the building up of such a manhood comes within the compass of this theme.   The whole domain of character, the whole sphere of morals, is embraced within the scope of that spotless life and those perfect precepts.

But Jesus was also 'God manifest in the flesh'. All that we can comprehend, all that we shall ever know of God we shall know in him and through him as the Word, the Revealer.

Jesus Christ is the Redeemer from all evil.   He is the great Comforter, the great Burden-bearer, the Friend by whose sympathy every sorrow is soothed, and whose sustaining arm supports under every cross.

In Him is the power of victory over sin.   The tempted, the struggling, the slaves of vice, the outcasts from society, aye, even 'the devil's castaways', all may find in him the hope and energy for a new life.

Jesus Christ is the conqueror of death. The mysteries of the endless future are unfolded through Him who brought life and immortality to light.

Jesus Christ is the head of a perfected society, the founder of the kingdom of God in whose triumph lies the only hope for the reform of governments, for the reconciliation of the antagonism of labor and capital, for the bringing together of rich and poor, for the elevation of the masses, and for the solution of the desperate problems at which social science stands aghast and which sometimes threaten the overthrow of the existing civilization.''

He was preeminently an *educating* preacher, leading those whom he reached to examine, compare, judge, and determine largely after his own method. He readily brought his people to view duty, in a measure, as he did. Thus it came about that his church was so thoroughly educated and trained that its strength could promptly be united and directed to any worthy undertaking. The year just preceding his first year as pastor of the Sixth Church, the total contributions of the church to the various Boards was $1486.00. The last year of his pastorate the contributions amounted to $3083.00, and certainly with no increase of contributing wealth represented in the congregation. Large increase of contributions for various objects as well as wholly new objects of church activity, not through the Church Boards, had also been made. Dr. Worcester's ideals of Christian life and responsibility were high. Courageously and persistently he pressed these ideals upon his people, until, in good measure, they accepted them. The great increase in benevolences was directly the result of the education which he had carried forward by his preaching, by his pastoral labors, and above all, which he had enforced by his personal example of systematic giving. His earnestness of spirit and directness of purpose together with his admitted sincerity made his preaching impressive. The orderly and natural arrangement of his discourses ; their careful division into propositions for consideration ; their logical structure and compactness made them easily remembered and easy to call up months, and even years, after their delivery.

His preaching was mainly from manuscript, although he often preached without.   It cannot be said that he was, as a rule, as successful in his unwritten discourses as in those that were written.   Still even here he was remarkably strong.   In all of his preaching and in his prayer-meeting talks he made large demands on his hearers.   Everything he said was so organically related to the rest that no one could hear portions of what he said with interest or with profit. One must hear it all,—must think it all, feel it all to get what was meant or even to become interested in it.   Neither a lazy nor a listless hearer would or could keep up much interest in his preaching.   It has sometimes been said, possibly truly, that Dr. Worcester's preaching and teaching demanded more of his hearers than can be given by many people of every ordinary congregation.   Whether this were true or not, those who tried to follow him and strove to appreciate him soon found their interest growing and made very rapid progress in ability to profit by his teaching.   His sermons never disappointed.   He often surprised those even who admired his preaching most.   As a result many of his sermons, by special request, were printed and distributed among his people.   He delivered several courses of sermons and these were exceptionally strong.   Very many beyond his own congregation read with great interest as well as with much profit his " Sermons on Womanhood" and " Sermons on Money."   So careful was he in the preparation of his discourses that, when he was asked to furnish them for printing, no material change had ever to be made to prepare them for the compositor.

As a *pastor* Dr. Worcester was a model of fidelity.

He constantly sought the highest good of all whom he was called upon to counsel. His reserve of manner coupled with a hereditary bashfulness and timidity, not common with one of his recognized ability, prevented his making acquaintances and friendships as quickly as might have been desirable. His thorough loyalty to his own heart forbade any effusiveness of expression and made impossible a display of feelings which he did not entertain. It also, many times, prevented the full expression of deepest feelings which he did entertain, and led to judgments concerning him, by those not fully acquainted with him, which did him injustice, and made them the losers.

He was a man of very tender heart, and of very keen and deep feeling. He loved his people with a fervency which he had little power to put in words. It was in times of trouble and sorrow or bereavement that his lips were opened and the fulness and tenderness of his heart had free expression. He had learned in the school of experience what it is to have the family circle broken. Out of this experience he could speak words which often calmed the tumult of grief and grew sweeter and more sustaining when the overwhelming tempest of acute grief had passed by.

He had no time for mere visiting,—no taste for idle gossip or fruitless chatter. He was intensely in earnest and awake to the importance of time and the responsibility of his ''calling'' even in his pastoral visits. Formal religionists and those who lived on a low plane of experience undoubtedly did not appreciate or highly value his society, but the hungry soul he fed, and gave courage to the fainting heart.

It is not necessary to deny that had he possessed in larger measure the faculty of becoming more interested in the ordinary affairs of people less gifted and thoughtful, as well as less earnest than himself, it would have increased his usefulness. Could he have removed some of the restraint and spoken, at times, more freely of his feelings and sympathies, it cannot be doubted his influence and helpfulness would have been greater at the time. It will not be questioned, however, that his pastoral work, even more than his preaching, survived his separation from his people. No scepticism can brush aside his consistent life and example. No doubt can long live in the presence of the recollection of his steady faith. No shocks of faith from the failures of fulsome professors can triumph over his transparent, downright consistency. He will be longer remembered for his sincerity than for his power of logical statement ; longer for his consecrated earnestness than for his gifts of oratory.

He was always and on all occasions a consistent minister of the Gospel. His " daily walk and conversation." never belied his pulpit ministrations. An *every day* Christian, his influence is felt and acknowledged as much as it was when he walked our streets and went in and out before us.

His service to the Church at large was the same in kind as for the individual church of which he was pastor. He had come to feel an intense interest in the great city where his lot had been cast. He saw its need of Christ as the solution of all the problems growing out of the conflicting interests which disturb its peace. He saw the danger of its great wealth, beget-

ting selfishness and tending to indulgence ; the perils of
its wretched poverty, breeding hatred and tending to
despair or lawless rebellion.

Firmly did he believe that the religion of Jesus
Christ accepted in the heart and lived in conduct, and
nothing else, could make rich and poor live together in
loving bonds of brotherhood, mutually helpful to one
another. This, and this alone, would make the prosperous awake to their responsibility ; would nerve the
poor and the unfortunate to bear their burdens. As a
Presbyter, therefore, he was prominent in all the work
which the Church undertook for the evangelization of
the city. An enthusiast on the subject of Missions,
Home and Foreign, he was equally energetic in his
work for the needy, the ignorant, and the vicious
directly about his own door.

The Presbyterian League has for its object the
support of the Gospel in communities which, but for
its assistance, would be in danger of abandoning church
work already begun. It helps feeble churches by timely
assistance until they can meet their obligations and
carry on their work without such outside help. Into this
important work Dr. Worcester put his heart and his
energy. In its service he spent much time. All associated with him in this branch of work greatly regretted
his departure from the city. In the regular work of the
presbytery he was noted for his promptness, regularity
of attendance at meetings, punctuality in meeting engagements for committee work, fidelity, clear judgment, and exceptional ability in the discharge of all of
the duties required of him by his brethren. He was
not given to much speaking in the public deliberations

of presbytery, but when occasion demanded he was prompt to respond, and was listened to with the greatest respect, and by most of the members with decided deference. His judicial habit of mind, his judicious treatment of men and measures ; his great candor and admitted fairness ; his clear statements and forceful style won the closest attention of his associates. He was regarded as one of the ablest debaters and soundest thinkers among the very able men who make up the presbytery of Chicago.

In 1891 he was chosen one of the Commissioners to the General Assembly which met at Detroit, in May of that year. It was a meeting of great and grave importance to the church. Questions affecting the peace of the denomination were to come before it. The relation of one of the great theological seminaries to the General Assembly must be considered. It was a time when clear heads and dispassionate judgment were at a premium. He was known to possess both. It was a time for courage and for moderation and he was an embodiment of both. It was every way fitting that the great presbytery of Chicago should send this man of iron will, calm judgment, clear mind, and loving heart to share in the responsibility and to perform his share of the grave duties of the hour.

The church had been disturbed by certain utterances of Dr. Briggs of Union Theological Seminary. Many thoughtful men had grave fears regarding the effect of these utterances. There seemed to be serious danger of the church becoming divided into Briggs and anti-Briggs factions. Revision of the Standards had been a prominent question in the presbyteries and must come before the General Assembly. So important a meeting brought together leaders in thought of the Presbyterian denomination. The gravity of the situation was felt by all thoughtful men. The "*Interior*" sounded the note of warning in its issue just preceding the meeting as follows :

"The contending brethren agree upon the Scriptures as the only and infallible rule of faith and practice.

They agree upon the Confession of Faith as containing the system of doctrine taught in the Holy Scriptures.

Both parties in the terms of warmest affirmation declare their loyalty to the Scriptures as the supreme and to the Confession as the subordinate, standards of our faith. Neither the one party nor the other can with any Christian propriety challenge the sincerity of the other in these affirmations.

Now it seems plain to the plain and unlearned Christian that here is a platform of agreement upon which we may stand with sufficient harmony, calmly to consider, reduce to a minimum, and adjust within limits of toleration and forbearance, all existing real differences. Or failing in this, that, having reduced those differences to the minimum, we can calmly and as charitably consider whether any of them are beyond the limits of safe toleration."

Whatever part Dr. Worcester took in the deliberations of the Assembly, he did not appear prominently before that body nor the world until the discussion came up on the report of the *Committee on Theological Seminaries*, through its chairman Dr. Patton, of Princeton.

That report proposed to disapprove, by refusing to
sanction, the action of the directors of Union Seminary
in transferring Dr. Briggs to the chair of biblical theology. The directors held that as the original appointment
of Dr. Briggs as a professor in Union Seminary had
been submitted to the Assembly and had been approved,
there was no need of seeking approval in a matter of
transfer from one chair to another in the same institution. The committee contended that the transfer
needed the sanction of the Assembly as much as though
it had been an original appointment.

It would not be in place here to review the proceedings of the Assembly. Many speeches had been
made on both sides of the question under discussion.
Extreme positions had been taken on both sides. Judge
Breckinridge, of St. Louis, had made an argument the
day before on the legal aspects of the case, supporting
the report of the committee. At the close of his speech
Judge Breckinridge fell from an attack of heart trouble
and expired before he could be removed from the
church.

It was under these sad and subduing circumstances
that Dr. Worcester took the floor at the opening of the
session on the following morning. He had been importuned to take part earlier, but he kept hoping that
some moderate measures would be proposed by some
one else, and that wiser counsels would prevail. He
only spoke when he felt that he must. As showing the
temper and the spirit of the man this speech will be of
interest. He first offered a substitute for the amendment proposed the day before by Dr. Logan, and then
addressed the Assembly on the question of adopting his

substitute. We give the whole as reported in the
" *Interior* : "

Mr. Moderator : I desire to offer a substitute in
place of the amendment of Dr. Logan. I desire also
to move this paper as a substitute for the entire report
of the committee:

The Assembly recognizes that the present relation
of our theological seminaries to the General Assembly
was brought about through the voluntary and generous
concession by Union Seminary of a portion of its independence, in the interest of a better adjustment for all,
and it recognizes that in the recent transfer of Professor
Briggs to the chair of biblical theology, the directors of
Union Seminary acted in perfect good faith, upon a
possible construction of their powers under the act de-
fining those relations. It recognizes also that the present widespread uneasiness and agitation in the church
has grown out of utterances of Professor Briggs subsequent to that transfer. At the same time it regards these
utterances as certainly ill-advised, and as having seriously disturbed the peace of the church and led to a
situation full of difficulty and complication ; yet the Assembly desires to act in the spirit of the largest charity
and forbearance consistent with fidelity to its trust, and
of the most generous confidence in the directors of Union
Seminary. Therefore,

Resolved, That a committee be appointed by this
Assembly, consisting of eight ministers and seven ruling
elders, for the following purposes, to-wit :

1. To confer with the Directors of Union Theological Seminary in regard to the relations of the said
Seminary to the General Assembly and report thereon

to the next General Assembly.

2.   To request the directors of Union Seminary to reconsider the action by which Dr. Briggs was transferred to the chair of biblical theology.

3.   To advise that in any case Professor Briggs be not allowed to give instructions during the year previous to the meeting of the next Assembly.

On these propositions Dr. Worcester said :

Under the circumstances under which we are met this morning, any attempt at excited rhetoric would be out of place, even if I were capable of it.   In the presence of that solemn providence by which our hearts have all been startled and I trust calmed, the only kind of discussion that seems to be in place is quiet, dispassionate, matter of fact reasoning together.   I do not stand here as the advocate of Dr. Briggs, though I honor his learning and respect his piety.   Still less do I stand here as an opponent of Dr. Briggs, though as my brethren of the Presbytery of Chicago know, he has said many things with which I totally disagree and the spirit of which I utterly disapprove.   I stand here as an advocate of peace.   From the day I was elected a commissioner to this Assembly one word of Holy Writ has come to my mind as often as I have thought of the responsibilities which would confront me here,—"Study those things which make for peace and things wherewith one may edify another."   Most earnestly have I hoped and most sincerely have I prayed that this Assembly might be guided to a conclusion in this grave and painful affair which would unite this Assembly, which would unify this agitated church, which would allay this threatening bitterness of strife, and which would send this church forward, a united phalanx, to more glorious and peaceful victories under the banner of our Lord Jesus Christ. And I do not believe Mr. Moderator, that in this hope and in this prayer I stand alone. I believe there are multitudes of calm and thoughtful men on both sides of this question, if you call them sides, so far as men's sympathies with Dr. Briggs are concerned, that there are multitudes of calm and thoughtful men in this Assembly who have been looking and who have been longing and have been praying for some safe middle course which should avoid extremes and keep the church in harmony. And when I heard, as I did on arriving, necessarily a day late at the meeting of the Assembly, that this matter had been intrusted to some of the clearest brains in this Assembly or in the Presbyterian Church for their report, I felt reassured—I felt that we should get just such a deliverance, moderate, mediative, on which we could all stand. And it was with profound disappointment and sorrow that I listened to that report when it was presented to this Assembly. Because, Mr. Moderator, say what you will, the course proposed in this report is an extreme course. It strains the authority of this Assembly over Dr. Briggs to its utmost limit.

Dr. Patton told us yesterday that this was the very least this Assembly could do. Mr. Moderator, what more could this Assembly do ? You cannot hang Dr. Briggs, you cannot imprison him, you cannot cast him out of the church, you cannot depose him from the ministry. You cannot, in this Assembly, impeach his orthodoxy or touch his moral character. The one thing that you can do is to veto, bluntly, absolutely, without a reason, his appointment as professor of biblical theology in Union Seminary.   That is the utmost you can do.   Even upon your power to do that, the committee themselves admit that there rests a shadow of a doubt, a shadow sufficiently distinct and perceptible to make them think it necessary to appoint fifteen wise men before another year, to clear it away.

But in the meantime—and I wonder if I am the only commissioner to whom the relation of the two resolutions in this report was a surprise—in the meantime while we admit that there may be some question about our authority to do this thing, we will behead the man and then we will confer with the directors of Union Seminary as to whether we had the right to do it.

And I object to this report because it is an arbitrary report, because it says simply that we disapprove of this appointment, and gives no reason for this disapproval.   Judge Breckinridge said yesterday, and we all recognized its force, that a judge might often give a very wise decision founded on very poor reasons, and that, therefore, it was better never to give reasons if you could help it.   But in a matter which touches the standing of a man, in a matter which affects the reputation of a man, in a matter which may prejudice an ecclesiastical trial already in progress, you cannot help it ; you have no right to help it.   If I remember rightly, it is not a great many years since there was a great political controversy in the United States over the question whether the President of the United States had a right to behead even a postmaster without giving some reason ; and we propose to behead officially a theological professor without giving any reason whatever. Now we are told that a great many reasons might be given. Why didn't the committee give a reason? Mr. Moderator, I fear it was because they knew that no one reason that could be given would carry a majority of this Assembly with it ; I fear that had some influence on the minds of the committee ; at all events I believe that to be true.

I listened with the greatest attention when Dr. Patton set forth the reasons, the possible reasons that might have been assigned. He admitted that it would not do to say that it was on account of the idiosyncracies of the professor that we disapprove this appointment ; he said that theological reasons, not amounting to a charge of heresy, might have been given; but he admitted with all his power of lucid statement, in which he has not in this Assembly a peer, those theological reasons would be so intricate and so obscure that very few would be able to distinguish them from a charge of heresy. He admitted that it would not do to disapprove of Professor Briggs on the ground that he is not sound in the faith, because that would be anticipating the Presbytery of New York; and the only reason that I could discover that he would urge as a practical reason that might have been given, was that Dr. Briggs is under suspicion. He is under suspicion, and Mr. Moderator, shall we disapprove of this appointment because the professor is under suspicion, when we know that steps have already been initiated to sift this suspicion and ascertain whether it is right or wrong ? Is it not the part of an Assembly of the Presbyterian Church, is it not one of the foundation principles of the Presbyterian

churches, to stand by a man who is under suspicion until the suspicion has been sifted to the bottom ?

At all events, Mr. Moderator, I protest against the
bare, blunt disapproval of this election without any
reason given, and I protest against it because, as Mr.
Ramsey has just so eloquently said before you, it will
inevitably, say what you may and do what you may,
have an influence upon the judicial proceedings already
initiated in the Presbytery of New York. The world
will know, will believe, the Presbytery of New York
will believe, that if this Assembly had not, down in its
heart of hearts, suspected Dr. Briggs's serious departure
from the faith, it would never have taken this action,
and the only way in which you can prevent this impression being made on the mind of the church and on
the mind of the country is to give some other reason
with those resolutions. Now, the committee feel this ;
the committee see that it would be very desirable to
take some milder course if it were possible. They have
said so in their report. Dr. Patton said the same thing
in his address, and Judge Breckinridge said the same
thing in tender words of deep feeling, in that dying
speech that he made to us yesterday. It is simply a
question whether any middle course is possible. I cannot believe that a great Assembly like this, desiring to
avoid extremes, desiring to do nothing which can in
any way cast a shadow of unjust suspicion upon a man
who is under trial, desiring to find some middle path
out of this difficulty in which we are all involved, will
sit down helpless before a problem like this.

It must be possible for this Assembly to find some
middle way out of this difficulty. I would have been

satisfied personally, notwithstanding the technical objections of Dr. Patton, and notwithstanding the legal argument of Judge Breckinridge, I would have been satisfied personally to vote for the amendment of Dr. Logan, and I would not have introduced this substitute for Dr. Logan's amendment at this stage if I had not perceived that the technical difficulty really weighed upon the minds of many judicious men of this Assembly, who have just the same desire for peace for which I stand here. But I saw that there were technical questions involved here. I felt the force to a certain degree, although I did not feel that it was absolutely conclusive, of Dr. Patton's point that we must approve or disapprove *simpliciter*, that it is not possible for us to interpose a qualified veto. Therefore, I propose that we reach the same result in another way, about the legality of which there can be absolutely no question. The only question that can arise is about its safety, and on that question I will touch in a moment.

Certainly it is within the power of the Assembly, if it chooses to waive its authority in this case, not to exercise, in view of the position in which Dr. Briggs stands before his own presbytery, the power of disapproval which under other circumstances there might be no peril in exercising, and instead of that to go to the directors of the Union Seminary and say to them, ''In view of these utterances which have been made since your action and since the inauguration, we ask you to reconsider in the light of the present this whole matter of your appointment.'' Now, what do you gain by this course ? You avoid, as I have already pointed out, prejudicing Dr. Briggs before the Presbytery of New

York ; and Mr. Moderator, I think this Assembly ought
to heed very carefully the words of Mr. Ramsey.   As
he has pointed out, the prosecutors in this case are in a
trying and difficult position ; they stand for those who
object to anything that may seem to be novel or hereti-
cal in the utterances of Dr. Briggs ; they stand for the
faith once delivered to the saints.   Shall we as an Assembly, who stand for that same faith and who are
animated above all things by loyalty to the hearts of
the church and to the Word of God, shall we do anything to prejudice their position and to make their task
more difficult ?   You make your action consistent
with itself in that you will confer with the directors of
Union Seminary as to the relations of that Seminary to
the General Assembly before you act upon your own
construction of those rules. You take a course fitting to
conciliate Union Seminary rather than to alienate it.
Mr. Moderator, the directors of Union Seminary are loyal
Presbyterians ; they are wise and calm men, and they
are waiting with intense anxiety, as has been said, for
the deliverance of this Assembly on this subject. Nevertheless, as I know from personal conference with two
or three of them, they are not waiting for such a deliverance as is proposed in the report of this committee.
They feel—what shall I say ? They feel pained,
they feel hurt, they feel aggrieved at the haste of this
Assembly to rush to such an extreme action, as if it had
no confidence in their wisdom in this case.   You conciliate the directors of Union Seminary by going and
asking them to do in their own wisdom and in their
own loyalty to the church what you claim that you
would have the right to do if you chose to exercise it ;

and above all, you give time for a calm and thoughtful consideration of this case, and you give time for a great deal of new light to be thrown upon it.

But what is the objection to this course ? I was touched with the way in which Judge Breckinridge put this matter yesterday. He referred to this very course. He said: "There are two courses before us, to approve or disapprove. Now," he said, "It may be suggested that we take a third course, to refer this matter back to the directors of Union Seminary, and," he added, "I have wished that such a course might be taken ; I have tried to see that it was possible, but it does not seem to be possible." Why ? Because in that case we would lose our control here of this matter. We lose our control! Now if we refer this matter back to them, there are but three things that the directors of the Union Seminary can do. They can reconsider it and revoke the appointment of Professor Briggs. Then your whole difficulty is removed and removed in a peaceful way. They can reconsider it and re-appoint Dr. Briggs, we will suppose ; then he comes to the next General Assembly in precisely the same condition as he comes to this. That appointment being made subject to the approval of the Assembly, will be subject to the veto of the Assembly then, and you are in the same position as you are to-day, except that by that time you will know a great deal more about the theological views of Professor Briggs than you know to-day, and that that Assembly will have a report from this committee of fifteen making clear the matter of the relation of the Union Theological Seminary to this Assembly. The only other thing that they can do will be, in the face of this earnest request of this Assembly and its committee of fifteen, to refuse to reconsider the case at all, and that is the only peril this Assembly exposes itself to by this action.

Mr. Moderator, is it possible that there are ten men in this Assembly who are frightened by any such specter as that? Is it possible that this Assembly believes for a moment that men like Dr. Dickey and Dr. Erskine White and Dr. John Hall and these other men whose names were read over to you by Dr. Dickey, that these men, when the Assembly says to them, "We request you to re-open this matter, we request you in the interests of peace, and in the interests of our church, to look again at the subsequent utterances of Dr. Briggs," that they will snap their fingers in the face of this Assembly and say : "Gentlemen, you have lost your control, and we will do as we please." If that is the feeling we have in regard to Union Seminary, the sooner it is cut loose from the church the better. If we have not faith in the integrity and in the honor, and in the character and wisdom of the Presbyterian ministers and elders who compose the directory of Union Seminary, then we had better say : "We want nothing more to do with Union Seminary, and the sooner it is cut loose and turned adrift the better for the church." But, sir, we have not only the integrity and honor of these men as a pledge in this case ; we have an action taken at the last meeting of the board of directors of Union Seminary ; an action which was an olive branch held out to this Assembly ; an action which was taken unanimously, Dr. Dickey informs me, and which is spread upon their records. What was that action ?   We understand from this committee that there is, as I have said, the shadow of a doubt growing out of the way in which Dr. Briggs was inducted into this chair.   There has been a question as to whether this Assembly had authority over a case of transfer like this, and some of the directors of Union Seminary are very strongly persuaded that the Assembly has no authority in the case ; and, yet by a unanimous vote and without reservation or qualification, they agree to waive that matter entirely, and to come before this Assembly without raising any technical question of that kind.   That overture of peace on the part of the directors of Union Seminary, we submit, this Assembly can afford to meet half way.   We can afford to go to the directors of Union Seminary and say to them, "Gentlemen, since you meet us in this spirit, since you offer in this way to waive your views of your rights under the compact which exists, we will meet you in the same spirit, we will waive our right to the veto, and now you sit down with our committee and together let us come to an understanding in this business."

[*The stated clerk said no such paper as Dr. Worcester has referred to has ever been communicated to this Assembly.*]

Dr. Worcester:—I don't know whether it is before the Assembly.   I give you the statement on the word of Dr. Dickey that it is spread upon the records of Union Seminary, and I think it is sufficiently before the Assembly to refer to it.

But Mr. Moderator, I was about to say one more thing.   Even in that extreme case—that the directors

in their haughtiness and in their independence, and in
their insolence, for it would be scarcely less than that
—should defy this Assembly and say, "No, we will
not reconsider this election, though you ask us to do
it;" still this case has not gone beyond your control,
unless Dr. Briggs can vindicate his soundness of faith
to the Presbytery of New York first, to the Synod of
New York second, to the General Assembly of 1892
third. If there is any real reason in the theological
opinions of Dr. Briggs, if there is anything beyond
those idiosyncrasies of Dr. Briggs which Professor Patton says are not a sufficient reason for such a measure
as this, if there is anything in the theological opinions
of Dr. Briggs which in 1892 shall seem to call for the
interference of this General Assembly, this Assembly
will have all that before it, and set before it in a regular way; it will have it before it under all the safe-
guards and under all the light secured by a triple
judicial inquiry. And that will be your advantage in
settling this question in 1892. And so it comes to
this: Have we confidence enough in the directors of
Union Seminary to waive our right of veto and say to
them: "Brethren, we ask you to adjust this thing
yourselves; you did not know when you appointed
Professor Briggs to this chair what his views were upon
many of these things; you did not anticipate such an
inaugural address and such subsequent utterances as
have so disturbed the church. You see into what a
state of agitation the church has been thrown; now
we ask you to relieve the church from its perplexity,
we ask you to do the thing which shall be for the
honor of God and for the peace of the church of Jesus

Christ." Mr. Moderator and brethren, I beseech you
to take heed what you do to-day ; I beseech you to
remember that it is easy to do in a day what you can
never undo in a generation ; I beseech you to remember that the Presbyterian church has erred many times
in the past, with all its wisdom and all its prayerful-
ness, and it may err again. Let us not repeat here
the follies of our fathers ; let it not appear that we
have learned nothing from the repeated and bitter lessons of the past. I have often found that I have
erred through acting too hastily ; I have seldom found
that I have erred through acting too deliberately. The
Presbyterian church has never been wanting in courage and loyalty to her Master. She has sometimes
been a little wanting in Christian charity and forbearance and brotherly love, and that has been the secret
of the sad schisms which have rent her in the past.
Oh, brethren, it is a divine voice which bids us endeavor to keep the unity of the spirit in the bond of
peace. We have listened to the thrilling appeals of
our home and of our foreign missionaries during these
days that we have been together. We have seen how
God has thrown wide open the doors of the whole
world for the introduction of his truth. His own great
providence is calling us to march forward to grander
victories than any of the past, in his name and for his
kingdom. Let us take an action to-day which shall
deliver us from strife and from contention, and which
shall leave us hand free and heart free to respond to
this divine call."

No clearer idea of the man could be put in words
than is revealed in this characteristic speech. It is

Worcester in every sentence.   Whether it is to be set
down to the credit of the Assembly that his counsels
were unheeded need not be passed upon here.   The
press of the country, almost without exception, pronounced it the greatest speech of the Assembly   It is
no wonder that it was heartily cheered, and that at its
close a general call for the " question " was made from
all parts of the house.   The manifest fairness and candor of the man ; his clear comprehension of the subject under consideration ; his masterful power of
analysis ; his great love for the Presbyterian church,
and his desire to find an honorable way of settling difficulty and avoiding rupture in the denomination were
evident to all who heard him and appreciated by all
who had not already fully made up their minds to follow another course.   It was believed by many that
had a vote been taken at the close of Dr. Worcester's
address his substitute would have carried.   It will be
clearly seen in this speech how earnestly he sought to
find an honorable middle ground where the contending
parties might meet and on which they could stand with
safety and honor.   He had great faith in time as a
factor in solving difficulties.   While he would not,
could not accept many of the utterances of Dr. Briggs,
and deplored the seeming belligerent tone in which he
expressed them, he could not, and would not be a
party to any action by the Assembly which must prove
in the nature of a decision prejudicial to his case which
was soon to be the subject of judicial inquiry.

   This speech at once gave him a prominence which
hitherto he had not enjoyed.   It is true that his speech
proved him to be a great man both in mental power

and in moral purpose. But his speech was no surprise
to those who knew him best. They had been accustomed to his clear statements ; had become familiar
with his generosity in stating the question under consideration from the side of those he was compelled to
oppose ; were prepared to expect from him moderation
and pleading for charity and fairness.

The Theological Seminary of Hartford, Conn.,
elected him to the chair of systematic theology for that
institution in May, 1891. After mature deliberation he
declined and decided to remain with his church in Chicago. But this decision was soon disturbed by his
election, in July, to the same position in Union Seminary, N. Y. The decision reached in regard to Hartford Seminary would have enabled him to reach a
prompt decision in regard to Union Seminary had the
conditions been alike or nearly so. But the difference
was great. Hartford Seminary is under the control of
the Congregational denomination and Dr. Worcester
was a Presbyterian. He was under no special obligation to leave his church and abandon preaching, for
teaching, at the call of an institution under control of
another denomination. With Union Seminary it was
entirely different. That is Presbyterian. He had
been trained for the ministry there. Its relation to the
General Assembly was seriously strained. The peace
of the Presbyterian Church had been threatened. The
position which many of the great men of the church
had taken as to the right of the trustees of Union Seminary, without submitting their action for the approval
of the Assembly, to transfer Dr. Briggs from one chair
to another, in the late meeting in Detroit, and else-

where, prevented their being considered for the vacant professorship caused by the death of Dr. Van Dyke. The position taken by Dr. Worcester was acceptable to the directors of the Seminary. It was no less satisfactory to the most thoughtful men of the denomination everywhere. It was known that he was thoroughly loyal to the Assembly. Of his theological soundness no shadow of doubt existed. He was therefore acceptable to the Seminary and to the Assembly as well.

Leading men of the church, from all parts of the country, urged his acceptance in the interest of peace. Coming to him in this way his election presented a question of *duty*. This, and this alone opened up anew the question of his leaving his pastoral charge and entering upon the work of teaching.

At one time he earnestly hoped that he might find that God did not call him to the ministry,—had seriously thought of teaching as a profession. But long ere this all doubt about his proper sphere of work had been cleared away. He was, and for long time had been, entirely satisfied that preaching was his mission and he felt highly honored that it was so. Teaching in a theological seminary he had never sought—never desired. It was a great struggle between choice and duty which he was called on to pass through. Well satisfied as he had been that he was where God would have him when he was preaching, if it could be made clear to him that it was duty to leave the pulpit for the professor's chair, he would do that. The voice of duty is the voice of God. That voice he had obeyed when he entered the ministry, although then he would have welcomed a different work. That voice he would still follow when it called upon him to lay down the work to which it had once summoned him and still obedient, take up another.

As a child he had suffered from palpitation of the heart, so that his parents did not dare allow him to play as other boys did. But as he grew older and stronger it was supposed he had entirely outgrown the trouble. One year, shortly after he came to Chicago, he had a slight return of it, but only for a short time, and as late as 1889, when he was examined for life-insurance, his heart was pronounced perfectly sound.

Early in the summer of 1891 his old difficulty returned in connection with the Detroit Assembly. The necessity of deciding upon the two calls which have been mentioned, aggravated the difficulty. The doctor considered it simply the effect of nervous excitement, and it entirely disappeared during the vacation which soon followed, as the probable effect of rest and sea-bathing. It has already been stated that he was a man of highly nervous temperament, although he was able, as a rule, to conceal from others its outward manifestation. On his return to Chicago from his vacation, the trouble returned, and in addition to palpitation, he suffered from oppression in the region of the heart, and once or twice with such sharp pain as to make it necessary for him to stop in walking. The disease which had manifested itself in his childhood, it will be seen, had only slumbered. It was not dead. He had not been cured.

Probably few will understand what it cost this man to resign from the Sixth Church to accept the chair to which he had been elected in Union Seminary.

Few knew him well enough to measure the struggle through which he passed, but all who knew him at all, knew that it was no ordinary conflict. He had become satisfied that duty called him to New York. He asked his church in the following letter to unite with him in the request that Presbytery dissolve the pastoral relation to enable him to accept.

"*To the Congregation of the Sixth Presbyterian Church of Chicago, Dear Brethren and Friends:*

When I declined a few weeks since a call which would have taken me away from you and from the pastoral work which is increasingly dear to me the longer I remain in it, it was my sincere hope that I might not soon be disturbed in this decision, but might be left free to devote myself with undivided mind to the preaching of Christ and the work of the ministry among you.

The kind expressions which came to me from so many at that time but strengthened this desire, and knit closer the strong ties of many years, and made it harder than ever to think of separation.

Yet, even then there were indications that this wish to be left undisturbed in my work was not to be realized, and after an earnest and prayerful study of the question of duty, prolonged through several weeks, I am now constrained to ask you to unite with me in a request to Presbytery to dissolve the pastoral relation existing berween us, that I may accept a call to the vacant chair of Systematic Theology in Union Seminary.

If this comes as a surprise to any, it is only because the expressed wish of the Directors of the Sem-

inary that nothing should be made public prematurely
compelled me to consider the question mainly in
silence.

How hard it is for me to make this request I am
sure you cannot know. My heart is bound to you by
the strongest ties of personal affection, gratitude, and
Christian fellowship. The work of the gospel in
mighty, growing Chicago calls out all my enthusiasm,
and to preach Christ in a pulpit of my own is the thing
I love best in life.

Yet as far as I can understand the leadings of
God's Spirit and Providence, he is calling me to leave
all these, and undertake a different service. And with
whatever shrinking from a work so difficult and for
which I feel myself so ill prepared, I must needs follow
His call.

May I not carry with me the assurance of your
loving prayers, which I shall so greatly need ; as you
certainly will have my most earnest prayers that God
will speedily fill my place among you with a man after
His own heart, richly endowed for the great work which
there needs to be done?

With deepest love and warmest gratitude for your
constant loyalty and your abounding kindness to me
and mine,

Your affectionate pastor,

J. H. WORCESTER, JR.

Burlington, Vt., Aug. 3, 1891.

To this request the church made a prompt although reluctant affirmative answer, as will appear in
the resolutions adopted. They are as follows :

73

Your Committee appointed to present resolutions appropriate to the resignation of our pastor, Rev. J. H. Worcester, Jr., D. D., respectfully beg leave to report :

The relation between pastor and people is, next to that of the family, the most tender and the most sacred of all our earthly relationships. When, as in the present case, the relation has been one of uninterrupted harmony, growing stronger and more endearing every year, an unmistakable call of duty can alone justify its dissolution. We are fully convinced that such a call has come to our pastor, and we should prove ourselves unworthy his most faithful instruction during all the years he has been with us, should we not reverently and loyally bow to its demands. In consenting to the separation of the tie which has bound us together, we rejoice to know that we are called upon to make the sacrifice only in what is believed to be the interest of the whole of the great Presbyterian Church of which our's is but a small part.

Dr. Worcester has endeared himself to us by his simplicity, his open candor, his tenderness, liberality, and eminent Christian consistency. He has commanded our admiration by his wonderful power as a preacher and teacher. His loyalty, sincerity, zeal and devotion to his work as a minister of the gospel, ever since he came among us, have been one continued pleading for nobler living. Now therefore,

Resolved, That we consent to the resignation of Dr. Worcester, as pastor of the Sixth Presbyterian Church, only because we are fully persuaded that he regards it as his duty to assume other labors in another field.

Resolved, That we bear cheerful testimony to his splendid ability as a preacher : to his wonderful power as a teacher ; to his skill as a leader in Christian work ; to his Christ-like character in every relation he has sustained while living among us ; to his fidelity as a pastor, tenderly sympathizing with every sorrowing one, and ever ready to " rejoice with them that do rejoice."

Resolved, That we recognize in the unity, harmony, and strength of our church the fruit of his faithful preaching,—the result of his consecrated, unselfish life. In him the poor and neglected have always found a sympathetic friend ; the needy a prompt and ready helper. By the bedside of the sick his words have given courage, or have taught resignation. In the house of mourning his counsels have ever been balm to the wounded heart, while faithfully pointing out the source of the only comfort that sorrowing hearts can know.

Resolved, That the multiplied activities of our church ; the increase in our beneficences, the greatly increased interest in missions, both Home and Foreign, are the result of Dr. Worcester's inspiring leadership and faithful service as a minister of Jesus Christ.

Resolved, That we highly appreciate the efficient work and noble Christian character of Mrs. Worcester, and that we feel a personal loss in her removal from among us.

Resolved. That we congratulate the Presbyterian Church at large, on having secured so able a man and so gifted a teacher, for such an important position in one of our leading Theological Seminaries."

It may seem strange that a man so greatly beloved as he was, admired for his gifts of preaching and loved for his sterling Christian manhood, should not have been importuned by his church, or at least by many of his personal friends, not to resign. The explanation is not difficult, and is a tribute to the man. Every member of the church knew that he never would have asked to have the relation dissolved if he had not already become thoroughly satisfied that it was his *duty* to do so, and that he believed he was following divine leading. So thoroughly had he trained his people in the sacredness of duty that there was no word which any one who properly understood him could speak without flatly ignoring his teaching and his example. The church regretted his leaving. The individual members regretted parting with a personal friend and beloved pastor and able minister, but what could they do ?—all were convinced that remonstrance would not only be unavailing, but unacceptable to him.

There can be no doubt but that his anxiety for the peace of the Presbyterian Church, seriously threatened as he believed, and the struggle through which he had to pass to reach his decision to resign his pastorate for a professor's chair, had much to do with the development of the old difficulty which had been supposed to have been overcome.

When he finally left Chicago for New York his heart difficulty increased so much on the train that the first thing he had to do, on his arrival, was to seek a physician. He was treated first for muscular rheumatism and of course without success. He was finally led to consult a doctor who was regarded as authority

in heart troubles, and for a time, he was more or less
helped. Still the doctor never seemed able to determine just what was the matter. From this time on
there followed a constant succession of ups and downs
in health. Every indication of improvement inspired
hope in his family, and was hailed with delight by his
friends.

His work in the seminary was entirely new, and
was unavoidably a great strain upon him, for he could
not permit himself to do any work which was not thorough and exhaustive. His ardent love for preaching
led him to continue to occupy some pulpit almost every
Sabbath so long as he was able to do so. Still he
claimed that this did not tire him especially when his
sermons were already prepared, and to those nearest
to him it seemed that it often did him good, physically,
to preach, as he would seem brighter and better after.
His general system was much run down as was shown
by carbuncles and boils during the winter of 1891-' 2.
Still his indomitable will would not yield or permit those
difficulties to interfere with any of his engagements.
He kept on with his work until the end of the seminary
year. It was hoped that the long vacation of four
months would restore him, but he gained little at any
time during this vacation, and toward the close of it he
was very sick, and for the first time since he reached
the years of manhood was compelled to absent himself
from service when the seminary year opened. He was
unable to take his place and begin his work until about
two weeks after the Seminary opened. He resumed
his regular work with his classes Oct. 13.

A change of physicians became necessary, owing

to the feebleness of the one he had hitherto consulted and his own inability longer to go to his house for treatment. The new doctor was at first quite sanguine and gave much encouragement. After a thorough examination he expressed himself as decidedly hopeful. Other physicians, friends of Dr. Worcester, saw no reason why he should not recover, and in time be as well as he had ever been. He entered upon his work with cheerful courage and did work outside of his regular duties. On November 7 he addressed the students of the University of New York delivering one of the monthly course of Monday lectures. His topic was "Not Transferable" (relating to character.) As he was to speak extempore he felt some anxiety, and had a good deal of trouble with his heart at first, but after he got started all went on well.

The next day—November 8, he was compelled to stand in line for an hour in order to cast his vote, but he endured the trial in order that he might discharge his duty as an American citizen. November 13, he preached his last sermon, at the Broadway Tabernacle— the church of Dr. W. M. Taylor. He had not preached before since August. He was assisted in the service by Dr. Hastings of the Seminary. His theme was "Borrowed Burdens," from Matt. 6:34. Although enfeebled and suffering it would not have occurred to any one who did not otherwise know, that he was not well. As showing his great delight in being able to serve God in the pulpit his diary record of this his last sermon will be of interest. His diary had become a bare record of facts. Of this, his last public church service he wrote : "Had great comfort in being able to deliver this one

more message, and was greatly encouraged to find that
no reaction followed.'' So late as the early part of
December his physician was hopeful and told him that
there was a fair chance of his being ultimately as well
as he had ever been. Christmas day was spent quietly
at home with his family and he enjoyed himself playing
games with his children as he always did. That night
he slept but little owing to the disturbed action of his
heart. From this time on he often had difficulty of a
like nature at night, It may safely be said that one
main reason for his unbroken health during most of his
life, as well as accounting in large measure for the great
amount of hard work he could endure, was that he had
always slept well at night. When wearied he could
throw himself down and sleep for ten or twenty
minutes at any time and awake refreshed. Now though
weak and weary he found it almost impossible to sleep
in the day time, and often difficult to sleep at night
owing to the pain in his heart.

The last day of 1892 he read a paper before the *Chi
Alpha*, a gathering of ministers. His paper was a review
of Prof. Stearns's ''Life of H. B. Smith''. His diary
records : ''It was more kindly received than I expected, but I had extraordinary difficulty in reading it,—
pain in my heart all the time,—a new experience and
very embarrassing. I had to stop once, and ask a
breathing space.'' At the urgent request of his pastor
he led the prayer-meeting one night during ''the week
of prayer''—January, 1893. He spoke on ''Earnestness
of the Church'' and with much earnestness, although
then suffering much pain. This was the last time he
spoke in public. It was a fitting close to his public

services that he, who had been so profoundly in earnest
all his life, should urge earnestness in the church as his
last message to its membership. The continuance of
pain in his heart and his inability to get rest and sleep
led to grave doubts in the mind of his physician. About
this time he told Mrs. Worcester, privately, that though
Dr. Worcester *might* be much better he would never
be really well again, but would always be at least, a
semi-invalid.

The brief Christmas vacation, instead of bringing
renewed strength, left him weaker than it found him.
He was now compelled to take a carriage to the seminary, being unable to walk the short distance to the
horse cars.

He did not attempt to attend Faculty meetings,
but he felt that it was best for himself to have his mind
occupied with other thoughts than his own condition,
and he did not see who could take his place should he
drop out. He was particularly unwilling to give up his
work of instruction as several of the faculty were in poor
health. Several times the doctor called intending each
time to tell him he must quit work, but after talking
with him, changed his mind, feeling that for a man of
his temperament it was better to keep on as long as
possible.

He was advised, finally, to go to Lakewood and
his colleagues urged it. He consented to go for a little rest, but several things had to be attended to first
so that it was a week after deciding to go before he
could do so. On January 25 a consultation of
physicians was held, and the decision reached that he
must stop work at once.

"In view of the complications at the Seminary and the number of others in the faculty who are *hors du combat*, it is very hard for me to accept this" is the entry in his diary, and the last he ever wrote in it.

The doctors said he must stop *for the present*, but he confidently hoped that after two or three weeks at Lakewood he would be able to resume teaching and at least be able to carry the Seniors through. His work was growing in interest to him all the time. The students could not realize how ill he was, as his mind was constantly so active and alert in class.

Mrs. Worcester says: "We left New York Wednesday, February 1st. One of the students kindly went with us to the cars, and Mr. Worcester was much pleased to hear him tell how much sympathy the students felt for him, and how they appreciated his heroism in keeping up against such odds. Speaking of it afterwards he said to me, 'I am glad if they think I am practicing what I preached when I told them not to whine if they were sick,' referring to an address on "Manliness" he had given them. The long ride of seven miles over the rough streets before reaching our ferry was somewhat exhausting, and on reaching the boat we had to give him stimulants, (although he hated to take brandy) and apply smelling salts. He said it was a new experience to have people look at him as a sick man. After we were once in the cars it was less fatiguing, but he felt much wearied on reaching Lakewood.

We sent for a doctor that evening and he changed the medicines, and Mr. Worcester slept better, I think, than he had for several weeks, five hours without waking once, and his head on but one pillow. He had been taking nitro-glycerine to relieve the pain in his heart for some time, but now the effect was beginning to pass off so soon that often he could not get to sleep before another season of pain would come. Thursday morning he felt so decidedly better that we both felt greatly encouraged, thinking that perhaps the change of doctors and of scene were going to work wonders. As we had met a friend the day before who reported that she had gained seven pounds there in two weeks, Mr. Worcester proposed our weighing ourselves that morning, that we might see how much we should gain, and was surprised to find that, though he had lost much flesh he still weighed 164 1-2 pounds. We spent the day quietly, but pleasantly in the house, as it was rainy, and hoped for another good night, but were disappointed. Medicines seemed to have very little effect upon him, or the beneficial effect was very transient. Friday the Lakewood physician told me that his condition was very serious, and that he thought he would never be a well man again. But I had no idea that the end was so near. Friday afternoon we took a drive of four miles about the lake, and Mr. Worcester enjoyed it, and did not get very tired. He was in the reading room part of the evening, and, for a little while, at a concert in the music-room, but the effort of walking up stairs caused him severe pain. Another bad night followed, and every day saw him weaker, so that even in getting about the house he used a cane. Saturday, though bright, was, to his disappointment, too cold and windy to make it prudent to drive out, but we spent the morning pleasantly in the

sunny corridors, among the plants and birds, and I
read aloud to him.   When Dr. Stone came in to see
him about 5 p. m. I begged him to give him something,
if possible, that would cause him to sleep, as I felt that
a few more such exhausting nights would break him
down utterly, and then, following him out into the
hall, I asked him if I should send for my husband's
parents.   But he said no, he saw no indication whatever that it was necessary.   And then he pressed my
hand, and bade me be brave, and I never saw him
again.

In regard to Mr. Worcester's parents coming to
Lakewood, we had thought of the possibility of it, but
thought it inexpedient, unless absolutely necessary, in
view of the inclement weather, and their age and lack
of strength.   But Mr. Worcester cautioned me, if they
did come not to let them stay in the room more than
three or four minutes at first, adding, 'I don't know
but even that would be too much for this poor heart
of mine.'   Saturday night he again suffered much,
sleeping but a few moments at a time.   It was early
Saturday morning, I think, that I was getting something
when he asked if I had just knocked over a vase, and
when I answered no, he said that his naps were so very
short he could hardly tell when he was awake and when
he was asleep, adding that he always meant to be
patient, and that he thought he should be, but if he
was not I must always remember that it was delirium.
All through his illness he was very patient and uncom-
plaining, though the marked change was a very sad
one, from such vigorous health to such weakness.

When I told him that Dr. Stone had given out

through over-work, and another physician was coming to take his place, he exclaimed, 'How everything works against me !' He kept his room all day by the new doctor's orders, being dressed after having his breakfast in bed, but whether sitting up or lying on the bed, he said he could find no comfortable position, and his weakness increased rapidly. He said he thought he had never felt so completely exhausted before. Retiring after a light supper, he said as he wound his watch, that he couldn't wind it many more times if he continued to grow much weaker. The doctor came in four times during the day, being in the house, and wishing to observe closely the effect of the medicines (which were almost powerless,) but it was not till his nine o'clock visit that he looked particularly serious, and then when I questioned him he said that he could not tell, but that he thought the end was very near.

"Well, dear, you wont have much longer to suffer." "The doctor thinks that I am going, does he ?" "Yes." "Then let us send telegrams." "Yes, this is death. I hear the death-rattle." "There is so much that I want to say, but so little breath to say it." "Oh, I didn't know it was so hard to die. Death by suffocation is hard. Lord help me to be patient. Come, Lord Jesus, come quickly."

When he first knew he was going, and Mrs. D. asked if she should stay with us he answered with a grateful smile, "No, we will watch it out together." I could only hold his hand and wipe the moisture from his forehead. He was drenched with perspiration, he coughed a great deal so that it was impossible to speak, and his breath came like groans. But often he looked at me and smiled, as if to cheer me. When I asked if he were ready to go he said, "Only as I trust in my Redeemer." He sent messages to the children telling them to trust in their father's God, and adding that they had always been an unspeakable comfort to him, and sent tender messages to his parents. He began repeating "Leave thy fatherless children," adding "you know the rest," and for me he repeated in full the beautiful benediction, "The Lord bless thee and keep thee : The Lord make his face shine upon thee, and be gracious unto thee : The Lord lift up his countenance upon thee, and give thee peace.'''

And so, just before midnight, Sunday, February 5, 1893, this servant of God closed his eyes on all earthly scenes to open them on the beauties of his celestial home. He, who had so patiently suffered so much, passed through the gates and into the city where there "shall be no more pain ; for the former things are passed away."

Without murmuring, and without repining this heroic soul ended its conflicts with disease and with sin, and joined the "ten thousand times ten thousand, and thousands of thousands," forevermore to be numbered among those "which came out of great tribulation, and have washed their robes, and made them white in the blood of the Lamb. Therefore they are before the throne of God, and serve him day and night in his temple ; and he that sitteth on the throne shall dwell among them. They shall hunger no more, neither thirst any more ; neither shall the sun light on them nor any heat. For the Lamb which is in the midst of the throne shall feed them, and shall lead them unto living fountains of waters ; and God shall wipe away all tears from their eyes.''

When news reached Chicago that Dr. Worcester was "very near home," it found Presbytery in session, and produced a feeling of deep but chastened grief. Although he had passed away before the report that the end was near reached them, his former associates in Presbytery suspended the order of exercises and spent the time in most earnest prayer. The loss was felt to be a personal bereavement to all who had known him.

Brief memorial services were held at Union Seminary on Tuesday, and the final funeral exercises were held Thursday, February 9, 1893, at the home of his father and in the church where as a child, student, and young man he had worshiped.

Rev. Simon J. McPherson, D. D., and Rev. James Lewis D. D., represented the Chicago Presbytery at the funeral and participated in the exercises. The Sixth Presbyterian Church of Chicago was represented by one of its members, sent by vote of its session. The principal address was delivered by the president of Vermont University, *Rev. Matthew Henry Buckham, D. D.,* and is as follows :

"There are times—and this certainly is one of them —when our experience of life forces us back upon the great primary verities of religion ; times when all our little philosophies and theodicies fail us, and we are driven into that final stronghold whose solid foundation is in the wisdom and goodness of God. In our

days of calmness and prosperity, looking out over the
calamities of men, we can, as we think, do something
to justify the ways of God to man, but the time comes
to us all when we shrink from a task to which we feel
no wisdom is equal save that infinite wisdom which is
forever associated with infinite love.   When the fair
promise of a young life is suddenly broken, when
splendid powers of intellect, affection, and will, splen-
didly equipped for action are silenced just when they
have reached their highest point of efficiency, no mere
earthly vindications or compensations can bring to our
minds any repose or comfort.   And our trouble only
increases when we take the large and unselfish view of
such a loss, when we take into the account its effects
upon the common welfare, upon the interests of virtue,
religion, and humanity.   When we see a young man
thus fully equipped with the means of great power, go
into a certain city, not to buy and sell and get gain,
but to serve his generation, to teach and preach the
truth which the world needs, to help men and women
to find the true life, and when we see him gaining and
using more and more of this beneficent power, and virtue going out of him on all sides round, and the hearts
of all good men full of cheer and hope and gratitude
because of the grace of God in him, and then when we
see this power suddenly brought to a stand, this gracious gift withdrawn, this beneficent career ended, this,
I say, brings to its supreme trial our faith in God.
More, almost, than any other experience in life, it
compels us to ask, " Is God indeed wise, and is he
good." One of the worst possible answers to this question is that stoical resignation which is more than half

unbelief, which says, "I will not think, and I will not feel, because that way lies rebellion and despair." It is good to give to our natural human feelings their course and vent. Even as the tears of our Saviour drew from those around him at the grave of his friend the exclamation, "behold how he loved him," so let our affection, our grief, our sense of love, have all that flood of expression which nature prompts and which religion approves. Let us tell one another, as not feeling any restraint or rebuke from religion what virtues he had, what good works he wrought, what love he inspired, what example he left to his children, what inspiration his life brings to all who will read God's lessons in and through him. And so through our natural human feelings shall be opened channels through which the peace of God, and the comforts of the Holy Spirit, and the assurance of divine love flooding and driving out all doubt, and fears, shall enter in and possess our hearts.

The company gathered here to-day doubtless consists in large part of those who have known John Worcester from his youth up. And it is one source of comfort to us to recall that life, the whole of it—for I am sure there is in our memory of it no single act which we would wish to forget to-day. We remember his boyhood, bright, and. pure, and hallowed ; we remember how in early life, through that process which is the privilege of Christian nurture, almost unconsciously to himself he entered into the Christian life ; some of us remember the thoroughly boyish and yet thoroughly serious spirit, with which in this very room he engaged in biblical study : how before the establishment of

Christian Associations and Young Peoples' Societies, when the sentiment of youthful society in Burlington was not as strongly Christian as it now is, he stood with decision and enthusiasm, side by side with those who, not merely by passive sympathy, but by active effort, gave themselves to the promotion of virtue and piety in our city, and how some of those youthful activities are even now bearing fruit in the organized Christian Institutions which are doing so much to bring God's blessing upon our community.

Of his college course you will permit me to speak with freedom and feeling. College men understand, what others may not, how largely the intellectual and moral tone of college life is dependent on a few leading men in the student body. It frequently happens that a small number of such men, or even one man, will impart so much of their or his individuality to their class or their associates, that the whole life of the College is affected thereby. John Worcester was such a man. He lifted the intellectual level of the whole college of his time. Bright, facile, capable in all departments, susceptible of enthusiasm from great and inspiring thoughts coming from all good studies, he set a standard of attainment and of intellectual production which the better minds strove to reach and which even the less gifted were ashamed to fall far below. I feel sure that every student of his time will bear me witness that Worcester's brilliant career was then and still is regarded as one of the not few careers of which the Institution has reason to be proud, a success which, not depending on mere facility in acquisition and repitition, but based on solid attainments and revealing reserved power, gave promise of an equally brilliant career in after life.

It was the natural outcome of such a scholarly ambition and such a College reputation that after completing his theological studies and spending some time in study and travel abroad, he was invited to an instructorship in the University, and after proving his ability to succeed as a teacher that he was called to a permanent place in the Faculty. But feeling that a dispensation of the Gospel was committed to him, he declined the invitation and entered the ministry in which service he continued without interruption for twenty years and until called to the chair of theology a little more than a year ago.

Of his work in his two pastorates, first for eleven years in Orange, New Jersey, and afterward for nine years in Chicago, others will more fittingly speak. In these fields the main work of his life was done, and any adequate tribute to his memory should be mainly taken up with this period of his life. That in the pastoral office he steadily gained repute and influence, that his pulpit ministrations attracted large audiences, that the churches which he served and led became potent agencies for good in their communities, this we know. What we cannot know, what never can be estimated by human standards of success, is the sum of his spiritual influence ; the truth first vitalized in his own heart and life and then scattered broadcast to germinate and fructify in other lives ; the souls he helped upward in faith and holiness ; the hopes, and inspirations, and comforts of religion made real in human hearts and homes and societies. Doubtless some small

number of these fruits of his ministry will come to light
through personal letters and tributes of affection from
grateful and sorrowing hearts, but the largest and best
parts of them will never be known to men until the
time comes when the secrets of all hearts are revealed,
and when redeemed souls are permitted to acknowledge their eternal debt of gratitude to those who led
them into the way of everlasting life.

It sometimes happens in the career of a man
whose life is not passed on the great stage of the world,
that in connection with some great critical event the
whole life of the man flowers out into some characteristic which gives him henceforward the large place
in men's esteem which he had long merited. This was
eminently true of Mr. Worcester's action in the General
Assembly of the Presbyterian Church in 1891. The
occasion was one of those heated controversies which
show us how very far we still are from having attained
to that calmness of conviction which the conscious
possession of the truth always brings with it. Partisan
counsels were in the ascendant. Danger of serious
rupture was near and threatening. The time was ripe
for an irenic word. The hour had come for a large-
minded and sweet-spirited man to lift the issue into the
higher region of tolerance and comprehensiveness. Dr.
Worcester saw the crisis, seized the opportunity, and
did what one brave and clear-sighted man could to
turn thought and feeling into wiser and safer channels.
Those who were present tell me that his speech was a
great outburst of Christian magnanimity, which will
long be memorable in the history of the Assembly.
Defeated of its purpose by parliamentary tactics, it

nevertheless even drew to its author the regard and the hopes of all in the denomination whose supreme interest was for the peace and prosperity of the Church. It was therefore no surprise, when shortly after, Dr. Worcester was called to one of the most important positions in the Presbyterian Church, that of professor of theology in Union Seminary.

What Dr. Worcester would have accomplished in this high and difficult position, had life and health been spared to him, we can only conjecture. The bent of his mind had not hitherto been in the direction of systematic theology, but rather toward religion on its vital and practical side. Perhaps this would have given him a great advantage in his approach to the study of theology. Perhaps those who appointed him to the chair hoped that the experience of a twenty years' pastorate, mingling itself with the studies of a man still young and growing, might beget a style of theological teaching which would prove eminently helpful to the preachers and pastors of the new generation. Certainly we who knew him could easily believe that on the one hand his sympathy with those essential and vital doctrines of Christianity which have wrought themselves into the noblest and holiest lives, and on the other hand that spirit of sincerity and fidelity which leads one to value truth beyond all traditions and conventionalities, would have led him to strive to work out in his own mind, and to teach to students, a theology which would be at the same time dogmatic and evangelic, at once Johannean and Pauline.

Two great sorrows coming near each other cannot

but associate themselves in our minds. It would be flattery unworthy of him and of us to compare our friend with the great Churchman whom all Christendom mourns. No other man in our generation had gifts and influence at all comparable with those of Phillips Brooks. But as they have, both in the prime of life, passed out of the Christian ministry so near each other, it is a pleasing consolation to us to associate them in our minds as fellow workers in this greatest of ministries. Especially pleasant is it to think of each of them as being in his sphere a representative of a Christianity, large, tolerant, comprehensive, but none the less clinging with life and death earnestness to that essential Christianity which is the world's hope. Why the Great Head of the Church takes to himself those who, to our view, seem to be the most useful and the most needed of all his earthly servants, is his secret with which we may not interfere.

God is wise ; God is good ; what He does is best. There we rest. Beyond this we cannot go. May he help us to say, ' "thy will be done." '

IN MEMORIAM.

On Sunday evening, February 12, a memorial service was held in the Sixth Presbyterian Church and the house was crowded with a sorrowing congregation.

Mr. Charles J. Merritt spoke feelingly of his former pastor *as a man*, recalling his strong personality, his remarkable loyalty to truth, his sterling honesty of character, and his strong love for his pastoral work.

Mr. John S. Ford, Superintendent of the Sunday School, spoke of Dr. Worcester in his *relation to Sunday School work*, telling of his interest, sympathy, helpfulness, and above all his constant watchfulness for spiritual results from the labors of teachers and officers of the school.

Mr. W. B. Jacobs spoke in earnest and tender words of the relation of the departed to *Christian work in general.* His interest in work for souls knew no parish boundary, but embraced every activity and every form of service which had for its aim the rescue of perishing souls. He was never too busy to give time for any helpful service. He rejoiced in good done for the cause of Christ by whomever done.

Rev. Simon J. McPherson, D. D., pastor of the Second Presbyterian Church, spoke of his departed friend's work *in Presbytery.* He spoke of his great ability, his safe, clear judgment, his candor, rare fidel-

ity, promptness, intense earnestness, and exceptional
modesty. He was a safe leader. He commanded attention by his wonderful power for lucid statement,
and cleared the way for intelligent and loyal following
by his marvellous ability to set complicated questions
in a light so clear that they were made to appear
simple.

Mr. Alexander Forbes told the story of his last
illness and death.

A committee appointed by the Session presented
the following memorial, which was unanimously
adopted by the congregation, and ordered to be signed
by the Officers of the Church and the Church and Society, and a copy sent to Mrs. Worcester:

"In view of the recent death of our former beloved pastor, Rev. J. H. Worcester, Jr., D. D., the
Sixth Presbyterian Church of Chicago puts on record its
appreciation of his character and his services : Dr.
Worcester was preeminently a manly man. He exemplified in his whole life his deep-seated conviction,
often expressed, that ' Christianity is a virile religion ; '
that it develops those traits of character,—courage, integrity, fidelity to duty, sympathy, and tender love
that unite to complete our idea of the manly man.
His exceptional loyalty to conviction relieved him, in
very large measure, from the paralyzing effect of conflict between desire and duty. When duty was made
clear to him, discussion ceased. This freedom from
conflict within himself was one of the elements of his
greatness.

As a preacher he was, beyond question, great.
Gifted with a mind naturally faultlessly logical, he

readily comprehended the unity of his subject, and the proper relation of all of its parts. He was thus enabled to state his position with masterful skill and with surpassing clearness. The foundation for his argument was always laid broad and deep on truths easily comprehended and indisputable. The discussion he always conducted along lines obviously natural and generously straight-forward. His premises being granted, his conclusions were logical necessities. He was, at all times, and everywhere, a preacher of the Gospel. His great, controlling purpose was to lead to Christ and then build up Christian character in those in whose hearts a good work had been begun. So clearly, so faithfully, so successfully did he point to the 'Lamb of God' that those whom he reached were always carried beyond himself to the Saviour of men.

Thus it was (and it was to his greatest credit) there never was a party calling itself by his name in this church. He found no time or place, in this pulpit, for effort at mere literary display, polished and ornate though his discourses usually were. His whole purpose and work as a preacher were truthfully summed up in the text of his last sermon as pastor of this church: 'For I determined not to know anything among you save Jesus Christ and Him, crucified.'

In his pastoral work he was preserving, faithful, and tender. He never wearied waiting on our slow creeping, even when himself could soar, if only he could know that we were trying. The tenderness and the wealth of sympathy of his loving heart only those who were called to pass through deep waters of affliction ever fully knew. The depth of his genuine sym-

pathy was often obscured by an unusual modesty and
self-distrust. These qualities, together with his unswerving honesty, led him habitually to under-state
his feelings. To those only who live in an atmosphere
of over-statement could he ever have been regarded as
other than tender and loving.

In the death of Dr. Worcester this church profoundly feels itself bereaved. We sorrow that we
shall see his face no more. We are grateful for the
legacy which this servant of the Master has left us of
loyalty to God ; unselfish devotion to duty ; a domi-
nating purpose to win men to Christ ; a firm belief
that the religion of Jesus Christ, accepted and embraced, is the only sure antidote for the benumbing
discontents which so try us amid the conflicts of life.

To the bereaved father and mother we tender our
sympathy in this hour of their sore trial.

Our hearts go out in loving sympathy for our dear
Mrs. Worcester, in this hour of her loneliness and sorrow. We beg to assure her that she will ever be dear
to us for her own sake and for her work among us, no
less than for the tender relation which she sustained to
our beloved brother and former pastor.

To the children we can but say : ' Let your
father's God be your God ; his Redeemer yours ; and
his triumph shall finally be yours.' God's Word
abounds with special promises for the widow and the
fatherless, and we humbly invoke for Mrs. Worcester
and the children the richest fulfillment of all upon,
and unto them.''

The memorial service closed with a tribute to Dr.
Worcester by the pastor of the church, *Rev. Carlos*

Martyn, D. D. The excellent condition in which he
found the church after fourteen months without a
leader spoke in the strongest terms of the excellence
of the work of his predecessor. The church was thoroughly organized and all its activities carried forward
by a people who had been specially well trained for intelligent service.

The *Executive Committee* of the *Presbyterian
Social Union* appointed one of the members of the
"*Union*" to prepare a brief " minute " on the death of
Dr. Worcester and to present the same at the regular
meeting, February 20. The following was offered :

" The Presbyterian Social Union of Chicago has
been saddened by the death of Rev. John Hopkins
Worcester, Jr., D. D.—a member of this Union from
its organization until his removal from the city. In
view of Dr. Worcester's position in this Union as one
of its most valuable members and wisest counsellors,
as well as its third president, we deem it proper to
record our appreciation of him, and of his services.

In the death of Dr. Worcester the Presbyterian
Church has lost one of its choicest leaders, the cause
of Jesus Christ one of its most faithful and loyal servants ; and society, one of its purest men.

The greatness of Dr. Worcester consisted, in part,
in his surpassing clearness of mind ; in his marvellous
ability to analyze a complex problem, separating it into
its simple elements ; in his wonderful power of clear
and convincing statement ; in his supreme loyalty to
truth, and courageous advocacy thereof under all circumstances ; in his genuine humility of soul, never
seeking honor or prominence for himself ; in his sincer-

ity and open frankness; in his loving catholicity of
spirit, and, above all, in his thorough consecration of
himself and all his rare powers to the service of the
Master he so nobly served.

As Presbyterians we mourn the early death of one
so amply endowed, so richly furnished for large usefulness, so temperate in speech, so generously liberal, yet
so safely conservative, so judicious and so judicial in
word and act, and at a time, too, when our beloved
church so greatly needs this combination of rare qualities in its leaders.

As the best tribute we can pay to the memory of
our departed brother we here pledge one another more
thoroughly to imitate his example in all wherein he
imitated Christ Jesus, and more earnestly to strive to
emulate those virtues which endeared him to all who
fully knew him, and which made him so conspicuous
an example of dignified Christian manhood.

To his bereaved wife and children we tender our
sincere sympathy, mingling our tears with theirs, and
praying that they may ever have the assurance that
God's arms of loving care are underneath them to hold
them up; that His gracious hand will dry their tears.
We humbly invoke for them the comfort which the
abiding presence of God's loving Spirit alone can
give."

After a few remarks by the author of the minute
on the character of Dr. Worcester and the great loss to
the church and to the world, the minute was unanimously adopted by a rising vote.

The action of the *Chicago Presbytery* of which Dr.
Worcester was a member at the time of his death is

recorded in the following, offered by a committee through its chairman, Rev. J. G. K. McClure, D. D. :

" It is with a high sense of its privilege that the Presbytery of Chicago records its admiration and affection for the Rev. John H. Worcester, Jr. D. D. who passed to the presence of his Lord, Feb. 5, 1893.

He was our dearly beloved brother and friend. Coming into this Presbytery in February, 1883, to be the pastor of the Sixth Church of Chicago, he immediately became a leader in counsel and in work by reason of his inherent worth. Every interest of each and all of our churches was dear to him. He gave himself without reserve to the consideration and help of all subjects presented to our attention and left a positive impression of wise, fair judgment upon every matter to which he applied his thoughts. His character was so strong and complete that it is not easy to single out a special trait and say, this was the man. And still his exemplification of faithfulness in every relation of life, was most marked. In the family circle a truer man as husband, father, and son never lived. In the ties of friendship he was loyal with a loyalty that loved without counting cost. As a preacher of God's word he held to that word whithersoever that word might lead him. As a pastor he served those committed to his care with a watchfulness that made their spiritual health his unceasing effort. As a presbyter his regularity, his punctuality, his readiness for every duty, his conscientious attention to detail, were recognized by all. As a minister of the Presbyterian Church he responded to her needs with devotion and was ready at any crisis to lift his voice in her welfare.

As a seeker after truth he opened his life widely to the light, and when he saw the light he obeyed his conceptions of truth unmoved by praise or criticism. As a believer in God he held to God with an unswerving fealty even in the utter dearth of feeling, when life seemed without a glow or an aspiration.

This faithfulness animated a man of great mental power. He had an intellect that could weigh evidence without haste and without prejudice ; that was capable of long continued processes of analysis ; that penetrated beneath the surface of words and things ; and that reasoned with fairness, sureness, and force. His ability for clear statement was commanding. Whether he was explaining a matter of parliamentary law, or a case of casuistry, or an exegetical difficulty, or a philosophical problem, he always put his own crystalline thought into terse, strong, crystalline expression. His mere statement of a question and what was involved in it, often answered the question to thoughtful minds. United with his intellect was a very tender heart. He seemed strong enough in physique and in mental force to be self poised. But no man needed sympathy and trust and affection more than he, and no man craved them more. What he desired from others he stood ready to give to others. He loved and he wanted to be loved. His great heart was keenly appreciative of every expression of personal interest and was even dependent for its joy upon such expression.

He died as a member of this Presbytery though serving the church of God as Professor of Systematic Theology in Union Theological Seminary, New York. He went to that position urged thereto by the earnest solicitation of the members of this Presbytery who believed that a large opportunity awaited him in it of advancing the intellectual and spiritual life of the church, and who believed that he was sufficient, under God, for that opportunity.   He did not however sever his connection with the Presbytery, for here were the churches, the work, and the brethren to whom his heart still cleaved.

It is with very tender and very lonely feelings that we thus recognize the worth of this scholarly, consecrated, genuine man of God, who has gone home to his master and his friend.   We rejoice that he labored among us so long, and that we knew him so well.   We rejoice that every memory of him will always appeal to us to be earnest, to be brave, to be devoted.   We send our affectionate greetings to his parents, and to Mrs. Worcester and her three children whose welfare will always be our joy, and we bid the Saviour of mankind bind up their hearts and ours and help us all to make fresh progress toward the land of the vision of God.''

The minute was adopted by a rising vote and Rev. Herrick Johnson, D. D. led the Presbytery in prayer.

It is most fitting that this part of the volume should close with the able address of Dr. McPherson, at the Union Theological Seminary.

MEMORIAL DISCOURSE

Delivered by invitation of the Board of Directors of the Union Theological Seminary, April 13, 1893.

Lover and friend hast thou put far from me,
  And mine acquaintance into darkness.—Ps. lxxxviii. 18.

The memory of the just is blessed.—Prov. x. 7.

But . . . if we believe that Jesus died and rose again, even so them that are also fallen asleep in Jesus will God bring with Him.—1 Thess. iv. 14.

We are a company of bereaved brethren. We at once lament and celebrate a pastor, a colleague, a teacher, who was a faithful lover and friend to us all. For myself I can truly say that I never had, and I never expect to have, a more valued fellow in the Ministry of the Gospel than he. From the day on which I was ordained, through twelve happy years, to the day when he became a professor in this honored institution, it was my favored lot in Providence to serve parishes which immediately adjoined his own. I became intimately associated and acquainted with him. The better I came to know him, the more highly I estimated him as a rare type of Christian manhood, and the more warmly I loved him as a great-hearted companion. I felt the loss seriously when he left my side. Now, when communications with him are altogether interrupted, I sadly realize that a blessing, irrecoverable on earth, has been taken out of my life. Yet in the consequent loneliness, which is a shadowy premon-

ition of old age, it is consoling to think of him as a
vital attestation of Wisdom's words: "The memory
of the just is blessed." Friendship is heir to the rich
legacy of his life. Sweeter still is the white promise
of our hopes in him. As debtor through him alike to
the sacred past and to the unimaginable future, I am
thankful for the opportunity to place a handful of lilies
on his early grave. Do we not know that when the
perpetual Easter dawns he will greet us as radiant
"Angel" of the Lord and Giver of life ? Meantime,
may our motives be chastened and our lives consecrated by the vision of what he has already become.

Character is never an accident. Bringing forth
after its kind, it has so close a connection with ancestry
that the laws of heredity largely determine it. Influenced by the atmosphere in which it grows, personal
and family and social relations give tone and color to
its developments. Formed by its peculiar discipline,
it is a cameo carved and polished by the lapidary arts
of education. Still more is it a crystalization of inward
disposition, choice, act and habit. These familiar and
fundamental facts have a fresh illustration in the derivation, life and character of that Christian gentleman
whom we are commemorating this evening.

He was of English and Puritan lineage, but in the
eighth of the generations who have been at home in
the New World. Four of his seven American forefathers were ministers, and there is good reason to
hope that his gifted oldest son may become the sixth
in that sacred line. His name, which under two or
three different forms of orthography, is widely scattered
amongst Anglo-Saxons, is said to have, etymologically,

a martial meaning ; but the family coat of arms, we are
told, "signifies the first bearer to have been a priest,
or some religious person ; or else one that had done
much for the church." The family itself has certainly
favored both the church and the school.

The original settler in New England, Rev. William
Worcester, is mentioned in the Magnalia of Cotton
Mather. "A fugitive from persecution and tyranny"
he came, apparently, from Salisbury, England, in 1637
or 1638. He was at once appointed pastor at Col-
chester, which, in 1840, became Salisbury, the oldest
town north of the Merrimac River. Its church was the
eighteenth in the Massachusetts Colony, of which he
was made a freeman in 1639. A man of liberal education he is described as "learned, wise, meek and
patient,"—attributes distinctive of his descendants.

The next three in the line lived in Massachusetts ;
godly, industrious men, of stalwart character, devoted
to the public weal, and loving, as one of them said,
"to see a man manly." Francis, of the fourth generation, after being some ten years a pastor, became an
evangelist and did thorough work in revival meetings,
part of the time with Whitefield. Noah, his son, a
farmer and shoe maker, who settled at Hollis, New
Hampshire, entered the army of the revolution with
two of his sons, but lived to gather around his table
eighteen children, of whom five were ministers. When
he died he left seventy-eight grandchildren.

Throughout these five generations, we are credibly
assured, "one and the same character, essentially, appeared from first to last .   .   .   . There may be
ascribed to each an enlightened belief in God and his

Word ; a confiding recognition of his Providence in all
things ; a fervent spirit and a constant habit of devotion ; an undeviating reverence for the Sabbath and
every institution of the Gospel ; an irreproachable veracity and honesty ; an erect manliness and an un-
daunted courage ; with an inflexible adherance to convictions of duty, and a benevolent forwardness to mul-
tiply and extend, in every appropriate and practicable
manner, 'the glory and virtue' of the Church of God.''
What an index to the personality of Professor Worcester, and, indeed, to the Pilgrim race of New England !

In the sixth generation, two members of the family are of special interest to us. One of them, Dr.
Samuel Worcester, a graduate of Dartmouth and a
famous preacher of the day at Salem, was among the
most active of the organizers, and for about twenty
years the first Corresponding Secretary, of the American Board of Commissioners for Foreign Missions.
The other, Rev. Leonard Worcester, was the grandfather of our friend. He was a Trustee of the University of Vermont. At first an editor, he was afterwards, for nearly half a century, the pastor at Peacham,
Vermont, where his memory is still reverently cher-
ished.

Four of his sons, as I make it out, were ministers.
One of them, Rev. John H. Worcester, D. D., whose
namesake and only child your professor was, still lives
in Burlington, Vermont, a noble and most venerable
figure. He was the pastor, first, at St. Johnsbury,
where his son was born, and, later, at Burlington. For
some years subsequently he was occupied in teaching.
Burdened with defective hearing at his great age he

has passed his most recent years largely within his spacious and well-filled library, in refined and studious retirement. His patriarchal form, cast in the heroic mould which has been common in the family, his intellectual head and attractive face, his gentle and dignified manner, and his pathetic and controlled sorrow, too deep for tears and too great for words, would win and touch any heart, especially if it loved his son. His is a gifted and cultivated mind, stored with select and classified knowledge, and trained to think upon high and difficult themes. Withal, its forces are marshalled by a reverent and independent judgment, conservative of ascertained realities and hospitable to fresh aspects of truth from any quarter. We need not wonder at what Prof. Worcester was when we remember that he was not only the son but also, for a third of a century, the close companion of such a man.

To this heritage and family, John Hopkins Worcester, Jr., was born April 2, 1845. Clean, stimulating blood flowed in his infant veins. When self-consciousness dawned, he could look backward with a sense of privilege and indebtedness, and forward with a sense of opportunity and high obligation. He found himself tenderly welcomed in the membership of a respected, refined and unostentatiously affectionate Christian home. He had parents to whom he could look up, and who led his youthful vision towards the Father in heaven. His mother, Martha P. Clark, was the daughter of Deacon Luther Clark, of St. Johnsbury. She was the youngest of three sisters, and the only one that is not now living. One of her sisters married the late Judge Redfield, for many years Chief

Justice of Vermont. The other became the wife of Rev. Joseph S. Gallagher, once the skillful and efficient Treasurer of this Seminary. All accounts agree that Professor Worcestor's mother was a lovely woman, with fine intellectual endowments and a sweet Christian spirit. She died when her son was three years old, entreating him with her latest breath to love the dear Saviour. As he was carried away from her grave, he burst into tears with the bitter cry: "Now, I shan't have a Mamma any more." But it was otherwise ordered. He was favored as few orphans have ever been. When he was less than seven years old, the present wife of his father became a genuine mother to him. Of Scottish extraction, high attainments and beautiful Christian character, her training was invaluable to him.

In Burlington, as in St. Johnsbury, he was surrounded by a quiet, cultivated New England town. The glories of the Green Mountains and of the Adirondacks beset him round. The picturesque and historic Lake Champlain lay beneath his eyes. Temptations, like those of a great city, were nowhere obtrusive, and there was a wholesome inspiration alike in the human life and in the natural scenery environing him. The climate, like the moral standard of his home, was honestly severe, but the impulses of domestic, social and religious life were warm, true and inviting. It was a favored, happy lot, whose good influences abounded in him to his latest hour on earth.

As a boy, he appears to have been precocious, as he certainly was remarkably handsome. He knew the alphabet from picture-blocks when he was only two

years old, and by the end of his third year he had, with
a little occasional help, taught himself to read. But
his native capacity, industry and modesty, coupled with
wise training, kept him from being spoiled. The intellectual and moral atmosphere of his home were
unusually stimulating, in some particulars, perhaps, too
stimulating for an entirely symmetrical development of
his boyish nature. It was at first a parsonage and
afterwards a school. He was constantly in the company of older minds. It may be a question whether
his early years had enough either of playtime or play-
mates for jovial mental health. At any rate, there are
indications that he attained uncommon maturity in his
youth. He became a member of the Church in his
seventeenth year. That step, however, was by no
means forced upon him. It was the natural thing for
him to take it, for he never knew when he became a
Christian. His faith blossomed out like a flower in
spring time. Its fruits, too, were prompt to follow.
While still young, he was one of the original founders
of the Young Men's Christian Association in Burlington, and an effective leader in Sunday School and Mission Work. Nevertheless, his powers and his useful
activities continued to grow and to increase their
harmonious adjustments to the end of his life.

After completing his preparatory course under the
eye of his father, he entered the University of Vermont, from which he graduated in 1865. His college
career was notable both as a key to his character and
on account of the influence which it exerted upon him.
Still living at home, as he did, he may have become
less fully identified with the social features of that

microcosmic life than would have been good for him.
A cotemporary describes him as rather exclusive, genial
with a few friends, disposed to be choice in his society,
yet really warm-hearted and helpful towards all.
His mere acquaintances were disposed to whisper that
he had contracted a few harmless little airs from the
girls' school in his father's house, where he may have felt
semi-conscious superiority. I doubt the exactness of
the inference, but we can all understand the sort of
rallying to which this opinion of average college boys
would subject him, and which may not have been altogether injurious to him. Then, too, he was a fine
scholar, studious in all departments and brilliant in
some. Alike more gifted, more cultivated and more
mature than most of his fellows, he had then, as ever,
what amounted to a passion for accuracy. He was
one of the most effective writers and speakers. Yet
at that stage he had not acquired the simplicity which
marked his later and fuller manhood. Human nature
around him looked up towards him and excused itself
by dubbing him sophomoric. There is a tradition that
he was one day to deliver an original declamation before his classmates. Every one of them entered the
room with a dictionary under his arm. At the first
polysyllable that Worcester uttered, they all with one
consent began to scurry sarcastically through their dic-
tionaries to find its definition. But he scarcely winced.
For him, the fun merely raised an issue of moral courage, touched with indignation and pity. Yet, in spite
of such chaffing, the little college world admired him
as a gifted mind without conceit, a real scholar without pedantry, an earnest Christian without cant, and

an apostle of manliness without effeminacy.

It was one of the small colleges, set upon the Acropolis of the Athens of Vermont. He was not only well known to the unconventional students, but he enjoyed also the advantages, peculiar to a small college, of intimate association with ripe professors who gave him individual attention. He improved his opportunities and became truly educated. Indeed, he has added distinction to the institution. The honored president tells me that all who have known it intimately for the last thirty years would be sure to name him among the score, or even the ten, who have had the most brilliant and promising collegiate careers. As attesting her continued regard, the University of Vermont gave him his doctorate degree in 1885.

After graduating, he taught for two years in the school of which his father was principal. During this period, especially after an interval of severe illness, he laboriously debated with himself, like many another young man, the question of what life-work he should choose. He thought of the law, but abandoned the idea as a dream of ambition. His choice then lay between teaching and preaching ; but he said at the time that his conscience suggested the query whether it was any the less a contest between selfishness and devotion than before, " the selfishness having taken the form of a desire of ease, instead of a desire for distinction." Others thought that he ought to continue teaching. But, although, after he had completed his theological course, he acted as tutor, for three months, in his Alma Mater, he declined its Chair of Rhetoric and English Literature, to which he had been invited, and determined to enter the Ministry. Even then, however, he went forward somewhat reluctantly, driven by a pure sense of duty, not, as he said, that he recoiled from its probable obscurity nor altogether that he dreaded its pressure, but from an utter incapacity to realize "that souls would be won to God by anything that he could do or say." He set out upon his career, trusting explicitly upon the Spirit of God, satisfied that whether eagerly, like Paul, or reluctantly, like Moses, he would try to do whatsoever the Master should indicate. If more of us undertook the ministry of reconciliation after his manner, there would be more ministers of the right kind.

He entered upon his theological course here in 1867. At the end of his Middle Year he went abroad and spent a year or more in traveling and in studying at Berlin and Leipsic. Returning, he graduated from this school of the prophets in 1871 ; and up to the 5th of last February, on every day of his life, he was both an honor to Union Seminary, and an exalted type of the ministers whom she has trained for the church of God.

The chief work of his noble life was done in the pastorate, preaching the living Christ to dying men— to my mind the holiest and sweetest vocation on earth. In these days of frequent pastoral changes, occasioned in part, no doubt, by the exacting and exhausting demands of the work, but far more, I fear, by the restlessness of ministers and churches, let it be noted that in almost twenty years he had but two charges and that he left neither of them because he would or because he must, but solely in response to an impera-

tive summons of conscience. He was installed pastor
of the First Presbyterian Church of South Orange, New
Jersey, January 10, 1872, and left it in January, 1883,
to become pastor of the Sixth Presbyterian Church of
Chicago. His work as preacher and pastor was of a
uniform quality throughout, and the quality was uni-
formly high. It was all done on his honor as the servant of Jesus Christ. None of it was slighted, whether
it was public or private ; his study and his prayer-closet
were as faithfully devoted to their purposes as the pulpit or the platform. Every minister is master of his
own time. Every minister is likely to hear the effusive
praises of the friendly flatterer, and to be left out of
hearing by his average critic. Consequently the be-
setting sins of weak ministers are laziness and egotism.
But my brother was neither lazy nor egotistical, for he
was not weak ; he was faithful, sincere and virile.
For genuine fidelity towards God and man, he was
well-nigh matchless.

His preaching, as some of you know, was distinguished for thoroughness ; whether he read from
manuscript, or spoke extemporaneously, as he could do
with admirable completeness, clearness and finish, he
always brought beaten oil into the sanctuary. His
published sermons on "Womanhood" are in evidence.
Unusually intellectual, yet with the white light of great
emotions, and with a passion for saving the whole of a
man, he made large demands upon his hearers, at the
same time that he gave them large supplies of thought,
feeling and purpose. Partly for that reason, he was
not, in the common apprehension of the word, a popular preacher. He dwelt in rather too high and rare

an atmosphere for that. He appealed especially to the somewhat select class of thoughtful and educated minds. Yet he left indelible lines of life upon the soul of all regular attendants, even when they were unconscious of the fact. He was singularly unselfish in preaching. It was not a great name nor a conspicuous place that he was seeking, any more than it was a fat salary. His first desire seemed to be to fill the place assigned to him, to make Jesus Christ conspicuous in truth and love, and to leave permanent gracious impressions.

He was a "house-going" minister, and he did not confine himself to houses of any class, rich or poor, personally friendly or personally indifferent. To his great personal regret he could not easily win an entrance into the affections of a stranger or acquaintance. He was too thorough for that ; at a time when much of our pastoral visitation consists largely of small talk, he had no small talk at all. He had to make his way on his genuine merits, which he was not facile in exploiting. But in times of stress and burden, when death stood at the door or devastated the home, he was most welcome. There was enough of him to meet a crisis, and souls in critical situations had faith in him, and found strength and peace in his ministrations. I have often felt that if I were on my deathbed, I should prefer his ministry to any other. He would have told me the truth honestly, completely, simply and affectionately.

A good general test of his pastoral efficiency may be found in the condition in which he left each of his churches. I fancy that one of the surest tests of any pastor's career comes to light after he goes away. If a church then has parties who say I am of Paul, Apollos or Cephas, you may almost take it for granted that there was something radically defective or selfish in his teaching. For some pastors seem to brand the Master's sheep with their own initials. But our friend left the Master's high, unifying name in his parishioners' hearts. They thought of Christ rather than of him. They remained united and prepared to offer a common welcome to the succeeding under-shepherd.

Still further, he always did his full share in the consecrated work of the churches of the vicinage, as, for example, in the Presbytery. Two extremes are possible : to neglect the individual church, which is the pastor's primary and imperative charge, and to neglect the common cause. He did neither. Bearing his own burden he shared the common burden. This was true of him in South Orange, where he did his initial pastoral work in a charming, quiet field. When I went from Princeton Seminary into his neighborhood, I was quickened by the example set by his own parish, and I soon felt his personal sympathy and brotherly helpfulness. But Chicago, as a larger, needier, more exacting field, holds his greatest monument. There he would neither stoop to degrading competition nor neglect his own charge. But, at the same time, he became in many ways easily the leading spirit in the Presbytery, with the possible exception of that Nestor of North-western Presbyterianism, the Rev. Dr. R. W. Patterson. The Presbytery depended largely upon his judgment, and followed usually in his footprints. He loved our city and never tired of toiling for its evangelization. He was always prompt in keeping appointments, and he never wasted time with needless talk ; for, influential as he was in the later years, he would speak only under the compulsion of duty, and then he always spoke to the point and from his real heart convictions. His place is not yet filled, and we miss him day by day.

Such a man needed human sympathy—he got it. His brethren learned to love and trust him, and he had a sweet and hallowed domestic life. On Oct. 29, 1874, he married Miss Harriet W. Strong, a daughter of Edward Strong, M. D., of Auburndale, Massachusetts. Four children, two boys and two girls, were given to them, all born in Orange and all living still excepting little Martha, who is with her father. Let him who can believe in the celibacy of the clergy. Our friend found almost an ideal of the kingdom of God on earth in his family. Strenuous a man as he was, with deep-seated convictions, he was so tolerant of the rightful opinions of others, as I believe, he never once, during their eighteen years of married life, crossed any real independent judgment of Mrs. Worcester's. Nor was he ever dictatorial, unreasonable or merely suppressive toward his children. A strong man will be considerate and fair, if he be only strong enough. He was strong enough, and he had sufficient reason. His children are worthy of him. His wife was like-minded with himself. With the same Puritan blood and New England culture, with almost equal gifts of mind and heart, she loved to be in his shadow, but, more than she will ever acknowledge or even know, she directed and inspired his life. He owed her much and, through him, so do you and I.

It is not strange that such a man, with such gifts, such pastoral experience and such a home, should come to love with unspeakable ardor the ministry of the Gospel. He often said, to his nearest intimates, that he thought no other work in life comparable to it. He left it, therefore, with as much reluctance as he entered it. When he was called in May, 1891, to the Chair of Systematic Theology in Hartford, he was in actual distress until he concluded that it was his privilege to decline. He loved the pastorate, and although he had come from a Congregational family, he had an intelligent and discriminating love for the Presbyterian Church. Two months later came the call from you. He appreciated the great honor of it, as his friends did ; but he shrank from it, with characteristic diffidence, and the acceptance of it required no small degree of personal self-denial. It was not the line of life which he had chosen, nor the department of theological instruction which he preferred. He consulted his close friends and they, in spite of their wishes to keep him in the pastorate, advised him to accept, because they regarded him as an ordained leader of leaders and because they hoped that he, with his conservative temper, non-partisan theological attitude and independent yet progressive mind, might do something to aid a beloved institution, and to heal the existing lamentable breach between brethren in the same church. Now, that he has gone home, shall we not hope and pray that the breach will be closed ?

During the last eighteen months of his life, as his strength was failing and his life was fading away, some of us have wondered whether his coming was not a mistake. But he did not feel any such questioning. Trusting no human counsel for the final decision, he had prayed fervently for divine guidance ; he fully believed that he had been led by God's spirit, and that the transfer was a part of the gracious Father's plan for him and for us all. He died as he had lived, better than submissive, — acquiescent. Filial hearts, therefore, will not be impatient or complaining that his work here ended when it seemed only to have begun. Its influence, I am sure, will not be transient. I know his work among you was rapidly growing in interest to him. You know, as I cannot, how gifted, cultured, genuine, devoted and open-hearted it was becoming. It would naturally have special attractions for strong, candid and manly students. Doubtless, he was in the main a disciple of your epoch-making teacher, Dr. Henry B. Smith ; so true a disciple that he could be independent of his teacher in important particulars. He had the same reverent, discerning spirit, the same firm, conservative and delicate grasp of generic essentials, the same undisturbed sense of liberty as to all undetermined and incidental matters. Equally with that master, he spent his strength in strenuous seeking after truth, and he would dare encourage his pupils to think for themselves, and to besiege him with all sorts of honest questions. If he had lived, I am sure he would have filled his place with ever-increasing power and with indubitable adequacy and renown.

His faculty for criticism, analysis and inductive logic was large. He valued conclusions neither because they were old nor because they were new, but in proportion as they seemed to comprehend the vital truth. The bent of his mind was not negative, much less destructive, but rather positive, constructive, and at least in mode creative. In a trusted and congenial company he had almost peerless ability to hear a difficult and complicated case, and then, instantaneously, with comprehensiveness, exactness and finish of statement, to point out its defects and make plain its integral significance. In this respect, he had the endowment of a great jurist—an endowment far more rare and valuable than that of the ready debater who can seize upon and advocate one side of a question.

No one could accurately measure his intellectual processes without noting his predominant moral qualities. Remembering both, I call him a great man. But, lest my own estimate of him may be partial and faulty, let me adapt the words of another friend. His greatness consisted in his surpassing perspicuity of mind, in his rare capacity to separate a complex problem into its simple elements, in his wonderful power of thorough and convincing statement, in his supreme loyalty to truth and his courageous advocacy of it, under all circumstances, in his genuine humility of soul, which enabled him to see the truth easily, yet never permitted him to seek prominence for himself, in his sincere and unpretentious candor, in his loving catholicity of spirit and in the complete consecration of his unusual powers and acquirements to the Light of the World.

The key to his character, I believe, will be found in the fact that moral considerations controlled him. The chief defect which I have heard ascribed to him

was an apparent reserve of manner. His exterior gave to
the average person meeting him the impression that he
was cold. A few acquaintances have thought that he
was even haughty. But his intimate friends knew
that this view of his character was radically mistaken.
His heart was always warm. He had an ample capacity for true friendship. He depended upon the love of
friends, hungered for the good-will of all, and suffered
often because he could not facilely show his own good-
will. He could not tell you to your face that he loved
you. If his life did not show it, he was powerless. It
was one of his heavy burdens that he had to force his
way where many another could win an entrance to the
human heart. He was utterly unable to wear his
heart upon his sleeve.

This was due in part, perhaps, to his Puritan
blood. He was morally strenuous and never frivolous.
His eyes were so filled with the great duties needful to
to be done that, pushing straightforward, he overlooked the allied little things which might be engross-
ing others. He hardly made enough of the com-
plaisant arts of tact. It may also have been due
somewhat to the intellectual pressure put upon his
early life in which his mind and conscience developed
rapidly. Besides, in early boyhood he was rather in-
valid. Possibly his boyhood was cut short because he
did not romp and play as much as healthy children
who have brothers and sisters. It was, too, the constant habit of his accurate mind to state things mod-
erately and carefully; whereas most of us are contin-
ually overstating and exaggerating. It must be added,
that unless his latest years, which mellowed him, be

excepted, he was to some extent deficient in that sense
of humor which oils so many wheels in life and which
enables us instinctively not to fight the insignificant
things, but to pass over them with a convenient smile
or laugh. Nevertheless, the great reason for his apparent reserve is not to be sought in any of these secondary influences. It came fundamentally from his
native modesty, which led him to depreciation of himself and to embarrassment before others. This bashfulness resisted, so stiffened his manners that they
misrepresented his feelings. If self-assurance or conceit be a virtue, we may admit that he had one vice.
For he was meek and lowly in heart ; yet so that he dis-
dained the fawning of an Uriah Heep and was a
stranger to the false modesty which Emerson called
the haughtiness of humility.

As conscientious a man as I have ever known, he
was hard upon himself, but gracious and tolerant towards the sincere moral postures of others. For this
reason, questions which belonged to the pure ethical
realm appeared to give him unusually little trouble. He
was simply above the reach of many of the ordinary
temptations of life. When he perceived that a thing
was right or obligatory, his doubts about it were
settled.

If, in matters of expediency or questions of the
reason, he would sometimes hesitate, you might be sure
that conscientious scruples were at the bottom of his
hesitancy, and that he could not as yet make out his
moral bearings. The moment that he discerned distinctly what he ought to do, he became as bold as a
lion. It was a curious combination, timid as to his

own personality, even as to his judgment ; perfectly
fearless as to duty. The historic speech at Detroit is
an instance in point. To his intimates, it has always
seemed characteristic rather than exceptional in its intellectual power, its Christian spirit, its moral weight.
For days he had been urged to speak. But he shrank
from the conspicuous responsibility. Though he passed
almost sleepless nights over the matter, he still refused
to say a word. But things appeared to him to be going wrong. Finally, alone, upon his knees, it became
plain to him that the Master summoned him to the
task. Then his lips were touched with fire, and, even
if the whole world had been against him, nothing
could have swerved him, more than Isaiah, from the
purpose to utter his convictions boldly, tenderly,
mightily, under the resistless inspiration of the sense
of duty. That is why my friend's speech will live and
quicken after the mere controversies of that hour are
the forgotten dust of logomachy.

Contrary to the opinions of some acquaintances, he
had an enthusiastic nature. His later boyhood in
Burlington furnishes a typical illustration. It seems
that one evening, shortly after dark, fire broke out in
a building down near the lake shore under the little
bluff. The boys started for it instantly on a run. He
outran the others, and, in going over the side of the
bluff, he made a misstep, fell and broke his leg. When
the others overtook him, they wanted to carry him
home at once. But he said : " No, no, leave me here ;
go and help put out the fire ; take me home afterwards."

Under that calm manner and controlled temper,

there was an intensity of conviction, of purpose, of feeling, of courage, of ideal vision, which explains apparent anomalies in his finished career and which promised heroic achievements in the withheld second half of his life-time. It will teach us why he was constant and tireless in every form of faithfulness, to his conscience, to his father, his wife and children and his friends, to the churches which he served, to the Seminary, to the Lord Jesus Christ. He was faithful in the least and faithful also in much, faithful alike in service and in suffering.

What is all this but to say, by way of summary and pre-eminence, that he was a gifted, manly, true-hearted Christian. His life amply exemplified the title of one of my favorites among his sermons, "Christianity, a Virile Religion." He exemplified it also in the supreme hour. He died at Lakewood, New Jersey, alone with his wife and his Saviour. When it became plain to the physician about nine o'clock on that Sabbath evening that he was soon to enter into rest, she went to him and said: "Well, dear, you won't need to suffer much longer." "Then," said he, "you think I am going?" "Yes," she answered, with the simple truthfulness of their life. He waited half a minute, and then replied: "We should send some telegrams"; that is, to his children and father and nearest friends. Brave, self-forgetful, resolute to the end! A kind-hearted lady in the hotel came to the door to ask them if she should not stay with them during that awful ordeal. But it was he who, looking toward her with a grateful smile, answered: "No, we will watch it out together." Love was sufficient and triumphant. Presently, Mrs. Worcester asked if he felt ready to go. Observe the reply of that man of white character and noble life. He just said : "Only as I trust in my Redeemer." The Professor, like a little child, had learned by heart the central essential of all theology. Shall any of the rest of us, ignoring grace, dare venture into the divine presence upon the rights of our personal merits ? Conscious to the final moment of earth, he suffered terribly during the three closing hours from suffocation and the griping pain about his heart. They prayed together—he for patience, and she that he may be released from physical agony. I shall never think of that man and that woman, their children absent, sitting alone, hand in hand, before the King who waited with the crown, not a tear in their eyes, but praying with unbroken voices to God their Father, without rejoicing that heroism still lingers upon earth. He was a dying hero ; she was a living heroine.

No, character is not an accident. It is the bestowment and the evolution of the covenanting, atoning, cleansing, emancipating and inspiring Christ.

SERMONS.

CHRISTIANITY A VIRILE RELIGION.

For God hath not given us the spirit of fear, but of power and of love and of self-control. —II Timothy, 1 : 7.

The application of these words is a personal one. They are intended as a gentle admonition to Timothy not to be wanting in courage and firmness, and particularly not to allow shame or the fear of personal risk to deter him from visiting Paul in this his second imprisonment and near prospect of martyrdom.

One sees from the whole tone of this most pathetic and yet most triumphant of Paul's epistles, that, while he tenderly loved his "son Timothy," and while he had the utmost confidence in his ability, purity, and piety, there was just a shade of anxiety in his mind lest he prove deficient in manliness. And so throughout the Epistle we find him guarding this weak point by admonitions,—delicate as the admonitions of that consummate courtesy always were,—affectionate, as from that great loving heart they could not fail to be,—but unmistakable in their significance.

"Be not thou therefore ashamed of the testimony of our Lord, nor of me his prisoner ; but be thou partaker of the afflictions of the gospel according to the power of God." "The Lord give mercy unto the house of Onesiphorus ; for he oft refreshed me, and was not ashamed of my chain." "Thou therefore my son be strong in the grace that is in Christ Jesus." "Thou therefore

endure hardness, as a soldier of Jesus Christ." "But
watch thou in all things, endure afflictions, do the work
of an evangelist, make full proof of thy ministry."

In our text he grounds the exhortation to Christian
manliness upon the very nature of Christianity. "God
hath not given us the spirit of fear, but of power and of
love and of self-control."

The Spirit of Christ, the Holy Spirit that dwelleth
in us, is not a spirit that prompts to timidity, to caution,
to shrinking from scorn and danger, and to a weak yielding to the tyranny of circumstances, but a spirit whose
fruits are "power" to do and dare, "love" that shrinks
not from self-sacrifice, and "self-control" that knows
how to endure. In other words Christianity is in its
very essence a virile religion, a religion that demands and
develops manliness.

The theme thus suggested to us: CHRISTIANITY A
VIRILE RELIGION, seems to me not unsuited to an occasion like this. *

We are here in the heart of a great city. And
what is a great city but a great throbbing center of masculine life and energy ? When we think of a village we
think of a cluster of homes. Our imagination instantly
calls up visions of children at play and housewives busy
about their doors. But when we think of a city, though
indeed it is full of homes, it is not these that rise first to
our thought but rather the market, the forum, the ex-
change, with their throng of eager, jostling, earnest
men.

When therefore in the person of the ambassador of
Christ, Wisdom now, as of old, takes her stand "in the
top of the high places, by the way of the places of the
paths," when "she crieth at the gates, at the entry of

the city, at the coming in at the doors," her word
as of old must be : "Unto you, O men, I call, and my
voice is to the sons of men."

If it is not so, if the Christian preacher has not
something to say worth the while of hard-headed, keen-
witted, busy, practical *men* to stop and hear, if the religion which he teaches is not robust and virile enough to
lay its hand boldly and masterfully upon these currents
of manly activities, and give worthy scope and direction
to the energies which are here centered, then he is out
of his place in such a city and such a pulpit as this.

It is useless to conceal from ourselves that Christianity has sometimes fallen under suspicion, as though
it were wanting in those elements which should enlist
the sympathies and elicit the enthusiasm of the distinctively manly character. Thomas Hughes, in his essay on
"The Manliness of Christ," gives a striking proof of the
existence of this feeling, in his account of a proposed
Society to be called "The Christian Guild," the members of which, though they must be first of all Christians,
were to be selected as far as possible for some act of
physical prowess, the motive for such an organization
being that the Young Men's Christian Associations,
though increasing in numbers, were wholly failing to
reach the class which most needed Christian influence,
because of an alleged feeling that these associations,
however valuable in some ways they might be, "did
not cultivate individual manliness in their members, and
that this defect was closely connected with their open
profession of Christianity."

The same feeling has its silent but unmistakable witness in the marked preponderance of women to be seen
in the composition of any average Christian congregation, and in the membership of any ordinary Christian
church. It reveals itself in the conduct of those hus-

bands and fathers, by no means few, who encourage church attendance and church membership in their wives and daughters while themselves deliberately holding aloof from the latter, at least, if not from both.

There is reason to fear too that the feeling that religion, at least as represented by the Christian church is an affair for women, is gaining ground just at the present time. Things have not indeed reached the pass with us to which they have come in Catholic France, which may be roughly estimated as made up of a female population of devotees and a male population of infidels, but the tendency seems to be in that direction. The church seems to be losing rather than increasing its hold upon the masculine half of our population. It is an ominous fact, e. g. which I find quoted from a circular of the Brooklyn Y. M. C. A. that less than one-tenth of the young men of that city are in the churches and Sunday Schools.

This tendency, if unchecked, must inevitably prove fatal. If the defect be inherent in Christianity itself, and if it be not in its power in some way to renew its vigor and regain that lost hold, it must go to the wall. No religion can permanently retain its power over society through a hold on either sex alone. If missionaries never feel that the gospel has a secure foothold in a heathen land till it has gained the wives and mothers to its side, we, in this land, must equally recognize that its footing will be insecure from the day that it loses the support of the husbands and fathers.

This is not to assume that the masculine nature is superior to the feminine. I should be the last to make such an assumption. Nor yet is it to make the contrary assumption which in some quarters begins to be put forward as one of the great discoveries of the age,—a step forward in civilization. You may take either view

you choose of that question ; or, better still, you may
say that there is no question here of superior and inferior; but that either sex is the complement of the other. It
remains true that they are unlike, and that unless Christianity appeals to and satisfies that which is distinctively
virile, it must forfeit its hold upon men, and with that its
sway over the society and civilization of the future.

Nor yet is it anything to the purpose to say that the
reason why there are more women than men in our
churches is that the religious instinct is stronger in
woman than in man ; for that is only to say that, by
reason of that stronger instinct, she will be more easily
satisfied ; and that a more vigorous and perfect religion
is needed to command and mould the less impressible
masculine nature. Call it what you please then ; call it
a virtue or a defect in the masculine character, the fact
remains, that a religion which does not embrace certain
elements will not appeal strongly to that character, and
will not rally the manhood of an age beneath its standard. Does Christianity contain these elements? I answer confidently, yes, in fullest measure. To the young
men before me to-day I say unhesitatingly : the religion
of Jesus Christ challenges your attention, challenges
your respect, challenges your unreserved surrender, and
hearty enthusiasm just because it is through and through
a virile religion.

Thus in the first place, Christianity appeals to manhood as a religion of fact rather than of sentiment.
It addresses itself to the intellect and not merely to the
emotions. It has been said, not I think without force,
that if the characteristic womanly virtue is love, the
characteristic manly virtue is truth ; that is, not that
women are more deceitful than men, but that while
men come behind women in unselfishness, women
come perhaps as far behind men in the capacity to

deal with things as they are. That, at all events, is your boast, that you are accustomed to act upon fact, and not upon feeling. But that is the appeal that Christianity makes to you. It comes to you with a series of historical facts, the facts of the life, death, and resurrection of Jesus of Nazareth, and back of these a series of spiritual facts of which these are the attestation, and asks you to square your lives to these facts. It does not say to you : "Believe in immortality because it is dreary to think that death ends all", but : "Believe in immortality, because Jesus Christ rose from the dead." It does not say to you : "Worship, you know what, and cannot know, simply because there is an instinct of veneration in your soul that must have expression." It says to you :. "Worship God, who in these last times hath spoken unto us by his son and hath given the light of the knowledge of his glory in the face of Jesus Christ."

It is indeed a strange thing that men should, like our modern agnostics, capable of seriously proposing to secure to religion a new lease of life and power by denying to it all basis of fact and confining it wholly to the sphere of the emotions, substitute, for the historic Scriptures, the poetry of Tennyson and Wordsworth, and for the worship of a crucified and risen Redeemer a "worship chiefly of the silent sort" paid to an "unknowable First Cause." Men want a religion that courts light, and does not shun cross-questioning. They want a religion that touches bottom somewhere. Such a religion they find in the historic gospel of our Lord and Saviour Jesus Christ.

2. Again, Christianity challenges your attention and allegiance *because it is a religion of conscience* and not of ceremony. Men in general take but little interest in "ecclesiastical millinery ;" or to speak less disrespectfully, the love of ornament which is so strong in

woman, is too weak in man to give mere ritual, however imposing, any very strong hold upon his mind. It is the ethical element that appeals to him. The gorgeous temple, the pealing organ, the solemn chants, the splendid vestments, cannot save a religion from the neglect and contempt of the masculine mind, if the moral earnestness has gone out of it.

Give me a man, I care not how rude and ungrammatical his speech, how uncouth his attire, though it be but a garment of camel's hair, with a leathern girdle about his loins, how primitive his pulpit, thought it be but a dry-goods box at the street corner, or a rock by the riverside, who nevertheless, like John the Baptist, knows how to cut and clear his way through the veneer of conventionalism, the husks of flimsy excuse and unconscious hyprocrisy, straight to men's consciences, making them hear the thunder of the everlasting "Thou shalt," and "Thou shalt not," and you shall see the manhood of Jerusalem or of Chicago turning its back upon the splendor of the temple and the pomp of its ritual, and going out into the wilderness for to hear him.

To this one element, I take it, more than to all else, Carlyle owed his mighty influence over the most virile thought and life of two generations. Now it is as a preacher of righteousness that the Christian minister demands your hearing. Christianity though never presented with less of aesthetic adornment, never commanded more of manly respect and devotion than in the days of Knox, of Cromwell's Ironsides, and of the Puritans; and it did so by virtue of its vigorous assertion of everlasting righteousness.

3. Once more, Christianity appeals to you as men, because it is an *aggressive religion*. I lately heard a man say that he could conceive of no life more distasteful

than that of a soldier on garrison duty. It was an expression of the manly instinct for action, as against mere waiting and enduring. A religion which does not appeal to that instinct,—which does not offer a field of action broad enough, and enterprise grand enough to give scope to the intensest energy, is not a religion for men. But where will you find these if Christianity does not offer them? Its field is the world, its enterprise, the reconstruction of society, the emancipation of mankind from spiritual bondage, and the establishment of a universal kingdom of God.

It is sometimes laid as a reproach against the gospel that it inculcates only the passive virtues, meekness, patience, and resignation. It does inculcate the passive virtues. It needs to inculcate them, for they are the hardest to attain. It needed not only to inculcate them but to place them in the foreground, under an overwhelming emphasis of precept and example, in the face of Roman pride and Jewish vindictiveness, in an age when revenge was a duty, submission a weakness, and humility a reproach. But if it be said that it fails to lay stress upon the active virtues also,—courage, perseverence, benevolence, philanthropy,—where is the proof? God hath not given us the spirit of fear, but of power, not of tame submission but of energetic action. "I have written unto you young men" not because ye are patient, but "because ye are strong"—is its appeal. Its metaphors are full of energy. It is a warfare, a race, an athletic contest. Throughout, we hear the ring of the martial cry, and see the clash of the contending hosts of light and darkness.

It cannot have escaped any student of Old Testament history that religion had its strongest hold upon Israel in time of war. One reason for this is that war was its only mode of aggression. Spiritually it could not go forth to the conquest of the world till its Messiah came to lead it. The weapons of its warfare were carnal. Only in the conquest of the promised land—in the execution of Jehovah's wrath upon the worshipers of false gods, were the religious feeling and the active energy of the nation brought into union. And so in times of peace religious enthusiasm was apt to wane. The same is true of Mohammedanism to-day. It is decaying, its hold upon its votaries is weakening because the sword of Islam has fallen from its grasp ; and its only hope of revival, as friend and foe alike bear witness, lies in a new war of religious aggression. But Christianity with its spiritual weapons calls you to an unceasing crusade and its appeal to your manhood is not less, but more powerful, because this crusade is not one of brute force, but of truth and of character.

4. Yet again, Christianity appeals to you as men because it is a *heroic religion.*

What is heroism ? Not the mere power to face danger ; that is courage. Not the mere power to endure suffering ; that is fortitude. Heroism is more. A noble motive is essential to make a hero. The hero is he who faces danger, who endures suffering and hardship, for duty or for love.

> "So nigh is grandeur to our dust,
>   So near is God to man,
>   When duty whispers low, thou must,
>   The youth replies, I can."

That is heroism.

Where indeed will you find a truer analysis of it than in these words of our text : "God hath not given us the spirit of fear," the spirit of the coward, "but of power ;" there is the energy to undertake a difficult task ; "and of love." there is the unselfish motive that glorifies it ; "and of self-control," there is the victory of the willing spirit over the weak flesh, that carries it through.

God has given us that spirit. The Apostle assumes that by the very nature of his calling the Christian is a hero. The Spirit of God makes heroes of men.

What indeed is the central principle of the Christian life, as Christ himself taught it ? Is it not self-sacrifice for others ? And is not that the very essence of heroism ?

Far be it from me to picture such heroism to you as an exclusively or peculiarly masculine trait. Were I to do so the silent heroism of women's lives all about me would put me to instant shame. Indeed it is but true, that, as the conditions of life now are, while the demand for heroism is an occasional thing in the life of an average man, the life of many a woman is one long exhibition of heroism ending only with the grave.

What I do say is, that there can be no true manliness without this element ; and that if religion is to appeal powerfully to men it must address itself to that latent capacity for heroism which we find buried somewhere even in the man of flabbiest moral fibre.

Listen, O man, to that call as it comes to you today from the lips of Jesus of Nazareth, the grandest hero that ever trod the earth, a call to deeds of power, to deeds of unselfish love, to the endurance of hardship with manly self-control. Is there nothing in your bosom that kindles in response to such a call ? Stirs there no enthusiasm within you to follow such a leader ?

For turn with me now for a moment from considering Christianity as an abstraction to look at Christ himself. Is he a leader for men to follow, or not ?

I once read a Jewish sketch which purported to set forth the experience of an Israelite youth who embraced Christianity, but in a few years renounced it and returned to the faith of his fathers, because his manly instincts could not brook the leadership of the meek and unresisting sufferer of Calvary.

The test is a fair one. If Jesus is not a manly leader, then Christianity is not a religion for men. If there is in him anything weak, if anywhere in his career it is the spirit of fear rather than of power and of love and of self-control that shapes his action, then turn away from him and find yourselves a leader of sterner stuff.

But where is the weakness ? where is the unmanliness ? I grant he was womanly, too. And I grant that the painter's art, startled at the discovery in him of all those traits to which we are wont to do homage as the peculiar glory of womanhood, has too often lost sight of his manliness, and placed an effeminate figure upon its canvas. But I deny that the gospels are responsible for the portrait. I claim it the crowning glory of the Son of Man that in him a complete humanity, both compact strength and all womanly grace, found its consummate expression.

A meek and unresisting sufferer. Yes, but is that all ? Is there no manly independence in his calm defiance of bigotry, as in the synagogue amid lowering glances he heals a palsied man or a crippled woman on the Sabbath-day ? Is there no manly indignation in those woes against the Pharisees, and in that glance before which the money changers in the temple quail and flee ? Is there no manly courage in that unfaltering step with which month after month he walked with open eyes toward a cross ? Is there no manly breadth of view in that plan for the establishment of a society to last through the generations with no other foundation than attachment to himself, and no other bond of union than two simple rites ? Is there no manly power in that life-work which in little more than three short years, with out arms, without numbers, without prestige, turned the currents of history into new channels, and wins an enduring supremacy over men for which Alexander, Caesar, Napoleon waded in vain through seas of blood.

Is it then in the last tragedy that his manhood breaks down? "The meek and unresisting sufferer"! And what then? He should have resisted? He should have fought? He should, like Elijah, have called down fire from heaven to consume the band that came out to take him? Nay, there is something manlier than fighting; it is to die willingly that others may live. It is to have the power to save one's self and refuse to use it, because to save one's self would be to leave others to perish. ·

The other day a railroad train was rushing at express speed toward its terminus but a few miles away, when the passengers in the forward car were startled by the bursting in upon them of the engineer and fireman, followed by a rush of smoke and flame. The cab of the engine had caught fire from the open door, and fanned by the swift motion was almost instantly in a furious blaze. The fireman tried to reach the air-brake, but could not for the press. A few moments only and that train unchecked, uncontrolled, would have rushed to inevitable and ghastly wreck. The engineer turned, looked a moment into the sheeted flame, then set his lips and climbed over the tender. A tremor, a check, a stop, and in two or three minutes a scorched and blackened figure is seen slowly, painfully making its way over the tender again. They did what they could for him; but it was of no avail. The flame had done its work. For duty and for the lives dependent on him he had gone deliberately into fiery death.

That was manliness. But it was a grander triumph of that same manliness when Jesus is seen walking for months straight toward a death more agonizing. And when at last he came face to face with it, standing for hours in calm dignity, silent and motionless, his flesh laid open to the bone with the cruel scourge, while round him raged a wild storm of blind, vindictive fury showering buffets and insults and jeers upon his head, yet neither cringing nor cursing. Standing that, not because he cannot help it, for there are legions of angels at his call, and in his person slumbers a power which had quelled the storm and trod the waves,—and when at last the cruel cross finished the ghastly work, hearing unmoved the challenge to save himself, because to save himself would have been to leave a world full of perishing men and women to a fate more dreadful and to agonies more dire.

Where, if not here, shall we find the supreme triumph of power and of love and of self-control? Take from Agamemnon old Homer's noble epithet "King of men." Here is one who claims it by a higher right in a grander sense.

If, then, there is so much in Christ, so much in Christianity as it came from him to appeal to manly character and evoke manly enthusiasm, the fault,—if it shall ever lose its hold upon men,—must lie in the presentation.

And here, brethren in the ministry, this theme comes home to us with the burden of a great responsibility. The preacher of a virile religion has need to be a manly man.

More than once of late have I come upon hints of a popular impression that ministers are deficient in manliness, "that they are not to be counted on in great emergencies where physical courage and physical manhood are demanded"; that, in short, there is a shade of effeminacy about them. Brethren, we cannot afford to let such an impression prevail. God hath not given us the spirit of fear but of power. Go over in your thought the preachers of great power, the preachers who not simply amuse but move and hold men, and you will find that however they may differ in their theology, in their ecclesiastical relations, in their style of eloquence, with rare exceptions they agree in this that they are thoroughly manly men.

More than this, our *preaching*, if it is to hold men's attention, must abound in those elements of which I have spoken. It must be thoughtful preaching. Flowers of rhetoric, roseate clouds of mysticism, tender gushes of sentimentalism, will not long hold men. They must have hard, solid thought. Withal it must be intellectually bold preaching. "The spirit of fear" is not God's Spirit, in the pulpit any more than out of it. The preacher who would make men listen to him must not fear to grapple with their diffiulties. It will not do for him timidly to hug the shore ; he must show them that he has a compass with which he dares to sail the deepest sea. But it must be intellectually bold in another sense, he must not fear to take a position. I have no faith in nebulous, non-committal preaching as an expedient for holding the men who are drifting away from the church.

Our preaching again must be strongly ethical. If like Paul we would make men tremble and yet come again to hear, we must like him reason with them "of righteousness and temperance and judgment to come." The preaching of mere morality is a weak thing enough ; it is a ball without powder, but the preaching that leaves morality out is weaker yet ; it is powder without a ball,— a mere flash in the pan.

Again if we would hold men we must set before them something to do. We must preach an aggressive Christianity. Our sermons must be drum-beats.

And finally we must keep before them the heroic ideal. If we fear to preach sacrifice, fear to preach self-denial, fear to summon men to endure hardness as good soldiers of Jesus Christ, they may flatter but they will not follow us.

But, fellow Christians, this theme has a broader application than to the ministry. If there is any truth in the impression that the men are drifting away from our churches, it is not *all* the fault of the pulpit. A virile Christianity must be lived as well as preached.

Fellow Christians, it is a grave question for you to consider whether in Christianity as exhibited in the ordinary *church life* of to-day there has been any loss of power, any decay of manly vigor.

If a self-indulgent church settles itself in softly cushioned pews to listen to an intellectual treat, to the stirring tones of a manly minister, and thinks that he is going to catch men and hold them, it might as well send him in a straight jacket to save drowning men. He might better, far better, so far as his spiritual influence is concerned, go and take his stand like Whitefield in a meadow with no responsibility but to God above.

Whenever and wherever the faith of the church becomes a tradition rather than a reasoned conviction, the morals of the church an accommodation to conventional standards rather than an uncompromising imitation of Christ, the organization of the church a kind of sacred club, rather a band of earnest Christian, loving souls united for a sturdy grapple with ignorance and pauperism and every other great social curse, and for resistance unto blood if need be, striving against sin,—the life of the church finally, a life of decent compliance with certain becoming observances, but without sacrifice, without self-denial, without any high inspiration of unselfish motive,—then and there it will have forfeited and justly forfeited all power of influence over the earnest manhood of the time.

If these things or any of them are true in any degree of the church life of to-day, (and whether they are so, and how far, I leave it to you to judge) so far it has itself to blame if it finds something of that influence already gone.

What is it that enables the Salvation Army of England to-day to exert such astounding power over masses of men so low and so brutalized that the church had given them up as beyond hope? Not its banners, not its brass bands, not its queer terminology and queerer hymnology, not chiefly its masterly organization even, but these two things above all, that over against churches which are content to stand mainly on the defensive, it is a movement of intense, determined, deadly aggression upon the very strongholds of Satan's kingdom; and that over against the indolent self-indulgence which too often gets itself called Christianity, it means, for every man and woman who joins it, toil, hardship, and sacrifice, and danger day by day, for Christ's sake and the gospel's.

But I have a word also to say before I leave this inspiring theme to the men before me who are standing aloof from Christ. Men and brothers, in vain do you seek refuge, in such a position, behind any such blemishes as these at which we have glanced, whether in church life or in ministerial character. You know well that Christianity is older than the nineteenth century and its source higher than any church or any pulpit of to-day. If you refuse to be on Christ's side it is not because Christianity is not manly enough for you. Ah, I fear it *is* because *you* are not manly enough *for it.* Not that you are not summoned to a worthy enterprise under a heroic leader, but that, taking counsel of "the spirit of fear," you have not had manhood enough to grapple with the demon of Doubt until you could trample it beneath your feet and take your stand upon everlasting realities,—not manhood enough to break the shackles of conventionalism and be true to the response of conscience within you to the words of Christ,—not manhood enough to throw yourselves heart and soul into a determined fight with sin,—not manhood enough to face ridicule, to bear to be thought singular, to run the risk of hardship and sacrifice for such a leader and in such a cause.

God gives another spirit. He is ready to give it to you, even the spirit of power and of love and of self-control. Come, seek and use it.

I am but a recruiting sergeant. In the name of the man Christ Jesus, the conquering hero, "the captain of our salvation," "the prince of the kings of the earth," I bid you come and enlist under his banner. Come, bring a man's strong arm to his service; come, show a man's courage in his battles ; come, lay the devotion of a man's heart at his royal feet.

THE BAPTISM OF FIRE.

I indeed baptize you with water unto repentance: but he that cometh after me is mightier than I, whose shoes I am not worthy to bear. He shall baptize you with the Holy Ghost and with fire.— Matt. 3: 11.

Fire! Mighty, mysterious word. There is something in that symbol which lays hold of the imagination as almost no other is able to do. It stands for one of nature's subtlest and most potent agencies, for one of man's greatest blessings, and for one of his direst foes.

The geologist tells us that it is only through repeated baptisms of fire that this globe has been fitted to be the abode of the manifold joyous life with which it teems. And were it cut off from the daily baptism of fire poured upon it from the blazing reservoir of the sun, it would soon roll through space a silent charnel-house of rock and ice, without so much as a green leaf to adorn it or an insect's wing to stir its air.

Terrible as fire is to man in its uncontrolled rage,— agent and emblem of uttermost ruin and devastation, yet curbed and controlled it is his most indispensable ally and servant, without which he would sink to a level below that of the savage, and scarcely raised above that of the brute. There is no myth of classic antiquity more pathetic and suggestive than that which tells us how Prometheus, moved with pity for the wretched race of mortals, brought them the gift of fire in a hollow reed, bringing upon himself by this deed of mercy the dire vengeance of the jealous king of the gods.

The cloud of smoke which day and night hangs

above our city is an offense both to the eye and to the
lungs; yet quench the countless fires in factory, in
warehouse, on hearthstone, in locomotive, and in
steamer of which it is the visible token, and how soon
would these thronging streets become a grass-grown
wilderness.

It is not strange that in revealing himself to man
God should have chosen this agent, so subtle, so resistless, so ethereal, verging so closely upon the spiritual,
as the symbol of his manifested presence.

Now, it is the smoking furnace and the burning lamp
passing between the divided portions of the sacrifice,
that reveal to Abraham the presence of the covenant
God. Again it is the bush in Horeb, burning but not
consumed, which makes known to Moses the awful
Presence before which he stands with unsandalled feet.
It is the fiery, cloudy pillar that reveals at once Jehovah's mercy and his wrath, as it stands between Israel
and Egypt at the Red Sea. It is on fire-crowned, light-
ning-girdled Sinai that he gives forth his law to Israel.
In the Holy of Holies, it is a cloud of fire upon the
mercy seat that reveals his nearness to his covenant
people, to pardon sin and to answer prayer. It is in
the fire from heaven consuming the sacrifice on Carmel
that he answers the prophet's prayer for a revelation of
the living God. It is in chariots and horses of fire
encircling the horizon that he reveals to Elisha's
affrighted servant his protecting presence round about
his people.

When, then, in ears long familiar with such histories
as these John the Baptist cried: "I indeed baptize you
with water unto repentance; but he that cometh after
me is mightier than I, whose shoes I am not worthy to
bear, he shall baptize you with the Holy Ghost and
with fire," there was no misunderstanding these words.

They spoke not of two baptisms, but of one, and that divine, expressed first literally and then in consecrated prophetic symbol. "He shall baptize you with the Holy Ghost, and with fire."

It is true that as fire both purifies and destroys, so this emblem of fire has two contrasted aspects, an aspect of mercy and an aspect of terror. There is a fire of God's wrath as well as a fire of God's love. "Our God is a consuming fire."

And there are those who, misled by the words which follow in the next verse, "He shall burn up the chaff with unquenchable fire," would see here two contrasted baptisms,—a baptism of the Holy Ghost for those that believe, a baptism of consuming fire for those that believe not.

But such an interpretation misses altogether the force of the emphatic contrast which was the very reason for choosing this word *fire*. "I indeed baptize you with *water*, * * * but there cometh one mightier than I * * * He shall baptize you with * * * *fire*." Clearly this is one baptism in two-fold expression, the literal expression interpreting the symbolic, and the symbolic vivifying the literal, just as a description and a picture of the same scene interpret and vivify each other.

He shall baptize you * * * with fire. Dwell a moment on that word. Not with water, but with fire. Water and fire are both purifiers, but the latter how much more searching and thorough. Fire penetrates through and through and burns out the dross to the very core. Water bears away the impurities without destroying them, merely changing their place. Fire consumes and makes away with them utterly. Water must be applied again and again to the same surface to remove new defilement. Fire does its work once for all. A busy housewife years ago fixed this thought in my mind as a nail in a sure place. It was a morning of early fall when grate-fires were beginning to be kindled. She was busy about the room with broom and dust-pan, gathering up the rubbish which had accumulated in this corner and in that. At length she came with a pan full, tossed it upon the fire in the grate, watched it a few seconds first sizzle and blaze, then glow, then vanish, and turning to me she said: "When you come to be a housekeeper you will feel what the scriptures mean by their frequent references to fire as a purifier." And every housekeeper here will feel it. How much unsightly rubbish which it were hard to find a place for, which else must needs be carried off and deposited upon some heap of refuse, there to blow about and again get under foot, or to pester and pollute the air with its odors, does the fire take care of instantly and completely, so that it is never heard of again.

You and I, my friends, need more than a surface washing to make us clean. We need the searching of the refiner's fire. Nothing short of this can consume the earthiness and selfishness from our hearts, leaving only the pure gold of a holy character. "Two things," says McLaren, "conquer my sin; one is the blood of Jesus Christ which washes me from all the guilt of the past; the other is the fiery influence of that divine Spirit which makes me pure and clean for all time to come."

But again fire *warms*, it *melts*, it *enkindles*. It is in all tongues the ready symbol of zeal, of enthusiasm, of aroused emotion. We speak of kindling affections, of a soul on fire, of flaming eloquence, of a heart melted with love.

And this, too, is what the baptism of fire brings to the soul. Without this baptism the Christian life is a cold routine of duty; with it an enthusiastic service of love.

This it was that burned on the lips of Savonarola and in the heart of Luther, that sent Carey to India, sustained Judson in that frightful imprisonment in Burmah, brightened young Harriet Newell's dying bed on the Isle of France, and made David Brainerd what he so often prayed that he might be, a flame of fire in the service of his God. To the heart that has received this baptism, sacrifice for Christ is a joy, toil for souls a privilege, and death, come in what grim form it may, a triumph.

And, once more, fire energizes. To the chemist in his laboratory, to the mechanic in his factory, to the captain upon his vessel, fire stands for the compelling, moving power. It is a conquering element. Kindle it and it spreads. It seizes upon surrounding material and makes it its own. The resistless march of a forest or a prairie-fire is something never to be forgotten by any one who has witnessed it. So this baptism of the Holy Ghost is an endowment of power. "Ye shall receive power, after that the Holy Ghost is come upon you: and ye shall be witnesses unto me both in Jerusalem, and in all Judea, and in Samaria, and unto the uttermost part of the earth." When the Church received at Pentecost that promised baptism, it went forth on a career of world conquest which has never ceased. Without that baptism it could never have achieved that work. All the resources of wealth, all the arts of politics, all the charms of eloquence can never make Christianity a conquering religion where that fire has died out. Every revival is the fruit of such a baptism. Every successful missionary, every mighty evangelist, every true winner of souls is made so by the baptism of fire. Take the sermons of Whitefield and read them. You can find nothing there to account for the wonderful effect of his preaching. The sermons are in no way remarkable. It was the fire of the Holy Ghost that made them a power. But that fire dwelt in the man; you cannot find it on the printed page. So if you were to pick up a spent cartridge from which the bullet had just sped that laid low a noble stag, you might say, "I see nothing here to account for that missile's deadly work." No; for the fire which made it a power is no longer in it. Such was the baptism of fire of which John spake—a copious outpouring of God's Spirit, by which souls were to be cleansed from sin, to be inspired with zeal, and to be energized to victorious achievement.

Now see whence this baptism of fire was to come. "I indeed baptize you with water unto repentance; but he that cometh after me is mightier than I, whose shoes I am not worthy to bear. *He* shall baptize you with the Holy Ghost and with fire."

Christ alone can give this baptism. What humility is there in the contrast which the forerunner thus draws between himself and the One who was to follow him; what comfort and instruction also for the disciple of Christ.

The contrast as the Baptist presented it was two-fold, a contrast on the one hand between man's work, and Christ's work, and on the other hand between the old dispensation and the new. There is a contrast between man's work and Christ's work. John could show men their sins, he could lead them to a formal profession of repentance and outward amendment of life; but he could not impart the Holy Ghost. He could not melt the stony heart. Only God could do that. And in this very prediction there is a virtual ascription of divinity to the Messiah whom he heralded.

Ah, my friends, this is as true to-day as it was in John's day. I can baptize you with water. I can take your outward confession of sin, and on the strength of it can receive you into the visible church. But if that is all that has passed you are in no happy case. I fear the visible church contains to-day too many such man-made Christians. Christians whose conversion, or what passes for such, is a purely human change, based on their own human resolves, brought about by human motives, under the influence of human persuasions, without one spark of the fire from heaven. No wonder such Christians are hard to distinguish from the world around them, sharing the same tastes, running after the same vanities, and often returning after a little to the world altogether, as so many of the multitudes whom John baptized without doubt have done.

My friend, are you such a Christian? I charge you seek without delay, from the only one who can give it, the baptism with the Holy Ghost. "Except a man be born again he cannot see the Kingdom of God." But was not John a prophet of the Lord, and would not the Lord set the seal of his own blessing upon his work? Doubtless he would and did. The same spirit who spake by the prophets did in all ages make their word effectual to some real spiritual results. Still there was a contrast between the work of the Baptist even con-sidered as God's instrument and the work of Christ for which it prepared the way. The contrast here was one of degree. It was the contrast between a measure of the Spirit's influence such as John's baptism with water might fitly typify, and the overwhelming fulness of that influence expressed as a baptism with fire.

The Baptist still stood in the shadows of that elder dispensation whose characteristic instrument was the law, whose characteristic grace was repentance. The fulness of the Spirit, joy in the Holy Ghost, the spirit of adoption whereby we cry Abba, Father, these were among the better things reserved for those to whom was preached the gospel of an incarnate, crucified, and risen Redeemer. I know not how to illustrate this difference of degree between the measure of the Spirit enjoyed by holy men under the old dispensation and the fulness of the Spirit which is man's privilege under the new, better than in the words of Wm. Arthur in that book to which I gladly acknowledge my deep indebtedness, "The Tongue of Fire."

"A piece of iron is dark and cold; imbued with a certain degree of heat it becomes almost burning without any change of appearance; imbued with a still greater degree its very appearance changes to that of solid fire and it sets fire to whatever it touches. A piece of water without heat is solid and brittle; gently warmed it flows, further heated it mounts to the sky. * * * * * Such is the soul without the Holy Ghost and such are the changes which pass upon it when it receives the Holy Ghost and when it is 'filled with the Holy Ghost.'"

Thus to baptize men with the Holy Ghost, in fullest measure, was the end for which Christ both died and rose and ascended. John the Baptist said much more, if we are to judge by the fragments of his preaching recorded in the gospels, of this baptism of fire than of the sacrifice of the Lamb of God for the sin of the world. And with reason, Jesus himself ever led the minds of his disciples onward from what he would do for them upon the cross to what he would do for them upon the throne. Every step of that life from Bethany to Olivet, was a step toward that blessed consummation, the sending of the Comforter. Forgiveness of sins but opens the way to communion with God. The blood shed on Calvary was, we may say it without irreverence, but the price paid by the world's Redeemer for the privilege of baptizing with the Holy Ghost and with fire.

Suffer me then once more follow-Christian, to press this question: Have you yet received the baptism of fire? Granting that you are a true Christian, that you have been born of the Spirit, still I urge this question, Have you received this fulness of the Spirit, this purifying, kindling, energizing, by that divine fire which is your privilege in this gospel day? The tokens are not hard to discern. The question is not at all whether you are as good a Christian as you might be and wish to be. Even the fire of God's Spirit does not consume sin all at once. But are you a growing Christian? Are you a happy Christian? Are you an enthusiastic Christian? If not, surely there is something wrong. Why should you miss the very distinctive blessing of the gospel? Why in this dispensation of the Spirit should you still be living on an Old Testament plane and painfully plodding through an Old Testament experience.

The Christian life is too high a life to be lived successfully without this baptism. The task set before the wretched children of Jacob to make bricks without straw, was nothing compared to the task he sets before himself who essays to live as Christ calls him to live without this fire in his soul. As well expect a glacier to do the work of a river, clothing its banks with verdure, and making the fields over which it passes rich with the golden corn, as expect a disciple of Christ to bless the world with his presence, and bear abundant fruit to his Master's glory, whose cold, worldly, selfish heart has not been thoroughly melted down under a baptism of fire.

As American Christians we rejoice in our untramelled freedom to work out our problem of "a free Christian in a free state." As evangelical Christians we rest our hope upon a Christian membership based upon personal experience of saving grace. As Calvinistic Christians we exalt fidelity to the whole truth of God's Word. As Presbyterian Christians we lay claim to an ecclesiastical system combining in a rare degree liberty with order, stability with efficiency. Never perhaps in all history has a church had a grander opportunity, freer scope, ampler resources, or better facilities for fulfilling its grand commission to preach the gospel to every creature.

But one thing is lacking,—the baptism of fire! Yes, fire! That is what we need to solve the ever-recurring problem of debt, which our Boards of Missions are so often compelled to face. Improved schemes for revenue are well, but though we scheme and scheme until we die, nothing but fire from heaven will unlock the treasures held fast in the icy fetters of selfishness and worldliness, flooding the treasuries of the church with streams of gold and silver till there shall not be room to receive them, and making the desert to rejoice and blossom as the rose.

Fire! This is the one remedy for the divisions of Christendom — for the unseemly rivalries on mission-fields, sometimes abroad and oftener still at home, which waste the Lord's money and put a stumbling block in the way of souls. In this fire the sects, which like so many bars of iron, have lain side by side in frigid isolation or smitten upon one another in the angry clangor of polemic strife, would flow and fuse together in a glow of brotherly love like the molten metal in the fierce heat of the furnace.

My brethren, why have we not this baptism? Did not Christ, when he promised his last best gift, promise it as a comforter who should abide with us forever. Is the gift of Pentecost exhausted? Is the energy spent that made the progress of the apostolic church such a marvelous succession of victories?

Or are we, busied with our plans and our machinery, forgetting that all these are inert and powerless till energized by the fire of the Holy Ghost?

God grant that in answer to united prayer, that baptism may fall here and now upon pastor and people, to his glory and the salvation of multitudes.

THE WORLD'S PREPARATION FOR THE GOSPEL.

But when the fulness of the time was come, God sent forth his Son.—Gal. 4: 4.

In this one sentence is contained the substance of a true philosophy of history. It directs our thought at once to the incarnation of the Son of God as the one central and supreme event for which the ages waited, for which all foregoing history was the preparation, and which, brought to pass in the fulness of time, laid the foundation for that process of redemption, issuing in the elevation of humanity to the dignity of sonship to God of which all subsequent history is but the unfolding.

As this Christmastide turns our thought once more to that great event, the sending forth of the Son of God, "made of a woman," I have thought that we might find a fruitful as well as a fitting theme for our meditation in the suggestion of a single phrase in this far-reaching utterance,—"the fulness of the time."

These are pregnant words. They point to a preparation of the world for the gospel, which must be completed even before the Son of God could undertake his great work of redemption. They teach us that in the fulfillment of God's decrees the element of *timeliness* plays an important part. In his delays there is nothing arbitrary, nothing capricious.

Four thousand years had passed away since the first proclamation of the good news of a "seed of the woman" who should "bruise the serpent's head." The joy of Eve over her first-born was perhaps inspired by the belief that this was the promised seed in whom that prediction was to have forthwith its fulfillment. But alas, if this was her hope, how bitter her disappointment as she bent over the body of the murdered Abel.

When Abraham received Isaac, the child of promise, and with him such great and precious promises of blessing through him to the whole world, he may have thought that this was surely the promised Redeemer by whom the great deliverance should be wrought. But God showed him that there was a long, dark story of Egyptian bondage which must intervene.

When Moses led Israel out of Egypt dividing the Red Sea with his rod, bringing bread from heaven and water from the rock, and talking with God face to face, as a man talketh with his friend, the nation may well have supposed that now surely the fulness of time had come and that this great leader and deliverer would realize for it all that had been promised at the Fall.

But ere he ascended to his lonely grave on Nebo he could only point them forward to another Prophet like unto him whom at a late day God would raise up, and to whom they were to hearken. When Israel returned from Babylon and under Zerubbabel, the heir of the promises made to David's royal line, rebuilt their ruined temple many of them doubtless looked upon him as the Anointed One, the very Messiah who was to come. But it was not yet the fulness of the time. This restoration was but one more step forward in a long preparation which was not yet complete. Israel's peculiar mission was not yet fully performed. The failure of Gentile civilization, Gentile government, Gentile philosophy, and Gentile religion was not yet complete. Five hundred years must still roll away before the decree going forth from the palace of Augustus that all the world should be taxed, strikes the hour, and sets in motion that little caravan from Nazareth to Bethlehem from which history is to date a new beginning and the world to gain a new hope.

The preparation implied in these words, "the fulness of the time," was two-fold, providential and moral.

1. Let us look first at the providential preparation.

Christianity was intended for the world. It was not like the Mosaic dispensation, a religion intended for a small and localized people, the very design of which was to keep them separate and distinct. It was good tidings of great joy to all people, a proclamation of hope and deliverance for the race.

We should naturally expect therefore that in the Providence of God it would be introduced into the world at an era when its diffusion might be as speedy and complete as possible.

The establishment of the Roman empire was the opening of such an era, the like of which the world had never before seen. What steam and electricity have been doing in our own day to bring the ends of the earth together and surmount obstacles to the commingling of nations, Roman arms, Roman Government, and Roman roads had done in the first century on a scale quite as surprising in its advance upon preceding ages.

In the interest of that world-empire whose cohesion and endurance they well perceived to depend upon the maintenance of the most perfect facilities of intercommunication between the center and the remotest parts, these great conquerors and road builders had been literally, though unconsciously, fulfilling the prophetic demand; "Prepare ye the way of the Lord; make straight in the desert a highway for our God." From the golden milestone of Augustus in the Roman Forum radiated a net-work of imperial highways over which as far as the Danube, the Pillars of Hercules, or the Cataracts of the Nile, the traveler could journey over well-built roads, and find all along his route post stations for the change of horses, and inns for lodging over night. Over these roads and over the highways of the Mediterranean made alike safe by the protecting hand of a strong government was carried on a vast commerce, which poured the products of the whole world into the imperial city, and bore back to the remotest provinces the products of Roman art, learning, and civilization.

Still more powerful as a unifying bond was the common law, which insured to all the diverse races composing this vast organism a rude, indeed, but uniform and measurably fair administration of justice. To Gaul, to Spaniard, to Greek, to Alexandrian, to Jew, justice was meted out under the same statutes, according to the same forms, and with the same sanctions.

By such agencies as these,—roads, commerce, government,—the world was made one as it had never been one before. A fusion of races took place. Narrow national prejudices were broken down. A kind of cosmopolitanism took the place of the national exclusiveness which a few centuries before had made dwellers on opposite sides of the same mountain or the same lake regard each other as natural enemies. Men of all races eagerly availed themselves of the privilege of Roman citizenship now so extensively thrown open, and boasted not that they were Greeks, or Gauls, or Jews even, but Romans.

The soldiers recruited by the thousand from every subjugated people, and assigned to service always at a distance from the land of their birth soon came to know no country but Rome, and no tie stronger than their military oath. With this went also the diffusion of a common civilization. Even in far away Britain Roman conquest was speedily followed not only by Roman roads, Roman camps, and Roman courts, but by Roman towns, Roman dwellings, Roman temples, Roman theatres, and Roman baths.

With this fusion of races and civilizations, and of more importance to the diffusion of Christianity than these even, went also the spread of a common language, not the Latin (though that of course was everywhere, as the official language, more or less understood), but Greek, the language of letters, the speech of that more graceful, more finished civilization to which even in the hour of her triumph the rude soldier nation had bowed in homage and which it became her ambition to copy and transplant. What French once was to modern Europe, Greek was in the days of the apostles to the civilized world. Whoever could speak it could count upon making himself understood in any city of the Empire, in Europe, Asia or Africa. Not since the dispersion of Babel had the world come so near to being of one speech.

There is yet one more element to be considered in the providential preparation, viz., the dispersion of the Jewish people, following with the instincts of their race in the track of commerce, not only of Rome itself the great heart of the world of trade, but to the remotest ramifications of that vast system, so that the geographer Strabo declared: "It is not easy to find a place in the habitable world which has not received this race and is not possessed by it." Wherever they went they challenged attention by their peculiarities, their separateness, by such things as their scruples in regard to food and their Sabbath rest. And everywhere they carried with them two things, the synagogue with its worship of an unseen deity, and the Greek Scriptures of the Old Testament, thus bearing their witness in the face of heathenism, the world over, to the spirituality of the one living God, the holiness of his law, and the promise of a coming redemption, and supplying the heralds of the gospel wherever they went with a place in which to begin their preaching, and a written word on which to base their announcement of God's promise fulfilled and redemption accomplished.

Thus the three great nations of antiquity were each of them in the all-comprehending plan of God tributary to the world's preparation for the gospel. Not till Roman law, Greek letters, and Jewish Religion had gained in some sense a world-wide diffusion, was it "the fulness of time" for "the desire of all nations" to appear.

Then how swiftly did the bearers of glad tidings, under the sheltering wings of the imperial eagles, fly over those roads built for far other conquests, seeking out the synagogues of the Jews and there proclaiming in the Greek tongue to Jews, proselytes, and heathen, "Christ, the power of God and the wisdom of God."

2. But side by side with this providential preparation there had been going on a moral preparation for the gospel, not less necessary, and "the fulness of the time" implies the completeness of this preparation also. Indeed it is this to which this phrase of the apostle more immediately refers, as we see from the context in which he pictures man until the coming of Christ as a child in his minority, subjected to a strict preparatory discipline, not trusted as yet with the privileges of son-ship because the fulness of time, i. e., the maturity which should fit him for them has not yet come.

This moral preparation aimed chiefly at the developing of that profound sense of need without which redemption would have been offered in vain. This end

was reached along two lines, a positive and negative, a
a divine and a human.

God himself took one chosen people in hand, and by
the message of his prophets, line upon line, precept
upon precept,—and still more sharply by his own
dealings with them in their long history taught them
the two great lessons of his own majesty and holiness
and of the guilt and the desert of sin, so constraining
them to feel their need of a Savior who should free
them from the curse of a broken law and reconcile them
to a holy God.

Meantime he left the rest of mankind in great
measure to themselves, to learn by the utter failure of
all their efforts to improve themselves or to stay the
downward movement toward chaos and ruin, the same
great lesson of helplessness and need. When this two-
fold training was complete, and not till then, God sent
forth his Son. So far as the human side was concerned,
it would be hardly possible for human helplessness to
receive a more convincing demonstration, or human
despair to reach a deeper depth than in the gilded de-
bauchery and splendid misery of imperial Rome. There
was no human agency for uplifting the race that had not
been already tried and proved a failure.

a. *Government*, political institutions, had been
tried; and these had failed. The brilliant political history of Greece had ended in effeminacy and subjugation
to a foreign yoke. The vigorous organization of repub-
lican Rome had given it the mastery of the world but
could not give it the mastery of itself nor save it from
issuing in the wreck of the civil wars and the servile
cringing at last of a race of free men at the feet of a
despot, who himself found even imperial authority, put
forth in statute after statute, powerless to check the
growing corruptions of the time.

b. *Civilization* had been tried; and that had failed. In a form of consummate grace and perfection it had gone from Greece, and in the track of the Roman legions had overspread the world. Yet as civilization advanced, corruption kept pace with it; and elegance of life and refinement of manners proved but a surface adornment, which, like the iridescent film upon a stagnant pool, did but overspread a depth of putrescence which it could neither heal nor hide.

In Rome itself, the center of civilization, a state of morals had been reached of which a Seneca draws this picture: "Daily the lust of sin increases; daily the sense of shame diminishes. Casting away all regard for what is good and honorable, pleasure runs riot without restraint. Vice no longer hides itself, it stalks forth before all eyes. So public has iniquity become, so mightily does it flame up in all hearts, that innocence is no longer rare; it has ceased to exist."

Gone were the ancient simplicity, the ancient industry, the ancient pure and sweet domestic life. Marriage was despised, family life abhorred as a burden, divorce an every day occurrence; the life of the rich was passed in inane luxury and empty frivolity, the poor clamored only for "bread and shows," and all classes wallowed in a lewdness that forbids description.

c. *Human religions* had been tried, and these had failed. The immoral gods and goddesses of the old mythology had no restraining power over the conscience and were fast losing their hold upon the belief of their worshipers. Yet though the world has been ransacked for new ones none have been found to take their place. The sacred rites are kept up as a matter of public policy by men who laugh in their sleeve while they perform them; and the people betake themselves to the temples there to learn, in the impure orgies performed as an act

of worship, acceptable to the gods, new lessons in vice.
Till of the moral outcome of it all the Holy Ghost has
given the dark but sober picture in that terrible first
chapter of Paul's letter to the Romans, every line of
which its readers could of their own knowledge abun-
dantly confirm.

d. As the power of religion waned, *philosophy* was
tried. But for the deep-seated moral hurt of the world,
wherewith the whole head was sick and the whole heart
faint, it had no remedy but words, words, empty words.
It could preach, but it could not practice, still less
teach others to practice.

The same Seneca whose precepts sometimes remind
us of the apostle Paul, was openly accused of adultery
and unquestionably initiated his imperial pupil Nero
into the vilest sins. Writing in praise of Poverty he
amassed an enormous fortune and had in his house five
hundred tables of citrus wood some of them worth as
much as twenty-five thousand dollars. Inculcating in
his essays clemency and truth, he connived at the
atrocities of Nero, and wrote for him the lying defense
with which he pretended to justify to the Senate his
cold-blooded murder of his mother.

In the face of life's mysteries and under the burden
of its sorrow it offered through the calm lips of a Pliny
such cold comfort as this: "There is nothing certain
save that nothing is certain. The best thing which has
been given to man amid the many torments of this life
is, that he can take his own life." That indeed was the
last crowning word of philosophy, its panacea for all
ills: "If life is too much for you, the way out of it is
before you."

In the face of this fourfold failure, of government, of
civilization, of religion as they knew it, and of philosophy to make the world better or to keep it from growing

worse an awful despair had begun to settle down upon
the heathen world; a despair which in thoughtful minds
found utterance in a gloomy pessimism which proclaimed existence itself a mockery, and in the unthink-
ing multitude dumbly wrought itself out in sheer recklessness of living.

Out of this despair grew a dim longing for redemption. Men's minds turned to that mysterious Orient out
of which so many strange things had come and whence
were heard hints and presages of some expected deliverance.

Even the Scriptures of the despised Jew began to be
regarded with curious interest for their promise of a
Messiah, and the prophecies of Isaiah find a strange
echo in the poems of a Virgil.

On the other hand the *divine* preparation was also
complete. The Mosaic dispensation had done its work
for Israel and for the world. The revelation of law was
complete. Nothing now was left for those who had
learned its lessons, but to wait for the "consolation of
Israel."

The whole Old Testament, both as law and prophecy, was condensed into the mighty proclamation
with which John the Baptist, last and greatest of the
prophets, shook the nation: "Repent; for the kingdom of heaven is at hand."

There remained nothing more, nothing higher to be
said, till, pointing to Jesus as he walked, he could exclaim: "Behold the Lamb of God, that taketh away
the sin of the world."

As a witness to the heathen world, too, Israel's mission was fulfilled. Its testimony against idolatry had,
as we have seen, been carried throughout the world.
Beyond that it could not go. It could rebuke; but it
could not convert. There was no world-conquering

power, no world-embracing universality in Judaism. It
had met the dim groping of heathenism for a redemption with the divine promise of a Redeemer; but the
connecting link was still wanting. Then it was, in that
fulness of time, when heathen despair had reached its
darkest depth, and Israel's longing its greatest intensity, that God sent forth his Son. And as the heralds
of salvation went everywhere throughout the length and
breadth of that world-empire telling the story of that incarnate, crucified, risen Redeemer, the Son of God, yet
born of a woman, who had come into the world that he
might bear witness to the truth, who had borne its sins
in his own body on the tree, and who had risen from the
tomb, that, triumphant over the last enemy, he might,
to as many as received him, give eternal life, they gave
to a world weary of its old gods and incredulously asking: What is truth? a new faith to a world in despair
of the future, whether for this life or the life to come,
a new hope; to a world exhausted in its own fruitless
struggles, a new power.

My friend, whatever you think of Christ, whatever
you do with him personally, you owe as a modern man,
as an American man, an unspeakable debt to that event
which this day commemorates. This world is a different
world to-day; above all is this land a different land
to-day from what it would or could have been had there
not been born in Bethlehem of Judea a Savior, who is
Christ the Lord.

Yet the blessing which thus comes to you through
Christ's influence upon the world, through the new
direction he has given to the currents of human history
is as nothing to the blessing which will come to you if
Christ shall be born in your own soul. Has he been
born there? For that, too, there must be, in some
sense, a "fulness of the time." Christ will never be

born in your heart, he will never bring to you the unspeakable blessing of a personal redemption and a personal sonship to God, till in the depths of your soul you have felt your need of him, till the emptiness of life, the uncertainty of the future, the failure of your endeavors or the burden of your sins have driven you to cry out for help from above.

You have been tossing perhaps these many years on a sea of doubt and unbelief, where neither sun nor star has in many days appeared. Have you not drifted far enough? Is it not the fulness of the time for you to receive on board the pilot who will guide your soul into the sure haven of a steadfast faith?

You are growing old. You have led a busy life and played a part not unimportant in human affairs. But you realize that each year that part grows less. You feel that you are being crowded off the stage by a younger generation. And before you all is uncertainty. You can look forward to no new and higher work awaiting you, to no certain and lasting fruition of your life's labors. Is it not the fulness of the time for you to receive into your soul Him who said: "I am the Resurrection and the Life. * * * He that believeth in me shall never die."

You are saddened in these closing days of the year by the memory of temptation, yielded to, high purposes unfulfilled, and by a sad consciousness of moral failure. Is it not the fulness of the time for you to receive into your soul one who can change defeat into victory, and who having begun a good work in you will not abandon it till he shall present you faultless before the throne of his Father.

Oh, if my voice reaches to-day one hopeless, despairing sinner, who has lost all faith in his own goodness and all satisfaction in the pleasures of sin, I say to such

a one, Take heart! Your very despair is a sign of
encouragement, for this is the very fulness of the time
for God's salvation to come to you.

THE GENEALOGY OF SIN.

Let no man say when he is tempted, I am tempted of God: for God cannot be tempted with evil, neither tempteth he any man. But every man is tempted when he is drawn away of his own lust and enticed. Then when lust hath conceived it bringeth forth sin, and sin, when it is finished, bringeth forth death.—Jas. 1:13-15.

The transition from the immediately preceding verse to these which are now before us is sudden and startling:

"Blessed is the man that endureth temptation for when he is tried he shall receive a crown of life, which the Lord hath promised to them that love him." "Let no man say, when he is tempted, I am tempted of God; for God cannot be tempted with evil, neither tempteth he any man."

It is manifest that there has been a transition in the apostle's mind not only from one aspect of temptation to another, but from one class of readers to another.

Temptation has two sides, a good and a bad side. Viewed from one side it is a *test of character*, a wholesome discipline, leading to glorious and everlasting results.

It is this which warrants these congratulatory words : "Count it all joy when ye fall into divers temptations."

Viewed from another side, it is a *seduction to evil*, which, if yielded to may issue in fatal consequences. Which of these shall be the practical side depends upon how it is met. Too often in our own experience, as well as that of others, we have found it passing over from the former to the latter, and issuing in sin, by which character is broken down instead of matured.

Too many of his readers, James well knew as they read these words: "Blessed is the man that endureth temptation" would be forced to say: "That blessing is not for me—I have not endured; I have miserably yielded. *How comes it so?* is the question he now turns to answer, and in answering it he traces in striking metaphor what may be called the Genealogy of Sin. Shall those who failed to meet the test take warrant from this view of temptation as God's appointed discipline to throw upon *Him* the blame of their failure, who placed them in such circumstances and exposed them to such dangers? Never! To every such fallen one he cries: Beware how you blaspheme a holy God by making him responsible for sins which are your own act, prompted by your own lusts, committed of your own will, and bringing forth their own fruit in a death which is your own work.

The answer covers the whole ground. It tells us where the whole fault does not lie, and where it does. It forbids us to put the responsibility of our own defeat upon God, and fixes it where it belongs—upon ourselves.

1. *It forbids us to put the responsibility upon God.* With temptation considered as seduction, as solicitation to evil, God has nothing to do. He cannot have; for he is a holy God. There is in his being no sympathy with evil in any form. Too holy to feel its seduction himself, much more is he too holy to become the seducer of others.

It is natural to us all to make excuses for sin. We seek to shift the responsibility upon some one else. When the first man sinned, he laid the blame upon the woman ; and the woman in her turn laid it upon the serpent. So we all pass on responsibility from hand to hand, laying the blame sometimes on our fellow men, sometimes on our parents,—on "that rash humor which our" mothers "gave" us,—but with a constant tendency to throw it back at last, consciously or unconsciously, upon God. Practically, there is where in the end it must fall, if we throw it off ourselves. One of President Finney's most powerful sermons is upon this theme: "The excuses of sinners condemn God," in which, taking up one after another some score of the favorite excuses of sinners, he shows how each in one way or another, really puts the blame upon God. We should all be only too glad thus to fix the responsibility upon our Maker if we could, for then sin would cease to be sin. Then we should have a plea which we could boldly take to the bar of last account and face with it the Judge upon his throne.

It is not surprising therefore that human ingenuity should exhaust itself in attempts to do this very thing.

Sometimes this is done under the learned guise of a false philosophy. This is the secret fascination of some of the forms of error which have maintained the most powerful hold upon the minds of men. So it is e. g. with that subtle form of thought called pantheism, which has shown such marvelous vitality, which underlies some of the most powerful forms of heathenism, ancient and modern, and which is trying just now to make good for itself a place in the Christian church. For in making man himself a part of God, this system fixes upon God the responsibility of all man's acts, and so destroys the distinction between good and evil, saying virtually : There is no evil. What seems so is but the shadow of good. So the modern materialism, boldly advocated by some of the present leaders in the world of science, which teaches that man is essentially an automaton, that thought and will are but secretions of the brain, whose character is determined by the brain's structure and fibre, clearly throws back the only responsibility for which it leaves room, upon the Maker of the automaton.

The doctrine of moral evolution held by so many as a natural sequence of the doctrine of physical evolution, teaching as it does that sin, not simply temptation, is a necessary step of progress,—the stumbling by which a child learns to walk,—that, as it is sometimes put, "the fall of man was a fall upward," puts all the responsibility upon God, who has ordained such a mode of progress.

With others the Scripture itself is wrested to this end. Perhaps it is the mystery of foreordination behind which the guilty conscience seeks to shield itself. "It was decreed. What could I do ?" Or, as the apostle quotes the same excuse in his day : "Why doth He yet find fault ; for who hath resisted his will ?"

Or it is God's providence on which we lay the blame. Whenever we lay the blame of our sin upon circumstances, we virtually lay it upon the Providence which ordered those circumstances. So Adam hinted at a responsibility lying back of the woman's, when he said : "The woman that *thou gavest* to be with me, she gave me of the tree, and I did eat."

When we say as we often do: "I could not help it ; in the circumstances in which I was placed, I had to do it" what is that but to lay the blame upon Him who placed us there ?

Or we charge all to the constitution which God gave us. So Burns sang :

> "Thou knowest that thou hast made **me**
> With passions wild and strong,
> And listening to their witching voice
> Has often led me wrong."

Or we blame God for not surrounding us with greater restraining influences; like the rich man in the parable, who, in pleading that Lazarus be sent to warn his brethren, virtually accused God of allowing him to perish for lack of timely warning.

These are a few of the ways in which we seek to throw upon God the responsibility of our failures to overcome temptation. To all such pleas the earnest, practical James has one simple answer, a sweeping denial, and one conclusive argument; God is a holy God. Here is no philosophizing over the problem of God's government, no recondite speculation upon the origin of evil, no metaphysical hair-splitting concerning fixed fate, free will, "fore knowledge absolute," but simply the direct appeal to conscience: "Beware how you attempt to make a holy God an accomplice in your guilt." It is sufficient. An aroused conscience instantly owns the conclusiveness of the answer, and the fitness of the rebuke.

2. Having thus seen where the fault does not lie we are next shown where it does lie. "Every man is tempted when he is drawn away of *his own* lust and enticed." The aim of the writer here is still intensely practical. Therefore he does not concern himself at all with the theological question, how sin first entered the world. There is nothing here about the fall of the race. It is your fall and mine, which he is accounting for. Nor does he ever bring in the agency of Satan, real as that agency is; because he is seeking to fix attention upon that sinful inclination within, to which the tempter himself makes his successful appeal, and without which he would tempt in vain.

a. Every man is tempted when he is drawn away of his own lust. I hardly need to remind you that lust is used here, not in its narrow sense, of sensual desire, but in its broad sense, of every form of sinful inclination. This is what gives temptation its hold upon us. The enemy without would never compel a surrender, did not the traitor within the bosom open the gates. The scent of carrion which is abhorrent to a dove, is sweet to a vulture. Their nature makes the difference. A holy soul might be tempted, but in a different way from that in which you and I are tempted. When it is said that Christ himself was tempted in all points like as we are, it is not meant that he was tempted in the same way that we are. The outward temptation is there, but not the inward lust.

b. But this is not the beginning. This secret inclination to evil, while it gives to temptation its sinister side, is not yet sin in the full sense of voluntary, responsible transgression. To this something more is necessary, viz: the consent of the will. "Every man is tempted when he is *drawn away* of his own lust and *enticed. Then*, when lust hath conceived it bringeth forth sin." The strong, albeit repulsive, image in the apostle's mind is that of a man yielding to the embrace of a wanton. The regal self-governing power listens to the enticing voice of lust and from this unhallowed union of will and lust there is begotten that loathsome offspring, sin.

See how these steps are illustrated in the confession of Achan (as you will find it Josh. 7: 20-21). "And Achan answered Joshua and said : Behold I have sinned against the Lord God of Israel. . . . When I saw among the spoils a goodly Babylonish garment and two hundred shekels of silver, and a wedge of gold of fifty shekels' weight, then I coveted them and took them." "I saw"; there is temptation on its providential side, the outward occasion which tested the man. "I coveted"; there is temptation on its seductive side, the

inward lust of covetousness, roused into activity by the
outward occasion and alluring, enticing toward the for-
bidden treasure. "I took"; there finally is the consent
to the enticement of lust, issuing in transgression.

c. But we have not done yet with this terrible genealogy. Sin which is the child of lust, becomes in its
turn a parent. Sin when it is finished, when it is full
grown—"bringeth forth death."—There is something
startling in that expression: "Sin, when it is finished."
There is a parallel, which cannot have been undesigned,
with the foregoing : "When he is tried he shall receive
a crown of life." Evil, like goodness, has its maturity,
its consummation. Character is never stationary. There
is a law of growth in sin as in holiness. At first sin
seems like an infant, harmless in appearance, almost
winsome perhaps, easly managed. But it soon becomes
a full-grown master. See how the lust of covetousness
in Judas issued first in petty thefts, which doubtless
seemed to him of very small account, easily concealed,
easily forgotten, but soon that little sin grew to the
greater sins of conspiracy, treachery, murder and suicide.
So Cain's lust of envy, when it had conceived, brought
forth the sin of anger, and that sin was soon finished in
murder.

"Sin, when it is finished, bringeth forth death."
Here is no hint of any joint parentage. This final issue
is something with which our consent has nothing to do.
Lust conceives by the consent of the will. But sin
brings forth its issue alone. When it has reached its
maturity, it issues in death by a law which works inde-
pendently of us.

There is an Oriental fable which relates that the
devil once asked permission to kiss a certain king upon
his shoulders. The king consented and straightway from
either shoulder sprang up a serpent which fastened its

fangs in his brain. So it is with us. We consent to it
at first because we think it a little thing, almost or quite
harmless. And lo ! it leaps to life a full-grown serpent,
and slays us with its venom.

These words recall the words of Paul : " The wages
of sin is death." But they recall them with a difference.
Wages are earned. They point to a trial of some sort, or
an award. Paul's figure then suggests judicial penalty.
But this of James suggests natural consequence. Death
is what sin issues in by its own nature. The two are not
in conflict. The sentence of death is indeed God's, but
nature is made the executioner. Under God's government things are so arranged, in other words, that sin
punishes itself. It *brings forth* its penalty.

O that men would learn that sin, when it has run its
course, brings forth death as naturally, as surely, as inevitably as fire brings forth heat, or as the sunrise brings
the day. If we could get this view of penalty as the
natural consequence of sin, rather than an arbitrary sentence imposed like a fine or imprisonment, at the pleasure
of the Judge, we should be less easily deluded with hopes
of somehow evading the penalty while indulging the sin.

" Sin, when it is finished bringeth forth death."
But the death too, like the sin, is progressive.

You remember the melancholy words of Dean
Swift, when, pointing to a tree whose upper branches
were leafless and dry, he said : " I shall be like that
tree ; I shall die at the top "—words sadly verified in the
mental decay which made his closing years a blank.
The sinner too dies " at the top." His death is first of
all a spiritual death, the death of his higher nature, the
death of his nobler impulses and aspirations. First it
is his godward faculties,—that side of his being through
which he has fellowship with the unseen, which dies,
then the nobler human affections. See how the degra-

dation of these is portrayed in that terrible first chapter of Paul's letter to the Romans. There bodily decay and physical death coming as the direct manifest result of intemperance, of lust, or of other forms of "finished" sin. Then, last of all, comes eternal death, the second death, the casting of soul and body into hell. And this too is just as truly natural consequence as spiritual death and physical death. There are few more significant expressions in Scripture bearing upon that awful mystery than Peter's word concerning Judas, "that he might go to his own place,"—his own place,—the place to which his affinities draw him. Vice, even in this world, seeks its own level. You do not find the hardened debauchee, when free to choose his own surroundings, seeking the house of God, or the happy fireside of the Christian household. He chooses rather the saloon and the brothel. He is more at home there. So in the world to come the sinner will sink to his own level. His surroundings will shape themselves to his nature. "Sin when it is finished *bringeth forth* death."

Here you have a descending ladder with its three steps corresponding exactly to that ascending ladder, whose upward steps have been indicated in the previous verses. These steps were: Temptation resisted; character perfected; a crown of life. These are, temtation yielded to; sin finished; death.

At the head of that ascending ladder,—as of that which Jacob saw in his vision,—stands God, our Father, reaching out his hand to all who will lay hold of it to help them safely up. But if you take the downward road you take it alone. That hand does not thrust you down, and the ruin in which it ends will be your own work. To-day I write opposite your name, my hearer, the word temptation. Not one name in this company against which must not stand that solemn word. But what am

I to write after it,—yielded to ? Or resisted ? a step up or a step down,—which shall it be ? Has the step down been already taken ? Has lust already conceived and brought forth ? Then make haste to slay thy sin, ere thy sin, full-grown, slay thee. Some one has said : "The life of sin and the life of the sinner are like two buckets in a well, if one goes up, the other must go down. When sin liveth, the sinner must die." But make haste ! make haste ! You have not a moment to lose. Every hour that you hesitate, sin is gaining strength ; to break away is becoming harder ; and you know not when the last fatal blow will be struck.

It is related by a French writer, that the captain of a vessel was one day walking carlessly along a river's mouth at low water. As he looked about him, not minding his steps, he did not notice a great chain stretched on the ground before him, one end of which was fastened to a ring in a stone on the bank, the other to an anchor sunk in the river. Not seeing it he stumbled against it, and his foot passing through one of the links, he could not draw it back again. For a time he struggled to extricate himself, but in vain. He turned his foot this way and that but could not draw it out. Then he called for help and some men who were passing hastened to his assistance. But their efforts too were futile. The foot was beginning to swell and could no longer be extricated. What was to be done ? The chain was too heavy to be removed ; the tide was coming in ; deliverance must be speedy or it would be too late. "Let us call a smith to saw the chain " said one. One of their number was dispatched to the nearest village, two or three miles away, and at length returned with a smith. But it was found that the tools he brought were inadequate, and he was obliged to go back for others. At last he returned ; but in the meantime the tide had risen, till the waves which at first barely wet the feet of the unhappy victim now reached to his waist The smith saw that he could do nothing. But one resource was left. The unfortunate man must part with his leg if he would save his life. O the agony of that moment ! But there was no time to be lost. Yes, yes, anything for life. Quick ! bring the surgeon ! He is brought with utmost haste, his case of instruments in hand. "O doctor," cries the wretched victim, "make haste, save my life !" But the tide is rushing in with terrible force, the doctor must get into a boat, and it is only by strong strokes of the oar, that he can reach to the side of the perishing man, who is now in the water up to his chin. "It is too late !" cries the surgeon in despair, and before anything can be done, the waves have gone over the man's head ; he is lost !

Impenitent hearer, you are that man ; sin is that chain, and you are fast in its links. If it holds you a little longer the result will be death. You have tried to break away alone, and you cannot. Sin is too strong for you. Its grip is tightening day by day.

You must have help, help which only One can give. But, blessed be God, that help has not to be fetched from afar. It is at hand. You have not to wait till one ascend into heaven to bring Christ down, nor till one descend to bring Christ up from beneath. "The word is nigh thee, in thy mouth and in thy heart," that blessed word of faith and hope, "that if thou shalt confess with thy mouth the Lord Jesus, and shalt believe in thine heart, that God hath raised him from the dead, thou shalt be saved."

But even with that help stern measures may be necessary. Remember the word of that very Saviour : "If thy hand or thy foot offend thee, cut them off and cast them from thee. It is better for thee to enter into life halt or maimed, rather than, having two hands or two feet, to be cast into everlasting fire."

Whatever it be, be it the dearest thing on earth, which keeps you fast in sin's horrible chain, cut it off, let it go. Stay not for parley ; seek not to compromise. Cast yourself at once and altogether upon the saving mercy of the divine Redeemer.

THE UNKNOWN FACTOR OF LIFE.

Go to now, ye that say : To-day or to-morrow we will go into such a city, and continue there a year, and buy and sell and get gain. Whereas ye know not what shall be on the morrow. For what is your life? It is even a vapor that appeareth for a little time and then vanisheth away. For that ye ought to say : If the Lord will, we shall live and do this or that. But now ye rejoice in your boastings : all such rejoicing is evil. —James 4: 13–16.

After the discovery of the planet Uranus in the latter part of the last century, astronomers found themselves much perplexed by the irregularity of its movements. It was found repeatedly to disappoint their calculations and to appear at some other than its appointed place. It was evident that there was some unknown factor concerned in the problem of its motion, which must be found and determined before its place could be successfully predicted. The hypothesis that this disturbing force was another and more distant planet led to a search and eventually to the discovery of the planet Neptune on the outermost rim of the solar system.

Life, like astronomy, has its calculations. There can be no wise conduct of life without plan and forecast. The greater part of our activities look toward the future. The higher we rise in the scale of intelligence the more distant are the results for which we toil. But this toil for the future involves some sort of a plan and anticipation respecting results. The incentive to effort is measured not merely by the value of the results aimed at, but also by the measure of certainty with which we contemplate them as attainable. Unless man could look forward with reasonable assurance to such and such results as the reward of such and such efforts he would remain a savage subsisting upon the spontaneous fruits of the earth, and the products of the chase, living from hand to mouth, seizing the good of the moment and leaving the future to take care of itself. No man would plow or sow in the spring, had he not a right to look for a harvest in the summer. No man would invest his capital or send forth his ships in the ventures of trade and commerce had he not a reasonable prospect of profitable returns. No one would curb the frolicsome impulses of youth to years of laborious study, had he not strong confidence that the education so acquired would prove in after years a source of power, influence, and emolument. Present sacrifice for future good is the law of all life.

In life-plans however, as in mathematical calculations, absolute certainty is impossible unless all the factors that enter into the problem are known. So long as there remains a single unknown element, it is liable to upset all our calculations, and lead to a result widely different from that to which we looked forward. But in human plans the unknown element is never absent. However perfect our science, however consummate our shrewdness, however ripe our experience, there will always remain something which defies calculation and which is liable at an unlooked for moment to upset and bring to naught the best laid plan.

This is the theme which our text suggests to us: *The Unknown Factor in Life.*

1. We shall appreciate this better if we trace it, by way of illustration in some of the common affairs of life. Look at it e. g., in agriculture. However good the seed which the farmer employs, however careful his attention

to the proper conditions of soil and season, however unremitting his industry in cultivation, he is never absolutely sure of his harvest. Because that harvest depends not simply on what he does, but on what he does and what nature does taken together, and because in the workings of nature there is an element of uncertainty as much beyond his forecast as it is outside his control. No weather prophet, no government bureau, no science of meteorology, within the reach of man, can forwarn him of the drought which may parch his wheat, of the premature frost which may cut off his corn, of the hail storm which may bring to nought in half an hour the labor of months. No entomologist can forecast for him the sudden increase of some species of grasshopper or caterpillar against the onset of which he shall be as powerless as against a destroying flood, and which in a single day may leave his green and flourishing acres as bare as the valley of the Nile after Pharaoh's plague of locusts. There is an unknown factor in the workings of nature that is liable to defeat all the plans of the husbandman.

See the same thing again in navigation.

The most thorough seaman, in command of the staunchest vessel, is never sure of reaching the port for which he steers. In the hurricanes that sweep the ocean, in the icebergs that drift with its shifting currents, in the fogs that gather and disperse, and in the uncertain workings of the human brain at outlook and helm, are elements of uncertainty against which no human skill or vigilance can guard. Few thoughtful men, I take it, entrust themselves even to that thing of power, that masterpiece of human invention, an ocean steamer, under, it matters not how tried and trusty a captain, without a vivid consciousness of the unknown possibilities which that captain can no more forecast than can the little child that toddles about the deck,—with which that mighty floating castle can no more cope than could an egg shell.

A few years ago the "Ville du Havre" was returning to France with a full complement of passengers, including many choice men who had been attending as delegates the meeting of the Evangelical Alliance in New York. They were nearing port after a prosperous voyage, the sea was calm, the night was clear and illumined by a brilliant moon, the passengers had retired in the best of spirits, when suddenly at dead of night, there was a crash; a sailing vessel which had been seen for an hour by the officer on the bridge struck the steamer amid-ships, and in less than half an hour she went down, bearing scores of her passengers to a watery grave. It was all the result of a moment's bewilderment, such as will sometimes befall the most expert and cautious. The officer, a seaman of long experience, had miscalculated. Thinking that he had plenty of time, he had disregarded the rule of the sea which gives to the sailing vessel the right of way, and had undertaken to cross her bow, thereby steering his ship to inevitable destruction. That was the unknown factor in the working of the human brain, against which it is impossible to guard in any affair which depends upon man's control.

Our railroads are multiplying and perfecting their precautions against accident every year; but the worst accidents are the accidents which arise from this uncertain working of the human brain, the momentary heedlessness of a switch-tender, the one blunder in twenty years perhaps, of a telegraph operator, the sudden recklessness of a careful conductor; and against these accidents no system of checks and automatic signals within the power of man to construct can provide a safeguard.

"Until General Sherman came to New York to live," said a friend of the General the other day, "and was wrapped up in business and social life, he spent much of his time reading military history. As an army officer he was compelled to travel a good deal about the country, and in his trunk he always took several volumes when about to start from St. Louis to Washington or New York. One book was taken in his hand. I remember in the summer of 1875 coming with him from St. Louis to Utica, where he was to preside at a big gathering of war veterans. He wore a long linen ulster, and in a pocket was a heavy book that pulled it down on one side. We were the only passengers in the palace car. After a few minutes' conversation the General pulled the book out of his pocket, settled himself in a corner of the seat, and didn't speak for hours. The book was O'Meara's *"Letters from St. Helena."* How many times he had read the book the General said he didn't know. He had read everything he could find to read about Napoleon, for whose genius he expressed the most enthusiastic admiration. As I remember our desultory conversation he held the opinion that Bonaparte was the greatest military commander the world ever saw. His admiration of the strategy the Emperor showed in the later years of his career, when he was fighting on the Rhine, before his first abdication, and in the struggles in front of Paris, as well as his arrangements for Waterloo, was unbounded. "Napoleon ought to have won at Waterloo," he said, "if there was any faith to be placed in human foresight."

In commerce the unknown factors are almost beyond numbering. When Bassanio would dissuade his friend from risking his life by acceding to Shylock's demand of a pound of flesh as the forfeit of his bond, Antonio replies: "Why fear not, man; I will not forfeit it! Within these two months,—that's a month before this bond expires,—I do expect return of thrice three times the value of this bond." Yet within that three months his ships have all miscarried, his creditors grown cruel, his estate has run very low, and he has nothing but his pound of flesh to pay. It is a poet's picture of the uncertainties of commerce—uncertainties arising from elements, from tempest, fire, and flood—uncertainties arising from the weakness of human character, the breakdown of which in the presence of temptation may ruin the strongest bank and sweep away the profits of the largest business,—uncertainties arising from the fickleness of fashion, suddenly revolutionizing the conditions of supply and demand and reducing a costly stock to practical worthlessness,—uncertainties arising from the very genius of man leading ever and anon to inventions and discoveries which by introducing cheaper substitutes for certain necessaries, or cheaper methods of production, may render worthless a manufacturing plant representing the accumulated wealth of a life time, or reduce to nothing the industry of a whole community. All the business sagacity of the world has never yet eliminated the unknown factor from business nor found the secret of so clipping the wings of riches that their possessor can be sure that in an unlooked for moment they will not fly away as an eagle toward heaven.

In war, the most skillful generalship cannot ensure victory. A storm rendering the ground too heavy for the manouevres of artillery, a sudden panic seizing the best disciplined troops, the treachery of a trusted officer, are contingencies against which human foresight can never guard, and which may change the fortunes of a campaign.

Science is perpetually striving to extend the area of the known and the calculable by bringing the irregular and the uncertain under some formula of law; but there will still remain, after her best endeavors, an unexplored region whose boundaries she may narrow but cannot abolish.

The unknown factor can never be eliminated ; for if
we found it in nothing else we should still find it con-
fronting us every where in the uncertainty of human life.

"Go to now ye that say: To-day or to-morrow we
will go into such a city, and continue there a year, and
buy and sell and get gain. Whereas ye know not
what shall be on the morrow. For what is your life? It
is even a vapor which appeareth for a little time and then
vanishes away."

When you can build a castle of clouds, can quarry
them, hew them, and lay them up in solid, enduring
walls, then and not till then may you fashion a certain
and lasting success out of that fleeting vapor, a human
life "The ground of a certain rich man brought forth
plentifully, and he thought within himself saying :
'What shall I do, because I have no room where to bestow my fruits? And he said, this will I do, I will pull
down my barns and build greater, and there will I bestow
all my fruits and my goods. And I will say to my soul,
Soul, thou hast much goods laid up for many years; take
thine ease, eat, drink and be merry.' But God said unto
him, ' Thou fool ! this night thy soul shall be required of
thee ! Then whose shall those things be which thou hast
provided?'"

Here is an unknown factor which confronts every
man in the working out of his life plans. He does not
know how long time he shall have to work in, or whether
he shall live to reach the goal of his desire.

What would not the capitalist, busied with his great
railroad scheme, the statesman, working out his national
policy, the scholar ardently pursuing some great discovery in science, give to be sure of twenty years of life in
which to complete his work? But that assurance he can
never have. To-morrow even he cannot count on as his
own. "Boast not thyself of to-morrow, for thou know-

est not what a day may bring forth." Science has no secret for measuring the length of a human life. Death comes unannounced. And he waits for no man.

2. Now for this omnipresent unknown factor men have invented a name. They call it luck. It makes no difference, they will tell you, how hard a man may work, if his luck is against him. In other words the unknown factor may neutralize all his industry. Success, they will tell you, is the resultant of pluck and luck, i. e. of individual energy plus a happy turn of those conditions which are beyond individual control. But the Bible has another name for it, to-wit, the will of God. "For that ye ought to say: If the Lord will, we shall live and do this or that."

Have you ever asked yourself why God puts this constant element of uncertainty into human affairs? It is because God chooses to reign. He does not choose to put into the hands of finite, fallible man the power to shape events at his will, either on a large scale or a small. He does not choose that man shall say: "This, that or the other having been done, this result must follow." The unknown factor is God's reserved power of veto.

Two hands are busy in the working out of every life-plan, a visible and invisible. All the unknown factors, the unknown workings of the human brain and the human heart not less than the movements of the earthquake and the hurricane, are in that invisible but overruling hand; and on the movement of that hand depends the final outcome.

A Sisera gathers a mighty host and goes forth to subdue and make an end, once for all of the people of God ; but "the stars in their courses fight against" him. The unknown factor, this time in the shape of unlooked for panic, scattering his mighty host, and a woman's unsuspected treachery ending his life, frustrates his design and Israel is free.

A Belshazzar, secure in the impregnability of Babylon's walls, laughs in the face of the invader and feasts in anticipation of his assumed victory; and the invisible hand becomes for a moment visible, to write before the eyes of the trembling monarch the sentence of doom : " Mene, Mene, Tekel, Peni."

A Haman weaves his snare with consummate art for the destruction of the man he hates; and so near is he to success that the gallows is already erected which is the destined instrument of his vengeance ; when the unknown factor, the measure of a woman's influence over the fickle mind of a despot, frustrates the plot and sends the plotter to die on his own gallows.

A Sennacherib prepares to lay siege to Jerusalem, and, confident in the overwhelming strength of his resources, rejoices in his boastings over the little city which he thinks soon to devour ; and lo! in the night, death, the unforseen, unheralded confounder of the mighty, stalks in some mysterious form of pestilence through his camp ; and on the morrow he is in retreat, his army annihilated, his prestige gone, hasting homeward to meet an ignominious death at the hands of his own sons.

But whatever the agency,—from broken pitchers in the hands of Gideon's three hundred to the mighty death-angel that swept over the Assyrian camp,—back of them all is ever the will of God.

" In the battle of Waterloo," exclaims Hugo, " there was more than a cloud, more than a storm. God was passing by." " Was it possible," he exclaims, " for Napoleon to gain this battle?" We answer no. Why? Because of Wellington? Because of Blucher? No. Because of God.

The shadow of a mighty hand hovers over Waterloo. It is the day of destiny. A force above man decided that day.

3. Now then, this being so; that there is always this unknown factor entering into the working out of our plans, and that this is nothing else than the invisible hand of God, working either with us or against us, it is plain that we can make no greater mistake in life than to leave that factor out of the account,—to reckon without God,—to assume that we are masters of the situation, that we hold the key to the future in our own hands, and to go on planning and executing with no reference to any higher will than our own. This is the mistake and the sin which God rebukes in the words of our text: "Go to now ye that say: To-day or to-morrow we will go into such a city and continue there a year, and buy and sell and get gain. Whereas ye know not what shall be on the morrow. For what is your life? It is even a vapor that appeareth for a little time and then vanisheth away. For that ye ought to say: If the Lord will, we shall live and do this or that. But now ye rejoice in your boastings. All such rejoicing is evil." Aye, verily; doubly evil; evil in its impiety, as well as in its folly. It is an evil, withal, which sometimes meets with startling rebuke.

In a cemetery in Central New York, so it is said, stands a row of eight grave stones which tell a strange story. A physician of the place during an epidemic of diphtheria, had such success in the treatment of the disease, that he believed himself to have mastered the problem, and even went so far as to say that he would "defy the Almighty to produce a case of diphtheria that he could not cure." Within a short time the disease attacked his youngest child. He fought it with all his skill, but in vain. One after another his eight children from the youngest up to a married daughter succumbed to the dreadful scourge, and were laid side by side in the graveyard. The community looked upon it as a direct judgment of God for his impious boast. Whether they were right or not, certain it is that that row of grave stones is a monument of warning to any who presume to boast that they hold the key of the future in their own hands.

4. But then how shall we take into the account an unknown factor? What is there to do but to ignore it, do the best we can with the known factors and take our chances? If the unknown factors concern simply the hidden form of nature, the waywardness of man, and the uncertainty of life,—if, in short, what we had to reckon with were merely luck,—we could do nothing more. But if all these run back at last to one,—and that one the will of God,—then there is much more that we can do. We do not indeed know what God wills, but we know what God is. We cannot read the book of his decrees ; but we know the principles upon which they rest, and the goal toward which they tend. We cannot forecast the movements of the unseen hand which weaves with ours the web of life, but we can have that hand with us or against us, as we choose.

We can take God's will into the account by allying ourselves with it, through the great Reconciler, Jesus Christ.

How then shall we ally ourselves with that will? (1) By choosing God's ends as our ends, entering our little life-plan into God's great world-plan ; by obeying God's command ; and by submitting ourselves to God's ap-pointments. This is the pith of the exhortation in the text : "For that ye ought to say, If the Lord will, we shall live and do this or that." Of course there is noth-ing in the mere saying by itself. The mistake of leaving God out of the account in our life-plans cannot be recti-fied by the repetition of any formula, however pious. But there is everything in cherishing the spirit of which such language is the natural and instinctive expression.

The rebuke here is aimed not simply at a boastful confidence regarding the future, but at the worldly spirit which underlies that confidence. Such a spirit is forgetful of dependence upon God because intent upon things with which God has nothing to do. But he who sets himself to work for God, will be constantly reminded that he must work with God, and he will be willing, nay desirous, that God's unseen but unerring hand should work with his own, furthering what is wise, frustrating what is foolish, mending what is imperfect, and bringing out of all, the desired results,—God's glory and the triumph of God's kingdom.

So long as God's hand and yours are at cross purposes, what can you expect but confusion and failure? But when the two are working together for the same great end, what can the issue be but harmony and triumph? Then your working out of your life-plan becomes like the writing of the little child, too young to form its own letters, whose father takes the tiny hand in his own, and guides it across the page, letter by letter, syllable by syllable, till the child's whole thought stands, expressed in letters fair and round.

If we thus ally ourselves with God, entering our life-plan into his greater plan, morning by morning, asking : " Lord what wilt thou have me to do?" offering the day to God and asking him to direct and bless all its activities, we shall still be no nearer than before to eliminating the unknown factor, in life; but without eliminating we shall have secured it. We shall be no nearer than before to knowing whether life is to be long or short, whether health or sickness, gain or loss, is to be our portion, whether the friends whom we trust will prove true or disappoint us, but we shall know, that, come what may, "all things work together for good to them that love God."

Like Paul we shall be sure that the unknown factor, however it may turn, "shall turn to our salvation," that Christ shall be magnified in our body, whether it be by life or death.

> "He always wins who sides with God,
> To him no chance is lost."

The unknown factor will thus be robbed, not only of its danger, but of its sting.

What matters it to one whose prayer of prayers is: "Thy will be done," if his own plans are crossed, if his own work is undone? What are such things but the erasure of the false touches in the pupil's picture by the more skillful hand of the master, by reason of which the finished work will show the fairer at last?

"For me it cannot be! It is too late! I have lived too entirely for myself. I have left God out of the account too long"!

Nay, my friend, but it can be; God has made a way. "God was in Christ reconciling the world unto himself," and he now beseeches you by us, his ambassadors: "Be ye reconciled to God." Throw away the old plans. Let the old life go. Begin anew with Christ for your corner-stone; and beyond and above all the uncertainties which overhang the earthly future, you may like behold, a mountain peak, rising clear and glistening above the clouds through which your path must lie, an assured and eternal triumph.

The key of the future is in Christ's hand, and if that hand is with you, then "Whether the world or life or death, or things present or things to come, all are yours, and ye are Christ's, and Christ is God's."

THE HOLINESS OF GOD.

Exalt ye the Lord our God and worship at his footstool; for he is holy. —Ps. 99: 5.

There is no one word more characteristic of the Bible than this word *holy*. There is no one declaration concerning God which means so much as this: "He is holy." It is the central truth in that revelation which he has made of himself to man. It is the most exalted thought of him which the mind of man can form. It is his supreme title to adoration and worship. "Exalt ye the Lord our God and worship at his footstool; *for* he is holy."

The very loftiness of this attribute makes it hard to define. Holiness is the one word which sums up God's moral perfections. It expresses all that God is as a moral being. Negatively, it denotes his absolute freedom from the least taint of impurity or moral evil; positively, it describes his possession of love for and delight in all good. This quality of holiness attaches to all God's attributes. God's love is a holy love; his justice is a holy justice; his patience is a holy patience; his wrath is a holy wrath.

The seven colors of the rainbow are all different, but they are all light, and together they make light in its perfection. So the various moral attributes of God, which shine through the prism of his word, though all distinct, are all holy; and together they make up his perfect holiness.

As a holy God, the God of the Bible stands alone. This is his distinction when contrasted with the gods of the heathen. Heathen religions may be searched in vain for such a deity. Their gods are often monsters of depravity, from whose immoralities as portrayed in myth and legend even their own philosophers have recoiled in loathing. The vile armours of Jupiter, the barbarities of Odin, the lies and thefts of Kirshna, are familiar examples which need but to be hinted at. No wonder that Plato declared the popular mythology of Greece unfit to be taught to the citizens of his Ideal Republic."

Or if, here and there, a purer conception of the deity has been formed, still it has hardly risen above that of a just governor,—an impartial judge. The idea of that intense moral purity which we call holiness as constituting the very brightness of the divine glory we owe to the Bible. The word holy in the classic tongues plays but an inconspicuous part in religion and bears no deep significance. It has rather an external meaning, of something separated, set apart to sacred uses. The overwhelming weight of meaning which it bears in the song of the seraphim: "Holy, holy, holy, Lord God of hosts," is poured into it by God's use of it in that Word in which he makes himself known to man.

It is a remarkable fact that even Mohammedanism, though founded on ideas borrowed from the Old and New Testaments, so much so indeed as to have been sometimes called a corrupt Christianity, and retaining many very exalted ideas of God, has almost lost the conception of his holiness.

The title "Holy" which is given to God almost oftener than any other in the Scriptures, is applied to him but once or twice in the Koran. His holiness is there quite thrown into the background by his power.

Still less does the modern philosophy of unbelief find its way to the conception of a holy God. In seeking to maintain God's infinity, that philosophy loses its grasp upon his personality. But an impersonal God cannot be holy. Such a God may be indeed "a power that makes for righteousness." But that power cannot be itself righteous. Before the mystery of an "Unknown First Cause" we may stand in awe; but we can no longer "give thanks at the remembrance of his holiness."

In its subtlest, most fascinating form of Pantheism, philosophy identifies God with nature,—and then proclaims the indifference of nature to all moral distinctions. Look where we will, we look in vain for that God "whose name is holy," till we come back to this Word. But here we not only find his holiness clearly revealed, we find it his supreme distinction, his crowning glory. He names himself "the Holy One of Israel." The praises not only of earth but of heaven find in his holiness their sublimest inspiration. "Where," exclaims Charnock, "do they find any other attribute trebled in the praises of it, as this? 'Holy, holy, holy, is the Lord of hosts.' Where do we read of the angels crying out, eternal, eternal, eternal, or faithful, faithful, faithful Lord God of hosts? Whatever other attribute is left out, this God would have to fill the mouths of angels and blessed spirits forever in heaven."

Only this of all God's attributes is wrought into the Triune name itself, the most sacred and most wonderful of all the names of God, "the Father, the Son, and the *Holy* Spirit." His holiness is that which makes God worthy of the *worship* of his creatures. A God of power might be feared. A God of wisdom might be admired. Only a God of holiness might be *adored.* "Exalt ye the Lord our God and worship at his footstool; for he is holy." Without holiness God would cease to be God. Were that holiness marred with the least taint of evil he would become an infinite monster before whom we might *cringe*, but whom, though he should blast us with all his lightnings, we could never sincerely *worship*.

This holiness of God is no mere passive purity and stainlessness. It is an intensely active principle. It determines all that God feels, all that God wills, all that God does, as Creator, Ruler, Judge. "He is righteous in all his ways and holy in all his works."

His holiness is a consuming fire, at once of love and of wrath. It makes God by the very necessity of his being,—a necessity which can never change and never cease,—the enemy of all sin, of all evil, wherever in the universe it is found, and it makes him by the same necessity to desire and delight in the holiness of his creatures above everything else in earth or in heaven.

Let us remember this. There can be no such thing as holiness without hatred of sin. The intense expression of his word, "I, the Lord, hate evil," "Do not the abominable thing which I hate," are no mere figures of speech, no mere accommodations to human modes of thought. They are expressions of an awful reality, a reality inseparable from the very nature of holiness. Between moral opposites there exists an inevitable repulsion.

On the other hand God can find no work more worthy of himself, none in which he shall take greater delight than to call forth, to foster, and to perfect in his creatures the image of his holiness. To this all the processes of grace converge. In this all the resources of the God-head are expended. To form this image in the lowliest is a diviner work than to create an orb like Sirius.

If holiness is such an active principle in God it

must impress itself upon all His works. And so it does. It impressed itself upon nature. It is only a superficial view that nature seems indifferent to moral distinctions. A closer study of her laws reveals indeed a "power that makes for righteousness." The laws even of nature, work in the long run on the side of good and not of evil.

It impressed itself yet more clearly upon man. "God made man in his own image," and though the fall has defaced that image, yet in that inner voice which we call conscience and in all those laws of our moral being which make it a costly and a bitter thing to do wrong, we have still the witness that we are the offspring of a holy God.

Holiness has impressed itself most clearly upon God's Word. We may indeed say that it is the one purpose of that word from beginning to end to show men God's holiness and to persuade them to imitate it. The Mosaic revelation began, it is true with very much that conception of holiness which we recognized a moment ago as the heathen conception, an external separation or arbitrary sacredness, attaching to certain persons, places, times, set apart for Jehovah's use. Thus we read of holy utensils, holy garments, etc. But it began there only to lead Israel on and up from that point to a view of holiness essentially moral. The whole design of that ritual, with its elaborate and varied sacrifices, its distinctions of clean and unclean, its washings and purifications, its guarded approach to God in the awful mystery of the holy of holies, was arranged to impress upon the worshiper the conception of a God of moral purity, to whose presence sin was the great barrier that needed to be removed.

As we pass on from the giving of the law to the prophetic period in Israel's discipline, we find this revela-

tion of the divine holiness growing more and more
intense and spiritual, till at length it bursts forth in all
its splendor in him who was "holy, harmless, undefiled,
and separate from sinners," and who "gave himself a
ransom for many."

The *cross* is the highest revelation to the universe of
the holiness of God, on both its sides of love and of
wrath. Never could there have been conceived such a
manifestation of the awful evil of sin in the sight of
God as was found in the necessity for the sacrifice of
God's only begotten Son before it could be forgiven.
Yet never could there have been conceived such a proof
of God's longing desire to redeem men from sin and to
make them sharers of his holiness as appeared in his
willingness to make that sacrifice.

Now I have brought this thought of God before you
not only because it is in itself one of the sublimest
which can occupy our minds, a thought of which the
angels in heaven never weary, but because I believe it
to be one of which our age, even the Christianity of our
age, peculiarly needs to be reminded. That which is so
supreme in God and so central in his Word, should
have the supreme and central place in our religious
thought and experience. Has it that place? I fear not
altogether. On the contrary there seems to be a distinct tendency in the thought of our day to undervalue
and to slur over the word of God. "There is something
in the air," one has expressed it, "which predisposes us
to think lightly of sin." Ours is an age of sentimentalism. We may see it in the mawkish sympathy
expended upon unrepentant criminals, in the disposition to regard vice as mere disease or misfortune, in
the excessive recoil from physical pain. On all questions the appeal is apt to be to feeling rather than to
conscience. To many it seems a worse thing that men

should suffer than that they should do wrong. Moral suasion, too often ineffectual, crowds out penalty wholly from the school and largely from the home. We begin to hear the hospital suggested as a substitute for the house of correction. Our theology and our morals are both subjected by this current sentimentalism to a gelatinizing process. We never weary of dwelling upon the love of God, but we too readily forget that it is a *holy* love. The love of God as it is often presented in the literature, and even the sermons of the day, is a mere desire to see his children have a good time, of which a human father of any strength of character would be ashamed.

How different the love of God as presented in his word! *That* is a love the whole scope and aim of which is to make his children holy, and which spares no discipline, however sharp, that will lead to that result. The very forms of our devotion too often betray, in their tone of easy familiarity and excessive endearment, an utter absence of that profound reverence for a holy God which thrills through the heavenly song, as it caught the ear of the rapt seer of Patmos.

We need to come back to the Bible and to study God as there revealed alike in the Old Testament and the New; we need to linger before the cross and read its inmost meaning till our whole souls are filled with a sense of the unspeakable holiness of Him "with whom we have to do."

For indeed this truth that God is holy means everything to us. Here is a searching test of our spiritual state. How am I affected, let me ask myself, by the thought of God's holiness? Am I in sympathy with that joyous outburst of the Psalmist in another Psalm, "Rejoice in the Lord ye righteous and give thanks at the remembrance of that holiness."? Does the remembrance of his holiness fill me with thankfulness, or with dread? Would an eternity in the presence of a holy God be to me an eternity of blessedness or of torture? These, *these* are questions that we cannot afford to put by. Sooner or later we must face the answers to them. For unless we do indeed love to think of God as a holy God we could never attune our voices to the harmony of heaven and could never breathe in its atmosphere. "Without holiness no man shall see the Lord." It is only the true Christian who can give thanks at the remembrance of God's holiness. But he can and will, even though he seem to see in himself as yet an utter lack of conformity to it.

There is indeed nothing more humbling than a clear view of God's holiness. When Isaiah had a vision of it, it wrung from him the cry: "Woe is me, for I am undone; because I am a man of unclean lips and I dwell in the midst of a people of unclean lips." And when Simon Peter got a glimpse of it in Jesus Christ his first impulse was to cry: "Depart from me, for I am a sinful man, O Lord."

It is not uncommon in these days to hear sneers at the language of intense self-abasement in which many of the holy men of Scripture speak of themselves, as exaggerated and unbecoming. Unbecoming it certainly is in those who repeat it without feeling it, as a mere cant of devotion. But for my part I have no doubt, that could we but see the holiness of God as those men saw it, we should find the intensest of their utterances none too strong to express our feeling of our own unworthiness. A God before whom even seraphs cover their faces is not a God before whom of sinful men can stand unabashed. Yet, humbling though it is, the thought of God as Holy is at the same time full of comfort. What a terrible thing for the world, could there be the least suspicion of unholiness in its Ruler and Governor. Who then could lean upon his promise? Who could trust himself in his hands? Who could bow to his disposal of events? But because he is holy, we know that he doeth all things well. Because he is holy we know that all things work together for good to them that love him. Above all, because he is holy we know that we can lean upon him in our own battle with sin.

There could be nothing more hopeless than that battle, did we not know that God cares infinitely more for our victory than even we ourselves. But, knowing that, there is nothing more hopeful. With the Father's love to enfold us, with the cross of Christ to redeem us, with the indwelling Spirit to sanctify us how can we fail? We cannot *if we seek*.

Here then is the conclusion of the whole matter. "Be ye holy," so God speaks to us in the Old Testament. "Like as he which hath called you is holy, be ye yourselves also holy in all manner of living," so he speaks to us in the New.

"The sum of all religions," it has been said, "is to be like the God we worship." A holy God must have holy worshipers. Since the least taint of sin is hateful to him, our fellowship with him cannot be complete till the last trace of it is gone from our souls. *Salvation*, as the Word of God presents it, is God's way of cleansing us from sin, and restoring in us his holy likeness. The promise of a salvation which shall free us from penalty while leaving us to wallow in sin is the devil's lie. While God lives, while eternity lasts, no power in the universe can separate *forgiveness* from *holiness*, so that it shall be possible to possess and enjoy the one without seeking and beginning to possess the other.

For this Christ died; for this therefore we should live. For this his Spirit dwells in our hearts. If we do not work *with* that Spirit for this end, we are working *against* him; and no insult to God could be greater than to resist the work on which he has set his heart.

O, for more of the spirit of William James when he wrote, "I want holiness so much that I might say I want nothing else. One additional grain of holiness * * * with the consciousness that God was pleased with it would outweigh a universe of every other kind of good."

Is this your longing my brother? Then there is a precious promise for you. "Blessed are they which do hunger and thirst after righteousness, for they shall be filled." Then with the Psalmist you may sing: "I shall be satisfied, when I awake, with thy likeness."

GOD OUR MAKER.

Know ye that the Lord he is God. It is he that hath made us and we are his. We are his people, and the sheep of his pasture. —Ps. 100: 3. R. V.

So God created man in his own image, in the image of God created he him; male and female created he them. —Gen. 1: 27.

Short as it is, this 100th Psalm is truly a wonderful Psalm, of which it has been said, with as much truth as beauty: "This Psalm contains a promise of Christianity, as winter at its close contains the promise of spring. The trees are ready to bud; the flowers are just hidden by the light soil; the clouds are heavy with rain; the sun shines in his strength; only a genial wind from the south is wanted to give a new life to all things."

This is no exaggeration. From out the bosom of the Jewish Church, with its national sanctuary, its separating rites, its exclusive call, comes this voice of universal religion, bidding all the earth rejoice in Jehovah. Paul himself did not preach a broader gospel. Here is no word of the Abrahamic covenant, no word of the Levitical sacrifices. The temple is here indeed; but its gates seem to stand wide open to the nations. And the appeal by which men are summoned to worship is that simplest, most elementary appeal which comes home to all alike, the claim of God as *Creator*.

Last week we listened to an inspired invitation to worship God for what he is in himself. "Exhalt ye the Lord our God and worship at his footstool, for he is holy." Here we are again invited to worship him for what he is to us. "Serve the Lord with gladness; come before his presence with singing; know ye that the Lord he is God; it is he that hath made us and we are his; we are his people, and the sheep of his pasture."

It is this claim of God upon us as our Maker, that I ask you to consider this morning.

Where did the Psalmist learn this truth? He learned it from an old book, already venerable and already sacred when he penned this song of praise, wherein it stands written: "So God created man in his own image: in the image of God created he him; male and female created he them." How grandly does that record stand out in its simple dignity, whether against the grotesque and puerile myths of heathen antiquity, or against the speculations, now degrading, now presumptuous, concerning man's origin, even of this boasted century of enlightenment.

Ever since there have been upon the earth beings who could think and question, one of the questions which has deeply engaged their thought, has been the question, Whence. Whence am I? How came I here? History is preforce silent upon this question. Its beginnings find man already here. How he came here it can no more tell than our memories can carry us back to our own entrance upon life. Science is silent upon the question. In vain the chemist in his laboratory labors to bring life out of dead matter. He cannot bring so much as one tiny animalcule into being, save from a living germ. In vain the geologist searches the rocks for some trace of a "missing link." In vain the biologist labors to effect some transmutation of species which shall show us man in process of becoming. We trace back our ancestry, link by link, into the remote past; but the first link we shall never reach, save by a doubtful guess or the sure witness of One who made us.

Such a witness is offered us here. "But how do I know," you ask me, "that this record of man's origin is true? I want it demonstrated, I want it brought to the test of science, before I can believe it." My friend, how do you know that she whom you call by the sacred name of mother, whose gentle hand soothed your fevered brow in childhood, whose loving arms were your refuge in every trouble, whose serene face is the benediction of your manhood, and whose silver locks are a very halo of sainthood in your eyes, was indeed the author of your being? She told you so? But what if after all you have been the dupe of selfish imposture practiced to gain reverence and filial duty? Will you not demand some crucial test, before you again breathe that sacred name and bestow that filial kiss? Will you not at least have the physician and the nurse brought into court and put upon their oath to confirm that unsupported testimony? "Ah," you say, "it needs no such confirmation. That transparent sincerity and truth which I have learned to know all these years, those tender tones that have so often thrilled my very heart, that exhaustless fountain of mother-love which no waywardness or ingratitude ever checked in its flow, that self-sacrifice without weariness and without end, which have followed me all my life through, these are their own sufficient confirmation. I ask no other warrant of her claim to all the devotion due from a son to her from whom he has drawn his life."

Well, then, here is a book that speaks to me in the name of God, a book that bears upon its face the stamp of sincerity, a book that searches my very heart, that appeals to my inmost being as no other book ever did or could, a book whose very pages seem to throb and glow with paternal love, and which culminates in a revelation of uttermost sacrifice for the race of man, such as had else never entered the heart of man to conceive ; and that book tells me God is my Maker, that my humanity came from his hand and bears his image and likeness. That answer satisfies the highest demands of my reason and meets the deepest wants of my heart. It imparts a meaning to the confused riddle of history, and pierces with a beam of prophetic light the dark mystery of destiny. Accepted as true it raises man to the loftiest moral stature of which he is capable. What other confirmation does it need or could it have?

" God created man."

Look first at the fact itself ; then at its bearings for us.

I. *The fact.* *God* created man. "Stop ! stop !" cries the materialist, "that is mere unscientific mythology. Matter evolved man. That is the scientific account of his origin." And what then is this *matter* out of which have come the thoughts of a Milton, the discoveries of a Newton, the visions of a Raphael ! Nothing can be evolved from matter which was not in matter to begin with. An acorn could never develope into an oak if all the potentialities derived from a foregoing oak were not wrapped up in that germ. If man is the spontaneous outcome of matter, by however long a process, then thought, feeling, will, personality, all must have been properties of that matter from whence he sprung. If they were not, that matter was wrought into form and quickened into life by a living God.

"God created man." Nay, says the Buddhist catechism, which has already gone through two editions in Germany, there is no God. The Bible idea of creation is "a delusion." Man was his own maker. "Everything originates through and out of itself, by virtue of its own will, and according to its own inner nature and constitution." Such is the boasted "light of Asia," for

which some, it seems, even in Christian lands, are impatient to forsake the "light of the world!" How vain
are such imaginations! Man himself, even as he is in
this, his fallen condition, is still a witness for the being
of a Creator. Intelligence, personality, conscience in
man witness to a First Cause, intelligent, personal, holy.

"Where then is this Creator?" cries the sceptic
again. "Show him to me and I will believe." And
yet this same sceptic tells us of the atoms of which matter is composed, estimates how many there are in a cubic
inch of gold, how many in a cubic inch of hydrogen;
pictures their groupings; describes their motions. Has
he ever seen an atom? No. Has any man ever seen
one? No. Can any man ever see one? No. Why
then affirm their existence? Because they explain the
phenomena which we see. O strange infatuation, that
can believe in invisible atoms because they account for
a few things, and cannot believe in an invisible Creator,
though he accounts for all things!

But again, "God created *man*." Man then is a distinct being. He is not an emanation of the divine essence itself, "co-existent and co-eternal with God," as
the Christian science (falsely so called) of our day in express terms declares; building its whole system upon
this primeval falsehood, centuries old, that God and man
are one, "inseparable, harmonious, infinite and eternal."

In vain does this old falsehood of pantheism, which
always in all its forms strikes at the foundation of responsibility, destroys the distinction between good and evil,
and makes man the object of his own worship, seek thus in
these days by tricking itself out in detached phrases of
scripture, to pass itself off as God's truth. It founders
upon the immovable rock of this declaration imbedded
in the very first chapter of divine revelation, "God created man." This sets man over against God, the creature

over against the Creator, the finite over against the Infinite, as a distinct being with a distinct responsibility to the God who made him.

"God *created* man." Again I look at this declaration. I open my Hebrew Bible and I find that this word *created* is a word used in this form only of God. I find it sparingly employed even in this story of beginnings. It occurs here only at three points, which are confessedly the greatest crises of the story;—at the beginning of all things—"In the beginning God created the heaven and the earth," at the first appearance of animal life, and at the appearance of man. Elsewhere, even in this creation-story, a commoner and broader word, *formed* or *fashioned*, takes its place. There must be a significance in this. It seems to mark the introduction of something new. It introduces man to us as a new order of being, not a mere link in a chain of evolution, but the product of a distinct creative act. But this view of man does not turn upon the testimony of a single word, or upon a possibly doubtful point of lexicography. We turn to the next chapter, and there we read: "And the Lord God formed man of the dust of the ground and breathed into his nostrils the breath of life, and man became a living soul." Here is a new life, a soul, direct from God. Even if science shall sometime succeed in proving, as by its own confession it has not yet done, save by doubtful inference, the derivation of man's body from the lower orders of creation, still the soul, which reaches out into the infinite, which feels and owns the eternal law of righteousness, and even in its blindness gropes upward toward "an unknown God," witnesses to another origin and points upward to a divine original.

"God created man *in his own image*." It were mere childish trifling to interpret this sublime declaration which underlies the whole Scripture, forms the basis of every appeal to man's conscience, and marks the goal of the whole stupendous scheme of redemption, as having reference to man's body, form and features. God is a spirit; and it is in the spirit of man that we must seek his likeness, in that spirit which "thinks God's thoughts after him," as it reads them in the rocks and in the stars, that spirit which knows what it is to delight in goodness and to be indignant at wrong, that spirit which is capable of truth, of justice, of benevolence, and which rises to its highest glory in self-sacrificing love. However sadly defaced, traces of that divine image may still be found everywhere. I see them in the aroused conscience of the trembling Felix, in the penitent tears of the woman who was a sinner, in the trustful prayer of the thief on the cross. Wherever the spiritual nature of man asserts itself above the clamor of his animal passions, there I catch a glimpse of that divine image in which he is made. But I find that image in its unmarred completeness only in the man Christ Jesus, the one perfect man, and therefore the perfect image of the invisible God, through whom, I, too, may be "renewed in that image," "putting on the new man which after God hath been created in righteousness and holiness of truth."

II.   What now does this truth that God is our Maker, and that he made us in his own image, mean for us? It means, first of all, that *we belong to God absolutely.* "It is he that hath made us and *we are his.*" No right of ownership can be more absolute than that which comes by creation. Even that claim has its limits. God has no right to deal unjustly, even with the work of his own hands. But neither can he deal unjustly, for he is holy. Within the limits set by his own holiness the Creator's sovereignty is absolute. He made us for himself. He had a right so to make us, and the being that we received from him we are bound to devote unreservedly to his service. Go where we will, this claim follows us. We can shake it off only by ceasing to be. Not a breath we draw is our own. Not a faculty we possess is ours to dispose of at our will. Each one is his gift, and he is entitled to its use. Though we despise his authority, trample upon his law, deny his being, still the unalterable fact remains: "It is he that hath made us, and we are his."

He made us for himself—but how? That we might know him, love him, serve him, rejoice in him, reflect his image, and share his glory for ever and ever. The creative impulse was an impulse of benevolence; God made man that there might be those upon whom he could pour out the rich treasures that are in himself and who could share his own ineffable blessedness. Since this is the end for which we were made, we can only be happy in fulfilling it ; and it is suicide as well as robbery to set ourselves against this purpose of our Maker and the laws of that being which he gave us.

Since God is our maker, again, *we have no right to complain* of the way in which he has made us or the lot to which he has appointed us. "Woe to him that striveth with his maker ! Let the potsherd strive with the potsherds of the earth. Shall the clay say to him that fashioned it, What makest thou? Or thy work, He hath no hands? " If God were not holy as well as omnipotent this reasoning would not hold. But since he is not only our Maker, but a Maker in his very being incapable of wrong or injustice, every mouth is stopped, every murmur is silenced. Criticism by the creature of the Creator's work is blasphemy. Unquestioning submission is all that is left us to whatever that act of creation involves.

It is easy to complain, Why did God make me thus? Why did he impose upon me this weakness, that limita-

tion? Why did he subject me to this terrible law of
heredity? Why did he place me amid such surroundings
of temptation? It is easy to say, If I had been offered
my choice to be created such as I am or not to be created
at all, I should have chosen rather not to be. Easy! But
how useless and how sinful! "It is he that hath made
us and not ourselves," as the old version has it. He
made us in wisdom. He made us for good, but he took
counsel therein with none but himself. He made us
"according to the good pleasure of his will." How much
chafing at our limitations, how much fretting at our lot
might we spare ourselves, did we but remember this.

The old monk, Roger of Wendover, tells this story
of one of the German emperors : "The Emperor Henry,
while out hunting on the Lord's day called Quinquages-
ima, his companions being scattered, came unattended
to the entrance of a certain wood, and seeing a church
hard by, he made for it, and feigning himself to be a soldier, simply requested a mass of the priest. Now that
priest was a man of notable piety, but so deformed in
person that he seemed a monster rather than a man.
When he had attentively considered him the emperor
began to wonder exceedingly why God, from whom all
beauty proceeds, should permit so deformed a man to
administer his sacraments. But presently, when mass
commenced and they came to the passage, "Know ye
that the Lord, he is God," which was chanted by a boy,
the priest rebuked the boy for singing negligently, and
said with a loud voice, '*It is he that hath made us and not
we ourselves.*'   Struck by these words and believing the
priest to be a prophet [*i. e.*, I suppose, inferring from
what seemed the reverent significance of the utterance
an unusual holiness in the man.] the emperor raised him,
much against his will, to the archbishopric of Cologne,
which see he adorned by his devotion and excellent virtues."

But on the other hand, since God is our Maker *we can trust his care.* "We are his," is a word of twofold meaning. It means not only that our Maker is entitled to our service, but that we are under his protection. Even the relation of Creator and creature, reverently be it said, is a relation of mutual obligation. God is not a drowsy Brahm, who in a moment of disturbed repose has called a race into being, straightway to forget them in profounder slumber. "We are his people and the sheep of his pasture."

It is natural for the maker of anything to feel a peculiar interest in his own work. The author confesses to exceptional tenderness for the creatures of his own fancy. The sculptor looks with almost paternal fondness on the statue conceived in his own brain and wrought by his own chisel. The poet loves his own verses and hears with a thrill of joy that they have found lodgment "in the heart of a friend." So God delights in the works which he has made. "His tender mercies are all over his works." Even the birds of the air and the lilies of the field are the objects of his care, because he made them. How much more that one creature whom he made in his own image, and who is therefore not only his creature but his child. Surely we need never urge in vain the plea of the Psalmist : "Forsake not the works of thine own hands ; " and we need never fear to rest in that assurance of the Saviour : "Fear ye not, therefore, ye are of more value than of many sparrows."

The only conceivable danger that can threaten us in the hands of a Maker who is also our Father is the disobedience to his will. So long as we obey that will, so long as we yield to that control, we are secure. The power that made us may be trusted to keep, and the love that made us for a destiny of glory may be trusted to work out that destiny, unless we defeat its purpose.

For with perfect power and perfect love goes perfect knowledge. Because God made us, he knows us through and through. All our thoughts, all our motives, all the labyrinthine windings of our natures, all the unfathomed depths of our hearts are "naked and open" to him. Thus he understands just how to deal with us. Are our souls disordered by sin, he alone can be trusted to provide an adequate remedy. Is his image in us defaced and lost, he alone knows how it can be restored.

Let us suppose that in the rummaging in some neglected attic you have come upon an unpublished symphony of Beethoven, but alas, in a sadly mutilated condition. Many leaves are gone, and what are left are so stained and blurred and torn that it is only here and there a fragment of the score that is legible. You play these fragments and you are entranced with the power and beauty of the theme. You are tantalized beyond endurance by the hints of harmonies that you can no longer reproduce. You take the fragments to musician after musician, to composer after composer, asking them if they cannot divine the master's thoughts sufficiently to complete the work. But each, in turn, declines the task. Only the master himself could complete the fragments, fill the gaps, and restore the broken harmonies. Human nature in you, in me, in the race, is like that mutilated symphony. It is blurred, defaced, imperfect. Call it what you will, the ruin of a once perfect creation, or the fragments of a creation, still unfinished, the fact of incompleteness is beyond dispute. It meets us everywhere. We catch here and there a hint of a majestic theme, a broken strain of a divine harmony. But only he who made us can complete these fragments and restore the perfect music.

One more thought and I have done, but this the

grandest, blessedest thought of all. Because God made us in his own image *it is possible for us to know God.* Not indeed thoroughly, as he knows us. The less can never comprehend the greater. The creature can never measure the Creator. Yet we may know him truly, as like is only known by like. Many things he has made, living, conscious things, which can never know their Maker. His image is not in them, and therefore they have no glass in which to see him. But you and I may find in every whisper of conscience, in every noble impulse, in every high aspiration, in every hard-won virtue, in every pure affection, a voice to interpret to us that Father in heaven who said: " Let us make man in our image, after our likeness."

And when we see all these scattered traces gathered together in our elder brother, who is bone of our bone and flesh of our flesh, and who is yet " the brightness of the Father's glory and the express image of his person," when we hear him say : " He that hath seen me hath seen the Father," then indeed we feel with awe of what a blessed and perfect union between the Creator and his creature this divine image in man is the foundation. And coming to God through Jesus Christ we find every stain removed, every defect supplied, every weakness strengthened, every longing satisfied, every aspiration realized, and in a blessed and ever growing experience we learn the deep truth of our Saviour's own word : " This is life eternal, that they may know thee the only true God, and Jesus Christ, whom thou hast sent."

THE MERCY OF GOD.

And the Lord descended in the cloud and stood with him there and proclaimed the name of the Lord; and the Lord passed by before him and proclaimed, The Lord, the Lord God, merciful and gracious, longsuffering and abundant in goodness and truth, keeping mercy for thousands, forgiving iniquity and transgression and sin, and that will by no means clear the guilty, visiting the iniquity of the fathers upon the children and upon the children's children unto the third and to the fourth generation.—Ex. 34: 5-7.

This is one of the most wonderful scenes of the whole Old Testament. Exactly what took place in the solitude of the cloud-wrapped mountain top language was inadequate to describe and imagination is powerless to picture. But this we know, that it gave Moses an insight into the innermost being of God which it took the whole Old Testament to unfold, and which only the incarnation of God in Jesus Christ could fully express.

It is indeed one of the striking proofs of the divinity of the Scripture, that here, away back in this early time, amidst the crude religious ideas which prevailed over the whole world, we have a description of God which to this day has never been surpassed. Moses could never have reached such a conception if God himself had not revealed it to him.

Moses you remember was at this time in an extremity. He had just passed through a terrible struggle. He had come down from Mt. Sinai to find the nation which Jehovah had just redeemed from bondage and taken into solemn covenant with himself, in flagrant apostasy. With all the severity of a righteous indignation he had

first rebuked and punished their sin, and then with all
the intensity of a yearning compassion he had interceded
for their forgiveness. His intercession had prevailed;
the coveted assurance of reconciliation had been given.
But now for the first time Moses recognized the full
magnitude of the task he had undertaken. He had to
stand as mediator between God and a people not only
ignorant and undisciplined, but stiff-necked and rebell-
ious. The burden of responsibility was overwhelming.
He felt that he must sink under it unless he could have
the support of a vision of God, of an insight into God's
"way" such as he had never yet obtained.

It was this, and no mere idle curiosity, which forced
from him the entreaty, "I beseech thee shew me thy
glory."

Already Moses had one great revelation of God to
prepare him for his mission to Pharaoh. In the name
proclaimed to him at the burning bush, "I am that I
am," God had made known his majesty as the one
infinite, eternal, uncreated Deity, high above all the
gods of Egypt. But now he felt that he needed something more. God understood his prayer. He saw the
need and so he granted the request, so far as it could be
granted to a sinful mortal.

There is an intensity of light which the human eye
cannot endure. To attempt to gaze upon it would
destroy the sight forever. So there is a glory of God
which the flesh could not support. Under the disclosure
of it this mortal frame would sink. No man shall see
God's face and live.

What Moses *saw* when that request was granted, he
does not tell us. Perhaps he could not. It seems
probable, that here, as before in Horeb, the revelation
was accompanied with some manifestation to the senses.
But that was mere drapery. The substance of the

revelation was in what he *heard.* It was in that wonderful "name" of God, which was there proclaimed: "Jehovah, Jehovah God, merciful and gracious, long-suffering and abundant in goodness and truth, keeping mercy for thousands, forgiving iniquity and transgression and sin, and that will by no means clear the guilty; visiting the iniquity of the fathers upon the children and upon the children's children unto the third and to the fourth generation."

The "name" of God in Scripture stands for his being, and in this "name" we have God's highest attributes, his inmost essence, disclosed to us.

And in that disclosure *Mercy* occupies the foreground. The whole import of this revelation was to assure Moses that Jehovah was before all else a God of mercy. We have justice here also it is true, justice in its sternest form of retribution, but it appears only as a qualification of mercy, put in to guard against confounding the divine mercy with a weak indiscriminate indulgence. First we have an accumulation of all the words by which mercy in its various aspects can be described, "Merciful, gracious, abundant in truth, keeping mercy for thousands, forgiving," and there, only as the background against which this seven hued bow of divine mercy may shine the brighter, the dark cloud of retributive justice.

These words are the key note of the whole Old Testament revelation of God. Law, ritual, history, prophecy, from Moses to Malachi are but the unfolding of this precious name of God. This text sustains the same relation to the Old Testament that the corresponding text, Jno. 3:16, "God so loved the world," sustains to the New Testament.

Mercy then is the very "glory" of God.

But what is mercy? Mercy is that particular manifestation of God's love which is called forth by *sin*. If there were no sinners in the world there would be no room for the exercise of mercy. Though it would still be an essential part of God's perfection, it would lie unrevealed in the unfathomable depths of divinity. For there would be nothing to call it forth. When a jury have found an accused criminal *not guilty*, they never "recommend him to mercy." *Justice* is his need and his sufficient protection. It is the guilty one for whom mercy is needed. So to a world of sinners the mercy of God is the great concern. It is their only hope and their only plea. Thus mercy differs from goodness and from compassion. Goodness has reference to need, compassion to suffering; mercy has reference to guilt. It differs from forgiveness, because it is broader. Forgiveness is a part of mercy, but not the whole. Mercy is shown even to the impenitent and obstinately guilty, in the forbearance which suspends their sentence, in the providential blessings daily showered upon them, in the offer of salvation made to them, in the helps to a better life afforded them, in the tender pleadings with them of God's Spirit. All this is mercy, pure mercy. "It is of the Lord's mercies that we are not consumed." There is not a sinner upon earth who does not experience God's mercy to the last hour of his life. Yet it is in forgiving and justifying that mercy finds its fullest and sweetest exercise, and it is only the forgiven and redeemed sinner who can know in all its length and breadth what God's mercy is.

No wonder then that in a book for sinners, such as the bible is, mercy should have the central place. There is no attribute of God which it so much concerns us as sinners to understand; while at the same time there is no other attribute upon which, till God himself speaks, we are more in the dark.

We need no Bible to assure us that God is just. Conscience tells us that. Such a book as Plutarch's treatise on the "Slow Retribution of the Deity" is the voice of natural religion, witnessing to the absolute certainty with which the guilty conscience looks forward to a meeting with a righteous judge. But there is no such certain looking for of mercy. There cannot be; for mercy is in its very nature spontaneous and not necessitated.

So as a matter of fact this is the side of God's being respecting which natural religion and heathen systems are most shadowy and unsatisfying. The tendency indeed is to shut out mercy altogether, and to insist that in his dealings with man God gives each in the end just what he earns, nothing less and also nothing more. But even though we should be persuaded that God is merciful, this would not meet our need, since we could never tell without his own assurance how far his mercy would go. and whether it would reach as far as the full forgiveness of all our sins or not. A vague hope in some possibility of divine mercy would be, apart from any clear word of God himself, the utmost length to which we could go.

In this great uncertainty — and what uncertainty could be sadder — God himself steps in and proclaims: "The Lord, the Lord God, merciful and gracious, long-suffering, 'and abundant in goodness and truth."

Through the whole Old Testament (which only those who are unacquainted with it conceive as harsh and vindictive) runs this unfolding of God's mercy. Nowhere have I seen the spirit of the Old Testament better expressed than in certain sentences of Prof. Briggs, which many of you no doubt have lately read:

"The mercy of God is the theme upon which the historians and the prophets, the singers and the sages alike delight to dwell. The greatest of the theophanies granted to Moses was in order to reveal God as the gracious, compassionate, the long-suffering, abounding in mercy and faithfulness. The love of God rises to its heights in the fatherly love of Deuteronomy, and the earlier Isaiah and Jeremiah; in the martial love of Hosea, Zephaniah, and the second Isaiah — a love to an unfaithful wife, who has disgraced her husband and herself by many adulteries; and a child who rewards the faithful father with such persistent disobedience, that he must be beaten to death and raised from the dead in order to be saved. The love of God as taught in the Old Testament is hard for the Jew or the Christian to understand. It transcends human experience.

None could have taught such love who had not seen the loving countenance of God, and experienced the pulsation of that love in their own hearts. The love of God in the Bible is an invincible, a triumphant authority, that invokes the loving obedience of men."

And when in the New Testament we see this mercy of God actually stooping from heaven and making its abode among men in the incarnate Son of God, breathing itself out upon the guilty in words of sweetest, fullest forgiveness, lavishing itself upon the unworthy and ungrateful, in every form of unwearied kindness, and finally offering itself upon the cross, a priceless sacrifice for the sin of the world, then we know indeed what Moses dimly perceived and what prophets and Psalmist vainly struggled to express. This glorious name which God proclaimed to his faithful servant finds its only complete interpretation in the cross of Calvary.

The sceptic who would close this book little thinks that in doing so he would blow out the only light that sheds upon our pathway here a beam of hope. He fondly supposes that he can retain the beam while extinguishing the lamp from which it streams, — as I can remember trying, when a child, to grasp and imprison in my clenched fist the beam of light that streamed through the room from a crack in a closed blind. But he cannot. Quench the lamp, and we are left in darkness, shut up to the one immovable certainty that God is just.

If then we must go to God's word for our knowledge of the very fact that mercy is God's peculiar glory, much more must we go thither for our knowledge respecting the quality and conditions of that mercy.

There we learn that God's mercy is sovereign. None can dictate its exercise. None can prescribe its terms. When God was preparing Moses for this gracious manifestation he declared to him: "I will have mercy on whom I will have mercy and will have compassion on whom I will have compassion."

In this mercy is unlike justice. There is a *necessity* of justice; but mercy is in its nature free, else would it not be mercy. When a condemned criminal stands before a judge to receive his sentence, exact justice demands a certain definite penalty, no less and no more. But if mercy steps in, she may modify that penalty in any one of a hundred ways. And how and how far she shall modify it is optional with him who pronounces sentence. It cannot be otherwise. Nothing is mercy which the guilty can stand up and demand as a right. *That* is simple justice. The only compulsion which God is under in the exercise of mercy is *from within*. It is the compulsion of his own fatherly love.

Moreover God's mercy is a *righteous* mercy. It is a mercy not inconsistent with divine justice. That is the significance of these last stern sentences of this wonderful proclamation. They are a warning against presuming upon God's mercy as mere weakness or indifference. There is a so-called mercy among men which is cruelly unjust to society. It is that mercy which refuses to punish crime, which deals lightly with defiant lawlessness. Nothing is more dangerous, nothing is more disturbing, than such indiscriminate indulgence toward wrong doers. We have had examples in high places here in our own city of that sort of "mercy" to criminals, — examples which make the cheeks of honest men tingle with shame and indignation. *Such is not the mercy of God.* He is and must remain forever just, and unless he can find some way to reconcile mercy with justice, mercy must stand aside. "Righteousness and judgment are the foundation of his throne." Mercy itself is cruel if it strikes at those everlasting foundations. "Be just before you are generous," is *a saying* which in principle holds true for God as well as man.

But how can mercy be reconciled with justice? Are they not in their nature contradictory and exclusive? If we take justice in a narrow sense, yes. If we take it in a large sense, no. Looking at the individual sinner by himself, of course justice and mercy do exclude each other. If he receives justice he can not receive mercy and *vice versa.* But taking justice in the large sense, of that which conserves the interests of the whole and maintains the supremacy of righteousness, there is no such necessary conflict. If God had not found a way to show mercy to sinners without injustice to the universe, he would have shown no mercy at all. Such a way God did find, through the sacrifice of his only begotten son, "whom God had set forth to be a propitiation, through faith in his blood, that he might be *just,* and the justifier of him which believeth in Jesus."

God's mercy is a righteous mercy because it is not a

weak indulgence of sin nor an indiscriminate pardon of
the repentant, but offers forgiveness only on the righteous conditions of repentance and faith in an atoning
Saviour.

Is mercy narrowed by these conditions? Not by a
hair's breadth. On the contrary "that mercy is bound-
less." The mind of man cannot grasp it. It is as high
as heaven, "Thy mercy reacheth unto the heavens and
thy faithfulness unto the clouds." "As the heaven is
high above the earth, so great is his mercy toward them
that fear him." Words like these assure us that if we
will but comply with the conditions of that mercy we
shall find it absolutely without limit. As the highest
mountains are overreached by the heavens, which are
still infinitely beyond them, so, though our sins were
piled mountain-high, the mercy of God still outreaches
and infinitely surpasses them.

What! are you afraid that your sins are too great
for God's mercy to blot out? Then are you not also
afraid that, as the earth turns over, Mt. Blanc will
knock down the stars from the sky? That mercy is
measureless in its results. "As far as the east is from
the west so far hath he removed our transgressions from
us." How far is that? So far that the breadth of the
universe lies between them. So far that the forgiven
sinner and his sins can never be brought together.

And God's mercy is measureless in its duration. "I
trust in the mercy of God forever and ever," sang the
Psalmist, and well he might, for "the mercy of the
Lord is from everlasting to everlasting upon them that
fear him." The time will never come when a forgiven
sinner will have outlived his dependence on the mercy
of God. He has deserved an endless doom and he
stands in need of an endless mercy. But thank God
his mercy is endless, and no soul that trusts in it will

ever find that refuge to fail.

And now, my friend, what are you going to do with this mercy of God?

There are but two things you can do with it,—accept it, trust it forever, on God's conditions, just as they are made known in his word, or reject it and trample it under foot.

There is no third alternative. You cannot change the conditions. You cannot dictate terms to the divine mercy. This is what millions are trying to do. But it is impossible. Mercy makes its own terms. Take it as it is, or refuse it. To build your hopes upon the mercy of God while persisting in sin or turning your back upon the cross, is as reckless as it would be for a conquered army to expect amnesty while deliberately violating the terms of surrender.

Surely you are not insane enough to spurn God's mercy altogether. Surely your conscience is not so dead that you will venture to throw yourself upon the naked sword of God's justice.

Then there is but one thing left, to come penitently, believingly to the foot of the cross and seek humbly as a sinner for the mercy of God in Christ. Will you do it? You cannot come too soon. To-day mercy invites; to-morrow judgment may summon. The storm is gathering. You need a refuge. Yonder is the Rock of Ages. Hide in it now.

GOD OUR JUDGE.

So then every one of us shall give account of himself to God.—Rom. 14: 12.

Somebody once asked Daniel Webster what was the most important thought that ever occupied his mind. If there was anything trifling in the spirit which prompted the question, the answer must have effectually startled it away. "The most important thought that ever occupied my mind," said Mr. Webster in his slow, solemn way, "was the thought of my individual responsibility to God." That is the thought which here occupied the mind of Paul, and which in these weighty words he seeks to lay upon the minds of his readers, "So then every one of us shall give account of himself to God."

This fact of accountability is indeed the most tremendous fact of existence. Nothing in the future, not death itself, solemn as it is, can compare in significance with this certainty that sometime, somewhere, you and I, every one of us, each for himself, must meet God face to face, and give an account of every deed, every word, every thought.

> "This burden of responsibility,
> Too heavy for our frail humanity,
> Crushes me down as at His judgment bar.
> Why! death is naught to this! If we should pray,
> If we should tremble when that hour draws nigh.
> So should our hearts be lifted all the way,
> *To live hath greater issues than to die!*"

There flits through your mind in a moment of reflection some memory of the past which you hastily brush aside, saying to yourself: "That chapter is closed. There was much in it that was bad enough; but thank God it is done with now!" Done with? No, not done with. That closed chapter must be read again, every word. Left behind? No, not left behind, but gone before to wait for you at the bar of last account. Your whole past and mine, is there; and every day brings us nearer to the hour when we must face it. Buried? Aye, but buried where? Buried in the bosom of God, who will call it forth in his own time.

No wonder men shrink from this thought of accountability and often seek refuge from it in Atheism, Materialism, Pantheism, Fatalism,—anything, in short, that effaces the personality of God, or destroys the free agency of man, and so does away with this idea of an account to be given. For in fact there is no other escape from this thought. Accountability is involved in the very essence of man's relation as a creature to God as his Creator. Men talk sometimes as though judgment were an arbitrary thing, a prerogative which God may lay aside if he pleases, in fact a wanton exercise of tyranny of which a God of love can hardly be thought capable. Whereas, in truth God can no more cease to be a Judge than he can cease to be a Sovereign. To lay aside his prerogative would be to abdicate his throne. Given a Creator, personal, holy, and a creature endowed with a moral nature, i. e., knowing good and evil and free to choose between them, and judgment by that Creator upon the conduct of that creature is an inevitable necessity. Judgment, I say, and remember that this judgment by the Creator means two things, an *estimate*, and an *award* based on that estimate.

Judgment in the former sense of an estimate is in-

separable from the possession of a moral nature. You
and I cannot regard the good and the evil with the same
feelings, and the higher we rise ourselves in loftiness and
purity of character, the more impossible does such moral
indifference become.

Judgment in the latter sense of an award, is inseparable from the possession of authority. A father who
puts no distinction between the obedient and the dis-
obedient child, shirks the very first responsibility of
fatherhood. A government which deals a like with the law-
abiding and the law-defying earns for itself only the contempt of both. A holy God who has brought into being
creatures capable of holiness and capable of sin cannot
regard the holy and the sinful with the same feeling, and
he cannot justly repress, (unless it be for a time, in the
exercise of a merciful forbearance,) the expression in his
dealings with them of the opposite feelings with which
he regards them.

The nature of man makes judgment a necessity. We
say of man that he is a *responsible* being. This is what
distinguishes him from the brutes. But responsible
means *answerable*. He is a being who can answer for his
conduct, who can be held to an account of himself, because he is *free*. But to whom is he answerable? To
himself? Yes, certainly. He must answer at the bar of
his own conscience for every choice he makes. But that
is not all. To whom else? To society? Yes, assuredly.
Society has a right to hold him to a reckoning, to exact
payment, to insist upon penalty for everything in his conduct which harms his fellowman.

But that is not all. Beyond both these tribunals
there is another, at which man can cease to be answerable only when it ceases to be in his power to do right
and avoid the wrong,—the tribunal of God his Maker.
This is his dignity, this is his distinction as a being made

in God's image, that he is capable of good or ill desert, and therefore answerable to the Judge of all.

Our own conscience demands that God should judge. It demands this with regard to others. There is an instinctive looking-for of divine vengeance to overtake the wicked, so strong that when disappointed it recoils against the very foundations of religious faith. The prosperity of the wicked is one of the potent arguments of the atheist. So Diogenes long ago complained that the success of Harpalus in his treachery would witness against the gods, and the infidel lecturer of to-day points to his own unpunished blasphemies as proof that there is no God. The fact that in the world we see no equal and exact judgment has always been one of the great stumbling blocks to faith. It is the difficulty stated with such power in the Book of Ecclesiastes, for which the royal sceptic found refuge only in the assured expectation of such a judgment hereafter, so sure are we that a God who does not *judge*, is really no God at all. And the same conscience which thus demands judgment upon others teaches us to look for it for ourselves. That deep foreboding of judgment to come it is which makes us shrink back from the mystery of death, and clothes an unknown eternity with dread. That voice within which utters its stern "You ought, you must," witnesses to my soul of a God above who lent to that voice its authority, and to whom, sooner or later, I must answer for every deed, every word, every thought.

Let us try to grasp this fact. There is much in the drapery of it, in the plan, the time, the manner of this accounting that is shadowy and mysterious. But the fact is as simple and intelligible as it is solemn. Here are two beings, God and I. We are not unknown to each other. God knows me altogether, for he made me. He gave me life and gave it for an end of his own. He

gave me reason and endowed me with gifts and powers
in the use of which I might seek that end. And he has
made himself known to me in conscience and in his
word. He has given me a perfect law to be my guide.

And the time will come when for my use of that be
ing and those powers which he gave, for my obedience
or disobedience to that law which he revealed, for my
reaching or failing of that for which he made me, I
must give account to him. He is just. He holds the
balance exactly true. There is no bias, no partiality, no
respect of persons with him.

He knows all,—every act, every word, every
thought, every wish, every motive. All the palliations
of my conduct are known to him ; the inherited weakness, the infirmity of the flesh, the strength of the temptation. But so also are all the aggravations, the light
disregarded, the warnings of parents and teachers despised, the pleadings of the still small voice unheeded.

He has all power. The sentence which he passes
he is able to execute. Resistance on my part will be
worse than idle. He is supreme. There will be no appeal from his judgment. No power can reverse his sentence and no hand can stay its execution. And he is
everywhere. Many a transgressor of human law gives
justice the slip by suicide. But God is on the other side
of the grave as well as on this. To seek by suicide to
escape his judgment would be as if one should betake
himself to the other side of the ocean to escape the penalty of a crime committed in this land, only to meet, as he
steps ashore, the officers of the law, whom the telegraph
has informed of his flight and who are ready to hand
him over at once to offended justice.

Such is the Judge to whom we must give account.
And these perfections assure us that that judgment will
be just, searching, resistless, final, inevitable. And in

that judgment every one of us must stand practically alone. Though the whole universe should be summoned together before that tribunal, it will make no difference. Every one of us will have his own past to face, his own soul to answer for, his own eternal destiny to be fixed by his own decisions. "If thou be wise, thou shalt be wise for thyself; but if thou scornest thou alone shalt bear it."

"Every one of us shall give account of *himself* to God." Many influences may have helped to make or mar us. Many others may be entitled to share in the credit or in the blame. But ultimately each man's life is in his own hands; each man's character is the fruit of his own choices, and each must give his own account. If another has tempted me to sin he must answer for it, and God will hold him to the same strict account, whether the temptation was successful or unsuccessful. But *I* must answer for myself alone as to whether that temptation was yielded to, or overcome. The man, the woman, the serpent all shared in the guilt of the first sin, but each had an individual account to render and an individual sentence to receive.

Now we must distinguish carefully between this fact as it is in itself, and the aspect which it wears to a disturbed conscience. To a sinner the thought of God as a judge cannot but be a thought of terror. But in itself that judgment is a thing to rejoice in. The criminal on trial for his life, as he looks at the judge before whom he is arraigned, may feel his knees smite together with fear. That judge appears to him an enemy by whom his life is endangered. But the citizens who watch the progress of the trial, who observe how evenly the balance is held, how calmly and dispassionately the facts are inquired into, and how gravely and sorrowfully sentence is pronounced, see in that same judge the embodied majesty of law, the refuge of innocence, the support of liberty and order.

What sort of a world would this be to live in, if there were no righteous Judge upon the throne ? Who could endure the constant spectacle of unpunished villains and unrighted wrongs, if he did not know that because God is a God of judgment these things must end sometime ?

What would life be worth if instead of being a trust from a Creator's hand to be accounted for to him who gave it, and gloriously rewarded if rightly used, it were a mere accident, so to speak, without purpose and without result ? There is nothing which gives to life greater dignity than the knowledge that it is a gift so precious and so measureless in its possibilities that God himself will make strict inquiry as to its use. Better a thousand times the certainty of judgment with the possibility of eternal life beyond, than the certainty of no judgment, the irresponsible life of the sparrow or the butterfly, with nothing beyond it but an infinite blank. And this is the alternative. Privilege carries with it responsibility. Fellowship with God is possible only to beings endowed with that moral nature which makes them accountable. Eternal life is the crown of moral victory won.

Society pays a tribute to the dignity of manhood in every court of justice which it establishes. Why is it that when a fox steals chickens or a tiger kills a man we shoot it without ceremony, but when a man steals or kills we put him on trial with every safeguard for the meeting out of exact justice ? It is because we recognize the worth of a man as an accountable being. And this is what makes the sin and the shame of lynch law, that it deals with accountable men as if they were dangerous brutes to be put out of the way by sheer butchery without law or justice.

Not only does this fact of an account to be given to God lend meaning and worth to life as a whole, but to every trivial act and detail of life. Nothing is unimportant which God thinks worthy of record in his book of remembrance and of review before his judgment-bar.

You know the story of Huss, that when examined by the inquisitors he at first answered carelessly and without reflection : but that suddenly hearing the scratching of a pen behind a screen, and perceiving that his words were being written down, he began at once to weigh them with the uttermost care. When Jesus said, " For every idle word that a man shall speak he shall give account thereof at the day of judgment," he meant to teach and he did teach that there is nothing in life so small as to be unimportant or unmeaning.

This thought of God as our Judge is not only an ennobling but a liberating thought. It sets men free at once from all forms of time-serving and sycophancy, from the tyranny of majorities and bondage to public opinion.

What a manly independence, what a noble freedom was that of Paul when he said to the Corinthians, " To me it is a small thing that I should be judged of you or of men's judgment. Yea, I judge not mine own self ; but he that judgeth me is the Lord."

Such independence is essential to any really worthy life. The man who dares not stand alone, who dares not be true to his own convictions of duty in the face of popular clamor, is a coward and a slave. The vessel that, without rudder, drifts at the mercy of winds and currents is destined to wreck at last. And the life that without the government of a controlling sense of duty is swayed this way and that by the shifting breezes of human opinion is destined to the same fate. But the voice of the multitude is powerful. To stand alone against it needs

bracing by a mighty thought. Sometimes men gain a
measure of this freedom by setting over against the
clamor of to-day the thought of the calmer judgment of
to-morrow. But the judgment of posterity is uncertain,
and it has besides this drawback that he who appeals to
it will not be there to hear its verdict. It is the thought
of God's judgment that sets us truly free. He who carries with him the ever present consciousness of an account to be given to God, will care very little for human
praise or human blame.

There is sustaining power also in this truth that God
is to be our Judge. There is no element of the unap-
'proachable human character of Jesus more marvelous
than his *patience*. Never was he provoked by misrepre-
sentation, opposition, persecution, insult, anguish, to so
much as even a single revengful act or angry word. He
suffered unto death without once taking his cause into his
own hands or lifting a finger to strike back. Would you
know the secret of that amazing patience. His disciple
will tell it to you. "When he was reviled he reviled
not again ; when he suffered he threatened not, but committed himself to him that judgeth righteously." On the
certainty of that judgment he rested. For that he was
content to wait.

The communities in which there is least of private
revenge and lawless resort to force are those in which
the administration of public justice is surest and most
impartial. Men are willing to wait and to endure in proportion as they see that they can safely leave their cause
in other hands stronger and steadier than their own. So
when we look above all human tribunals, even the most
august, to a throne of absolute justice and of infinite
power, before which every strife must be adjusted and
every wrong set right, then it is that we learn to suffer
wrong with meekness and in silence, and to wait in

calmness and in patience for the righteous judgment of God.

Again the thought of God's judgment inspires charity and forbearance in our judgments of our fellows. This is the particular use the Apostle is seeking to make of it here. "So then every one of us shall give account of himself to God. Let us not therefore judge one another any more. But judge this rather, that no man put a stumbling block or an occasion to fall in his brother's way."

There is a sense in which we cannot help judging our fellowmen. We cannot help regulating our dealings with them by some estimate of their character. But it is God alone to whom they are accoutable. He alone has the material for a just judgment. The underlying motives, the stress of temptation, the earnestness of the struggle, which must all be taken account of in such a judgment are hidden from all but God. If there were no judge up there, perhaps it might be necessary for us ill-equipped as we are for the work to assume some prerogative of judgment. But since there is such a judge we may well leave our fellowmen in his hands. There is responsibility enough for each of us in preparing for the account we must render for ourselves. Aye, when we consider what measure of clemency and forbearance in that judgment we ourselves shall need, and remember that word, "With what judgment ye judge, ye shall be judged," how dare we be exacting and severe in our judgment of our fellow servants.

It is clear then that if we could but be delivered from those personal fears which to a guilty conscience are inseparable from the thought of God's searching judgment, that thought would bring nothing but comfort and strength and inspiration to our souls. But ah, that *if!* The past is past. No tears, no prayers, no promises can change one line of the unalterable record. And there is enough in that past, even with the best of us all that may well make us afraid when we think of meeting a holy God.

Who of us dare say that, when called to that last account, he can meet the summons in the confidence of stainless integrity, and await as his due an approving judgment? Not one. "For all have sinned and come short of the glory of God."

Well then, if we cannot have *this* confidence, is there any other confidence that can divest that great day of its terrors? Yes, there is. Though the best of men cannot hold up his head before that bar and plead "Not guilty," the very chief of sinners may there hold up his head and plead, "Christ died for me." The soul that is hidden in Christ has nothing to fear even from the most searching judgment of God. None need ever fear to face God as his *Judge*, who has learned to know *God* as his *Saviour*. You remember that when the three Hebrews were cast, at Nebuchadnezzar's command, into the fiery furnace, his servants beheld them with amazement walking in that white heat unharmed, and with them a fourth like unto the Son of God. So the soul that has the Son of God for its companion and protector will walk unscathed amid the consuming fire of that last tremendous day. "The blood of Jesus Christ cleanseth from all sin." The soul that has been washed in this blood will stand spotless as the purest angel before that bar.

And so, hidden in that refuge, washed in that crimson fountain, it is possible for the child of God to look up and rejoice that God is a Judge, to say, as one did say, when told that some were looking for the judgment as close at hand, "If I were sure that the day of judgment were to come within an hour, I should be glad with all my heart. If at this very instant I should hear such thunder-

ings and see such lightnings as Israel did at Mt Sinai, I
am persuaded my very heart would leap for joy."

With the Psalmist of old such an one can sing:
"Make a joyful noise before Jehovah the King. Let the
sea roar and the fulness thereof, and the world and they
that dwell therein. Let the floods clap their hands and
the world and they that dwell therein. Let the floods
clap their hands and the hills be joyful together before
Jehovah, for he cometh to judge the earth. With righteousness shall he judge the world and the people with
his truth."

CALVARY INTERPRETED BY ITSELF.

Now from the sixth hour there was darkness over all the land unto the ninth hour. And about the ninth hour Jesus cried with a loud voice, saying: Eli, Eli, lama sabachthani? that is to say: My God, My God, why hast thou forsaken me? Some of them that stood there, when they heard that, said: This man calleth for Elias. And straitway one of them ran and took a sponge and filled it with vinegar and put it on a reed and gave him to drink. The rest said: Let be: let us see whether Elias will come to save him. Jesus, when he had cried again with a loud voice, yielded up the Ghost. And behold the veil of the temple was rent in twain from the top to the bottom; and the earth did quake and the rocks rent, and the graves were opened; and many bodies of the saints which slept arose and came out of the graves after his resurrection and went into the holy city, and appeared unto many.— Matt. 27:45-53.

Who can read this story of Calvary without feeling that he is looking into a great deep of mystery. That which caused careless on-lookers who no doubt had gazed with morbid and unfeeling curiosity upon many a public execution to turn homeward in silence and with smitten breast, and drew from the stern Roman centurion, inured to spectacles of judicial torture, the awed confession: "Truly this was the Son of God," was no common incident such as a thousand times had stained the pages of history, of judicial murder to appease a popular clamor.

Something is here unique, awful, — which constrains us to pause before it and ask, What meaneth this? One of the most impressive deaths recorded in history is that of Socrates as it is drawn by the master hand of his great disciple. But place it side by side with this story of Calvary, and who but must cry with unbelieving yet honest Rousseau: "Socrates died like a philosopher, but Jesus Christ died like a God."

One of the most painfully impressive things in life is the indifference of nature to human anguish and human guilt. Generation after generation has made the earth to reek with crimes and cruelties the very tale of which if told without concealment were enough to freeze the blood in human veins; yet the old globe has rolled on without a tremor, like the fairest planet in the sky, and still the seasons come and go; spring spreads over all its gay carpet of flowers, and winter shrouds all in its mantle of spotless white; and from all nature there is no sign of horror or of sympathy. While dungeon walls echo and reecho with the shrieks of tortured victims the still glory of the dawn creeps up the sky. The sun looks smiling down and floods with noontide splendor the scene where martyrs breathe out their souls in flame, and sets in all his glory of crimson and gold upon battlefields where truth and justice and freedom have been crushed out in blood. And over the field of carnage on which the wounded writhe in lonely anguish and the dying call in vain for a cup of water to moisten their parched lips, the stars look down with the same undimmed eyes and the moon sails on in the same silvery brightness as over the bowers where lovers whisper their vows or the cottages in which mothers croon infants' lullabies.

But here is one who dies and above his cross the heavens veil themselves in blackness, and at his expiring cry the earth shudders to its foundation! It is nature's response to the supreme court of history. And yet not nature's.

The skies had no eyes to see that uplifted cross.

The earth had no ears to hear that dying cry. It is the response of the God of nature, signifying by supernatural signs his presence and his sympathy at the death of His beloved Son.

In the threefold miracle, of the darkness, the rent veil, the opened graves which accompanied the crucifixion of Jesus we have God's witness to the supreme importance and God's hints of the inner meaning of that event.

Miracle I call it. For there can be no alternative between denying the veracity of this narrative and admitting the supernatural character of these three accompaniments of the tragedy of Calvary.

It was no eclipse that darkened the heavens; for the passover moon, then at its full, rose that evening in the east as the sun was setting in the west. It was no earthquake that rent the veil of the temple in twain from its top to the bottom. Earthquakes rend rocks and overthrow solid walls, but they cannot rend asunder loosely suspended tapestry.

The earthquake itself, opening the rock-hewn sepulchres round about Jerusalem was no mere natural coincidence, frequent as such things are round that Dead Sea region. For though a convulsion of nature might rend the sepulchres, it could not reanimate the dust they held, to walk the streets of the holy city.

These signs were supernatural, and they had a meaning. They were not arbitrary signs, simply to call the attention of the universe to what was there taking place. They were a revelation from God, — answering to the revelation of his book and through the lips of Jesus himself, all pointing in one direction, all pointing to the glorious mystery of vicarious sacrifice as the central meaning of the cross, — and confirming the testimony of the divine Sufferer himself: " The Son of Man came to give his life a ransom for many."

We may call them, taken together: *Calvary inter-preted by itself.* It is true that these signs taken by themselves would be an insecure basis on which to build up a theology of the cross. When God wishes to convey new truth, above all, truth on which the soul's salvation hangs, he does it in words too plain to be misunderstood. Yet when we find supernatural events responding to the inspired words, the very heaven and earth as it were pointing to the cross, and echoing the words of the last of the prophets: "Behold the Lamb of God, that taketh away the sin of the world," the witness comes home to us with a solemnity and impressiveness that nothing else could give.

Look then with me at this threefold supernatural witness to the meaning of Calvary.

1. It begins with that mysterious darkness. "Now from the sixth hour there was darkness over all the land until the ninth hour. And about the ninth hour Jesus cried with a loud voice, saying: Eli, Eli, lama sabachthani; that is to say: My God, my God, why hast thou forsaken me?"

Surely this darkness has been nothing else than the frown of God, the outward symbol of his awful displeasure against sin. It might well seem to be directed against the impious city that had rejected its King with the cry, Crucify him! Crucify him!— to be the dark shadow of the doom already hanging over that city for this its crowning guilt, and soon to fall with crushing weight. Or it might seem to be directed against the world, the depth of whose fall and apostacy from God was first fully revealed in this its impious murder of one whose only crime was that he was sinless. But that cry of Jesus himself, uttered just as the darkness was passing away, and put by both Matthew and Mark

in close and evident connection with it, points to a
still deeper and more awful meaning. It points to a
hiding of God's face from his own Son. "My God,
my God, why *didst thou* forsake me?" is the closer,
more literal rendering, which points to a darkness in
the soul of the Redeemer already passing away with the
outward darkness which was its mysterious reflection.
During that darkness he had been silent. What the
experience, what the inner struggle of that soul was
during those three awful hours no human imagination
can ever fathom. Only when it passed away with the
outward darkness that so fitly symbolized it, and there
came again to that mysterious and patient sufferer the
sense of his Father's presence and his Father's love,
did he give a hint of what it had been, uttering himself, as God-fearing souls ever love to do, in the
inspired words of that treasure-house of devotional
utterance fitted to every phase of spiritual experience,
the Psalms of David. But in that cry; "My God, my
God, why hast thou forsaken me?" there was more than
an apt use of Scripture language. There was an application of Messianic prophecy. These were the opening words of a Messianic Psalm, in which the agony of
the cross is portrayed with a minuteness scarce surpassed by the gospels themselves.

In that utterance then, thus deliberately supplied by
the Holy Spirit centuries before, and deliberately applied by Jesus himself to the unfathomable experience
of those silent hours, we have the interpretation of that
supernatural darkness.

That darkness was indeed the frown of God, the
outward symbol of his awful displeasure against sin, —
but a frown directed toward the sin-bearer, the symbol
of that hiding from him of God's face which was the
bitterest drop in the cup of vicarious suffering.

Once lose sight of the truth that Jesus was there offering himself a sacrifice, bearing our sins in his own body on the tree, and a cry like this becomes inexplicable, the one blemish in that matchless scene, the one contradiction, utterly irreconcilable with the steadfast courage, the unfaltering submission, and the unshaken faith revealed in every other act and word of that heroic sufferer. Either God did actually hide his face from his Son, either Christ did suffer in that hour the sense of separation from God, unspeakably more dreadful than any bodily anguish, which is sin's supreme penalty, or else we can make nothing of this cry but the incoherent utterance of tottering reason or of reeling faith.

Either God did actually withdraw from his Son the sense of his presence and support, or else Jesus momentarily lost his hold upon all this through the failure of his self-possession or a temporary eclipse of his faith in God. To say this would be to impute to him a weakness to which many of his followers have risen superior, who have passed triumphant through all the agonies of martyrdom with songs upon their lips not for one instant losing their consciousness of God's nearness or their trust in his faithfulness.

But if that hiding of God's face was real, then but one explanation of it is possible. Christ was taking the sinner's place. He was suffering the darkness of God's frown that you and I might walk forever in the light of God's countenance. And that darkness over the land was the symbol of the more awful darkness enshrouding his soul as he tasted death for every man.

2. If this was true, if our sins were indeed laid upon this sinless Lamb of God, then they must have been put away completely and forever. Then the way must be fully open for sinners to return to God. So indeed it was, and this, too, had its supernatural attest-

ation following close upon the other. "Jesus, when he had cried again with a loud voice yielded up the Ghost, and behold the veil of the temple was rent in twain from the top to the bottom." The words of that dying cry Matthew does not give; but John has recorded them. "When Jesus, therefore had received the vinegar he said: 'It is finished!' and bowed his head and gave up the Ghost."

"It is finished!" The veil of the temple was rent in twain. Surely it needs no interpreter to unfold the meaning of a sign so eloquent. We have only to recall what this veil itself was, and what it stood for in the God-given symbolism of the tabernacle to see in an instant what was meant when God's own hand rent it asunder. That veil was the curtain which closed the entrance to the Holy of Holies, the presence chamber of Jehovah, where on the mercy seat between the cherubim rested, till the sins of the people grieved it away, the Shechinah, the luminous cloud which was the visible symbol of his presence with the covenant people. To that presence the veil barred the way. It was a perpetual proclamation to the worshiping people in the courts without, that sinful man is not fit to enter the presence of a holy God. One hand alone might lift that veil, — the hand of the high priest, the appointed mediator for sinners, — and that but once a year, when he entered with the blood of the sin-offering by which atonement had been made for the sins of the people, to sprinkle with it the mercy seat. Thus that veil, hanging before the mercy seat as at once a doorway and a barrier, shutting out the worshipers from the immediate presence of God, and yet admitting one to intercede for them and present on their behalf the atoning blood, spoke at once of reconciliation possible and of reconciliation incomplete. It spoke of God's gracious purpose toward man, and yet it proclaimed man's need of a more thorough cleansing from guilt than any which those typical sacrifices could effect. After the sacrifice had been offered, after the blood had been sprinkled, the veil was still there.

"The Holy Ghost this signifying," says the Epistle to the Hebrews, "that the way into the Holiest was not yet made manifest."

When then that veil was rent by God's own hand it proclaimed more loudly than even a voice from heaven could have proclaimed it, that atonement was at last "finished," that a sufficient sacrifice had at length been offered "once for all," that the old preparatory dispensation was done away and that henceforth there was free access for every penitent sinner to the mercy-seat of the King of Kings. No need now for any farther bloody sacrifices. No need now for any human priest. The rending of the temple veil was God's response on the instant, his seal set without delay to that cry from the cross, "It is finished." If the darkness over all the land proclaimed the awful reality of Christ's vicarious suffering, the rent veil proclaimed its glorious sufficiency. The penalty has been borne; the atonement has been accepted; henceforth for all who trust in that atonement the way to the mercy-seat is open and free.

3. But if these two things are true, if sin's penalty has been borne, and if the way to God is now open and free, then we look for a removal of the curse. The sentence, "Dust thou art and unto dust shalt thou return," must be revoked or the work of Calvary will not be complete.

But here again God bears a mighty witness in the third miraculous event of that wonderful day. "And the earth did quake and the rocks rent, and the graves were opened and many bodies of the saints which slept arose and came out of the graves after his ressurection."

Here is more than a mere shudder of nature at the expiring groan of its Lord. Here is the opening of death's prison that his captives may go free. It is a proclamation of victory through seeming defeat, of death conquered by dying. If the veil of the temple rent in twain showed us a dying Redeemer opening the way for sinners to the mercy-seat, these opened graves show us that Redeemer entering the very stronghold of our last enemy, bursting its bolts and bars and leading forth his captives into life eternal.

This is not only a proclamation but a prophecy. These opened graves are the first trophies of a splendid triumph. These risen dead, (following, not anticipating Christ's resurrection) are the first fruits of a mighty harvest still to be reaped. It was fitting that an earnest should thus be given of the finished redemption wrought upon the cross, a pledge also for all time of "the power of Christ's resurrection." Could any miracle bear plainer witness to Christ as the life-giver and to the cross as a power to cancel the curse of sin?

Then my brethren we have in the supernatural events which surrounded that scene on Calvary and marked the death of the Sufferer as something strange and apart from all other deaths, a kind of miracle-gospel speaking to us of God's displeasure against sin visited on the sinless, of a way thus opened for sinners to draw near to God, of death vanquished, the grave robbed of its prey, and life eternal won — for all who follow that victorious leader.

And you too, fellow-sinner, this is the gospel which I offer to you to-day, — a gospel whose three mighty terms are atonement, reconciliation, eternal life. That darkened heaven, that rending veil, those opening graves, are God's mighty voices to you proclaiming

that the debt is paid, that access to God is free, that
death is swallowed up in victory, inviting you to walk
henceforth in the light of God's countenance, to enter
boldly, not into an earthly holy of holies, but to the
very heavenly mercy-seat itself, to enter here and now
upon the possession of eternal life.

When the very skies and the very graves are thus
vocal will you be deaf to those voices? In the presence
of a tragedy of expiation and a revelation of divine
love at which the very rocks are rent asunder will your
heart, harder than the rocks, refuse to break? And like
those curious, careless, callous bystanders, awed but for
an hour, will you too, return to your house the same
unyielding, impenitent sinner as before?

NEGLECT OF SOULS.

No man cared for my soul.—Ps. 142: 4.

"If I had ever heard as much about Jesus Christ before I came to this place as I have since, I should not be here." Such was the bitter reply of a condemned felon as he lay in his cell awaiting execution, to the ministers, Y. M. C. A. committees, and devout women, who visited him day after day, and pleaded with him to take Christ as his Saviour before the hour came that should launch him into eternity. Not only bitter, but probably untrue. That he now would have nothing to do with that Saviour but thrust him sullenly away, showed what he would most likely have done had he heard of him before.

It is not hearing of Jesus Christ but believing on him that keeps men from prison and gallows. But however worthless a justification of himself, the words were a severe arraignment of the Christian city that had suffered him to grow up within sound of its church bells, yet had done nothing for his soul till he lay under sentence of death in a felon's cell.

And they are startlingly suggestive of the reproaches against Christian neighbors, friends, aye kindred even, with which the walls of the most awful prison house may one day resound. "If you had spoken to me of Jesus Christ, if you had warned me of the wrath to come, I should not have been here."

"No man cared for my soul." In the life of the Psalmist according to a common Hebrew mode of speech, "my soul" meant simply "me." He refers to the neglect and indifference of his friends when he was hard pressed by his enemy Saul.

But since the soul is the true self, since there are no interests to compare with its interests, no perils to compare its perils, it is not perverting the words, only intensifying them to take them in the sense which they first convey to an English ear. It is thus that I ask you to consider them to-day, as the complaint of the sinner who is left to take the downward road unheeded and unwarned, when he at last awakes to the fact that he is lost.

Three things concerning this complaint we have need to consider.

1. Who have cause to make it.

2. Against whom it justly lies.

3. Why it is that souls are thus neglected.

I. Are there any in this day of missionary and evangelistic zeal who can justly complain : "No man cared for my soul ?" Alas, yes ! In heathen lands millions have cause to make it. The question asked by a convert of a missionary : "Where was your father, that my father died without the gospel ?" is a home question for those Christians who are living at ease and doing nothing to obey the Saviour's bidding to give his gospel to every creature. I do not deny that a heathen might be saved who had no distinct knowledge of Jesus of Nazareth. But neither Scripture nor experience encourages the hope that many will be. And yet despite all that the church has yet done for the spread of the gospel, there are millions in the world to whom that name above every name is an unknown sound.

The heathen too often have reason to think that Christian nations care for everything else that is theirs rather than for their souls. The black man found that

the Christian cared for his bone and sinew. The red
man found that the Christian cared for his lands. The
Chinaman found that the Christian cared for his trade.
But alas, they are still only beginning to be convinced
that Christians care for their souls.

But it is not far-away heathen alone who have cause
to make this complaint. The unevangelized classes in
our own land, yes in this Christian city, have cause to
make it. That condemned felon whom I have just quoted
represented a class who though living within the sound
of church bells, and having dealings all their lives with
Christian people, have scarce so much as heard the name
of Christ, unless it be in blasphemy, much less have ever
heard from the lips of any disciple of Christ, a loving
invitation to come to him.

It seems incredible that in a land where missions
and churches abound, where Sabbath Schools and mission schools are scattered broadcast such can be found.
Yet they can be.

England is a land of as many churches and bibles,
of as much gospel light and Christian activity as our
own. Yet a minister walking across the fields in the
west of England one Sabbath day and pausing at a little
cottage to inquire his way found there a solitary old man
of eighty years, and falling into conversation with him
asked at length: " Do you know Jesus? " " Jesus? Jesus?
no I never heard of him. Do he live about here ? " " I
mean Jesus who lived eighteen hundred years ago and
died for you and me on the cross. You know him ? "
" No I don't. I never heard of him." And so the minister sat down and told him that old story, from Bethlehem to the opened sepulchre, and behold it was all as
new and he listened to it all with as much wonder as if
he had been an untutored savage in the heart of Africa,
aye, and received it with the simple faith of a little child.

His mind was clear. He could talk intelligently of his own past life. He had heard of witches often enough, could tell many a tale of their pranks, and had horse-shoes upon his doors to keep them off. But of Jesus he knew absolutely nothing.

Suppose ye, my friends, there is none such in this land ? I tell you there are thousands, heathen, unevangelized heathen, though living almost under the shadow of church spires. And when from drunken deaths, starved deaths, bloody deaths, they go up to their last account, it will be a sad tale they will have to tell, albeit one that will not cover their own sin, "No man cared for my soul." But these are not all. The impenitent in our own homes and congregations too often have cause to make this complaint. To them the gospel message is indeed familiar. They are taught it in childhood. They hear it from Sabbath to Sabbath seated in their own comfortable pews. The invitation of the gospel has been pressed upon them from the pulpit not once but many times. Oh they have light enough, opportunity enough. But it has all been of a general sort. The invitation has come to them as part of an undistinguishable mass, not personally with a warm grasp of the hand and a tender utterance of their name. "No man cares for my soul," they often say to themselves. No one takes any interest in my individual salvation.

Let me give you an illustration of what some of them are thinking.

A pastor called upon the daughter of one of his church members to talk with her of the concerns of her soul. Among other things he said to her : "It would give your father great joy if you should become a Christian." "I do not think it would" she replied. Thinking she must have misunderstood him he repeated his remark. "I do not think it would," she still replied.

"You do not think so? Why not?" "Because I think if
he cared anything about it he would have spoken to me
on the subject, and he never has."

Not only is this indifference noticed, it is often
keenly felt, by those who are not Christians. They may
have no sense of personal danger, but they are sensitive
to the apparent want of sympathy and interest. It is no
uncommon thing for those who do speak of these things
to the irreligious, to be told in reply in a tone half grateful, half reproachful: "you are the first person that has
ever spoken to me on this subject." For years perhaps
that man or woman has been wondering why it was that
among all these Christian friends and acquaintances no
man seemed to care for his soul.

II.   But who is responsible for these neglected souls?
The parable of the Good Samaritan answers that question. Those who might have cared for them and did not.
The guilt of this neglect lies at the door of every Christian who fails to show an interest in the souls of others
as he has opportunity. This applies even in the case of
those who know the way of salvation and will not take it.
That does not excuse us from seeking to win them, since
that very effort might be the one they needed to end
resistance.

It is no excuse to say: "They have churches and
bibles and sermons." These are not enough. What
every man needs above all things is to be made to feel
that the gospel is a personal matter, that Christ came to
seek his individual soul. And nothing helps him to feel this
like the pressure of the hand, and a word of personal entreaty from a Christian friend. He cannot lose himself
in the crowd then, and let the words aimed at his conscience slide off upon some one else. It is no excuse to
say: This is the business of ministers, elders, Sunday School teachers. I am only a private Christian.

Suppose a case like this. You are on board a vessel. A man has fallen overboard. At your feet lie a pile of life preservers: but you do not lift a finger to throw one to your drowning fellow creature. When remonstrated with you say: "I am only a passenger. It is the business of the ship's officers to guard the lives of those on board." But if this plea would not serve you in such a case how much less in the case of a soul sinking into hell. It is a question for each one of us to bring home to himself then: "Do I care for the souls of the perishing around me, and do I let them know that I care for them?" If some soul from my neighborhood, within my reach, should go up to the bar of God to-day to meet an awful doom, and should cry out in its despair: "No man cared for me," would any part of the guilt of that neglect and ruin lie at my door?

Few of us can ask these questions without some degree of self-reproach. Ours may not be a total indifference to the souls about us; but in most cases how feeble our interest when compared with the worth of a soul or the greatness of its peril.

This being so we cannot help asking the third question:

III. Why is there so little concern for souls among Christ's followers?

Two words tell the story; unbelief and selfishness.

I. Unbelief. We cannot feel concerned for those we do not feel to be in danger. Unbelief in the threatenings of God is a chief cause for neglect of souls. That old lie of the father of lies: "Ye shall not surely die" is afloat still, doing the work of the burglar's chloroform in stupifying the Christians who should be on the watch, while the enemy makes sure of his booty.

It is not that the words are obscure. No warnings could be plainer or more terrible than those of Jesus

Christ. It is not ordinarily that Christians have reasoned themselves into a definite belief that the words mean something else than they seem to mean. It is simply a feeling that such threatenings cannot be true.

I put it to you to-day, Christian hearer. Do you believe that at the last day the judge will say to those on his left hand: "Depart ye into everlasting fire?" If you do, what are you doing to rescue souls from that fire? If you do not, why do you reject the plain words of Christ?

But souls are neglected too from unbelief of another sort, unbelief in the promises of God. If too hopeful a view of the case of sinners relaxes effort, too hopeless a view paralyzes it. How often do we excuse ourselves from effort for a soul by the plea, "There is no use. He is beyond reach." Beyond whose reach? Yours? or the Holy Ghost's? Have you a right to set bounds for God or to limit the power of prayer?

O, for more faith in the power of God's truth attended by God's Spirit to break the hardest heart! O, for more of that faith for spiritual combats that David had when with five smooth stones from the brook he went boldly forth in the name of the Lord of Hosts to meet the Philistine champion. Where would have been the work of such a man as Judson or such a woman as Fidelia Fiske, where the hundreds of Burman and Nestorian souls, that now glitter as stars in their crowns of rejoicing, if they had ever allowed themselves to know such a thing as hopeless cases.

It might seem that these two kinds of unbelief are at least not likely to be found together. Yet the reverse is true. It is no uncommon thing to find doubt as to the real danger of the impenitent united with doubt of the possibility of doing them any good,—the two together rendering the Christian a passive looker-on at the most solemn of all tragedies, the ruin of a soul.

Yet our neglect is not all due to unbelief. The irreligious sometimes, seek a false comfort here. They say: Christians do not belive their own teachings concerning God and eternity. If they did they could not be as unconcerned as they are about their friends and neighbors who must be in danger of the wrath to come. And if they do not believe these things, why should we trouble ourselves about them? But the reasoning is not sound. All experience teaches that it is quite possible to believe in the reality of an evil and yet do nothing to relieve or avert it. The comfortable citizen unfolds his morning paper and reads perhaps of a famine in Asia, so many human beings a week dying of starvation, babes pining to death on their mothers' bosoms, men groping in the dust by the wayside for a few grains of rice to keep soul and body together a few hours longer. He does not say: "This must be exaggerated! I don't believe a word of it." He does not doubt the facts. He exclaims: "This is horrible!" and then he falls to and eats his plentiful breakfast with no loss of relish and then goes his way not perhaps contributing so much as a penny to the relief of that unquestioned suffering.

Such is the power of *selfishness*. And that, alas, is the other great secret of our neglect of souls. Oh, there is a fearful amount of this selfishness in the church of Christ. The heartless answer of the priests to Judas when he came to them in an agony of remorse crying: "I have sinned in that I have betrayed innocent blood." "What is that to us? See thou to that," is what the conduct of too many who think their own salvation secure seems to say to the unsaved about them. Monstrous! that one should not care what becomes of others if his own soul is saved. Yet just this monstrous thing, I fear. is too often actually realized.

Even our concern for our own families, if it stops
with them, is proved to be only a selfish concern. They
are so much a part of ourselves, so necessary to our happiness, that we may well be filled with distress at the
thought of eternal separation from them, on purely selfish ground, without a particle of that love for souls
simply as souls or pity for the lost simply as lost which
drew Christ down to earth to seek and to save.

One may even be unselfish enough to feel some motions of sympathy for the impenitent and some desires
for their salvation, and yet be too selfish to do anything
for them. Effort for souls involves self-denial. Timidity must be overcome for one thing. How often does the
Christian allow his nearest neighbors, whom he meets
every day, to gain the impression from his silence that he
cares nothing for their souls simply because he is not unselfish enough to be willing to risk repulse or a sneer.

Effort for souls, too, takes time, and we are econ-
omical of time in these driving days. Withal he who feels
the burden of a perishing world as the apostles felt it,
and esteems the rescue of souls the most important work
in which he can engage will have little money to spend
in pampering himself and little heart for the mere frip-
peries and frivolities of life. Yes, we must get rid of self in
all its forms, pride, covetousness, love of ease; we must
be ready with the Saviour of souls himself to deny ourselves and take up our cross, if we would be free from a
share of the reproach : "No man cared for my soul."

IV.   If these are the causes of the neglect we are
considering, they themselves suggest the remedy. It lies
in holding before our minds the facts by which unbelief
and selfishness may be overcome.

Three facts especially :

I.   The worth of the soul. Do the bodily sufferings
of men appeal to your sympathies? If you stood on a

battle-field, your ears filled with the groans of the maimed and the dying, would you feel that you *must* do what you could for their relief? Yet what are pains of body to soul suffering? Even if the body were to last forever its well or ill being would be a secondary matter. The true well or ill being would be that of the soul. How much more when it is but a handful of dust which in a few days will return to the earth as it was?

Or are you interested in your neighbor's affairs, anxious to see him prosperous, willing to make some exertion to put him in the way of advancement? This, too, is most praiseworthy. But what is outward prosperity to a ruined soul? What is adversity to a soul sure of eternal life? The career of the most successful will soon end, the troubles of the most unfortunate will soon be over, unaided by wealth, unsupported by friends, unattended by fame. the soul must go alone, a soul in Christ or a soul out of Christ to the presence of its Judge. Would you do good that will last; you must do it for souls. All joys, all miseries, all pursuits, all studies, all relationships, all things that awaken our interest and call forth our sympathy for our fellowmen have meaning only as they bear upon the destiny of their souls.

II. The second fact is the peril of souls. The doom of the willful sinner is not a pleasant subject of contemplation, but it is a needful one, if we would feel that yearning for them which Christ felt. It was that sight which drew him to leave the bosom of the Father, lay aside the glory of the godhead and endure the agony of the cross. Are we more tender than he that we can feel what he felt though we close our eyes to what he saw? Look at the completeness of the ruin which awaits an impenitent soul, banishment from God, exclusion from heaven, the utter extinction of God's image within and degradation to the level of fiends. Look at the misery of it, memory a worm that never dies, the star of hope blotted out in the blackness of darkness. Look at the eternity of it—endless remorse, endless self-loathing, endless despair. O, my friends can you see a soul exposed to such ruin, and care nothing for that soul?

III. But against this dark back-ground we need to keep constantly in view the love of Christ. "The love of Christ constraineth us." His love to us. Should not that constrain us ? Shall angels take an interest in the fate of human souls, shall they shout for joy when one sinner repents and shall we alone their fellow· sinners bought by the same blood, rescued from the same bondage, look on without concern while they die in their sins? But think also of his love for them.

Perhaps these souls are uninteresting in themselves, besotted with ignorance or repulsive with vice. We can find in them nothing to awaken our interest. But stay ! These are souls for whom Christ died. Is there nothing in that to invest them with interest? What, am I a disciple of Christ. a friend of Christ, and shall I care nothing for that which he loved even unto death ? Nay, shall I not rather go to the ends of the earth if need be, or dig down into the lowest strata of society, anywhere, everywhere in short, where there are souls to be found that we may find these gems for which he came on such a quest and lay them as our tribute of love and homage at his feet. Surely he who brings one soul to Christ makes a richer and more acceptable offering to Him than he who lavishes a fortune in his service or rears the most splendid temple to his praise.

Two or three practical remarks now, and I have done.

1. The first is that if we are guilty of neglect of souls we are neglecting the main business of life. What is a Christian but a follower of Christ? And how can

we be followers of Christ unless we live for that for which
he lived. But he came to seek and to save that which was
lost. That was his business here. And he has left that
work now to his people. Why is it that Christ does not
take his people to heaven as soon as they repent? You
say he leaves them here for their own discipline. True,
but not for that alone. He also leaves them here for
usefulness, that they may make known the glad tidings
to their fellow-sinners. And shall we busy ourselves
here and there, and neglect the very thing for which we
are left in this world of dying men?

2. If we are guilty of this neglect we are also
found false witnesses for God. "Ye are my witnesses,"
said Christ. What are we to witness to? To the truth
of the gospel. And chief among these is that men have
immortal souls to save, and that these souls are lost
without Christ. Do we witness to any such truths when
we suffer souls to go to destruction without a word of
warning or an effort to save them? No, but the very
opposite. In that case we say to men by our lives that
their souls are of very little value, and that if they die in
their sins they run very little risk.

3. I remark again that it is useless to look for any
great awakening of sinners till Christians awake to a
real concern for their souls. If those who see are insensible to the peril in which souls are lying, how shall
the blind be expected to realize it. As well expect a
temperance movement to begin among drunkards, as expect a revival to begin among the ungodly. "These
Christians know more about this matter than we do,"
they reason "and if they are not alarmed for us, why
should we be alarmed for ourselves?

But while this is all true, I cannot dismiss this subject without an earnest word to those before me who are
neglecting their own souls. My friend, if it be true that

no man cares for your soul, there is the more need that
you care for it yourself. You have but one soul to lose
or to save. If you lose it the misery will be yours no
matter on whom you throw the blame. "If thou be wise
thou shalt be wise for thyself but if thou scornest thou
alone shall bear it."

But it is not true that no man cares for your soul.
However it may be with others, One cared for it. He
sought it with many tears. He poured out his blood for
it. If you will go to destruction you must go over the
bleeding body of your Redeemer. How then, when you
have done that can you meet that Redeemer enthroned
upon the judgment seat, and looking upon those pierced
hands attempt to justfy yourself to his face with the plea :
"No man cared for my soul?"

CHRIST MADE PERFECT THROUGH SUF-
FERINGS.

For it became him, for whom are all things, and by whom are all things, in bringing many sons unto glory, to make the Captain of their salvation perfect through sufferings.—Heb. 2:10.

The apostle is here dealing with "the offense of the cross." He is seeking to remove for sincere but wavering Jewish believers, the "stumbling block" which the Jew always found in the conception of a *suffering Messiah*.

Such a conception was so perplexing to them, so foreign to all the ideas in which they had been trained that they evidently felt lingering misgivings about it, even after they became Christians. It is to meet these that the apostle affirms that such a way of redeeming man was every way worthy of God. "*It became Him* for whom are all things and by whom are all things, in bringing many sons unto glory to make the Captain of their salvation perfect through sufferings." It was suitable, it was worthy of God, and harmonious with his perfections, that he who had all ways and all expedients at his disposal, who was not constrained or limited in his choice of methods, should choose just *this* way of lifting up sinful men to a share in his glory.

But with the change and growth of Christian sentiment in the lapse of centuries, it has come about that these words introduced to remove one stumbling-block, have themselves given rise to another. With our firm belief in the absolute divinity, and the faultless perfection at every stage of his earthly life of our glorious

Redeemer, it has come to be not a little perplexing to us that He should be here presented as needing to be *made perfect.* We can easily see that a sinful nature like ours needs the discipline of chastisement to correct its waywardness, that the impure ore needs the refiner's fire to purge away its dross. But *He* was pure gold from the first. What could the refiner's fire do for Him? This is the point for our study this evening: *Christ as our Redeemer made perfect through suffering.* I say Christ as our Redeemer for you notice that he is introduced here not simply by a personal but by an official title, the Captain of our Salvation; that is, the author, or better perhaps the Pioneer of our Salvation. The word here rendered Captain is one seldom used in the New Testament and denotes not as our word captain would suggest, a military officer, but rather one who is at once a leader and a model, breaking the path in which others follow and furnishing the pattern by which they regulate themselves. It is in this capacity for this work, that he who undertook it was perfected by suffering.

1. First of all, he was perfected as *man.* It was assuredly worthy of God to redeem man through man. The first condition for the Son of God in undertaking our case was that he should assume our nature. And throughout this epistle, particularly, you find great stress laid upon this oneness of nature, this full brotherhood between Redeemer and redeemed. This oneness was entire. It is of the utmost importance that we hold fast to the genuine and complete manhood of our Saviour Jesus Christ, and that we never allow his divinity so to overshadow his humanity in our thought that the latter shall cease to be real, or that we shall doubt or lose sight of his full participation in everything that belongs to an *unfallen* humanity. But the idea of

growth, of progress from immaturity to maturity, is inseparable from the idea of manhood. There are two kinds of imperfection by no means to be confounded with each other, the imperfection of blemish, of defect, and the imperfection of immaturity. You pluck an apple from the tree in early summer, and you say: See how perfect it is! No worm has punctured it, no speck can be found on its surface. Divide it with your knife and you will find there all the parts proper to an apple, — the flesh, the core, the seeds. But will you eat it? Will you give it to your children? Will you plant its seeds expecting it to grow? Why not? It is not ripe yet. In that sense it is not perfect. It will take many days of sunshine to soften its pulp, to sweeten its juices, and to mature its seeds so that they can germinate and grow.

You see a babe of six months old crowing on its mother's knee, and you say: There is a physically per-fect child. See how well formed its limbs, how regular its features, how intelligent its expression. It lacks no part, no sense, no faculty. Could you make it trans-parent and study its brain and internal structure, you would very likely find all as perfect as its outward form. But will you give it an ax to wield? Will you bring it a problem for solution? Oh no; it is still an imma-ture babe. It has yet to be make perfect, physically by years of study, spiritually by years of discipline.

Just so Christ was spiritually perfect at every point of his life, perfect as child, perfect as youth, perfect as man. Yet the perfection of the child was not the same as the perfection of the man. There was no sin in the child Jesus, but there was immaturity; and there was advance from this to the maturity of the man who at thirty years of age began to preach the kingdom of God. This is not theory; it is the literal teaching of Scripture.

"And Jesus increased in wisdom and stature and in favor with God and man." It could not be otherwise and Jesus still be true man.

And following out this same thought, if Jesus was perfect as a man at his baptism he was perfect in a still higher sense at his crucifixion. And this highest perfecting was the fruit of the sufferings and struggles of those years of struggle with Jewish unbelief and Pharisaic bitterness. This is exactly what is said a little farther on in this Epistle, (5:8) "Though he were a Son, yet learned he obedience by the things which he suffered." Though he had from the first the filial spirit, the steadfast purpose of obedience, that Spirit was intensified, that purpose of obedience was confirmed and solidified by the discipline of suffering.

You watch a smith tempering a piece of steel. He alternately heats it in the fire, and cools it by a sudden plunge in cold water. For what? Not to purify the metal; that has been done already; but to toughen it that it may be bent double without breaking, so that it may be driven against the flint rock without turning its edge. It is this temper, this toughening of character, which is wrought by the discipline of suffering. And we know no other way in which it can be wrought. Other ways God may have for the angel, for the little child who dies before it has encountered any of the storms of an earthly life. But if so, we know not, nor can we even imagine what they are. No man's character is ever throughly welded, here, till it has been through the fire. There is no robust, stalwart virtue which has not been beaten upon by storms of temptation.

And this was as true of the ideal man Christ Jesus as of any of his brethren. And only then when he was thus perfected as man was he ready for that final victory over the powers of darkness by which he set Satan's captives free. "Though he were a Son, yet learned he obedience by the things which he suffered, *and being made perfect* he became the author of eternal salvation unto all them that obey him."

As our *Example*, again, Christ was made perfect by suffering. This is an important part of his work as Saviour, which is by no means to be overlooked, because it is not the sole or the chief part. Christ saves us by making us holy, and one of the influences by which he makes us holy is the influence of his own holy example. We needed to have the law embodied in a life. We needed to have the ideal manhood set before us in a personal form. In the example of Christ this has been done. And in this sense he is peculiarly the leader, "the pioneer" of our salvation, bringing us to glory by the path of obedience to the Father which he has trodden unfalteringly before us.

But it is easy to see that as an example he must needs grow to perfection. He could not have furnished us the example we need in a single act. Had he appeared from heaven for a single day and then gone back again, that day however perfectly lived, would not have given us the needed example. That example must be a *life*. And it must be a life long enough and varied enough to touch our lives at all vital points. Now one of the most vital points, one of the crises at which we most need the encouraging influence of example, is the experience of suffering. This is a phase of life which we have all to pass through. It is one which peculiarly tries our faith and submission. Of how little use to us in that experience would be the example of one, however pure, however sinless, who had known nothing of sorrow or of struggle, who had been always happy, always prosperous, always outwardly successful and fortunate. Such an example would fail us at the very moment of greatest emergency. And so you find that the appeals to Christ's example in the New Testament are chiefly to this very aspect of it, his endurance of suffering. "Consider Him that endured such contradiction of sinners against himself, lest ye be wearied and faint in your minds." "Christ also suffered for us, leaving us an example that we should follow his steps."

3. But not only was our Redeemer thus made perfect through suffering as man and as example. He was also made perfect as *Propitiation*. We stand here in the presence of a great mystery. The necessity of propitiation in order to forgiveness, I, for one, do not profess to comprehend. Here and there I see a ray of light upon it. But it lies deep in the counsels of the Godhead, one of those things which the angels desire to look into. But the fact is as clear as God's word can make it that a propitiation was demanded, i. e., that something was needed, *not* to *incline* God to forgive, that inclination is as eternal as his fatherhood, but to make it fit, to make it consistent with his attributes for Him to forgive.

Over and over again in language the most varied, does God's word set forth that forgiveness could not be bestowed until in some way the ill desert of sin had been fully manifested and the holiness of God completely vindicated. But this can only be through the suffering of some one for sin. Propitiation and suffering therefore go together. Even had it been possible for Christ to be perfected as man and perfected as example not suffering, he could not have been a perfect propitiation. He could not have been a propitiation at all, had He not "suffered for sins," the just for the unjust. We need a *blood-bought* pardon. Only by another's stripes can we be healed. Call it purchase, call it substituted penalty, call it what you will, the fact

stands sure upon the testimony of the Saviour himself
that not till His body had been broken and His blood
shed could remission of sins be offered in His name.
The Scriptures everywhere link together these two
things, a suffering and an atoning Saviour. All the
sufferings of the Redeemer contributed toward the
efficacy of this propitiatory work, but it was not till the
cross had been endured that He could cry: It is finished, and offer with pierced hand a free pardon to all
who would receive it.

4. Finally; not only was the Captain of our Salvation by his sufferings made perfect as man, made perfect as example, made perfect as propitiation: He was
also made perfect as *Priest*, i. e., as Mediator between
God and man. When we speak of Christ's priesthood
we include under that term all that Christ is now doing
at God's right hand to carry on the work of redemption,
all that he is doing in reclaiming the lost and reconciling them to God, all that he is doing in strengthening
the weak and encouraging the despondent. But in
order to be perfectly qualified for this helpful office, he
must have something to commend him to men's confidence. He must be presented to them in such a way as
to draw out their faith and love. And this he is able to
do because he comes to them as one who has suffered as
they suffer, who has been tried as they are tried, and
who has come off victor through the conflict. A suffering Redeemer appeals to our love and to our confidence
as no other could. "For in that He Himself hath
suffered being tempted he is able also to succor them
that are tempted," (Heb. 2:18). "We have not an high
priest which cannot be touched with the feeling of our
infirmities but was in all points tempted like as we are."
(Heb. 4:15). These two passages distinctly ground
Christ's helpfulness and perfection as a sympathizing

high priest upon his sufferings. Yet there is always
something a little perplexing as we read them. For we
cannot help asking how after all divine knowledge
could gain anything from the teachings of experience.
If Christ was the Son of God what can he have known
of human need after his sorrowful sojourn in this world
that he did not know before?

But the difficulty is relieved when we consider that
it is needful not only that He should be able to sympathize, but to make us feel his sympathy. And to this
end He must have suffered himself. To whom do we
go among our earthly friends in our times of trial. Is
it not to those who have had the same trials? Here
and there you find a man who is justly called "a Son of
Consolation," who is a sort of unordained minister of
comfort to all the children of want and sorrow.
Instinctively the burdened turn to him for relief; the
perplexed and troubled open their hearts to him without
persuasion. And when you come to inquire what it is
that gives him this hold upon men you always find that
he is one who has been through deep waters himself.
This was his ordination. By these experiences he was
prepared for his blessed ministry of comfort.

Just so it is with our great high priest. Whatever
our sorrow we can always go to Him with the certainty
that He knows all about it, with the assurance of
sympathy which comes from the knowledge that however deep the waters through which we are passing He
has passed through deeper still. He is a perfect
Refuge, a perfect Support; and He was *made* perfect
through suffering.

Thus as Man, as Example, as Propitiation, and as
Priest was the Captain of our Salvation made perfect
through suffering.

It only remains that we linger for a moment in conclusion on those opening words: " *It became Him.*" It was worthy of God when he would bring sinners to glory to do it through the mediation of a suffering Saviour.

It *became* Him; for even if we suppose some other method had been possible, no other could have so gloriously manifested His love. Where else than in the sufferings of His own Son could God have given us a true measure of His condescension and the intensity of His yearning toward the work of His own hands!

It became Him; for no other way would have been so consistent with His Fatherhood. Suppose a choice had been open between such a method as this, and some other more external and mechanical, would not God as a Father, have chosen that which would show men most of His heart, and come home to them with the most force of personal appeal?

It became Him; for no other way is it conceivable that He could, so fully, have shown us the intense evil of sin. When we see it reaching in its effect even to the throne of God and dragging down the eternal Son of God from the bosom of the Father to a temporary share in the suffering which it has brought upon the race, then only do we realize how monstrous and how terrible is the thing of which we are so ready to make light.

Two questions now, growing out of this theme suggest themselves for our earnest thought.

If it became the infinite and Holy God to prepare for us a Saviour through such costly processes of suffering as this, how does it become us sinners to treat such a Saviour?

Remember, thoughtless hearer, ready now to dismiss this offer of salvation, as you have so often done before, with Felix's promise of attention at some more convenient season, it is no uncostly gift with which you thus trifle. He whom you are content to leave thus to stand at your heart's unopened door went through fire and water to rescue your soul. For that He wrestled in the wilderness with the arch-enemy, for that He was wrung with anguish in the garden, for that He cried upon the tree, "My God, my God, why hast thou forsaken me?"

Was it worthy of God to give up His Son to such suffering for you, was it worthy of Christ to go through all this that He might qualify Himself to be the Saviour of your soul, and is it worthy of a man to treat such a Saviour with neglect? Oh, surely there is but one becoming reception for such a Saviour as this, and that is the reception which enthrones Him forever in the contrite heart, and serves him with all the powers of a consecrated life.

2. And then the other question. If it became Him for whom are all things and by whom are all things; to make the captain of our salvation perfect through suffering, how shall we expect the saved themselves to be made perfect? If the one man who through his whole life was holy, harmless, undefiled, and separate from sinners, could, nevertheless, attain the perfection of His victorious manhood only by this discipline of trial and temptation, shall we whose very natures are stained through and through with sin think to be made perfect at any less cost, or by an easier process?

Christ was the Pioneer of our Salvation. He opened the path by which the "many sons" are to be brought to glory. There is no other path to glory for us than that which is marked by the prints of His bleeding feet. It was a hard and thorny path to Him. Shall we expect it to be made smooth and strewn with flowers for us?

Always, always these two things are put together, — a share in Christ's sufferings, and a share in His glory. The one is never to be separated from the other.

But then there is this other precious thought, that if we thus share in Christ's sufferings, we shall come to share also in the glory to which they lead, but, what is better, in the *fruit* which they bring. If there is a sense in which Christ's sufferings were unique and separate from all other suffering in God's universe, there is also a sense in which they are the pattern of what every one must pass through who would be made a helper and a comforter to others. There is but one anointing for that holy priesthood. It is the anointing of pain and sorrow. Do you remember with what eagerness Paul seemed to reach out after his Lord's cup of suffering that he too might drink of the same? And why? That he too might have some share in that unspeakable joy of leading many sons of God unto glory. "Therefore," he exclaims, "I endure all things for the elect's sakes that they may also obtain the salvation which is in Jesus Christ with eternal glory." Ah, was not that worth while?

Dear friend, has God put the cup of suffering to your lips? Has He laid the cross upon you? Take this high consolation — there is none higher — for your own, that He who thus prepared the Captain of your salvation for His great work is preparing you for some share in that same blessed ministry of healing and help. He is initiating you into the holy priesthood of comforters. He is conferring upon you an ordination that no human hands can give, and presently He will send you forth with a heart throbbing with sympathy, and lips touched with the fire of love to comfort others with the comfort wherewith you yourself have been comforted of God.

MEDIOCRITY.

"And likewise he that had received two, he also gained other two."—Matt. 25: 17.

This parable recognizes, without pausing to debate or justify it, the universal fact of *inequality* in the distribution of God's gifts. Look where we may, this inequality confronts us. In surroundings, in opportunities, in health, in physical powers, in intellectual keenness and grasp, in gifts of genius, in everything that tends to happiness and honor in life, men enter life with the most various equipment. One is born in a filthy cellar, to an inheritance of squalor and misery, another enters life in a home filled with all comforts and refinements. One is doomed to struggle from birth against the hopeless odds of inherited disease, while another begins his career endowed with the soundness and vigor of an infant Hercules. To one, study is the weary, ineffectual struggle of a dull mind with problems that perpetually elude its grasp, to another, the exhilarating play of a keen intellect which finds only pleasure in the exercise of its strength. A Raphael at twenty, paints pictures which bring the world to his feet, while another goes from master to master, from school to school, and labors through a life-time of painstaking diligence, only to spoil every canvas he touches and win the derision of the critics for his pains.

So the Sovereign Giver of all has disposed it, and who shall dispute his decree? Whatever men may say about *election* as a religious doctrine, the principle of a diffeaence put between men by God's sovereign disposal, a difference with which their merit has nothing to do, and for which he gives no reasons, runs all through life. There is no man who does not find himself hedged in from the cradle to the grave by limitations absolutely fixed by the measure of endowment and opportunity with which it pleased God that he should enter upon the race of life.

Now the result of this inequality is that most of us find ourselves, when we come to measure ourselves against our fellowmen, in the competitions of life, just where this man who received the two talents found himself, somewhere between the extremes, that is, in a position of *mediocrity*, neither extraordinarily gifted, nor extraordinarily lacking, neither giants, in other words, nor dwarfs, but, as the phrase goes, just " average men."

And yet though it is the very nature of the case the lot of the immense majority of the human race, this lot of mediocrity is one against which we all more or less rebel. We chafe under it as one of the hard conditions of life, and even find excuse for not doing what we might with the two talents entrusted to us, in the fact that they are but two, and not five like some fellow-servant's.

Mediocrity! The very word has the sound of a reproach. We say in a tone of disparagement concerning this one or that one : " He never rises above midiocrity." If this be the fault of his own indolence it is indeed a reproach. But what if God never meant him to rise above mediocrity? What if He himself did not raise him above mediocrity in the measure of endowment with which He sent him into the world? 1 think we may find in this subject of *Mediocrity* a theme of practical value for us as Christians to reflect upon to-day.

I. In the first place then, let me remind you that in the nature of the case the vast majority of the race must needs be mediocre people. Mediocrity is the unavoidable result of the variety in uniformity which is the underlying plan of the whole creation. The trees of a pine forest are all alike, and yet unlike. There is a uniform type or plan tending to the production of a tree of a certain shape and size ; yet each tree has its own individuality. And the result of this variety in uniformity is, that, while here and there a tall tree will stand out above the rest and here and there a short one fall below them, the great mass will vary but little, one way or the other, from an average line which marks the height of the forest.

The only escape from this phenomenon of mediocrity, would be by the sacrifice of variety to an *absolute, unvarying* uniformity. The condition called mediocrity, in other words, could be made to disappear by the introduction of absolute *monotony* in its place, and in no other way. If all men were equally brilliant, equally strong, equally well-balanced, there would be an end of eminence and of mediocrity at once, and we should have a world like a boy's company of pewter soldiers, all run in the same mould. This would be no gain in interest and picturesqueness of life certainly. It may well be questioned whether it could be any more of a gain in wholesomeness, in intellectual and moral vigor and development.

Opinions differ as to landscapes. I have heard some men say that to them a level prairie with neither hill nor tree was more beautiful than the Alps. But the general consent of mankind still awards the palm both in beauty and in healthfulness to the landscape diversified with mountain and valley, hill and plain. There is a significance in that phrase " a *dead* level " by which we characterize the absence of inequalities. Such a level is " dead," in more senses than one. But if there are mountains, there must be valleys ; if there are hills there must be plains.   Raise all alike and you have but a table-land instead of a prairie, the one is flat and monotonous as the other.

Society is like a landscape, unspeakably better and richer for "the diversities of gifts" which it presents in such endless variety.   Yet among these diversities eminence in any direction must needs be rare, else would it cease to be eminence.   The majority cannot rise above the humbler levels of mediocrity.   For again we must remember that mediocrity is a sliding scale.   What seems eminence within a narrow horizon, becomes mediocrity the moment the horizon is broadened.

Mt. Mansfield (at which I used to gaze in my boyhood) is a monarch as he stands among his fellows of the Green Mountain range, but put him with his 4,200 ft. of elevation, by the side of the mountains of the world, the Alps, the Andes, the Rockies, and he is a very humble and commonplace mountain after all.

Shall we then say that the many are sacrificed to the few,—that mediocrity exists simply as a *foil* to eminence? This seems to me to have been the idea of the Greek philosophy.   The multitude was to toil and spin that philosophers might study and scintillate.   But a more thoughtful view of life shows that the few exist rather for the many.   The mountain pierces the clouds and confronts the storms, that from its sides may burst the springs whose streams make the valleys laugh with verdure and the meadows teem with flocks.   It is on the plains that the world's harvests are reaped.   So it is by the many, the unnamed, unpraised multitude of "commonplace" men and women, that the world's great work is done.

Officers are needful to an army, but an army of officers would be a laughing-stock.   It is the common soldier who does the hard fighting that wins victories. It is the solid phalanx with fixed bayonets that is irresistible.

The solid fabric of civilization does not owe half so much to the men who make speeches and go to congress as it owes to the men who follow the plow in the furrow and the women who bear and rear the children at home. These are commonplace things but they *make the world*. And it is well that it should be so. There is safety in such life, if there is no glory. Few can bear the steady glare of the footlights. To be always on exhibition is a severe moral strain. For the most of us it is better that our work be done quietly and with as little of the theatrical as possible.

2. Well, we can agree to this without much trouble ; we can see that mediocrity is a necessary and useful thing in a perfect world ; we can admit that a world in which all were heroes and generals, poets and prodigies, would be a queer world to live in ; we are quite satisfied that the majority of the Lord's servants should receive but two or three talents, some of them even but one, provided only *we* can have five.

We have no quarrel with the principle of inequality, so long as that principle is so applied that it enables us to look down on others. It is only when, from the height of an eminence we have striven in vain to reach, they look down upon us, that it is hard to bear. There is something in us which chafes at the consciousness of being lost sight of in a herd. The desire to excel, the love of preeminence is rooted deep in human nature. Competition, the struggle to be first, is almost the first law of life. It is a useful instinct. Though few can realize their ambition, though but one in a thousand attains the eminence to which the thousand have alike aspired, still the whole thousand advance farther and

achieve more than if no such strife to be first had urged
them on.

A company of swimmers were enjoying themselves
in the ocean at some distance from shore, when a friend
who stood watching them from the beach, saw some
distance beyond them the sharp dorsal fin of a shark
protruding above the water. Not wishing to confuse
and paralyze the swimmers by telling them of their danger, yet eager to bring them to land as quickly as possible he snatched his watch from his pocket, and holding
it up cried, " I will give this to the one who first reaches
the shore." Supposing themselves challenged to a proof of
their skill, the swimmers struck out lustily, and reached the
shore before the shark overtook them. But *one* gained
the offered prize; but when they turned and saw the
danger from which they had escaped, those who lost
were more than consoled for their disappointment.

So it is that in life, for one who gains or has the
power to gain prizes of distinction for which so many
seek, hundreds are saved by the endeavor to gain it, from
miseries of ignorance, poverty, and even vice, to which
they had else inevitably fallen victims.

In youth we all hope to *excel*. We dream of some
eminent attainment, some rare achievement, some heroic
deed, which shall set us far above the common level. So
be it ! Properly curbed it is a wholesome ambition.   I
would not give much for the future of the youth who had
never felt it. And yet, almost without exception, we are
doomed to disappointment. For a time perhaps, we may
easily distance the little circle with which we measure
ourselves ; but as we grow older and measure ourselves
against larger and larger numbers of our fellows in tasks
more and more serious and difficult, as from the top of
each height that we succeed in scaling we discover others
farther and farther away,—the conviction is at last forced

upon us that we are not and never can be anything more than mediocre people, after all,—much better endowed, much more successful, doubtless than some, perhaps than many others ; but not better than thousands upon thousands of our race, not preeminent enough in any sphere to be conspicuous above the multitude of others whose measure of ability and achievement is fully equal to our own.

It seems a hard fate—to see others climbing the heights we hoped to climb, winning the prizes we hoped to win, shining with the brilliancy of stars of the first magnitude, and to accept for ourselves the lot of the undistinguished, the ordinary, the commonplace. It brings a sharp temptation, a temptation which appeals with power to the bad side of the universal desire to excel— the temptation, viz. to conclude that our work, because not conspicuous, is not worth doing,—the temptation to imitate, not the wisdom of this servant who received the two talents but the folly of that other who received but one, and refuse to turn to any account at all an endowment which is not large enough to yield brilliant results. What use, we exclaim, in wearing life away in the performance of these commonplace tasks which the world would never miss if they were undone, which it will never praise be they done never so well? No doubt there is something discouraging here. As Bishop Brooks has well said, the hero's is not the hardest task, for he works in the eye of the multitude, with their huzzas to cheer him on. Harder is the task of the common man who works on unheeded, with no consciousness of unusual achievement to sustain him, and no expectation of applause at the end.

3. What antidote can we find to this disheartening influence of the consciousness of mediocrity? The antidote lies in the very thought suggested by this parable,

the thought of *the relation of our life-work to God*, first as
being his appointment, second as being for his glory,
third as being under his eye.

a. First as being *his appointment*. The *sovereignty
of God*, once grasped with hearty acquiescence, is a wonderful moral tonic. It puts iron into the blood. It has
made the men who have believed it profoundly, always
and everywhere men of *grit*, men of moral fibre; staunch
as heart of oak to face the hard things in life. "May I
not do what I will with mine own?" "Shall the thing
formed say to him that formed it, why hast thou made
me thus?" are the questions which have power to silence
repining and rebuke envy. "God wills it," is, to one who
recognizes God's absolute authority and believes in his
perfect wisdom, a sufficient reply to all questionings concerning the fewness of the talents with which God has
been pleased to entrust him. You and I are soldiers on
the battle-field of life. As such it does not lie with us to
select our posts or choose our duty. If the commander
bids us lead a company in a brilliant charge which will
cover our names with glory, it is well. If he assigns
us to unnoticed duty at the rear, or bids us take our
place in line with a hundred others to receive a cavalry
charge and roll in the dust with the unnamed multitude
of the wounded and dying when it is over, again, *it is
well*.

b. For, again, we are not giving this warfare in our
own name or for our own glory. If the disposal is God's,
the cause is God's also. The servants who received the
talents, whether five or two or one, received them not to
enrich themselves withal, but to administer for their
master. To him each task had its value, the small and
obscure no less than the conspicuous.

This is the evil side so rarely absent from the ambition to excel, that that ambition centers so largely in

self. That by which we can win glory for ourselves we account worth doing, and nothing else. In a race, those who see that they are hopelesssly distanced, soon drop out. Why should they run it to a finish, when no glory can come to them as the result. Not so the mowers in the hayfield. He who cannot cross the field with the swiftest, still swings his scythe as he can ; for he knows *his* labor, too, will count in the harvest, and share, according to its sum in the reward. If life were a race run for glory, as many seem to take it, here too, it might be wise for the slow of foot to drop out. But life is a far other thing than that. It is serious work under God's leadership, which aims at his glory in a harvest of eternal value, in the bringing in of an everlasting kingdom, and in which each laborer, conspicuous or unnoticed, each task, great or small, has its distinct plan and worth. So that to one who has come to look at life from this point of view, to live it with this thought of God's glory as its end, this whole question of eminence or mediocrity drops out of the account. To him the important thing is the *work done*, not the glory reflected on the worker.

Charles Kingsley, in all the ardor of youth, thrilling with energy and conscious of intellectual power, finds himself set down on a bit of English moorland, scattered over which, in three little hamlets are some 8oo souls mainly stolid, lumbering farmhands and laborers, among them all not a grown man or woman who can read or write. And is this to be his work? Surely there is not much chance for honor or distinction here! A mere country rector, one among hundreds, that is all. There are men in the ministry who are spoiled for life by such an experience as that. What is the use, they say to themselves, of trying to do anything or be anybody in a place like this? Kingsley has told us how he felt about it. " I will confess to you," he says, "that in those first heats of youth this little patch of moorland in which I have struck roots as firm as the wild fir trees do, looked, at moments, rather like a prison than a palace,—that my foolish young heart would sigh ; oh, that I had wings,—not as a dove, to fly home to its nest and croodle there, but as an eagle to swoop away over land and sea in a rampant and self-glorifying fashion on which I now look back as something altogether unwholesome and undesirable. It is not learnt in a day, the golden lesson of the old collect, to love the thing which is commanded and to desire that which is promised,—not in a day ; but in fifteen years one can spell out a little of its worth."

And so accepting this obscure commonplace task in this spirit of desire to love the thing which was commanded, and doing it as unto the Lord, and not as unto men, he made of that prison a palace, as he himself bears joyful witness, transformed that golden community into a community of intelligent and reverent worshipers, and found his lowly task, accepted first for duty's sake, rich in unlooked for joys and abounding in soul-satisfying rewards.

c. And lastly, the antidote to this discontent bred of the consciousness of mediocrity lies in the thought that we are doing our work *under God's eye*. It takes no eminence of gifts to win *his* attention. He watches as closely and reviews as carefully the work of the servant to whom he gives two talents, as of him who has received five. For what to him is the difference between five talents and two which seems so immense to the servants themselves ? The loftiest pinnacle of human fame to Him is but the summit of an anthill, scarce visible above the plain on which it stands.

To him *fidelity*, in tasks great or small, is the one concern. For this he watches ; on this he smiles ; and this and this alone he will reward.   The thought of his interest and commendation can well console us for that absence of human attention and praise which is inseparable from the common, every day lot.

To him it matters not how splendid or how humble the endowment.   What he asks is that we make the most of it.   If we do that, then whether we have received five talents or two, or even but one, we shall be alike sure of a reward which will lift us to a glory above the highest pinnacle of earthly praise, and ensure to us an increase of gifts, an enlargement of opportunities beyond the scope of the loftiest earthly ambition ; the reward of hearing from the lips of Him who fixed the grade and set the measure of our work the word of approval : " Well done, good and faithful servant ! Thou hast been faithful over a few things ; I will make thee ruler over many things.   Enter thou into the joy of thy Lord."

DEBORAH'S ASTROLOGY.

They fought from heaven.   The stars in their courses fought against Sisera.—Judges 5: 20.

Have we then astrology in the Bible? Were our fathers right after all who believed a few centuries ago that human destiny was linked in some strange manner to the movements of the stars, that the life of every man was ruled by the influence of the planet under whose ascendant it began, and checkered with good or evil fortune according as the planet formed conjunctions with its fellows, now baleful, now benign?

Abraham, we know, when at the call of God he forsook the Chaldees, turned his back on a nation of star-gazers. Indeed from these very kinsmen of Abraham it was that, centuries later, through the medium of the Saracens our forefathers themselves learned this occult science, (and learned it so well that some of its technical phrases still have currency in our daily speech.) But the children of Abraham learned no such arts either from their father or their father's God. It was no such vain superstition as this which drew from victorious Deborah this exultant shout. In truth it was no defined influence of the stars which was present to her mind. We must not forget that we are here with poetry, and oriental poetry at that, and nothing more can safely be assumed than an intention of the poet to declare in the strongest possible form of speech, that Sisera, as the enemy of God, against God in the endeavor to oppress God's people, had all things in God's creation, whether things on earth or things in heaven, even to the very stars in their courses, arrayed against him.

But this was not mere poetry. It was truth, literal and exact truth. The imagination of the poet even in this loftiest flight has been quite overtaken by the patiently advancing steps of science.

I ask your attention this evening then, to the truth, veiled under this sublime poetic imagery ; that *he who opposes God has nothing less than the resistance of the entire universe to overcome.* The stars fought against Sisera because Sisera fought against God. But there are other ways of fighting against God than by leading forth an armed host to oppress and persecute God's people. Every man fights against God who undertakes to accomplish what God disapproves,—whose ends conflict, *wittingly or unwittingly*, with God's ends,—whose life says to God. reversing the words of Jesus in the Garden ; " *My* will not thine be done."

That man fights against **God**, for instance, who seeks to found an empire in duplicity and bloodshed ; that man fights against God who seeks preferment by tortuous methods of political chicane ; that man fights against God who seeks to make a fortune or rise to power by corrupt use of the machinery of a city government ; that man fights against God who attempts to build up a successful business by methods other than those of strict integrity ; that man fights against God who seeks to give currency to a false doctrine in religion or a false principle in government.

You and I, my friends, whenever we do these or the like of these things ; whenever we aid or abet those who do them ; whenever, in any way, we seek what God disapproves, or seek ends in themselves worthy by *methods* which God disapproves ; plant ourselves in opposition to *him*. and in so doing array against ourselves the resis-

tance, not passive merely, but active,—resistance which
may properly be called *a fight*,—of the whole material
universe. Observe, I say, the *material* universe. In the
world of mind there are powers of darkness which fight
on the side of such a man. But the world of matter and
of force, in all its grand totality,—earth, water, air, fire,
sun, moon, and stars, gravity, magnetism, heat,—all
things and all forces that are,—combines in one unceasing movement toward his defeat and destruction.

To see that this is no unfounded or extravagant
representation we have only to consider that stupendous
truth which it is the glory of science in our day to have
set forth in such clear light as it never stood in before :
the oneness of nature. Take e. g., the new doctrine
known to scientific men under the name of *"correlation
of forces."* The limits of this correlation are not yet
fully defined, nor is this the place to expound them in
detail. But without attempting to do this, it is enough
to say that many forms of force which were formerly
supposed to be quite distinct, such as light, heat, electricity, the momentum of moving bodies, the expansive
force of steam and gases, and the like, are now known
to be so many interchangeable forms of one thing, viz.
motion ; and that instead of force being "generated and
lost," as it used to be said, in the various natural and
mechanical processes that were all the time going on,
there is really only a change from one form of force to
another ; as when the heat of a fire is transmuted into
the expansive form of steam, and that into the motion of
a fly-wheel, which in its turn moves the flying lathes or
spindles of a factory.

A step farther in this direction shows us that the
ceaseless activity and change which is going on upon the
earth is kept up by the steady supply of this force of motive power, in the form of light and heat, from the sun.

What the heat is to the body, keeping in motion a current of blood through every part without which the vital processes could not go on ;—what the sea is to the world, supplying in the form of clouds the water which, descending as rain and gathering into streams, waters the crops, turns the mill-wheels, and bears the commerce of the nations, that is the sun to the earth, and to all the planets which circle around it. There is not a form of motion or of life that is not dependent upon its rays. Were its fire put out every living thing would die ; the seas would freeze to their very depths, and the bare earth, one mass of rock and ice, its very vapors congealed, its air stirred by no breeze, its echoes waked by no sound, would go careering on its way through night wrapped in the silence of eternal death.

But not only is the earth thus linked with the sun into the inseparable unity of a single system ; the moon also at whose bidding the tides ebb and flow ; the planets that, circling with it round a common center, by their attractions influence its motions, and thus its seasons, temperature, climate, are all parts of that same unity. This whole planet is, as it were, a single organism pervaded with a common life.

But surely in speaking of the universe as a unit, we must stop here. Surely when we have reached the orbit of the outmost planet we have reached a rim that shuts us in,—sun, planets, satellites together, an isolated island in the great deep of space, with no relations to what lies beyond,—nothing to bridge the chasm of emptiness which separates us from the fixed star. Nay, not so. Across this chasm messages come and go on a bridge of light, and by the chains of that subtle thing that we call gravity this island of ours is securely moored to all those other countless isles that crowd the shoreless ocean. Here, too, science is delighting us with ever fresh revelations. 'Tis but a few years since an instrument, the spectroscope, was invented, by which the messages that light brings us from those worlds so immeasurably far away, can be interpreted; and thus we have learned to recognize the presence in those distant orbs of the very same substances, the iron, the sodium, hydrogen, and so on, of which our own mountains and seas are composed.

In our own day, too, astronomers have learned that as the planets circle around the sun, so the sun itself is moving among the stars, swayed by some mightier attraction, in cycles that must be measured by æons around some center yet unknown; a center which devout astronomers, like Mitchell, have sometimes conceived of as the very pivot of the universe, the throne of the Creator. Yet sublime as is such a thought, it is more likely that that far away star itself, together with all the glittering host that stud *our* sky, forms but a subordinate part, a wheel within a wheel of a still vaster universe, the bounds of which thought itself faints in the attempt to reach.

But why dwell on these revelations of physics and astronomy? Simply to bring in as strong relief as possible the *unity of nature*, the oneness of this vast creation of God, to make not only clear, but vivid. if I may, the truth that this little earth, significant as indeed it is,— mere speck of dust in the wide waste of shining sands with which space is strewn—is yet the focus of influences radiated to it from every corner of the universe, even from the remotest star.

The error of the astrologer was not in his notion that the heavenly bodies influence human affairs, but in his notion of the nature of those influences, in supposing them occult, magical, supernatural. In rational, natural and to a large extent discoverable ways they do influence us daily. Not in those rare cases alone when sun and

moon stand still that a Joshua may complete the rout of
the enemies of Jehovah, or a star in the East guides the
wise men from the Chaldean plains to the cradle of the
new-born King, are these shining ones made the ministers of God's Providence. When the silent sunbeams in
the faces of one of two contending armies defeat the
plans of a skillful leader, when the pole star's steady light
guides the discoverer on his way, when the moon brings
in her wake the tide that floats a stranded bark, then it
is that the stars in their courses become executors of the
purpose of God.

Mark you, it is the stars *in their courses that play
thus* their frequent part in aiding or in crossing human
plans, not miraculously arrested or hastened or turned
aside, but moving steadily forward in the appointed path
which from their creation they have held unswerving.
Thus not the stars only but the winds and seas and clouds,
thus all nature in its uniformity acting always and only
in conformity to its unvarying constitution is still working out in the life of man the purposes of God.

I do not overlook the objection to all this, arising
out of this very uniformity. But let us defer the consideration of this objection till we have considered the
unity of nature in another aspect. This unity is a *unity
in time* as well as in *space*. In other words, just as all
worlds, all created things, are bound together by the
forces of nature into one whole, so all events that have
happened, are happening, and are yet to happen, are
linked by the law of cause and effect into a single chain,
rather let us say into a network of chains, crossing and
recrossing, uniting and dividing, so as to form a single
web, stretching without a break from the dawn of creation to the last syllable of recorded time. The events of
history must be looked at, not as so many distinct drops
of a falling shower, but as the drops of one broad, un-

broken current issuing from the throne of God and merging in the ocean of eternity.

It is a mistake therefore, to regard any event, or group of events, as standing by itself, disconnected from other events or groups. It is a mistake to speak of one fact as the cause of another in such a way as though the latter had no other cause. A profound theologian has called attention to this error in these words : "The talk so often heard about great events from small causes is a mere play of fancy, idle, but not so surely harmless, inasmuch as it withdraws the attention from that universal connection of things in which the cause really lies."

The practice here condemned is one familiar to us all. We speak thus, proverbially, of "great oaks from little acorns." But the acorn is no more the cause of the oak than is the foregoing oak of which the acorn itself is a product.

Just consider what an acorn is. Consider that it took an oak to produce it, weeks of sunshine and rain to mature it, that earth and air were both laid under contribution to furnish materials for it, and that even so it cannot produce another oak without the aid again of earth and sun and dew and rain, toiling with the little germ for years. Not a great result from a small cause, but one small part of the result of the unceasing labor of great causes, is the majestic tree which we admire. And this instance from the natural world represents fairly the fact regarding human affairs. Then, too, we are accustomed to speak of the merest trifles as effecting the most enormous changes, sometimes even as changing the whole course of history. But the trifles in question are themselves but parts of the result of previous events—if you please of the whole previous course of history, and again these trifles would not have the effect we ascribe to them but for the co-operation of a great many conditions

which are just as truly part of the cause as that to which
we arbitrarily apply the name, since to change any one
of them would just as surely change the effect. We can
all of us recall instances, if not of our own experience,
certainly within the range of our observation, where a
very little thing, the merest accident, as we say, an un-
expected encounter with a friend in the street, the sudden
occurrence of some text of Scripture, a bit of paper spied
in an out of the way corner, the flight of a bird, the falling of a leaf, the picking up of a pin—has seemed to
change the current of a life. But none of these things
occurred itself as it did without a cause, without a net-
work of causes, in fact, so intricate that omniscience
might trace it. Nor would any of them have had such
effects, happening to another person under other circumstances. These attendant circumstances, the character
and state of mind of the person, and the foregoing events,
must all be taken together before we fairly arrive at the
cause of the events which seem so important.

There is a book entitled "The Fifteen decisive Battles of the World," wherein are described fifteen great
battles, by which the destiny of nations and the subsequent course of human history seems to have been
changed. Yet a writer in the columns of some news-
paper a few years ago showed clearly enough that the
battle of Bennington—a mere skirmish, we may almost
say, between a British foraging party and a handful of
Green Mountain Boys, should be reckoned as a sixteenth
in this list, since it decided the Battle of Yorktown.
which, as virtually decisive of American Independence,
is reckoned among the fifteen. And why not? In
such a process, where are we to stop? Who is to say
what have been and what have not been decisive battles?
Rather, was there ever a battle fought that was not decisive, could we but trace with the eye of omniscience all

the effects that flowed out from it in every direction?
There is absolutely no limit to the illustrations that
might be given of this subject; but enough for our purpose. Now for the application.

This one great system of things, this universe that
has been, is, and shall be, a vast, enduring, organic
whole, one without a break, this is God's *instrument*.
For his ends it was made. Its ponderous machinery
moves in execution of his plans. In this system man is
placed with the power of choosing his own ends. If he
chooses God's ends as his own, he has all this vast
machinery on his side. If he chooses ends that clash
with God's, he has it all against him, and its whole momentum must be overcome before he can succeed. What
a railway train is to him who takas his place in it, wishing to go just where it is going, that is the universe to
him who seeks God's ends. What the same train moving at full speed would be to him who, taking his stand
in front of it, should attempt to turn it about, that it
might carry him in an opposite direction, that is the universe to him who seeks ends other than God's.

For since nature is one it must be all for, or all
against. Since it is God's it must be all for his friends
and against his enemies.

And now with this oneness of nature in view we are
prepared to notice the difficulty before referred to, viz.
that as a matter of fact we find nature in helping or hin-
dering man's design quite indifferent to the goodness or
badness of them,—that the friendly veil of night is spread
as often over the thief as over the refugee ; that the same
unsetting star and the same favoring winds that guided
the Mayflower, guided also the slave-ship to our new-
world coast ; that the same remorseless flames devoured
Chicago's churches with her gambling hells, and overwhelmed in a common ruin the upright, liberal dealer

and the grasping knave ; that whether the sun's blinding
rays defeat the one or the other army depends not at all
on the cause at issue but solely on the time of day and
the position of the battalions. This is all true. So, long
ago, the perplexed philosopher complained that "all
things come alike to all," and many a thoughtful mind
since his day has stumbled at that stumbling-stone.

But the solution lies in that very view of nature as
one whole which we have been developing. This seeming confusion arises from viewing events piece-meal, dis-
regarding their relations to the one great whole. It is no
part of God's purpose that at every step, in every instant, right should triumph and wrong should fail ; that
every good deed should be rewarded, and every evil deed
punished on the spot. Christ himself declares that God
makes his sun to rise on the evil and on the good, and
sends rain on the just and on the unjust. This seeming
injustice, this delay of justice—makes up a part of our
probation here. In this very thing, therefore, nature is
but God's instrument. And when this ceases to be his
purpose, when in his wisdom the time arrives to bring to
nought evil counsel, he knows how to do it, and to do it
through the instrumentality of nature without the slight-
est interference with her unvarying laws.

And be sure that time is *coming*.

> "Though the mills of God grind slowly
> Yet they grind exceedingly small.
> Though with patience he stands waiting,
> With exactness grinds he all."

But if still it is said that God's plans develope so
slowly that meanwhile there is a chance for any amount
of success and triumph in fighting against him,—if it
is said that greedy men do get wealth, ambitious men
power, and bad men of every sort their wicked ends, in
defiance of God ; let it be remembered that "the tri-

umphing of the wicked is short," and that inexorable
nature, if she does not triumph over them before, will
very soon triumph over their graves. Thither the robber
cannot carry his gold. There the usurper cannot wear
his crown.

And as with themselves, so with the works they leave
behind them. These, too, must all wax old and perish.
The same inexorable nature will not rest till it has oblit-
erated them all. Every revolution of those mighty
wheels unravels a thread of the web which it took a life-
time to weave. And this is real defeat. Consciously or
tacitly all men build for eternity. It would have been
small gain to Sisera to have won his battle with Israel
with the certainty that the next day or the next year he
must fight it over again and lose it. Let not appearances
deceive you then. When you make the stars in their
courses do your bidding, when you can stop the earth in
her career, pluck the moon from the sky, and quench
the light of the sun, then, and not till then, may you
hope to win enduring victories fighting against God.

Is this what you are doing my friend? Oh, then, be-
think you how near at hand is the night when these
revolving stars shall look down upon your grave! Cease
building breast-works against the ocean which the next
tide must sweep away, and set your life in harmony with
the music of the spheres. Plant it so in the line of God's
purposes that you may triumph over nature in her last
triumph over man. Cease pulling down God's building
in the vain hope to rear with the stones some miserable
monument to your own glory which the mighty torrent
of events moving in the eternal channels of God's purpose will soon sweep away, and build with God, that so
your work may remain, glorified forever in that fair city
which shall stand unmoved when the heavens themselves
shall be rolled together as a scroll.

But if this theme has thus its warning, it has also, for the friends of truth and right its mighty inspiration. Deborah and Barak and the people of the Lord who fought with them sang this song of triumph after a hard-fought battle. You may be in the thick of the fight to-day, my hearer, and to you it may seem that things move very slowly and that Satan wages still a most successful war. Have patience! Wait! The stars still swing onward in their courses, the great wheels of the universe are ever turning, and presently the hour of your deliverance will strike. "It is good for a man to both hope and quietly wait for the salvation of God." What though you do see evil triumphant and unchecked in the walks of trade, in the pursuits of politics, in the places of power? What though a foe assail you of tenfold Sisera's prowess, and with ten thousand times his host, and though the battle has lasted long and you are tired and faint? Yet wait! The hour is at hand when all this shall be reversed! And when the fullness of the time is come, when the favorable conjunction of the stars take place, when the right point is reached in this great unfolding which since the beginning of time has been going on, some weak woman, it may be, and with a hammer and a nail will finish the work. Behold the husbandman waiteth for the precious fruit of the earth, and hath long patience for it, until he receive the early and latter rain. Be ye also patient ; stablish your hearts ; for the coming of *the Lord* draweth nigh.

THE ALLEGED WASTE OF FOREIGN MIS-
SIONS.

To what purpose is this waste? —Matt. 26:8.

Comparing John's account of this incident with that of Matthew it is plain that this question was asked by different persons for different reasons. John speaks only of Judas as the fault-finder and tells us plainly what his motive was. "This he said not that he cared for the poor, but because he was a thief, and had the bag, and bare what was put therein."

Matthew gives to understand that the disciples generally chimed in with the murmur, yet certainly they neither shared in nor suspected its real inspiration. The criticism had a plausible sound, and they evidently caught it up and echoed it in mere thoughtlessness.

It did seem like a waste, when there were so many hungry and naked ones whom it would have clothed and fed, to make this lavish expenditure as the mere expression of a love which might have been shown in some less costly way. Nevertheless, Jesus himself did not so look upon it. He promptly silenced both classes of objectors with the words: "Why trouble ye the woman? for she had wrought a good work upon me. Let her alone. She had done what she could."

In our own day the question is often repeated in circumstances like these. "To what purpose is this waste," the question is often asked, even by sincere follow. ers of Christ, concerning various forms of self-sacrifice,

and of expenditure of life and treasure, in Christ's name —
to what purpose is this waste when the same expenditure
might have been made to do so much more good in
some other way. Especially is it said of the expenditure of life and treasure in the work of *foreign missions*,
"to what purpose is this waste" when there are so
many ·poor at home to be cared for, and so many
heathen at home to be brought to Christ? When a
youthful Bishop Hannington, on the threshold of the
service for Africa to which he had given his life, falls
a victim to the rage of jealous savages, instantly the
finger of criticism is pointed, "to what purpose is this
waste" when the same zeal expended in behalf of
England's unchurched masses might have been crowned
with years of fruitfulness.

When our own church calls for a million of dollars
to be expended in carrying out her marching orders,
"Go ye into all the world and preach the Gospel to
every creature," we hear it again. To what purpose, —
when there are such multitudes still unevangelized in
our great cities, and such fields yet unoccupied in our
own newly peopled states.

Now, too, as of old, this question is asked by different classes of objectors for different reasons and in a
totally different spirit. It is asked by many from
motives as sinister as those of Judas. When the testimony of travelers and residents in foreign lands to the
waste and failure of missions is glibly quoted as conclusive, it is forgotten how far from disinterested is much
of this testimony. It is not to be wondered at·that men
of immoral life who rejoice in the freedom found in a
heathen community to indulge passion and revel in vice,
should seek to discredit the missionary who does more
than any one else to thwart their iniquity and expose
their vileness.

Half a century ago the islands of the Pacific were a paradise of lust for the seamen of every civilized nation. Is it strange that when the missionaries came teaching chastity, and turning those abodes of unrestrained license into orderly, God-fearing communities, they should, by such men be pilloried as hypocrites, their work branded as a failure, and the money expended in it jeered at as a waste?

As Richard H. Dana said after a visit to the Sandwich Islands. in which he did his best to arrive at the truth in regard to the work of the missionaries : "The mere seekers of pleasure, power, and gain do not like their influence ; and those persons who sympathize with that officer who compelled the authorities to allow women to go on to his ship by opening his ports and threatening to bombard the town, naturally are hostile to missions."

To a young man who was expatiating to him on the inefficiency of missionaries in China, Dr. Ellinwood said: "Whom did you see in China principally?" "Oh, the young men of Shanghai and other ports, clerks in warehouses, and others." "Do you not think some of those young men were leading lives which threw them out of sympathy with missionary operations? Were not some of them a little lax in their morals?" "Some of them! Every one of them," was the quick reply. "I do not know of any exception." "Well, but do you think that such testimony as theirs is quite conclusive in regard to the work of missions?"

Some years since a noted English traveler and author stated in one of his books that the missionaries at a certain African station had accomplished nothing and that their station was useless. Whereupon the leading missionary at the station referred to, wrote in reply that his station could hardly be considered *entirely* useless, since it had been a refuge for the native women from the drunken attacks of the traveling companions of this very critic. Instances need not be multiplied to prove what the well-informed have long understood that much of the testimony to the *waste* of missions by which many are misled would be found, if sifted, to be inspired by the Judas spirit.

Then again this criticism is often prompted by *selfishness*. There are those who do not like the pressure upon their own conscience of the claims of the heathen world, and so they are ready to welcome and accept without examination any alleged evidence of *waste* which may justify them in shirking self-denial. There is still much professed sympathy for the poor, which in reality, as in Judas' case, is but tenderness for one's own purse. When I hear Christian people put aside the appeal on behalf of foreign missions with the response: " I do not believe in wasting money on the heathen, when there is so much to be done at home," and then those same people, (as sometimes happens, though not always) dole out of their abundance for the cause of home missions an insignificant pittance, one-tenth, perhaps, or one twentieth of what they would expend to build a new club house, I am involuntarily reminded of the words: " This he said not because he cared for the poor, but because he —— had the bag." But while this cry of *waste* is often originated in some such sinister or selfish motive, I have no doubt that the vast majority of Christians at least, who take it up, do so in mere ignorance and thoughtlessness.

The first two classes of objectors, the malignant and the selfish, it is of little use to try to convince; but the other and larger class need only to have the case fairly put before them to see how unjust is such a criticism.

To do this as it should be done, — to tell in language worthy of the theme the thrilling story of heroism and sacrifice, of patience and triumph, under equatorial suns and amid poplar snows, on fever stricken coasts and on cannibal islands, face to face with the hoary civilizations of Asia and with the naked savagery of Borneo and of Pategonia, — would demand a tongue of fire. Only the inspired pen which recorded the Acts of the Apostles could worthily attempt this nineteenth century continuation of the same stirring story of the cross.

Yet let me give you, as best I may, four reasons why this work of foreign missions is not a *waste* either of money or of life.

1.   And the first is the same with which the Master Himself silenced this ill-timed cavil of the disciples. "Why trouble ye her? She hath wrought a good work upon me." That alabaster box of ointment, very precious, was not wasted, because it was poured upon *His* head, as the expression of a love that would give Him its best. Where in our day should we look for the highest expression of this same supreme love to Christ, if not in the treasure poured out, in the lives devoted to this work of making Him known to the world for which He died? Other causes appeal to a variety of motives, motives of self-interest, of patriotism, of natural compassion. Even the irreligious, out of mere humanity, give freely to build hospitals for the sick or to buy coal for the poor. Even the skeptic will give toward the building of a church in his own community, as a safeguard to property and a bulwark of order. But here is a work which appeals to one single motive, love for Him who gave His life that a lost world might be saved.

If one were asked to name the highest expression in this our day of that love to Christ which is willing to lay all at his feet, he would instinctively turn to the lives of those devoted men and women who, leaving home and native land, turning their backs forever upon the delights of culture and the allurements of ambition, have gone only for the love of Christ to bury themselves for life among filthy savages or sordid Asiatics, enduring the daily spectacle of their physical squalor and their moral leprosy, that so they may win jewels for His crown. In such lives Christian consecration touches its high-water mark. And he, to whom no fragrance is so sweet as a consecrated life does not count the precious ointment wasted.

When Henry Martyn died at thirty years of age alone in the heart of a heathen land, the flaming soul which had known but one thought, one passion fairly consuming the frail tenement in which it was confined, while as yet scarce one convert had rewarded his earnest toil, it seemed indeed like a waste of precious ointment; but who will doubt that He who said of Mary as the highest praise: "She hath done what she could," has written over against that devoted life the same satisfying eulogy?

2. This work is not a waste, again, because of *the mighty impulse* which the church has drawn *from the examples of heroism and consecration* it has called forth. "Wheresoever this gospel shall be preached in the whole world, there shall also this that this woman hath done be told for a memorial of her." Surely that was not a waste which, like a seed dropped into the ground, should have power to reproduce in other lives generation after generation the same devotion to the Master and the same spirit of sacrifice. But is this not also true of these missionary lives and offerings, which are mourned over as so sad a waste? What life next to that of Christ has done most to impel Christians to a

high standard of fervor and sacrifice? What but the
life of Paul, the great foreign missionary of the primitive church? When the pure soul of Harriet Newell,
dying, a young bride of nineteen on a foreign isle, ere
she had so much as set foot among the people whom she
longed to tell of a Saviour's love, left its frail tabernacle
and exhaled heavenward like the perfume from the
broken box of alabaster, even devout souls, staggered
by the mystery of God's ways, cried out in their perplexity: "To what purpose is this waste?"

Yet *was* it a waste, when that short and simple story
of a woman's love and sacrifice touched the heart of all
England and America, and moved hundreds out of
lukewarmness and lethargy to be up and doing for the
Master? When whole communities, even, are revived
and churches are brought into being as the result of the
reading of that simple story? Who shall say that the
longest life of service among the heathen would have
been as fruitful of results as was that early death
through its influence upon the Christian· Church?

When Theodore Parker, certainly no blindly partial
critic of evangelical enterprise, laid down the life of
Adoniram Judson he said, and justly, that if the missionary enterprise had done nothing but produce that
life, all its costs were repaid. But Judson does not
stand alone. This work has produced scores of other
lives as noble, as inspiring as his. With equal emphasis
may it be said that if the missionary spirit had done
nothing for this nineteenth century but to illumine it
with one such heroic life as David Livingstone's it would
have been worth all its cost. But what a galaxy of
heroes and heroines has this enterprise of foreign missions given the church! We need not go back to the
early centuries for our saints and martyrs. They have
lived and walked with us, they have gone forth from our

houses and our churches, men and women of whom the
world was not worthy, who even though dead, still

Yea, and will live to rouse the careless, to convince
the doubting, to stimulate the half-hearted till the
church's last battle is fought, her last victory won.

What Christian has ever laid down the life of Fidelia
Fiske, or of Dr. Grant of Nestoria, of Dr. Calhoun of
Syria, of Dr. Morrison of China, of Carey or Duff of
India, or of Bishop Patteson of Melanesia, without a
new conception of the grandeur of the Christian life
and a new impulse to more thorough consecration.

3. Once more, this work is not a waste because of
its *general uplifting and civilizing effects.*

The critics of missions have one standard of
measurement by which they assume that their value is
alone to be gauged, *the statistics of conversions.* Are
these in any given case but small; the question is
triumphantly asked: "To what purpose is this waste?"
But the standard is too narrow, granted that conversions are the result at which this whole work aims, yet
if this were never attained, there would still be, in the
indirect results alone, compensation many times over
for their cost. We have already seen how true this is
of their effect on the churches at home. It is no less
true of their effect upon heathen communities abroad.

The passengers and crew of a California vessel
wrecked among the Fiji Islands, when daylight came
found themselves to their indescribable horror ashore
upon what they took to be a cannibal island. Knowing
that they must perish if they remained where they were,
they summoned all their courage to face an unknown
fate, and made for the nearest hut. On entering, the
chief officer saw lying on a board a dark colored object

that fixed his attention. It was neither a spear nor a club, it was — yes, it was a Bible. Turning to his comrades: "We are safe," he exclaimed. "Where that book is there is no danger."

And so it proved. The influence of the missionaries had transformed these whilom cannibals into hospitable friends, who showed the shipwrecked crew no little kindness and sent them on their way rejoicing. Think you that crew needed to enquire for statistics of church membership before deciding whether the missionary money expended on that island had been wasted?

If missions in the Pacific had done nothing else than make savage and cannibal islands safe for the sailor and the castaway, — and that they have done in fifty years for substantially the whole of Polynesia, that alone would be worth all their cost.

And such results have followed in the track of the missionary all around the globe. Do you ask where are the witnesses? They are at hand, a great cloud of them, men who can speak that they do know and testify that they have seen. Shall we summon a few of them? We will call no missionary, no secretary, no minister, lest their testimony should be suspected of bias. We will call only scholars, travelers, diplomats, who shall tell us what they know of the influence of missionaries: Shall we call scholars?

Few names carry greater weight for *candor* than that of Charles Darwin. In his voyage around the world he visited Terra del Fuego and found its savages "the lowest of the human race," scarce one degree above the brutes, so degraded, indeed, that when he heard that a mission was to be attempted among them he pronounced it a hopeless undertaking. But when a British admiral told him of what he had seen of the fruits of that mission, this man who had abandoned all his faith in Christ

and the Bible conceived such faith in missions as an
elevating power, that he made haste to enroll himself as
a subscriber to a work which he pronounced next to
the renaissance of Japan, the greatest wonder of the
century.

From the other side of the globe we may bring his
co-laborer in science, Alfred Russel Wallace, to tell us
how in the island of Celebes the missionaries have
changed "a wilderness" of "naked savages" into "a
garden."

Shall we summon such travelers as Henry M. Stan-
ley and Emin Bey to tell us why they call so loudly for
missionaries as the great hope of Africa? Shall we call
government officials to the stand? From India with its
hoary and inflexible civilization comes Sir Charles
Aitchison, governor of the Punjab to tell us that missionary teaching and Christian literature are leavening
native opinion in a way and to an extent quite startling
to those who do not take the trouble to investigate, and
declares that, "apart altogether from the strictly Christian aspect of the question" he would as an administra-
tor "deplore the drying up of Christian liberality to
missions in this country as a most lamentable check to
social and moral progress, and a grievious injury to the
best interests of the people."

Sir Barth Frere, late governor of Bombay, steps
forward to declare that the teaching of Christianity is
effecting in India "changes moral, social, and political
which, for extent and rapidity of effect, are far more
extraordinary than anything witnessed in modern
Europe." But these (and they are representations of a
great number in like position to judge) are Englishmen,
and themselves Christians, at least traditionally.

Let us hear a Brahmin, the Hindoo reformer Chun-
der Sen who, while deliberately rejecting christianity as

inferior to the old Vedic Theism which he seeks to restore, still proclaims: "It is not the British army that deserves the honor of holding India. If any army can claim that honor, it is the army of Christian missionaries headed by their invincible captain Jesus Christ."

There is no harder mission field, none where direct results have been more tardy, than China.

A certain Lieutenant Wood of the United States Navy after studying the missions there from the deck of a man of war, has sent broadcast through the newspapers the sad intelligence that they are a total failure. We may leave him, however, to settle matters with our minister to China, Col. Dinby, who says, "the tourist who sneers at the missionaries or fails to give them his unqualified admiration and sympathy, is, if earnest, simply ignorant. He has not taken the trouble to go through their missions as I have done. It is idle for any man to decry the missionaries or their work. I do not address myself to the churches, but as a man of the world talking to sinners like myself, I say that it is difficult to say too much good of missionary work in China."

But time fails to name even the witnesses of like character and standing who might be summoned from all parts of the globe. I add the testimony of but one, General Lew Wallace, ex-minister to Turkey, who from the position of unbeliever in Christianity was brought by the examination of the New Testament to that attitude of mind which reveals itself in Ben-Hur and who, from a like unbelief in the work of missions, was won over in a similar way, and confessed on his return that though he went to Turkey prejudiced against the missionaries, he had found them an admirable body of men doing a wonderful educational and civilizing work outside of that which was strictly religious.

4. But finally and above all, this work is not a waste *because of its direct and eternal results*, in *souls* turned from darkness to light and from the power of Satan unto God.

Is it a waste of life and treasure that has given us in India one hundred thousand native communicants, thirty-five thousand in China, some thirty thousand in Japan, one hundred thousand in Polynesia, a million in the heathen worlds; to say nothing of those already gone, some of them from the dungeon and the martyr-flame, to join the great multitude whom no man can number before the throne of God and the Lamb?

Is it waste which, according to the showing of the government census of India, multiplies the native Christians by 67% while adherents of other religions are increasing from 10% to 13%? It looked like waste in China while Morrison was waiting for seven years for his first convert; but it did not look like waste to our missionaries when they found that during the last decade the increase in all the Protestant missions had been almost one and one half fold or 140%. It may have seemed like waste to the Moravian missionaries in Greenland during the fifteen years that they labored without one convert but it does not seem so now to those who find not a single avowed pagan in the district covered by their labors. It seemed also like waste for a time to the Baptists of the Lone Star Mission in India as years of labor passed by with almost no visible result, that they were almost ready to withdraw from the field in despair; but when in 1878 ten thousand converts were baptized in three months there was no more thought of waste then.

Judson, as he sat by the wayside waiting wearily day after day for even a listener, must often have been tempted to ask of his own life "To what purpose is this waste?" had not his been the mighty faith which to the question, "What are the prospects of success?" could answer "As bright as the promises of Almighty God." But even Satan can hardly have tempted him to ask such a question after he had been permitted to welcome two hundred in one year to the church of Christ.

Foreign missions a waste! Then was the blood shed on Calvary wasted. Then were the labors of the apostles wasted, then were the lives of the martyrs wasted, then was it waste when Latimer and Ridley lighted with their flaming bodies England's candle which has never been put out, then is all sacrifice for Christ and all toil for souls a waste, the gospel itself a fable, and heaven a dream.

But if at God's right hand there sits a Christ to whom the Father has promised the heathen for his inheritance and the uttermost parts of the earth for his possession, and who will accept and crown every deed of love and every sacrifice laid at His feet as He accepted and crowned this deed of a loving woman of Bethany there is then no work on earth which holds the promise of larger, more glorious, or more imperishable returns!

WHAT SHALL WE DO?

Now when they heard this they were pricked in their heart and said unto Peter and to the rest of the apostles: Men and brethren, what shall we do? Then Peter said unto them: Repent and be baptized every one of you in the name of Jesus Christ for the remission of sins.—Acts 2:37-8.

The day of Pentecost was a day of wonders. It was a day of *power*,—the manifested power of the Holy Ghost. But of all the manifestations of that power which was the mightiest? Was it the mighty rushing wind? Was it the flames of fire resting on the heads of the disciples? Was it the new tongues in which these unlearned men were heard to speak? No : far beyond either of these was that which is here recorded. "Now when they heard this they were pricked in their heart." "And the same day there were added about three thousand souls." The wind and the fire were phenomena of matter, the tongues a phenomenon of mind, but here was a moral miracle, an exhibition of divine power over the spiritual creation.

It is the tendency of our minds to wonder at the outward and spectacular rather than at the inward and spiritual. As in our Saviour's life-time the multitudes wondered far more at the multiplication of the loaves in his hand than at the gracious words which proceeded out of his mouth or at the sinless life he led, so still we are prone to appeal to his miracles, rather than to his life and teachings in proof of his divinity ; and yet it is in the teachings and the life far more than in the miracles that the full splendor of the Godhead is revealed. So, too, the Ten Commandments given to Moses upon Sinai at the first glance excite our wonder far less than the spectacle of the mount itself quaking and smoking and thundering, amidst which they were given. Yet it is in that law itself infinitely more than in any of these marvelous accompaniments of its delivery that we see the proof that Moses had indeed talked with God, and that he spake by a divine authority. One can hardly fail to be reminded in this succession of phenomena, the mighty wind, the fire, the outward miracle of the tongues, followed by the inward prick of compunction in so many hard hearts, of that impressive lesson, so like in the progress of its events,—the earth-quake, and after the earth-quake a whirlwind, and after the whirlwind a fire, and after the fire a still, small voice,—in which Elijah was taught the same great truth, that God is seen more in his secret workings than in spectacular displays; more in the voice with which he speaks inwardly to the heart of man than in the mightiest convulsions of nature or the most overwhelming judgments upon nations.

What is it to teach the unlearned to utter his thoughts in a strange language compared with teaching a hardened sinner to see himself in a new light, to feel toward God a new affection, and to shape his life by a new purpose. "Behold he prayeth" was a more wonderful thing to say of the fierce persecutor than if it had been said that he spake with all the tongues under heaven. The piercing of a hard heart is the greatest miracle God ever works.

And consider *how* hard were these hearts,—how against all human probability it was that they should be pricked with anything like compunction under this sermon of Peter's

Remember this was in Jerusalem. These are in part the very men who had often listened to wonderous words of Jesus himself in their temple and in the streets of their

city. Some of them had seen his miracles. They had
heard of what had happened at Bethany within the last
few months, how he had there raised to life one who had
lain four days in the grave. Some of them had joined in
the cry : "Crucify him ! crucify him !" of that tumultu-
ous throng before Pilate's judgment seat, and had gazed
upon the cross, had felt the earth-quake, had stood
under the shadow of the darkness, had smitten their
breasts and returned, awed but still unconvinced. Surely
hearts that had resisted such influences as these, must
have become hard indeed. And accordingly we find them
running together out of mere curiosity at this new sight,
and some of them like the mockers who in our day gather
to make fun wherever the Holy Spirit's presence is
specially manifested,—with irreverent sneer, attributing
his work to the effects of new wine.

Shall we expect such hearts, hearts which had successfully hardened themselves against the life and the
words of the divine Master himself, to be penetrated by
the preaching of his unlettered disciple? Yet behold
these men now, *pricked in their hearts,*—their contempt
all gone, their indifference all gone, their scepticism
about the claims of Jesus to be their Messiah all gone,
turning to his disciples with the intensely earnest question : "Men and brethren, what shall we do?" What
but the almighty power of God could have wrought such
a change? The ax does not cleave the tree without an
arm to wield it. Peter's sermon could never have so
cleft these hard hearts had it not been applied by the
Holy Ghost.

But let us attend more closely to the nature of this
effect. "They were pricked in their heart." Their com·
fort was gone. Their peace of mind was gone. Insensibil-
ity had given place to uneasiness, to anxiety, to alarm.
Their question, "What shall we do?" is the expression

at once of conscious guilt and of conscious danger.   As
one who in a transport of rage has murdered a fellow-
being, awaking suddenly to a sense of what he has done,
cries out with a thought at once of the mischief which he
cannot undo, and of the penalty which he cannot
escape :   "Oh, what shall I do? what shall I do?" so
these men were pricked in their heart, they felt "compunction",—that is the exact force of the Greek word.—
as Peter's words brought home to them what they had
done. And what was it that his words thus brought home
to them? One sin alone. He had not sought to convict them
of theft, of blasphemy, of idolatry, of licentiousness, of
any sin but this that they had spurned their Messiah
and crucified their Lord. This was what they now perceived. The pain of self-reproach for this was what they
now felt. Blessed, hopeful pain! When, by diligent
chafing and cautious warming, sensibility has been restored to a frozen limb, you cry out with pain when no
pain was felt before. Yet you rejoice in that pain as a
promise of returning life. So there is hope for any man
so soon as he is pricked in his heart for refusing his
Saviour and resisting the Holy Ghost.

Would to God my impenitent friends, that Christians about you could see you pricked in the heart.
Would to God that my words might be made effectual by
the Holy Spirit to the awakening in you of compunction
for just this sin. I doubt not a thoroughly aroused conscience would convict you of various sins, some of you
of sins against purity, some of you of sins against truth,
some of you of sins against the law of love to your neighbors. But there is one sin greater than any of these of
which I *know* that it would convict you all. It is the sin
of rejecting a Saviour, of despising his love, of harden-
ing your hearts against the calls of his spirit. Could we
see you pricked in your heart for this sin, oh how should

we rejoice,—not at your pain ; but at the hope it would give that the hard heart might be softened and the lost soul saved.

Still it would be only a hope. Many a soul feels the prickings of compunction for its treatment of its Saviour, yet stifles them again and so becomes more hardened than before. Therefore I ask you to note it again as a still more hopeful feature in the case of these men that they asked just this question : " What shall we do? " They could have asked no question more to the point than this. They saw that this was a case that called for action. They were in a state of guilt,—something must be done about that ;—in a state of danger,—something must be done about that. Theirs was no case for idle waiting, no case for theological hair-splitting. It was a case for action,—prompt, energetic action.

My friends, it may be there are some of you who already feel compunction for your neglect of the gospel and ingratitude for a Saviour's love, but you are *doing* nothing about it. You are just waiting for things to take their own course. You keep your feelings to yourself and meanwhile go right on as before. I forewarn you that compunction so treated will not last long. It will soon give place to a state of things worse than before.

Satan does not care how many sermons you hear, how many tracts you read, how much you think about religion, how much emotion you feel, if only he can be sure that you won't *do* anything. In that case all these things will but help to rivet his chains by making your heart harder and more insensible.

> "Nothing either great or small
> Remains for me to do,"

is true as it was written and meant, but not true as it is sometimes quoted and sung. It is true that we have nothing either great or small to do toward atoning for sin, but it is not true that we have nothing to do towards turning from sin, it is not true that we have nothing to do toward fleeing from the wrath to come. "Nothing to do," thought the antediluvians when Noah warned them of the coming deluge, till at length the flood came and destroyed them all. "Nothing to do," thought Lot's sons-in-law when Lot warned them that God would destroy their city, till the fire and brimstone fell and they perished in the flames.

But the awakened jailer at Philippi thought otherwise when he fell down trembling before Paul and Silas crying: "Sirs! what must I do to be saved?" The awakened Saul of Tarsus himself thought otherwise, when, startled to find against whom he had been fighting, he cried: "Lord what wilt thou have me do?"

And Jesus taught otherwise when he said : "*Strive to enter in at the strait gate; for strait is the gate and narrow is the way that leadeth unto life, and few there be that find it.*"

I spoke to you last week, my friends, of the thing that God exhorts you *not* to do. "Harden not your hearts." I tried to show you something of the fearful responsibility and peril of such a self-hardening. But you remember I pointed out to you that so long as you simply *do nothing* that process goes on. You delude yourself wofully if you think that while you are doing nothing things will stay where they are.

A little swelling has made its appearance on your face. You heed it not at first ; but it increases, and at length you decide to show it to the physician. He examines it, shakes his head, and advises you to have it removed. You reply: "Oh, no; I don't think I'll do anything about it. I only want your opinion as to what it might be." Seeing that you are not sufficiently awake to your danger he tells you plainly that it is a *cancer*, and

that if it extends beyond a certain point it will be certain
death. You are greatly agitated, and see the gravity of
the situation, but you cannot make up your mind to the
painful operation, so you decide to let it go, to do nothing about it at least for the present. Think you that while
you do nothing that fatal growth will stop? Think you
that if you simply let it go, it will heal itself? Never!
While you do nothing that enemy will eat your life away.
In prompt action lies your only hope. Oh, my friend,
that is after all but a faint emblem of the fatal processes
going on in your soul while you do nothing, processes
which no anxiety, no compunction, nothing but right action will arrest. Do you see that you are in the wrong,—
that you are in danger? Lose no time, then, in asking
this question : "What shall I do"?

But of whom shall you ask it? This leads us to take
note of another hopeful feature in the case of these men.
They went to *the right place* to push their inquiry. They
addressed themselves to "Peter and the rest of the
Apostles."

Why did they not undertake to prescribe for their
own case, to decide for themselves what was the best course
to pursue? Or why did they not go away to their old
teachers, the chief priests, the scribes, the doctors of the
law? Ah, they had a good reason for doing neither of
these. They realized at least that they had been impli-
cated in the guilt of crucifying one who was their Messiah, and who would come to be their Judge. And they
saw that he alone, who was at once their accuser and their
judge, was to be trusted to tell them what to do. The
way that he pointed out, and that alone, they would be
safe in taking. And therefore they applied to his ac-
credited representatives, to the men who had been with
him as his disciples, and who stood now as his apostles,
or ambassadors, to tell them from him, what they
must do.

Was not this the part of common sense? But, alas, how many an awakened sinner fails here! He has sinned against God, yet he will not let God tell him what to do. He has rejected Christ, yet will not take Christ's way to be reconciled. He has grieved the Holy Spirit, yet he will not listen to the Holy Spirit's voice telling him how he may obtain his blessing.

Some think they can answer this question for themselves. "My own reason," they say, "is guide enough. That will tell me what to do." Some resort to this and that human authority for advice and obtain advice as various as the authorities to whom they apply. But God's answer is the only safe answer, and that is given in his word. Is there one here pricked in his heart, and thoroughly roused to the fact that something must be done to escape from the wrath to come? My friend, trust the *Bible alone* to tell you what to do. Go to Christ's ministers, go to Christian friends, if you will. They have traveled the road themselves and it is to be presumed they can give you wise direction. But *trust* it not even at their lips unless you see that it is grounded on the word of God. See that you have a "Thus saith the Lord," for every step. For just so surely as only God's instructions could guide Lot to a place of safety from the fiery rain that was about to descend upon the cities of the plain, just so surely can these alone guide any sinner to a place of safety from the judgment that is yet to come upon the world of the ungodly.

Many an awakened soul has been *fatally misled* by trusting to well meant but mistaken and unscriptural advice of some sincere Christian friend.

You see too, my friends, that though this question was put to all the eleven apostles, there seems to have been no disagreement about the answer. The reply of Peter spoke the sentiment of all. Eleven men but only one mind. So you will find it in the word of God. God spake by many messengers, but he gave but one gospel. The Bible is made up of many books, but they all give but one answer to the question: "What shall we do?"

More rudimentary indeed in the earlier and incomplete stages of religious development, and endlessly varied in form according to the needs of the particular individual who asks the question, that answer in its completed gospel-form never varies in substance from the one here given. I pray you mark it well, inquiring soul, for it tells you exactly what you must do.

"Repent and be baptized, every one of you, in the name of Jesus Christ, for the remission of sins." Repent! At this very first word occurs an instance of the danger of trusting to any guidance but that of God's own word. Open a Roman Catholic Bible and you will read there "Do penance." This is Rome's perversion of God's way. But you may say: The Roman Catholic Bible is a translation, and yours is a translation. How am I to know that theirs is not true. My friend, you may know it almost as certainly if you do not read Greek as if you do. You may learn what Peter meant by seeing what these men did. Do you read of any penance here, any scourgings, any vigils, any mortifications? None. "Then they that gladly received the word were baptized, and the same day there were added unto them about three thousand souls." When a German emperor insulted Pope Hildebrand, the so-called successor of St. Peter, the would-be vicar of Christ, he was compelled to stand for three days, barefoot and clad in hair cloth, in the cold of midwinter in an outer court of the castle at Canossa, ere he could receive absolution. But here are men whom Peter himself has just charged with complicity in the crucifixion of Christ, offered an instant pardon, baptized and taken into the full fellowship of the church in one day, with no hint of penances of any kind.   Not only so, but look all through the New Testament and you will find not one trace of such performances from beginning to end.   Of repentance you will find enough, of penance nothing. Rome, after diligent search through the Protestant Bible of King James, has detected some half dozen errors of translation to which she triumphantly points as exhibiting a doctrinal bias which discredits the whole work.   Yet not one of these is an error half so vital, or so monstrous, as this which, for the sake of bolstering up an evil practice, received by tradition from a corrupt age of the church renders by such a word as "Do penance" a word which every Greek scholar sees for himself to mean "change your minds."   But if Peter did not bid these inquirers, "Do penance" neither did his answer mean "Feel sorrow."   They felt that already.   They were already pricked in their heart. That was sorrow.   And out of that deep sorrow of compunction they had asked : "Men and brethren what shall we do?" It was to some new step Peter directed them,— something to which this sorrow and sense of guilt must lead them, but which was more than these.   That something was repentance, literally a change of mind—i. e., not a change of views or a change of feelings, though it includes both these ; but precisely what we mean when we say : "I planned to go on such a journey, but I changed my mind," viz., a *change of purpose*.   They had rejected Jesus as their Messiah.   When Peter said "Repent !" he bade them reject him no longer, but accept him, and bow to him as their Saviour and their Lord.   "Repent" in the Bible is a word of action.   It rests on feeling : it presupposes the sense of sin and sorrow for sin as the motive to action, but he who stops with sorrow and *turns not* from sin stops short of repentance.   John the Baptist came preaching repentance, and

314

when the people asked him what he meant he told them
very plainly, and it was neither to do penances nor to feel
sorry ; but to the publicans it was : " Exact no more
than that which is appointed you : " to the soldiers : " Do
violence to no man, neither accuse any falsely, and be
content with your wages ; " to all the people : " He that
hath two coats, let him impart to him that hath none,
and he that hath meat let him do likewise."

My friend, you have been resisting God's Holy
Spirit. Repent, by yielding to his influence and doing
whatever he prompts you to do. You have been rejecting Christ. Repent by accepting him as your Saviour,
your Sovereign, your all.

There is an Old Testament precept which expresses
the exact nature of that which is here required. You
will find it in Is. 1: 16-17. "*Cease to do evil; learn to do
well.*" But repentance will not make amends for past sin.
It was a startling discovery to those Jews to realize that
they had crucified the Lord of Glory. No repentance
could undo this deed. And therefore they needed, to
withdraw the iron that was rankling in their souls.
another word beside this word Repent. And it was
given. " Be baptized in the name of Jesus Christ for the
remission of sins." To be baptized in the name of Jesus
Christ was an act of faith in Christ. It was a personal
acceptance of him as their Lord. To be baptized for the
remission of sins was still more specifically an act of
faith in his atonement, an appropriation to themselves of
the benefits of the sacrifices of that " Lamb of God that
taketh away the sin of the world."

But this was not all that the apostles bade these
convicted sinners do. Here again I ask you to notice
the contrast between the *inspired* prescription for the
healing of troubled consciences and many of the prescrip-
tions of men. " Repent," says the rationalist, " and

that is enough. God is bound to forgive upon repentance." Not so say the apostles of Christ.

The deed is done. Repentance will not undo it.
The guilt of a crucified Messiah is on their souls. Repentance will not cancel it. Something else is needed,
some more potent solvent than tears to erase the record
in God's book of remembrance. That most potent thing
is the blood of Christ. Guilt calls for atonement as well
as for repentance. Therefore to the command "Repent"
is added the command: "Be baptized in the name of
Jesus Christ for the remission of sins," a command which
finds its commentary in the words of this same apostle in
another sermon preached a few days later. Neither is
there salvation in any other, for "There is none other
name under heaven given among men whereby we must
be saved." To be baptized in the name of Jesus Christ
is an act of faith in Christ. To be baptized for the remission of sins is specifically an act of faith in the atonement of Christ, an appropriation to one's self of the sacrifice of "the Lamb of God that taketh away the sins of
the world."

But baptism was more. Since it was an outward, a
public act, it was not only an act of faith but of confession. It was an open acknowledgment of sin, an open
acceptance of Christ, an open vow of allegiance to him.
Before friends and foes alike. it committed those who received it to the side of Jesus Christ.

So then we have in Peter's answer to the question.
"What shall we do?" these three things : repentance.
faith, confession. It is God who has joined these three
together ; and what God hath joined together let no man
put asunder. You cannot be saved by turning from sin
without an acceptance of Christ's atoning sacrifice : you
cannot be saved by accepting Christ's atoning sacrifice
without turning from sin, and neither your repentance nor

your faith will approve themselves genuine and complete
without open acknowledgment before the world of Him
by whom you hope to be acknowledged at last before the
Father and his holy angels.   " For with the heart man
believeth unto righteousness and with the mouth *confession is made unto salvation.*"   " Every one of you," so
Peter made answer to the various multitude who
thronged upon him with their anxious question " There
is no difference."   " All have sinned and come short of
the glory of God."   There is no softening of the conditions for the Nicodemuses who may wish to become disciples secretly.   There is no exclusion from them of the
priests who may have had a personal share in the guilty
plot against God's holy Son.   And those words are just
as applicable to-day and in this congregation.   " Repent
and be baptized, every one of you."

But you have been baptized already.   Your parents
gave you baptism in your infancy.   Then you have had a
great advantage and trifled with it, a great opportunity
and missed it, a glorious birthright and despised it.
You ought to have grown up a Christian child trusting
Christ and following him from your earliest years and
you did not do it.   What you have now to do is not to
be baptized anew. When Peter found that Simon Magus
had been baptized without a true conversion he said
nothing about a new baptism, but he bade him repent.
What you have to do is to supply the reality which is yet
lacking, and without which your baptism remains an
empty form.   Faith and confession, this is the spiritual
part of baptism, and these duties remain unfulfilled. Do
not think there is for you some new, some easier, some
peculiar way.   Repent, believe, confess, every one of
you. Turn about, change your mind from rejection of
Christ to submission to him.   Appropriate to yourself
the blood shed for many for the remission of sins, and

lay your burden of guilt on him who was wounded for
your transgressions and bruised for your iniquities. Own
him before the world as your Lord and Saviour, numbering yourself with his people here that he may make you
to be numbered with his saints in glory everlasting.

It is not recorded that all those who asked this earnest question accepted Peter's answer. In the form of the
record : "Then they that gladly received his word were
baptized," the contrary is rather implied. It is one
thing to be awakened and another to be converted, one
thing to ask in all earnestness: "What shall I do?"
another thing to do as we are bidden. Many a Naaman
has come to the prophet's door, and gone away in a rage.
Many a young man has come saying : "Good Master,
what must I do to inherit eternal life," and gone away
sorrowful.

It is midnight. The streets are deserted. The distant foot-fall of the watchman alone breaks the stillness.
What is this crouching form that I see lingering near the
steps of that quiet dwelling, hugging about her shoulders
a scanty shawl. She was a woman once. Let us not
name her now. And this was her childhood's home, and
weary of sin and shame she has come back to cast herself at her mother's feet and beg to be taken in. See,
she ascends the steps ; she lifts her hand to the knocker.
One moment more and the door will be opened, and she
will be clasped to a loving bosom. But no, she hesitates,
she withdraws her hand. Overwhelmed with the dread
of meeting those pure eyes, of facing brothers' and sisters' questioning looks, her courage has failed her, and
leaving the knocker unlifted she turns and glides away
into the darkness. Oh, had she but heard the voice at
that moment pleading within those walls for the erring
one ; had she but been told to take that one decisive
step! So near to rescue yet unsaved!

Awakened, inquiring. seeking soul, not far from the kingdom of God to-day, do not draw back from this one last step. " *Knock*, and it shall be opened unto thee."

THE ELEMENT OF DOCTRINE IN RELIGION.

*Till I come, give attendance to * * * * doctrine.—*
1 Tim. 4:13.

It is characteristic of the religious tendencies of the
day to depreciate *doctrine*. Doctrinal preaching, doctrinal study by Christians for themselves, doctrinal teaching of children in the Sunday school or at home, all
these are decried and disused. "The life! the life!" is
now the cry.

Preaching should be the exhortation of men to a
good life. Let us study the Bible only for its pure
morality and its good examples, skipping the hard
places such as the fifth and ninth chapters of Romans,
just as we skip the hard names of the opening chapters
of Chronicles. We accept the Scriptures as profitable
for "reproof, for correction, for instruction in righteousness," but not "for doctrine," since doctrine itself
is no longer found profitable. And we say of the individual, "No matter what he believes if only he is
sincere."

This is a natural reaction from an extreme of doctrinal rigidity and polemic heat, but, like most reactions,
it is itself an extreme. The pendulum has swung too
far. Of course, if religion be only a sentiment, if to
stand in rapt admiration before the Sistine Madonna;
to apostrophize the soaring lark; to compose a melting
symphony; to grow pensive at the sunset, if this —
though all the while you be a liar, or a profligate — is
religion; — if to love — anybody or anything, no matter

whether worthy the devotion of a rational spirit or not, is religion, then religion has nothing to do with doctrine. Poetic rhapsodies on the divinity of beauty are the preaching it demands. Or if religion be a matter of conduct alone, the practice of virtue as between man and man, — honesty, integrity, doing as we would be done by, — then doctrine has no place there. Panegyrics upon the virtues, in the manner of Seneca, are the preaching for such a religion.

But if religion is an affair of the whole soul — if intellect, feeling and will are all concerned in it; if it includes our relations to God in even a higher degree than it does our relations to each other, if religion consists in knowing, loving, and obeying God — and nothing less than this is worthy to be called religion, — then the great doctrines concerning God and man, concerning sin and redemption, concerning eternity and retribution, are its very bone and marrow.

Therefore we find the Scriptures replete with doctrinal teaching, and insisting strenuously on doctrinal study.

The shorter catechism sums up truly the substance of Scripture in the statement " The Scriptures principally teach what man is to believe concerning God, and what duty God requires of man."

This exhortation of Paul to his son Timothy was consistent with his own practice. His epistles are doctrinal sometimes to abstruseness. His sermon to the Athenians on Mars' Hill is full of doctrine.

John, the apostle of love, whom we are wont to contrast with Paul as expressing the emotional, rather than the intellectual side of Christianity, rivals Paul in the prominence he gives to doctrinal teaching, and furnishes perhaps the severest denunciation of doctrinal heresy to be found in the New Testament (2 Jno. 9-10), a denunciation which would win for any theologian who in these days should repeat it literally, the titles of bigot and fanatic.

But, it is claimed, that in this particular, the disciples swerved from the example of the Master. This dogmatism was their great mistake. Jesus himself taught precepts, not dogmas. We hear much from those who reason thus of the Sermon on the Mount ; but less of the discourses to Nicodemus, to the woman of Samaria, to the multitude that followed him for the sake of the loaves, to Martha on the way to the grave of Lazarus, to the disciples as they sat together at the last supper, of such chapters as the 25th of Matthew beginning with the parable of the Two Virgins and ending with " *These shall go away into everlasting punishment; but the righteous into life eternal,*" and of the Great Commission with which, after his ascension, he sent his disciples forth, " *All power is given unto me in heaven and in earth.*"

The truth is that a careful analysis of even the few fragments of the Master's teachings which these four brief gospels have preserved to us, reveals there the germs of all the doctrines wrought out in more systematic form in the epistles. No narrowing of the limits of inspired Scripture can eliminate the doctrinal element. Not only does it remain in the gospels when you have rejected the epistles, but even when in the desperate attempt to get rid of it you have tampered with the gospels themselves throwing out the fourth and mutilating the others till, if you choose, the Sermon on the Mount alone is left, which is exalted by many as the sum total of the Gospel, even then you shall find the same interweaving of the two elements, the woof of precept inwrought and held in place in a warp of doctrine. The being of God, his personality, his perfection, his power, his providence, the possibility and power of prayer, man's sin, his ac-

countability, the rewards and punishments of a future
state, and the possibility of forgiveness, all these *doctrines*,
either presupposed or directly asserted, are, in this one
discourse, appealed to as motives for the observance of
those precepts which it is the main drift of the discourse
to inculcate.

Those who raise this protest against doctrine, do
not seem to realize that questions of doctrine are in
reality simply *questions of fact*. We have a great respect
for the scientific man who devotes his life to a laborious
investigation of the facts of chemistry, of geology, of
astronomy. We dwell with delight on Franklin flying
his kite to determine whether it is a fact that the light-
ning is caused by electricity, and read with enthusiasm of
the new discoveries that are made in our own day in the
rocks and in the stars. Shall we then regard these facts
with profound interest, and hold the investigators of them
in deserved esteem, yet treat as indifferent and even im-
pertinent all inquiry into the facts of the spiritual world?

Whether there is or is not a God ; whether if there
is, he is a person or only an essence ; whether, if a person, he concerns himself at all with our affairs ; whether
it is of any use to go to him with our needs, our troubles,
our requests ; whether he holds us accountable for our
conduct ; if so, whether we are just now in a position to
gain his approbation ; whether we are in reality good at
heart, or bad ; and whether what we need is a development of our characters as they are, or, before all, a radi-
cal change of character ; if any change is needed, how
it is to be brought about ; whether there is a life beyond
this, and whether our conduct here will make any difference with our condition there ; and if so, precisely
what are the conditions of future happiness ; whether the
Bible is the word of God, containing his own authorita-
tive answers to these questions, or whether it is a simple

human production containing "guesses at truth";
whether Jesus was a teacher worthy of belief, and if so,
what he was; whether or not he rose from the dead as
his disciples claimed; whether he was or was not something more than a man; whether we may or may not pray
to him now; whether he is or is not at this moment gov-
erning the world and answering the prayers that are addressed to him; these are all questions of *fact*. In reference to each one of them there is a truth and there is a
falsehood.

And, more than this, it is of the last importance that
we should know what is the truth and what the falsehood.
Not only is it facts that are at issue here, but they are the
facts of all facts that it most vitally concerns us to know.

The human mind is so made that all facts interest it
whether they seem to have any practical bearing or not.
Questions concerning the laws of electricity, the motions
of the stars, the constitution of the sun,—all these have
an interest, an absorbing interest for us, but what are all
these questions, what are all the discoveries of science and
all the inventions and the strides of material civilization to
which they lead, compared with these vast, these wide-
reaching, these infinite questions which affect our immortal spirits? By so much as spirit is higher than
matter, and the unseen world more real and more enduring than the world that is seen, by so much are these
questions touching the spiritual and the unseen, these
questions of theology, these questions of *doctrine*, the
vital and overshadowing questions of human life. No
man releases himself from the dominion of facts by indifference to them. The facts remain and they govern his
life. If he does not accommodate himself to them, they
will make him miserable. We are all of us in the spiritual world, whether we will or not. Shutting our eyes to
it will not take us out of it. The only effect of shutting

our eyes will be to make us stumble and fall.

It is a great mistake to suppose that in this respect the conditions of our spiritual life are in any wise different from those of our natural life. In both worlds there are laws, to violate which, is to bring certain penalty upon themselves. A man cannot afford to be ignorant of any of the laws of his being. There are certain laws of health, the observance of which promotes soundness and strength of body, and the neglect of which begets disease. Just as truly are there laws of spiritual health, the observance or neglect of which is attended with corresponding results.

In neither case does the sincerity of one's error make any difference with the result. The inflexibility of law is a truth that science is bringing ever more and more into relief. A certain course of conduct is followed by certain effects, which depend not at all on the design of the action but wholly on the nature of the act. The man who takes a draught of corrosive sublimate because he finds it in a bottle labelled sulphate of quinine, and believes it just the medicine he needs, will die just as quickly as the man who deliberately pours it out and drinks it, knowing what it is, with intent to kill himself. The man who overtaxes his system, in a self-denying struggle to keep his wife and children above want, will fall a victim to apoplexy or paralysis as quickly, as though he did it out of a selfish greed to fill his coffers with a miser's hoard. The deluded wretch who, in all sincerity, abandons himself to the lewd rites of an obscene religion, to the worship of the Cyprian Venus of the Syrian Ashtoreth will end by making himself as much a beast, and sinking as deep in the slough of moral pollution, as he who gives himself up to like practices in conscious defiance of all religion.

Mr. Beecher used to be pointed out as a shining

example of the improved style of preaching which leaves out the doctrines. Yet listen to his own statement and illustrations: "It is often said",—I quote his words— "It is no matter what a man believes if he is only sincere. This is true of all minor truths, and false of all truths whose nature it is to fashion a man's life. It will make no difference in a man's harvest whether he think turnips have more saccharine matter than potatoes, whether corn is better than wheat. But let the man sincerely believe that seed planted without plowing is as good as with, that January is as favorable for seed-sowing as April, and that cockle-seed will produce as good a harvest as wheat, and will it make no difference?"

But there are no truths which have in them such power to *fashion the life*, as the great truths about God and Christ and the hereafter.

A man often falls below his creed, just as he often falls below his ideal. But he seldom or never lives above it. One may indeed put his creed away in some closet of his mind, lock it up, and never look at it. But so far as he uses it,—and a creed is made to be used and not locked up,—it shapes his life.

Will it make no difference with a man's life whether he acts on the belief that there is a God, that he is a sinner needing a Saviour, that Jesus is the incarnate Son of God who came into this world to save sinners, or whether he acts on beliefs the opposite of these?

Nay, it *will* make a difference, such a difference that if he acts upon the wrong beliefs in these matters, his life will be a blunder, a well meant blunder, if you choose, but a fatal and an irretreivable blunder, nevertheless. Indeed the more sincere one is, i. e., the more intense his convictions, the worse, if his convictions are wrong. For they will impel him the more powerfully in the wrong direction.

One of two things we must do. Either we must
shape our life according to some definite plan or we must
drift. To drift, beside being unworthy of a creature with
intelligence, is certain shipwreck. But to form a plan,
we must have made up our minds concerning great
spiritual facts, to form a judicious plan we must have
made up our mind upon them according to truth. Sailing by a chart is no safer than drifting, unless the chart
be *true*.

But some would put it another way. Instead of saying : no matter what one believes, so long as he is *sincere*, they say : no matter what one believes so long as
his life is right. Very well ; be it so. Without doubt
character is ultimate. It is the life, not the belief, that
is weighed in the balance. But *will* the life be right, can
it be right when belief on fundamental points is wrong?
"Oh God, though he doubted thy being, he lived thy
law," was the prayer of a so-called "liberal" minister,
by the grave of one who had said in his heart, "There is
no God." Lived God's law ! that law of which the first
great commandment is : "*Thou shalt love the Lord thy
God with all thy heart and with all thy soul and with all
thy strength and with all thy mind*."

The word of God itself says : "Without faith *it is
impossible to please him; for he that cometh to God must believe that he is, and that he is a rewarder of them that dili-
gently seek him*."

There, then, are at least two articles of creed laid down
as indispensable to the very beginning of a right life. It
is by first narrowing the definition of a right life so as to
leave out some of its most essential features that we so
easily persuade ourselves that the creed has nothing to
do with such a life. Life is shaped by *motives;* and
motives grow out of *convictions*. The aim of religion, it
is urged, is not to teach men what they ought to *believe*,

but what they ought to *be*. No, not that either. The aim of religion is not even to teach men what they ought to be, but to *make* them what they ought to be. 'Tis one thing to make men *see* their duty, and quite another thing to make them *do* their duty. For this, mighty motives are needed. And nowhere are motives so mighty to be found as in the great realities of the spiritual world as set forth in the doctrines of the Bible.

Socrates believed that sin was the result of ignorance, and that men only needed to be shown the better way to walk in it. But when he and his followers,—the wisest and purest philosophers of Greece, if not of the world,—had been pointing the way for four hundred years the world was no better than before ; and we still find the cultivated Roman poet, with all these teachings before him, cooly confessing : "I see and approve the better ; I follow the worse." And you and I, my friends, know only too well how many wise and earnest exhortations to duty we have heard and approved of and—neglected.

Mere exhortation will always be received so by the mass of mankind. Preaching which consists simply in imploring men to "*be good*", will always fail. Trying to move men so, is like trying to move a boulder by a direct push of the crowbar. First throw down a solid block of doctrine as a fulcrum, and then resting your lever of exhortation upon that you may work to some purpose. It was the boast of Christianity that she brought a purer morality to men ; but it was her prouder boast that she brought *men to a purer morality*. It was something to have given the world a more perfect code of ethics than all the philosophies and all the religions of antiquity could furnish. But often as her first defenders against the assaults of heathenism and scepticism appealed to this, they appealed yet oftener and with greater triumph

to her success in reducing that sublime code to practice,
and purifying a society that was festering in its own rot-
tenness. And this achievement she owed to her doctrines
of God, of man, of sin, of redemption, of the Holy
Ghost, of heaven and hell. It was the tremendous and
accumulated weight of these behind her exhortations,
driving them home to the very core of men's souls that
made them take hold as no exhortation of the mere
moralist had ever taken hold.

Armed with the power of these doctrines her missionaries have gone hopefully among the most debased
and imbruted of mankind, among savages so ignorant
thal they could scarce grasp the simplest processes of
multiplication, and so vile that the last vestiges of the
family had disappeared ; and there, where the moralist
would have stood aghast, when the most sanguine of
philosophers would not have had the hardihood to put
his system to the test,—there, waiting for no preparatory process of civilization, nor of education other than
education in these same doctrines which some think too
abstruse and recondite to be of profit to an American
congregation, they have wrought results by the side of
which there is nothing more wonderful even in the opening of the eyes of the blind and the raising of the dead to
life.

You may think, my friend, that *you* are so in love
with purity and virtue that you need no such goad to
your pursuit of them. Have you then found it so? Are
you making such rapid strides towards the goal of moral
perfection, and do you find the steep ascent so easy that
you can afford to dispense with anything that would support and quicken your steps?

"Give attendance to doctrine " ! It is a charge not
for the preacher only, but for every man and woman, yea,
and child. "*Add to your faith virtue, and to virtue,*

knowledge." "Whatsoever things are true—think on
these things."

The spiritual world is too real and too near for you
to put aside all question about it with easy nonchalance.
Its possibilities of evil and misery are too tremendous to
be dismissed with the sluggard's confidence that "*somehow* all will come out right." "Give attendance to
doctrine;" and let it be a reverent and earnest attendance. This is no field, and your brief life gives no time
for a dilettante scepticism. The great questions about
God and the soul, the solemn questions that men ask in
the shadow of the cross, and in the shadow of the grave,
are no riddles for an after-dinner exercise of wit. They
are questions to be pondered and wrestled with and
prayed over till the fulfillment of the promise is obtained:
"When he, the Spirit of Truth, is come, he will guide
you into all truth."

SONGS IN THE NIGHT.

" By reason of the multitude of oppressions they cry out;
They cry for help by reason of the arm of the mighty;
But none saith, where is God, my maker,
Who giveth songs in the night?"—Job 35: 9-10.   R. V.

The book of Job unfolds in a dramatic dialogue of
unsurpassed power and beauty the struggle of the human
mind with the problems presented by the divine government of this world.   On the one side are Job's three
friends, contending stoutly for the proposition, that under
the government of a just God suffering is always the penalty and therefore the proof of guilt ; and that when a
good man (in appearance) is overwhelmed with calamity,
it stamps him as a cunning hypocrite, who beneath a
mask of piety conceals a character rotten to the core. On
the other side is Job himself, in his conscious integrity,
repelling with indignation the conclusions of his friends,
yet so far accepting their premises that he is involved in
a hopeless mental conflict, in which he is brought once
and again to the very verge of an impeachment of God.
After Job has thus by his vehemence silenced his friends
without satisfying himself or finding a solution of the
problem, another party to the discussion presents himself, in the person of Elihu, the son of Barachel the
Buzite, who, despite his youth, essays to play the role of
umpire in the strife, and give a solution which shall place
both Job and his friends in the wrong.   This he accom-
plishes with but indifferent success, suggesting indeed
one important truth which the former disputants had

overlooked, and which does much to relieve the difficulty, to-wit, the disciplinary aspect of trial, yet leaving the matter still involved in darkness, till God himself draws near in the awful majesty of the storm, and speaks the final word.

It is in this discourse of Elihu that we find the words to which I have drawn your attention. They are a reply to the complaint of Job (set forth at length in chap. 24 : 1-12,) that God allows so much oppression and misery to go unrelieved and unavenged. "They pluck the fatherless from the breast," Job had complained, "and take a pledge of the poor, they cause him to go naked without clothing and they take away the sheaf from the hungry. . . . . Men groan from out of the city, and the soul of the wounded crieth out, yet God layeth not folly to them "—that is, he does not bring them to account for their cruelty.

Looking back to these words Elihu declares, that if the oppressed cry out in vain and obtain no deliverance, it is because they do not turn to the true source of relief. "By reason of the multitude of oppressions they cry out. They cry for help by reason of the arm of the mighty ; but none saith : where is God my maker, who giveth songs in the night?"

"*Songs in the night*"—let this then be our theme, and let us learn ever from Elihu's imperfect wisdom this great lesson, that he who would learn these songs must have God for his teacher.

Night! It is God's symbol of all painful and gloomy things. It stands in his word for sorrow and loss, as the light and the day for prosperity and joy. And as there is no land under the sun on which the shades of night do not fall, so there is no human life which has not its night of weeping, its deep shadows of trial. Of one land alone, and that a "land that is very far off," is it written,

"There shall be no night there," a prophecy which finds its counterpart and its interpretation in those other words : "God shall wipe away all tears from their eyes."

Life here is a checkered experience, of mingled light and darkness, smiles and tears. Sooner or later the brightest sun of prosperity, of happiness, goes down, and it is night. It may be the lonely night of bereavement, when one listens in the awful silence for a voice that is forever still. It may be the chilly night of misplaced trust and disappointed affection, when one sits in sack-cloth by the ashes of a desolated hearth. It may be the restless, tossing night of pain and sickness. It may be the bleak and wintry night of poverty and unsuccessful struggle. It may be the stormy night of oppression and persecution, in which the lightnings flash and the rain beats pitilessly on a defenseless head. In one guise or another the night comes to all. "Man that is born of woman, is of few days and full of trouble."

But while the experience of trouble is common to all, men differ widely in their way of meeting trouble. These words of Elihu suggest this difference. They describe a common way of meeting trouble, which brings no relief ; they point out a better way ; and they show the effect of meeting trouble in that better way.

Elihu makes first of all a sweeping assertion respecting the way in which men are wont to meet trial, in that particular form of it to which he was then referring—"By reason of the multitude of oppressions, they cry out; the cry for help by reason of the arm of the mighty ; but none saith, where is God my maker?" That is, few say this. The mass of men, when trouble comes upon them, meet it simply with groans and complaints. They turn every way for relief but the right way. They cry out, now in rage and now in despair, but they do not pray. They look upon their troubles perhaps as an ac-

cident, perhaps as an injustice, rarely as a lesson
set by a loving hand ; moaning in mere pain, as the brute
might, rather than asking after a deeper meaning. "None
saith, where is God my maker, who giveth songs in the
night, who teacheth us more than the beasts of the field
and maketh us wiser than the fowls of heaven?"

This is too true a picture of human life. Few things
are sadder than the rarity of true religion among those
who seem most to need its consolation. Take, for instance, the condition of the laboring classes in England
to-day. It is a condition of great, often abject misery.
It is misery resulting in great part from oppression, the
oppression of an unjust land system, and the oppression
of soulless capital. By reason of the multitude of these
oppressions the oppressed cry out. Yet none saith,
"Where is God my maker?" For if there is one thing
sadder than the physical condition of these masses it is
their spiritual condition. Of all classes in England they
are admitted to be the most destitute of religion, the
most inaccessible to the comforting message of the
gospel. This misery, when it has not hardened them
into a bitter hatred of a religion identified in their minds
with the oppressions under which they groan, seems to
have crushed out their susceptibility to spiritual influence.

The cry of "Bread, bread," which inaugurated the
French Revolution with its wild carnival of atheism,—
the cry of nihilism to-day, proclaiming on behalf of the
oppressed masses of Europe that "the first lie is God,
and the second lie is right," and demanding the destruction of all religion as well as all social order as the only
remedy for the ills under which they groan ; the cry of
communism, telling the toil-worn and the hungry that
Christianity has nothing to say to them, and preaching to
them a gospel of anarchy leading to a millenium of idle-
ness,—these are examples of the cry of which Elihu

speaks, a cry as old as the groaning of the Israelites under
their Egyptian task-masters, when they bade Moses and
Aaron go their ways and let them alone, because they had
made their case worse than before ;—a cry which brings
back no answer but its own wailing echo. If I have gone
abroad for illustrations, it is only because there the con-
trasts are a little sharper, the lights and shades a little
more pronounced.   Turn to our own city, go into its
wretchedest quarters, where the poverty is deepest, the
toil hardest and most ill-paid, the surroundings most
squalid and repulsive. You may see misery enough there.
You may hear groans and curses till your soul is sick.
But how few you will find asking : "Where is God my
maker?" How long must you listen for the "Song in
the night?"

Or turn in another direction. Go up the marble
steps of yonder mansion. Pass through that stately
portal. Enter those richly tapestried parlors. Without,
the sun is flooding the world with glory ; but within is
night—deep, dark night. For the voice that once made
those walls echo with glee is still. The golden hair that
once flashed like sunshine through those rooms is pil-
lowed in a coffin, and now this is a childless home. It is
night here ; but you listen in vain for any song in the
night. For this is a prayerless home. That mother is
weeping her life away in despairing grief. That father
is going to and fro, making no sign, mastering and lock-
ing up in his bosom by sheer force of will a dumb anguish
that is making him old before his time. But neither says :
"Where is God my maker?" Neither looks above for
comfort or strength. And so the blessings are all missed.
The sweet songs that that night of sorrow might have
taught are all unlearned.

Oh, the pity of it ! The pity of it ! Of all wastes of
which the world is full—wasted hours, wasted riches,

wasted labors, wasted loves,—what other so pitiful as this untold mass of wasted sorrows,—sorrows that teach no lesson, sorrows that bring no higher comfort, sorrows that come as heaven's messengers to bring back wandering souls, but that only end in driving such souls farther into darkness and rebellion?

Trouble so met sometimes leaves men bitter and defiant; sometimes it renders them stolidly indifferent; sometimes it drives them to despair and self-destruction; never does it leave a blessing behind it. Now and then one tries to rise above it, to sing in the night. But the song soon dies away into a wail or breaks into a sob. The broken heart cannot make its own music. The song in the night is a gift.

In contrast, then, with all these ways of meeting trouble,—the dull way, the defiant way, the despairing way, the humanly self-reliant way, there is but one true way of meeting it, but one victorious way, one way which can wring joy and blessing out of the very sorrow itself, and make music out of pain, and that is, to inquire after God.

To inquire after Him as teacher. Trouble is God's messenger. "Affliction cometh not forth of the dust; neither doth trouble spring out of the ground." We are in the hands of our maker. Day and night come to us by His command. There is no chance about them therefore, but divine meaning. The night comes for a purpose. It hides a lesson. It is part of the discipline by which immortal souls are trained. Hence no man meets sorrow rightly who does not seek to hear God speaking to him in it. When the voice came from heaven in answer to the prayer of Jesus in the temple, some of them that stood by said that it thundered; but Jesus himself heard the words of strength and comfort spoken to him by his Father. O brother man, on whose head the storm is breaking to-day, do not be content to hear in it merely the thunder of nature. Listen! Inquire! and you shall hear God's voice speaking its articulate personal message of instruction to you.

This is not saying that we are to try to trace in every trial some distinct connection with our own past conduct, some rebuke of specific sins. That was the very error of Job's friends, by which he steadfastly refused to be misled. It is not saying that we should seek to unravel all the mystery of Providence, and know why we are led in one way, others in another, why we suffer while others rejoice. These are questions it is vain to ask. Eternity alone holds the answer to them. It is one thing to ask such questions, and another to ask, What spiritual truths would God reveal to me, what lessons of experience would he have me make in this darkness into which he has led me apart? These are questions that will never be earnestly asked without finding an answer. They are questions the asking of which is essential to the right use of sorrow, and to true comfort in sorrow. For sorrow is endurable in proportion as it is intelligible, in proportion as we can hear in it a kindly voice, and see beyond it a beneficent aim.

God is also to be inquired after as Helper. There is a specific for the bearing of trial as distinct as any specific against a fever or a poison, and more sure. That specific is prayer. There is relief in it, there is strength in it, such as can be found nowhere else. Trials cannot be successfully borne alone, because they were never meant to be borne alone. They were meant to be cast upon God. They were meant to throw us upon His strength and to teach us its sufficiency. He who attempts to bear his trials without prayer makes the same mistake that one would make who should attempt to carry a heavy load all day without food. If every trial is God's messenger, a part of its message always is to call us nearer to Him. If every trial has its lesson to teach, one of these lessons is sure to be the lesson of our dependence upon strength from above.

See now what the gain is of thus coming to God. To one who thus comes to Him to be taught and to be sus-tained, He gives *songs in the night.* He does not at once dispel the darkness, perhaps, but he comforts in it. And so in the night, where nature can only weep, grace sings.

Songs in the night He gives ; not one song only, but many.

He gives the song of peace : " Thou wilt keep him in perfect peace whose mind is stayed on Thee." " In everything by prayer and supplication with thanksgiving let your requests be made known unto God, and the peace of God, which passeth all understanding, shall keep your hearts and minds through Christ Jesus."

He gives the song of trust. Listen to that song as it comes from the lips of the sweet singer of Israel : "Yea, though I walk through the valley of the shadow of death, I will fear no evil ; for Thou art with me, Thy rod and Thy staff they comfort me." "God is our refuge and strength, a very present help in trouble ; therefore will not we fear though the earth be removed and though the mountains be carried into the midst of the sea." Listen to it as it comes in strains scarcely less sweet from uninspired lips :

> I know not if or dark or bright
>   Shall be my lot,
> If that wherein my hopes delight
>   Be best or not.
>
>   . . . . . .
>
> My bark is wafted from the strand
>   By breath divine,
> And on the helm there rests a hand
>   Other than mine.

> One who has known in storms to sail,
>   I have on board.
> Above the raging of the gale
>   I hear my Lord.
>
> He holds me when the billows smite,
>   I shall not fall.
> If sharp, 'tis short: if long, 'tis light.
>   He tempers all.

This song of trust is peculiarly a song of the night. We can scarcely learn to sing it from the heart till the darkness gathers about us. And if the darkness brought us no other blessing than to teach us that song, it would I e worth all it costs.

But He gives also the song of hope. No night for the child of God is eternal. In the deepest darkness hope catches glimpses of a coming dawn. The horizon is bright with promises, which, like morning clouds, glow with the light of approaching day. And so in the deepest gloom the Christian can sing of heaven : "I shall be satisfied when I awake with Thy likeness." "Thou wilt show me the path of life ; at Thy right hand there are pleasures forever more."

Finally he gives—noblest song of all—the song of triumph. "Not only so, but we glory in tribulation." "Our light affliction which is but for a moment, worketh for us a far more exceeding and eternal weight of glory." "In all these things we are more than conquerors through Him that loved us." He enables us not only to rejoice in the face of trial, but to rejoice over trial, to "count it all joy when we fall into divers temptations," because we see before us not only deliverance from the trial, but gain through the trial, purer, more Christ-like character and a greater weight of glory as its result

And so God's children have always been known in the world by their songs in the night.

Hark ! And you will hear them coming faintly through the barred casements of many a dungeon ; as at midnight they come from the heart of that dungeon at Philippi where Paul and Silas lay with feet fast in the stocks. Hark again ! You will hear them as they ring out cheery and full of praise from the humble cottages of the poor. Hark again ! Can you not hear them rising in weak and tremulous tones, yet sweet and full of patient trust, from beds of pain? Aye, can you not hear them, sinking almost to a whisper, but that whisper a whisper of triumphant hope, on the lips of those who are fast passing into the shadows of the last night of death?

I hear one of those songs now, a glorious, a triumphant song. It is the voice of an apostle, and it comes from a Roman prison, where he lies waiting for the executioner to lead him forth to martyrdom: "I am now ready to be offered, and the time of my departure is at hand. I have fought a good fight ; I have finished my course ; I have kept the faith. Henceforth there is laid up for me a crown which the Lord the righteous judge shall give me at that day."

I hear another, coming sweet and clear from behind the bars of the Bastile. This time it is a woman's voice that I hear, the voice of Madame Guyon. imprisoned there for her faith.

> "A little bird am I,
> Shut from the fields of air:
> And in my cage I sit and sing
> To him who placed me there;
> Well pleased a prisoner to be,
> Because, my God it pleases Thee,
> Naught have I else to do;
> I sing the whole day long;
> And he whom most I love to please,
> Doth listen to my song,
> He caught and bound my wandering wing,
> But still He bends to hear me sing.

>   .   .   .   .
>
> My cage confines me round,
>   Abroad I cannot fly;
> But though my wing is closely bound,
>   My heart's at liberty;
> My prison walls cannot control
> The flight, the freedom of the soul.
>
> Oh! it is good to soar
>   These bolts and bars above,
> To Him whose purpose I adore,
>   Whose providence I love;
> And in Thy mighty will to find
> The joy, the freedom of the mind."

I hear that song again; this time from the dying bed of a minister of Christ, the venerable Dr. Payson, as amid the bodily sufferings and agonies indescribable of his last days, he exclaims: "The celestial city is full in my view; its glories beam upon me; its breezes fan me; its odors are wafted to me; its sounds strike upon my ear and its spirit is breathed into my heart. Nothing separates me from it but the river of death, which now appears but an insignificant rill that may be crossed at a single step, whenever God shall give permission. The Sun of Righteousness has been gradually drawing nearer and nearer, appearing larger and brighter as he approached; and now He fills the whole hemisphere, pouring forth a flood of glory in which I seem to float like an insect in the beams of the sun."

Ah what havoc would it make with our Bibles, what havoc with the poetry of Christian experience, were we to take out of them all the songs of the night.

There is a peculiar sweetness in the song of the night, a depth, a tenderness, a heavenliness, which other songs do not bear. The groves of old England are full of sweet songsters, which make the day vocal with their cheerful notes. But when the sun has gone and the gathering shades of evening have hushed the chorus into silence, then it is that richer, clearer, sweeter than all,—its notes thrilling with a passionate ecstacy,—the song of the nightingale floats out upon the dark.   It is nature's parable of the priceless lessons of affliction, of the song in the night, surpassing all other songs.

My friends, the night will come first or last, to us all. We cannot keep it away. I once read a pretty little conceit of two children who had been at play in the meadows and who had found the day so beautiful and perfect that they could not let it go, and so that the sun might not know his going down, they stole in and turned back the hands on the great clock in the hall. But while they were still rejoicing in their beautiful day, they found that the sun was sinking behind the hills, and the long, long shadows were creeping across the meadows, and the day was gone. As vain are all our efforts to put off the night of adversity.   It must come.   To some here doubtless it has come.   Others may not suspect it.   There are blind men whose eyes, like Milton's, are

" ———clear,
　　To outward view of blemish or of spot,"

and give no hint to the observer of the darkness in which the soul sits within.   So there are lives seeming serene and cheerful enough to those who know them only from the outside, which are yet wrapped in the blackness of darkness.   The night has come, and you cannot help it. You cannot bring back the lost joys. You cannot change your night to day.

But there is one thing you can do.   You can say, Where is God my maker?   You can listen for his voice. You can grasp His hand.   You can sit down humbly at His feet to learn the lessons He would teach you. You can cast yourself in prayer upon the everlasting arms.   Then He, who giveth songs in the night, will give them to you,—songs that no darkness can silence, songs that will rise ever clearer and richer through the night watches, till they are swallowed up in the glad shout of the resurrection morning, when "the day breaketh and the shadows flee away."